A hole of utter, mi ———————————————————— n-
ter of the stone wall, ri———————————————————— y
sucked air down, a sharp gasp. The hair on his a— —— ne
straight up and his back muscles tried to shudder and crawl
away down his spine, intent on running as far and as fast
as possible, with or without the rest of him.

The gate . . .

It pulsed open with a silent thunder, gaping wider, swallowing up more of the garden wall, which simply ceased
to exist where that blackness touched it. The edges scintillated in the glow from the gas lamps, shot through with
irridescent color. The fascination of it drew him, repulsed
him, left him trembling violently. What power did these
people from the future possess to open such a thing out
of sheer air and solid stone? Ancient names and half-recalled
incantations stumbled through his broken, sliding thoughts,
names of power and terror: Anubis, destroyer of souls . . .
Kur, the coiled serpent of the fathomless abyss, destroyer
of the world in flood and thunder . . .

The outward shudder of the gate's receding edges finally
came to a halt and it hung there, silent and terrible, beckoning him forward from his hiding place while his senses
screamed to run in the opposite direction and never glance
back. Then, as though such a thing were the most ordinary
occurrence in the world, the men and women in the garden began stepping calmly through it, vanishing from sight.

Lachley started toward the gate. Just behind him, a
woman's voice shrilled out, "My God! It's John Lachley!" He
jerked around and focused on a woman who stood not ten
paces away, who was staring straight at him, eyes wide in
recognition. She knows me! By God, she'll not stop me!
Lachley whirled and plunged toward the gaping black hole.
Behind him, the woman shouted, "Stop him! That's Jack the
Ripper!"

Screams erupted on his heels, then he was inside. Falling, rushing forward through time with dizzy speed.

THE HOUSE THAT
Jack Built

Robert Asprin
Linda Evans

THE HOUSE THAT JACK BUILT

A Baen Books Original

Baen Publishing Enterprises
P.O. Box 1403
Riverdale, NY 10471
www.baen.com

ISBN: 0-671-31965-5

Cover art by Gary Ruddell

First printing, January 2001

Distributed by Simon & Schuster
1230 Avenue of the Americas
New York, NY 10020

Production by Windhaven Press, Auburn, NH
Printed in the United States of America

THE HOUSE THAT
Jack Built

Chapter One

Skeeter Jackson wasn't in jail.

And that was so overwhelming a shock, he wasn't entirely sure what to do with himself. The one thing he *didn't* want to do was hang around the infirmary, where Bergitta lay in the recovery room after emergency surgery and where Senator John Caddrick sat bellowing like a wounded musk-ox, threatening to shut down the station around their ears. So he ducked past crowds of shaken tourists, wounded in the riot at Primary, slithered past news crews and the irate, fuming senator—who was still taking up a valuable medical technician's time to wash tear gas out of his eyes—and headed out into the vast crowds thronging the Commons.

He didn't really know where he was going or what he intended to do, once he got there. He didn't have a job any longer, and wasn't likely to find a soul on station to hire him, particularly not with the kind of trouble Time Terminal Eighty-Six had brewing. Skeeter threaded his way through the jostling crowds, ignoring the shocked gossip flying loose through Commons,

and wondered for perhaps the fifteen millionth time
what had become of his friends, young Julius, who'd been
born in ancient Rome, and—far more devastatingly—
down-time refugees Ianira and Marcus and both their
little girls. Ianira was the leader of the entire community
of down-timers stranded on the time terminal, Speaker
for the Found Ones' Council, and the inspiration for
the fastest-growing up-time religion in the world.

Not only major VIPs in anybody's book, but very
nearly the only friends Skeeter possessed. They'd all
disappeared in the middle of a riot, the first of many
to hit Shangri-La Station during the past week, and
despite massive searches, not a trace of them had been
found. Either they'd managed to escape down one of
the open time-touring gates or they'd been kidnapped
and smuggled out. Or—and he had to swallow hard,
at the thought—somebody'd cut them into small pieces
and dropped them down an unstable gate. Like the
Bermuda Triangle, maybe . . .

"Skeeter!"

He looked around, startled, and found Kit Carson
homing in.

Panic struck.

"Don't bolt!" The retired time scout held up a hand
as he hurried through the crowd. "I just want to talk."

Skeeter paused, gauging the expression in Kit's
eyes—a surprisingly friendly look—and decided not to
run. "Okay," he shrugged, waiting. After all, Kit had
stood up for him in the station manager's office high
above Commons floor, when Security Chief Mike
Benson had been chomping at the bit to toss him into
the nearest jail cell—or maybe through the aerie's glass
window-walls. A long shiver caught Skeeter's spine at
that too-recent memory. Mike Benson had dragged him
up from the station's subbasement battleground in
cuffs, facing murder charges. Neither he nor the

station's down-timer refugees had really had any choice *but* fight to the death, trying to wrest Bergitta away from her kidnappers, a group of Islamic *jihad* fighters.

The *Ansar Majlis* had styled themselves after the original *Ansar,* the religiously motivated nineteenth-century "dervishes" of the Sudan, famed for routing British forces and killing General Gordon at Khartoum. The terrorist members of the *Ansar Majlis* had dragged Bergitta down into the station's sub-basement, where they would've beaten her to death, after raping her. But that hadn't mattered a damn to Mike Benson.

If not for Kit's support . . .

He didn't even know why Kit had come to his rescue.

So he shoved his hands into his pockets, suppressing a wince where the cuffs had dug into his flesh, and waited for Kit to catch up. The world-famous time scout actually clapped him on the shoulder, startling Skeeter considerably.

"Come down to Edo Castletown with me," Kit said over the roar of voices on Commons. "I need your help."

Skeeter blinked. "My help? What for?"

Kit grinned at his tone, but the smile faded too quickly. "After you left the aerie, Ronisha ran computer records checks for everyone who entered the station today. I'm afraid the databanks are a mess, thanks to that riot Caddrick started." Kit shook his head and made a derisive sound of disgust. "Half the arriving tourists haven't even scanned their records in properly yet. But Ronisha thinks she's got a line on the *Ansar Majlis* leadership. A couple of businessmen, seemed legit enough. Came to open up a new outfitter's shop for the Arabian Nights sector. They checked into their hotel, nice and quiet, then tried to contact some of your pals from that murderous construction crew. By radio, mind."

Skeeter's brows rose. "Don't tell me, they tried to contact those little radio handsets Benson took off those bodies we left downstairs?"

One corner of Kit's mouth twitched. "You got it. Mike intercepted the call. That down-time kid, Hashim, who helped you with the rescue? He helped us out again, in a big way. He answered the transmission, told them there'd been trouble, but he'd meet them, bring them up to date." Kit thinned his lips. "They're in my hotel, Skeeter. I want them *out.*"

"Alive?" Skeeter asked softly.

Kit's eyes blazed, giving Skeeter a dangerous, top-to-toes assessment that left Skeeter sweating despite the bravado of his return stare. "Preferably," Kit said in a low growl. "With as little damage to young Hashim as possible."

"No argument, there. Where'd he agree to meet them? At the Neo Edo?"

Kit nodded.

"When?"

The retired time scout checked his watch. "About fifteen minutes from now."

Skeeter swore. "I'll need a good disguise. Get me somebody's headdress. And a tool belt." He paused. "You're sure you've got the right assholes? Not just a couple of innocent Arab businessmen looking for long-lost relatives?"

"We're sure," Kit said grimly. "They asked Hashim to bring schematics of the station's brig, so they could plan an attack. They aim to break their buddies out of jail."

Skeeter whistled. "That's bad."

"You're not kidding, that's bad. Right now, they're in room Four Twenty-Three, waiting for Hashim to show up with his pals."

Skeeter nodded. "All right, let's get this over with."

A quarter of an hour later, Skeeter and young Hashim ibn Fahd were walking softly down a carpeted corridor on the fourth floor of the Neo Edo hotel, the latter in Neo Edo livery. Skeeter wore a long headdress shrugged down across his shoulders and a toolbelt at his hips. The toolbelt hid an eight-inch Bowie knife and a snub-nosed revolver shoved into a paddle holster inside his trousers. Kit, too, wore a disguising headdress and tool belt, and carried a sleek little semiautomatic pistol. Security had closed off the corridor at either end, stationing officers in the stairwells and elevator.

The fourth floor was as secure as they could make it without evacuating innocents from adjoining rooms, which they *couldn't* do, not and keep the element of surprise. A bad situation to be sure, but letting terrorists like the *Ansar Majlis* continue to operate was a good deal worse. Five minutes earlier, security had reported the arrival of three additional men from the Time Tripper Hotel, also newcomers to the station. At a guess, the leadership of the *Ansar Majlis* had gathered for a high-level pow-wow. Once inside the room, Skeeter and Kit would probably have only moments before the leadership realized they were meeting with decoys. As Kit knocked, Skeeter told his hands to stop shaking.

The door to room 423 opened just a crack and a low voice spoke in Arabic. Skeeter's heart was pounding. He hoped like hell those incarcerated construction workers in the brig had given Hashim the correct code word to respond with. Hashim answered the challenge, his stance cocky and belligerent. A chain rattled, then the door opened wider. Hashim slipped to one side, out of the line of fire. Kit shoved the door open and strode in. Skeeter followed at his heels, raking the room with his gaze. He found only three men in sight. The door to the bathroom was partially closed. *At least one in there, maybe another in the closet . . .*

A well-dressed man of about fifty stared at them through narrowed eyes. He spat out something that Kit responded to with a gutteral monosyllable. At the doorway, Hashim let loose a voluble flood of Arabic, drawing attention to himself. Then the closet door opened and a new voice spoke sharply. The effect was electrifying. Weapons appeared with terrifying swiftness. The man in the closet grabbed Kit by the arm, clearly demanding to know who the hell he was.

The next instant, he was airborne, flipping arse about head past the end of one bed. A gunshot cracked as Skeeter dove toward the bathroom door, drawing his Bowie knife and slamming it into the unprotected thigh of the man between him and Kit. The man screamed. Another gunshot blasted loose, but Kit wasn't where the bullets impacted. He was across the room, then somebody else screamed and went flying into the mirrored closet. Skeeter kicked in the bathroom door, coming in low to the floor, and heard a yell of pain just as bullets tore through the doorway at head height. The door caught the shooter full in the face and sent him reeling back against the john. Skeeter kicked his feet out from under him. The man went down hard, struck his head against the toilet tank, reeled face-first into the shower stall and lay still. Skeeter disarmed him swiftly, then lunged back out into the hotel room.

Hashim stood on top of the man Skeeter had stabbed, grinding his wrist into the carpet and holding a gun he'd clearly just liberated. Out in the main room, the fight was over. Three men, dazed and bleeding, lay in crumpled heaps where Kit had tossed them. Kit was breathing hard, eyes narrowed down into slits, then let out a bellow that shook dust loose. "*Security!*"

Officers flooded into the room.

Kit stepped aside as handcuffs appeared and dazed men were wrestled into restraints. "Check the room next door," Kit said curtly. "Make sure nobody was hurt. Bastards got off several shots that went through the wall."

Skeeter stood breathing hard in the bathroom doorway, hardly able to believe it was over so quickly. He turned over his own prisoner from the shower stall, gratefully stripped off the headdress and tool belt, handed over the borrowed weapons, and gave Security his statement. "Do me a favor, will you?" he asked in a tight, controlled voice. "Find out what they know about Ianira's disappearance." Then, far too wound up from the adrenaline rush to just hang around, he headed out into the corridor, away from the stink of gunpowder and blood, wishing mightily for a glass of something cold to swallow.

"Skeeter."

He glanced up and found Kit heading his way, *sans* disguise. The prisoners were being dragged—or carried—out of room 423. The door to room 425 was open as officers checked the frightened occupants for injuries and reassured a sobbing woman that the danger was over. "Security will take it from here," Kit told Skeeter. "Hashim's going down with them to translate. Good work. If you hadn't taken those two out, I might've ended up with a bullet in my back. I don't know about you, but I could do with a good, stiff drink and a plateful of hot food. How about I treat you to supper at the Silkworm Caterpillar while we talk?"

Skeeter swallowed surprise—and an involuntary rush of saliva—and was overwhelmed by a sudden flood of hunger, accompanied by a spreading sense of euphoria that he was still alive to *be* hungry. He couldn't recall when he'd eaten his last real meal and didn't want to remember too closely what it had consisted of, either.

"Okay," Skeeter nodded, meeting Kit's gaze. "Thanks."

He wondered what the retired time scout had in mind as they crossed the world-famous Neo Edo lobby, heading for the *Kaiko no Kemushi,* the Silkworm Caterpillar. Kit's restaurant, at least, appeared to have survived the riot at Primary intact, but the hotel lobby bore mute testament to the tear gas and the panic. Hotel employees sponged down silk wallpaper in an attempt to remove the residues. The snarl of an industrial carpet shampooer broke the elegant hush. Workers were masked against fume exposure to the whitish, powdery film of chemical irritants left behind. What the cleanup would cost . . .

Beyond the lobby, decorative bridges across Edo Castletown's ornate goldfish ponds had been shattered, their railings smashed to splinters during the riot Senator Caddrick and his goons in uniform had instigated. Before the infamous politician's arrival, Edo Castletown had been one of TT-86's most picturesque sectors, with its Shinto Shrine and graceful pagoda-style rooflines. Skeeter clamped his lips as he traced the path of battle scars, broken shrubbery, and smashed ruin that had marred Edo Castletown's fragile beauty.

Too many of his few friends were missing, as a result of station riots.

Kit stood at Skeeter's shoulder, silent and grim as they watched cleanup crews trying to clear away the debris. Shopkeepers sorted through the wreckage of their merchandise. Rachel Eisenstein's medical triage teams, staffed mostly by volunteers since the trained medical personnel were all down at the infirmary, treating the seriously wounded, ministered to those suffering from tear gas exposure and minor injuries. Sue Fritchey's Pest Control crews huddled over a few small, dark shapes lying on the floor, trying to keep prehistoric birds and pterodactyls alive where they'd been teargassed, trampled, and almost drowned in the goldfish ponds. Sue, tears streaming down both cheeks, was setting the broken wing bones of a crow-sized

flying reptile while one assistant held the wing carefully stretched taut and another administered anesthesia
and monitored the animal's life signs.

"*Zigsi*," Skeeter muttered under his breath, using one
of his favorate Mongolian curses. "Doesn't Caddrick
know it's against the law for *anybody* to discharge tear
gas on a time terminal? Even law enforcement agents?"

Kit shot him a sidewise glance, mouth hard as
marble. "Men like John Caddrick don't care what the
law says. And neither do the kind of agents who'd come
to Shangri-La with him."

Skeeter shivered, afraid of Senator John Caddrick in
spite of—or maybe due to—his rough Mongol upbring-
ing. He recalled with satisfaction trading assaults with
Caddrick, back at the leading edge of that riot, but . . .
One of these days, Caddrick was going to calm down
enough to remember what Skeeter had said and done.

Skeeter knew about powerful men.

Apparently, so did Kit Carson.

"Come on, I need that drink." Kit steered Skeeter
past sliding rice-paper doors into the softly lit Silkworm
Caterpiller, with its smooth, polished wood floors and
delicate porcelain vases and its priceless bonsai cherry
trees, bathed in their full-spectrum grow lights and
grafted—rumor had it—from cuttings taken from the
National Cherry Trees of Washington. The scent of
expensive cuisine relaxed Skeeter a degree as he followed
Kit toward a private cubicle near the back, threading
his way past half a dozen Asian billionaires, two instantly
recognizable international singing stars, and a haphazard
collection of the merely wealthy, all of them discussing
the riot and Senator Caddrick's presence in hushed,
worried tones.

Kit motioned him into a chair. "Sit down, Skeeter.
You look exhausted." At his signal, a waitress glided
up, silent and lovely in a silk kimono and delicate

geisha's coif. Kit ordered for them both—in Japanese. Moments later, a steady parade of silk-garbed waitresses materialized, bringing an avalanche of delicate porcelain dishes heaped with the most fabulous food Skeeter had ever smelled and—more importantly—several glassfuls of liquid stress relief. Skeeter upended the first and felt better immediately. As attentive servers brought more whiskey and poured steaming green tea into tiny cups, Kit smiled, the corners of his eyes crinkling into weatherbeaten folds. "Dig in. Enjoy. You've earned it."

Skeeter had no idea what he was eating, but it was all fabulous. Even the stuff that was raw. He'd certainly eaten stranger stuff as a kid, stranded in twelfth century Mongolia. Kit let him eat in silence, paying attention to his own meal, then glanced up when a bellboy in Neo Edo uniform delivered a heavy leather briefcase. Kit nodded toward a chair and tipped the young man. "Thanks."

Skeeter frowned. "What's with the briefcase?"

"The real reason I asked you here," Kit said, his glance intent.

"Oh, great," Skeeter groused, toying with his chopsticks. "Make me feel better, why don't you?"

"Actually," Kit chuckled, "I hope to do just that."

Skeeter looked up from the dripping bite of whatever wonderful concoction was dangling from his chopsticks and waited, abruptly wary. He did not expect what came next.

"I want to talk about your future," Kit said, sitting back and toying with the edge of his plate. When Skeeter just stared, the grizzled former scout gave him that world famous jack-o-lantern grin and chuckled. "All right, Skeeter. You've been remarkably patient. I'll end the suspense." He dug into the briefcase and dropped a sheaf of computer printouts onto the table. Skeeter looked curiously into Kit's eyes, but the retired scout merely stuffed more of his expensive lunch into his weathered face, so Skeeter picked up the stack and riffled through it. And discovered he was holding copies of the arrest reports for each of the thirty-one crooks Skeeter had put out of business in the last seven and a half days.

Skeeter had, during the past week, managed a feat even he hadn't thought possible. He had stunned the entire 'eighty-sixer population of Shangri-La Station virtually speechless. He'd only had to make citizens' arrests of seventeen pickpockets, five grifters, eight con artists, and a bait-and-switch vendor to do it, the latter peddling fake copies of an inertial mapping system that kept track of a person's movements away from a known point of origin, like a time-touring gate. The real gizmos had saved lives. Substituting fake ones could kill an unwary tourist, fast.

Once La-La Land had recovered the use of its stunned, multi-partite tongue, of course, rumor had run wild. "It's a new scam," went the most popular version, "he's up to something." And so he was. Just not what the rumor-mongers *thought* he was up to. Skeeter had taken his new "job" far more seriously than either of the ones he'd lost, thanks to his frantic search for clues to Ianira's disappearance. To his own surprise, Skeeter Jackson made a profoundly diligent undercover detective.

Judging from the printouts Skeeter now held, that fact was not lost on Kit Carson. He just didn't know what Kit had in mind to do about it.

Kit was grinning at him, though. He leaned forward, still smiling, and tapped the printouts in Skeeter's hands. "Mike Benson, bless him, has been glowering for days over this. If he hadn't been so busy trying to keep this station from exploding into violence, I expect he'd have called you in to explain by now."

Belatedly, Skeeter realized he'd made the head of Shangri-La security look . . . Well, if not outright incompetent, downright foolish. Thirty-one arrests in seven and a half days was a helluva haul, even for TT-86. Kit was studying Skeeter intently, eyes glinting in the indirect lighting. "I must confess to a considerable curiosity."

Skeeter sighed and set the reports down. "Not that I expect you to believe me," he met Kit's gaze, "but with Ianira and her family gone . . ." He blinked rapidly, told himself sternly that now was not the time to sniffle. His reputation for playing on a rube's emotions was too well known. "Well, dammit, somebody's got to make this place fit for the down-timer kids to grow up in! I was thinking about Ianira's little girls the other day, right about the time I saw a pickpocket snatch that Chilean lady's wallet. It made me so flaming mad, I just walked over and grabbed him. Maybe you haven't heard, but Artemisia and Gelasia call me 'Uncle Skeeter.' The last time I was anybody's uncle . . ."

He shut his mouth hastily, not wanting to talk about the deep feelings he still harbored for little Temujin. He'd seen the child born nine months after he'd fallen through an unstable gate, the one that had dumped him at the feet of the khan of forty-thousand Yakka Mongol yurts, or *gers,* as the Mongolians, themselves, called their felted tents. Yesukai had named Skeeter his first-born son's honorary uncle, effectively placing his heir under the protection of the *bogdo,* the sacred mountain spirit the Yakka clan had believed Skeeter to be. He didn't talk about it, much. It was a deeply private thing, standing as honorary uncle to the future Genghis Khan. Skeeter's rescue by the time scout who'd pushed TT-86's Mongolian Gate had caused Skeeter to lose that "nephew." And now the *Ansar Majlis* had deprived him of his honorary nieces.

Ianira's beautiful children . . .

Kit's eyes had darkened; he spoke very quietly. "I'm sorry, Skeeter. We've all searched."

He nodded, surprised Kit had believed him, for once.

Kit pointed to the arrest reports with a lacquered chopstick. "What I'd really like to know is how you managed to catch thirty-one criminals in such a short time."

"*How?*" Skeeter blinked, caught off guard by the question. "Well, jeez, Kit, it was dead easy." He felt the flush begin at the back of his neck and creep up his cheeks. "I mean, I was good at that kind of thing, once. It's not hard to spot the tricks of the trade, when you know 'em as well as I do. Did."

"You realize," Kit said slowly, "a lot of people are saying you pulled the jobs yourself, then planted part of the 'take' on those people, so there'd be a fall guy to blame?"

Skeeter's flush deepened, angry this time. "Doesn't surprise me. Although it's the stupidest thing I've heard in a while. One of those jerks had a stolen money roll with ten thousand bucks in it. If I were still in the business, do you honestly think I'd've turned over ten *grand* to station security?"

Kit held up both hands. "Easy, Skeeter. I didn't say I agreed with them."

"Huh. You must be the only up-time 'eighty-sixer who doesn't."

"Not quite," Kit said softly. "But I have noted the problem. I've also noticed how hard you've been trying to get another honest job. At the same time you've been hauling in all these petty thieves and swindlers." He tapped the sheaf of arrest reports again. "And I know why you've been turned down, too." Kit sat back, then, studying him once more. "Tell me if I'm wrong, but it seems to me you're mighty dedicated to this, ah, new crusade of yours."

"Damn right, I am," Skeeter growled, looking Kit square in the eye. "Mopping bathroom floors never did exactly challenge me. And I don't want the kids on this station growing up where somebody with light fingers can walk off with everything they've worked hard to earn." He added with a bitterness he couldn't conceal, "I never did roll an 'eighty-sixer, you know. Family's family, whatever you think of me."

Kit didn't respond to that, not directly. "So you intend to keep up the vigilance? Continue making citizens' arrests?"

"I do."

The former scout nodded sharply, as though satisfied. "Good. It occurs to me that your, ah, unique talents could be useful, very useful around here. How much did that ridiculous maintenance job of yours pay?"

Skeeter blinked. "Five bucks an hour, why?"

"Five bucks? That's not a salary, that's slavery! Barely enough to pay station taxes, let alone rent. What were you eating, sawdust?"

Skeeter refrained from pointing out that a good many 'eighty-sixers subsisted on less. "Well, I didn't eat fancy, but I got by."

The retired scout snorted. "I can just imagine what you were living on. Tell you what, young Jackson. You take yourself upstairs to my office, fill out the paperwork, I'll put you on payroll for a month, trial basis. Special roving security consultant for the Neo Edo. Set your own hours as you see fit, minimum eight a day, starting at, say, twenty dollars an hour. At the end of a month, if your arrest record justifies it, we'll see about making it permanent."

Skeeter tried to scrape his jaw off the carpeted floor and failed utterly.

Kit's sudden, glittering grin was terrifying. "Know

of a better way to catch a con artist than send one of their own kind after 'em? My God, Skeeter, thirty-one arrests in a *week?* That's more than Security caught last *year.* I'm not faulting Mike or his people, but you've got a damned fine point about it being easy to spot the tricks when you've used 'em, yourself."

Kit shoved back his chair and stood up. "Come on, Skeeter, I'll take you upstairs, introduce you to the personnel clerk. Robby Ames is a good kid, he'll show you the ropes. Then go home and get some sleep. Tomorrow morning, I'd appreciate a guided tour of Commons. I want to let things cool down out there, before we take a look-see at what we're up against, with Caddrick on station. And frankly, I'd like to watch you work. Maybe we could hit the Britannia crowd when the gate opens in the morning? There's sure to be a pile of pickpockets on hand for that. We'll figure out strategy while we're at it, stuff like should you stick to the Neo Edo proper or follow potential thieves off premises when they follow hotel guests?"

Skeeter still hadn't managed to scrape his lower jaw off the floor.

"Oh, and you'll need a squawky with all the Security frequencies and a training class on codes and procedures. I'll talk to a friend of mine in security about it." He chuckled wickedly. "When Mike Benson finds out, he'll eat nails and spit tacks."

Skeeter Jackson suddenly realized that Kit was not only enjoying this, the offer was serious. For the first time since his return from Mongolia, somebody other than a down-timer *trusted* him. For a long, dangerous moment, he was blind, throat so tightly closed he could hardly swallow. Then he was on his feet, clearing his throat roughly. "You won't regret this, Kit. Swear to God, you won't regret it."

"I'd better not!" But he was grinning as he said it

and for the first time since Skeeter had known Kit
Carson, the threat didn't terrify him. Kit stuck out a
hand and Skeeter grasped it hard, suddenly finding
himself grinning fit to crack his face in half.

My God, he thought as he followed Kit Carson out
of the Silkworm Caterpillar. *A private eye!* Working
for Kit Carson, of all people, the man who'd once
threatened to shove him down the nearest unstable
gate, minus his privates.

La-La Land would never be the same again.

He wasn't entirely sure Shangri-La Station would
recover from the shock.

Jenna Nicole Caddrick had spent a full eight days
trapped in a little room at the top of a scrubbed,
wooden staircase, staring out the window into the
grimy, soot-filled working world of Spitalfields, London.
She was too ill to travel even as far as the kitchen.
Dr. Mindel's tinctures left her woozy and afraid for the
tiny life growing inside her, but the gunshot wound to
her head required treatment and she was too deep in
shock to protest necessity.

Her strength began to return, however, as the wound
healed, and with healing came the restless urge to *do*
something. She couldn't spend the rest of her life sitting
beside a window, disguised as a Victorian man in a
world she scarcely understood. And Carl's blood called
out for vengeance, Carl's and Aunt Cassie's, both,
murdered by her own father's hired killers. When Jenna
woke early on the morning of her eighth day in London,
she knew she had to do something to stop her father.
She lay staring for a long time at the ceiling, stained
where rainwater had seeped through the roof at some
point before Noah had paid to have it repaired, and
considered where she might begin.

The first thing they had to do, of course, was survive.

But there was plenty she could do, while surviving. And the first thing to enter Jenna's mind was the need to find Ianira Cassondra. The tug of bandages across the side of her head, where Dr. Mindel had shaved the hair close to treat the grazing path of a stranger's bullet, brought a deep shiver. It hadn't been one of her father's hired killers, who'd shot her. A down-timer had done that. A native Londoner who'd saved Jenna's life, then realized what Ianira could do, with her gift for prophetic clairvoyance. Her erstwhile rescuer had calmly shot Jenna in cold blood, then had disappeared into the drizzling yellow rain with the Cassondra of Ephesus.

Eventually, footsteps thumped up the wooden steps outside her bedroom. Jenna sat up, grateful for the lessening of dizziness from concussion, as Noah Armstrong pushed open the door with her breakfast tray. "Good morning." The detective smiled.

"Good morning, Noah." She didn't know, yet, whether the enigmatic private detective was male or female; but it didn't really matter. She owed Armstrong her life, several times over. If Aunt Cassie hadn't hired the best, before the *Ansar Majlis* had shot Cassie Tyrol dead in New York . . .

"You look better this morning," Noah smiled, grey eyes warm and friendly. Dresssed in a Victorian woman's long skirt and a plain brown bodice ten years out of fashion, its perenially high collar obscuring Noah's throat—and therefore any hint of whether or not Noah possessed an Adam's apple—the detective wore what might've been a wig or real hair pulled back into a bun at the nape of the neck. "Are you hungry?"

She nodded. "A little."

"Good."

The cereal was hot and filling, the toast nicely buttered, the bacon fried crisp. Steaming tea sent up a fragrant cloud of steam. "Noah?" Jenna asked softly a few minutes later.

"Yeah?"

"We have to find Ianira."

"Marcus and I are taking care of it," Noah said firmly. "You're staying right here. Where you'll be safe."

"But—"

"No." The detective held her gaze, grey eyes hard as marble, now brooking no disagreement. "You're far too valuable to risk, Jenna. And you had a damned close call, the last time you were outside this house." Noah touched the side of her head. "This is nearly healed, thank goodness. And without infection, which is a small miracle."

Jenna's lips twitched. "I thought it was all the carbolic you keep pouring over my scalp."

The corners of Noah's eyes crinkled slightly. "Cleanliness *is* next to godliness, they say, particularly around here. Be that as it may, I won't risk seeing you shot dead, next time."

She considered arguing. Then realized she was still too weak and shaky to do much of anything physical, anyway, so she subsided, at least for the moment. Maybe she could think of some way to help that didn't require leaving this house? "What are you and Marcus doing?" she asked, instead. "To find her?"

Noah sighed, sitting in a chair beside the window. The corners of the detective's mouth had drawn down slightly. "We know the man who took her is a doctor, and a man of means. Wealthy enough to wear a silk top hat and a good frock coat. He frequents the area of the Royal Opera and Covent Garden, yet he clearly knows the streets of SoHo. Well enough to lose himself in that maze of nasty little alleyways. If I have to, I'll check out the identity of every physician, every surgeon in London." Noah leaned forward in the chair and touched Jenna's cheek gently. "Don't worry, kid. We'll find out who he is and we'll get her back."

Jenna bit her lip. If—no, when, it had to be *when*—they finally did rescue Ianira, she would come to this house expecting a joyous reunion with her family, only to learn that three *years* had passed in her children's lives . . .

Jenna, herself, wasn't over that shock, yet.

Noah had been forced to stay down the Wild West Gate's timeline long enough to catch up to the Britannia Gate's timeline, which ran three years later than Denver's 1885. Would Ianira's little girls even remember their mother? *If* they could even find Ianira . . . London was a depressingly immense and sprawling city, teeming with more than five million people crammed in cheek-by-jowl, inhabiting everything from spacious palaces to ramshackle staircase landings and stinking gutters. The number of places to search would've overwhelmed even a die-hard optimist.

Outside, angry voices in the street were shouting what sounded like abuse at their neighbors. Jenna's startlement gave way to the beginnings of alarm as she stared from the window to Noah. "What's happening?"

The detective moved to look outside and scowled. "Bastards."

"What is it?" she asked sharply, trying to rise.

"A gang of unemployed dock rats, hassling Dr. Mindel."

Ugly taunts and anti-Semitic slurs slammed against the window like hailstones. At least it wasn't the pack of up-time killers looking for *them*. Jenna sank back down against the pillows and shivered. "But why? Dr. Mindel's one of the kindest men I've ever met."

Noah's jaw tightened above the collar of the outdated dress. "Annie Chapman was just found murdered, over in Hanbury Street. Along with a leather apron in a

basin of water. Half the East End now thinks a Jewish
boot finisher killed her this morning." The detective
glanced around at Jenna's involuntary sound and met
Jenna's shocked stare. "Get used to it, kid. The East
End is set to explode. Anti-Semitism's running wild,
because everyone's convinced it has to be a foreigner
killing these women. Which is another reason I don't
want you outside. You're disguised as a man, Jenna,
a foreign-sounding man. Those dock rats down there
are going to make life damned dangerous for foreigners
in these parts during the next several months. Believe
me, it's just too risky out there."

Jenna swallowed hard, listening to the ugly shouts
in the street. She wasn't accustomed to such hatred,
such naked prejudice. She touched her abdomen,
where Carl's baby grew, and realized she couldn't risk
herself. Not yet. Someday, her father would pay for
what he'd done, wrecking her life, ending Carl's and
Aunt Cassie's in a bullet-riddled pool of blood. But for
the moment, she had to survive.

She had never hated necessity more.

Ronisha Azzan was a woman with a major-league
problem.

Seated in Bull Morgan's office high above the snow-
choked valleys of the Himalayan mountains, with her
boss in jail and terrorists loose on station, she was preparing for a face-off with the most influential—and
dangerous—politician of the era. Ronisha studied
Granville Baxter, TT-86's Time Tours CEO, with whom
she shared a Masai heritage, and wondered whether or
not she had just made the biggest mistake of her career.

"Are you out of your mind?" Bax demanded as the
aerie's elevator hummed upwards with its first load of
reporters. "Letting a pack of *newsies* into a meeting
this critical?"

Ronisha held the Time Tours' executive's gaze steadily, one of the few souls in Shangri-La Station tall enough to meet Bax's gaze eye to eye. "This is one meeting that *has* to be public. And you know why."

The tall executive's lips thinned. "Bull's meeting was public, too!" It came out understandably bitter.

"Yes, it was." She was only too aware of her precarious situation. "Bull's meeting *was* public. But I'm not Bull Morgan. And Bull Morgan is not *me*."

Almost absently, she flicked invisible lint from her brightly colored suit, its rich African patterns reproduced in silk, rather than plain and ordinary cotton, and shook back over her shoulder three solid feet of intricate braids, most of them her own. Ronisha favored four-inch spike heels to go with her African textiles and elaborate coifs. She hadn't yet met the man she couldn't intimidate, given half a minute's time and a chance to crush his fingers in a handshake while she outmaneuvered him at his own game—whether that game involved matters of the bedroom or the boardroom.

Ronisha Azzan was deeply proud of her Masai heritage and at the moment, that heritage was very nearly her only weapon. The Masai were famed as lion hunters. And the biggest, nastiest man-eating lion in the universe had just strolled into her *kraal*. Ronisha smiled, not at all nicely. As Shangri-La Station's Deputy Manager, Ronisha Azzan was nobody's assistant *anything*—a fact Senator John Paul Caddrick had yet to learn. If she could manage to keep her knees from shaking visibly while she taught him.

Granville Baxter stared hard at her for a long moment, brows furrowed. Then her meaning struck home and he started to grin. A weak grin, given what they had yet to face, but a grin, nonetheless. "Woman, you are wasted in station management. You ought to be a tycoon someplace, rolling in money."

"Oh, I don't think so. Somebody's got to do this job."
The elevator doors opened with a faint *ping*, disgorging
a cluster of reporters, most of whom stared up at her
for a long, disconcerted moment. Newly arrived from
up time with the senator, they hadn't yet met her. She
rose from her half-leaning seat against the corner of
Bull's desk.

"Welcome to TT-86. Ronisha Azzan, Deputy Station
Manager. Yes, set up right there, that's fine, anywhere
along here. Glad to assist you. If you have any questions
about power connections and cables, my administrative
assistant can help you out. Bernie, see to it our guests
have what they need. No, I'm sorry, we'll have to wait
for the senator's arrival before I make any official
statements . . ."

From a corner of her eye, she saw Bax shake his
head and mutter, "Ronnie, I hope you know what we're
doing."

Deep inside, where she wouldn't have let anyone
see, Ronisha hoped so, too.

Senator John Caddrick arrived ten minutes later. The
elevator doors slid open with another soft *ping* to reveal
the red-faced enemy, eyes nearly scarlet from the
aftermath of the tear gas. Ronisha Azzan narrowed her
own eyes as Caddrick halted for just a fraction of a
second at the threshold between elevator and office,
taking in the glare of lights, the shining camera lenses,
and the small forest of microphones. Clearly, the senator
had planned on intimidating a suitably cowed and
trembling assistant manager, rather than walking into
a live press conference.

As he swept his startled gaze toward Ronisha, the
elevator doors attempted to close automatically. He had
to jump forward in unseemly haste to avoid the
embarrassment of being carried all the way down to
Commons again. Behind him, a staffer caught the doors

and reopened them as Caddrick stalked forward in silence, leaving his legislative aides and a whole pack of armed, stone-faced federal marshals to trail into the aerie behind him. The senator made a visible, valiant, and not very successful effort to ignore the electrifying presence of the press corps.

She took that as her cue to launch an offensive of her own.

"Senator Caddrick," she said coolly, "welcome to Time Terminal Eighty-Six. Ronisha Azzan, Deputy Station Manager. This is Granville Baxter, Shangri-La Time Tours CEO. On behalf of Shangri-La Station, please allow me to extend our heartfelt condolences regarding your recent losses. However . . ." and she let a hint of steel creep into her voice, "in accordance with up-time laws governing the safety of time terminals and their official residents and guests, I need to remind you of a few laws regarding conduct on time terminals."

Caddrick's eyes widened slightly, then narrowed with a dangerous glint.

Ronisha plunged ahead. "It is against inter-temporal law to incite riot, or to aid and abet the illegal discharge of chemical agents banned from use on any time terminal, whether by a private citizen or by a member of law enforcement." She flicked a gaze at the marshals, who carried short-barreled riot guns and stared straight through her as though she were vermin. Clearly, they didn't give a damn about breaking inconvenient laws on the other side of a time terminal's Primary.

She faced Caddrick again. "It is illegal, as well, to willfully endanger the lives and property of station guests and residents. Senator, your actions here have put at risk the lives of several hundred innocents on Shangri-La Station. You have also violated several endangered species protection acts by putting at risk the only living population of prehistoric birds and pterodactyls in the world. If any of those animals die, you can be charged with several serious felonies. This station cannot and will not risk a repeat of the incidents you have created since your arrival. Have I made myself clear on these points?" Without giving him time to respond, she added, "Now, then. What, exactly, brings you to my time terminal? Please bear in mind that your answers will be recorded for posterity. Or the courts." She nodded pleasantly toward the utterly enchanted newsies and tried to ignore the terrifying presence of those cold-eyed marshals and their wicked riot guns.

Speaking very softly, which in no way disguised the menace in his voice, Senator John Caddrick said, "Am I to understand you're going to put *me* in jail?"

Ronisha drew herself up to her full height, augmented by stiletto heels, and forced a smile down the full seven inches of her superior stature to the senator's furious grey eyes. "Not at all, senator. But you do realize, I hope, that my first concern must be the safety of this station and its residents and guests. I cannot permit *any* situation to threaten human or protected animal lives on TT-86, no matter how well intentioned the action. Surely you, of all people, must understand that?"

She could see it in his eyes, the look of shocked fury that said, *You devious, black bitch* . . . and coldly loathed him. Then he passed a hand across his eyes, a hand that visibly shook, and said in an unsteady voice, "Forgive me, Ms. Azzan, I'm not quite myself today . . . You see, I just received word that the *Ansar Majlis* brought my little girl onto this station. And with the press broadcasting riots and murders on TT-86, naturally we thought it prudent to bring along federal marshals . . ."

Oh-oh. Silent alarm klaxons sounded. If Jenna Caddrick had been dragged through one of TT-86's gates by her up-time kidnappers, Shangri-La Station was in more serious trouble than even she had realized. A man like John Caddrick wouldn't need any additional ammunition to shut them down for good. And he was damned effective at playing to the press.

So she played his game to the hilt, taking the senator's arm solicitously and guiding him to a chair. "Senator, please, sit down. There's no need for armed warfare between us. Everyone on TT-86 is in deep sympathy with your pain and loss." John Caddrick wasn't the only person in this room who knew the tricks of playing to the press. She wasn't Coralisha Azzan's grandchild for nothing.

Ronisha glanced over one shoulder, looking for her executive assistant. "Bernie, a glass of scotch and soda for the senator, please." Her assistant handed it over and Caddrick sipped, hand still trembling visibly. Ronisha waited for just a moment longer, keeping her expression carefully concerned, then said quietly, "Now, then, senator, why don't you fill us in on exactly what you've learned that's brought you to us? Tell us how we can help."

She seated herself in Bull Morgan's chair and composed herself to listen, switching on the digital pad that would send her handwritten notes directly to her computer, as well as turning on the room's meeting-recorder system. Cameras near the ceiling tracked silently, mirroring the swing of press cameras as Senator John Caddrick began to speak.

"Ten days ago," the senator said heavily, "tragedy struck my family. Again. You must be aware that I lost my wife several years ago to a drunk driver? She was killed trying to get home to my daughter's birthday party. Jenna . . ." He blinked rapidly, eyes reddened and wet. "My daughter and I never got over it, particularly poor little Jenna, she was so young when my wife died. My wife's sister, Cassie Tyrol, became a second mother to her. Jenna Nicole adored her aunt. Wanted to follow her onto the stage, was studying film . . ." He paused, wiped his eyes distractedly with unsteady fingers. "Jenna met her aunt the day Cassie died, at a restaurant in New York. Cassie had flown in from New Hollywood to see her. There was an atrocity . . ."

Ronisha knew all about the terrorist hit in New York. "Yes. I know. The *Ansar Majlis*."

"This crazy damned Brotherhood!" Senator Caddrick bit out, voice harsh. "They've declared open warfare on the Lady of Heaven Temples. I've tried for years to warn Congress something like this was bound to happen, letting down-timers onto the time terminals in whole-sale droves . . ." He shook his head. "Cassie was heavily involved in the Temple, you see, very public in her support. Her last film was about the Temple. It was a smash success and she donated the proceeds to the Templars . . . and now this Brotherhood . . ." his voice was breaking up, his eyes wet.

John Caddrick fought himself under control again with visible effort. "They sent a death squad after poor Cassie. Murdered her, right in the restaurant. Jenna disappeared. Kidnapped by the *Ansar Majlis*. The FBI has been working on it, of course, trying to track down *Ansar Majlis* ringleaders in New York, but I hired a detective, a good one. Sid Kaederman's been trying to trace my daughter's possible movements after that attack in the restaurant. Mr. Kaederman believes Jenna was forcibly brought to TT-86 by her kidnappers. Jenna's bank account and bank box were emptied, the same day her aunt was murdered."

He looked up, finally, and met Ronisha's gaze. "Some of her friends at college thought Jenna and her roommate had been planning a trip down time, against my express wishes, of course, but they thought she'd made arrangements to buy tickets and a false identity through some underworld mobster, so I wouldn't find out. Jenna's been hyped on film-making all her life, same as her aunt, wanted to make historically accurate films. God knows, it was something she might have done, buying a time-tour ticket to make some idiotic movie. So I put Sid Kaederman to work on the lead.

"When the *Ansar Majlis* forced Jenna to empty her bank account for them, they discovered her tickets and her false identification papers. They forced her to come here, to use them, so they could get out of New York without being detected. But even though we know they came here, and we know the names on the false identities she purchased in New York a year ago, we don't know which down-time gate they might have gone through. None of Jenna's friends knew which gate she planned to visit and we couldn't trace the mobster who sold her the time-touring tickets. She used a different source than she'd used to buy the phony identities and we never traced the ticket-scalper."

John Caddrick drained the rest of the scotch in his glass, then leaned forward in his chair. "What I want, Ms. Azzan, is simple enough. I want my daughter back, alive and unharmed, *whatever it takes.*" The rasp of steel in the senator's voice sent a chill of genuine terror down Ronisha's spine. "You may believe I've followed the reports of riots, kidnappings, and murders on this station with keen interest. If *anything* has happened to my little girl on this god-forsaken time terminal or down one of its gates, I will use my authority and influence to shut down this entire station. And you may rest assured, Ms. Azzan, these federal marshals *will* shut you down, if the situation warrants it."

Ronisha slipped a hand into her lap and pressed the buzzer under the lip of Bull's massive desk, the one that alerted security headquarters trouble was brewing in the station manager's office. She wanted Mike

Benson up here, stat, and kicked herself for not having summoned him sooner.

"Senator," she had to force her voice to steadiness, "I think everyone in this room realizes how serious the situation is. Fortunately, we've obtained a very solid lead on the terrorists you came here hoping to trace. We have several of their henchmen under arrest and are fully informed as to the *Ansar Majlis'* plans. My chief of security has men acting on this information right now, sweeping the station to arrest several of the *Ansar Majlis'* key ringleaders, who arrived through Primary today."

Caddrick's eyes shot wide. "You have information on their plans?" he echoed, voice flat with surprise.

"Yes, we do. Several of the station's resident down-timers discovered the plot and fought a pitched battle against the terrorists, subduing them. Thanks to the down-timers, we have enough information to arrest the entire *Ansar Majlis* operation."

Shock detonated behind Caddrick's eyes. "My God! Why, that's—that's incredible! But that still doesn't tell us where Jenna is." Shock gave way to calculating hostility.

"No, it doesn't," she agreed, stalling for time while thinking fiercely, *Shag your butt, Benson, I need you up here,* and played what she hoped would not prove to be her final trump card. "Because we're dealing with international and inter-temporal terrorism, I don't think it's unreasonable to call in an uninterested third party. To oversee the investigations which will have to be launched. I certainly don't want to give the impression this station has anything to hide. And I'm certain you don't want the investigation to take on the appearance of a personal vendetta."

A few of the reporters suppressed delighted gasps.

Senator Caddrick glared at her while a slow red flush crept up his neck.

"Of course," Ronisha added, "*we* know it isn't anything of the kind. But surely you, of all people, must know how appearances can be deceiving. The public has a right to the truth, obtained in a fair, unbiased manner. Thank you, Senator, for insisting on an independent investigation by an unbiased team. If I recall inter-temporal statutes correctly, that kind of fact-finding mission would fall under the jurisdiction of the Inter-Temporal Court of the Hague. I propose we send a representative of the Bureau of Access Time Functions through Primary at its next cycle and request immediate assistance from an independent team of evaluators appointed by I.T.C.H."

She and Senator Caddrick locked gazes across the desk. She'd just made an enemy for life and knew it; but John Caddrick had walked into this room already a mortal enemy, so no ground was lost by insisting on an unbiased review team. Under normal circumstances, the very last thing *anyone* on station would want was an investigation by the Inter-Temporal Court. Zealous I.T.C.H. officers had been known to shut down station operations over minor violations, putting stations under direct Court control until new management could demonstrate its willingness and ability to comply with the last dotted "i" and crossed "t" of the law.

But these weren't ordinary circumstances.

She was fighting for the life of the station.

Senator Caddrick nodded slow agreement, despite the fury seething in his eyes. "Of course, Ms. Azzan. It was never my intention to conduct an official investigation personally, although I certainly will demand that one be launched immediately. I shall, of course, conduct a fact-finding mission of my own while I'm here."

There being nothing she could do to stop him, short of throwing him into the brig—which would not improve the station's image—Ronisha simply nodded graciously.

"Now, then, senator, you said your daughter had obtained forged identification papers? She and her kidnappers are travelling under assumed names, then. What names? Any information you can give us will be critical in tracing them."

"Yes, of course." The senator was digging into a pocket for a CM disk, which he held out. Ronisha accepted the disk just as the emergency phone on the corner of Bull's desk jangled, its tones shrill in the hushed office. Ronisha glanced at it with a sinking sensation in her middle. Whoever was on the other end of that line knew what Ronisha was in the middle of, up here, how serious this meeting was.

"Excuse me, please," she said, picking up the phone. "Aerie, Azzan speaking. This had better be good."

"Mike Benson, reporting in!" The security chief had to shout above the roar in the background. "We've got the *Ansar Majlis* ringleaders under wraps."

"Fabulous," she said with a rush of relief.

"Do you still need me to answer that silent alarm?"

"Yes, please."

"On my way."

She hung up the phone and faced the expectant crowd in her office. "Now, then," she said pleasantly, "where were we, senator? You were about to give us the information on your daughter's forged identifications, I believe."

Caddrick stared at her for long moments, clearly expecting her to explain the interruption. When she didn't, he glowered for a moment, then said coldly, "This disk contains the data we've gathered so far. Mr. Kaederman believes the *Ansar Majlis* ringleader, a notorious intersexual using the alias Noah Armstrong, used one of Jenna's forged identities to bring my daughter here. Jenna's kidnapper was probably travelling under the name of Benny Catlin."

Across the room, Granville Baxter came out of his chair to tap commands into the nearest computer terminal, pulling up Time Tours' records of gate departures.

"Perhaps, senator," Ronisha suggested, "you might give us some insight into your daughter's interests and habits? Anything we can learn about Jenna, about the way she thinks, what she might do under stress, will increase our chances of locating her."

"Yes, of course. I brought some things with me, besides that disk." Senator Caddrick turned to an aide who hovered nearby. "Hand around those biographical packets, would you? And those photos of that bastard, Armstrong."

While Bax worked at the computer, a sweating senatorial aide passed dossiers around the room, first to Ronisha and the Time Tours CEO, then to the newsies, who struck like piranha. There were several photographs of Jenna Caddrick, all of them recent, as well as a photograph of the *Ansar Majlis* terrorist, Noah Armstrong. Ronisha realized with a start of surprise why the senator had mistaken Skeeter Jackson for his daughter's kidnapper. From a full-frontal view, they didn't closely resemble one another, but there were distinct similarities of bone structure and coloring. From behind or at an oblique angle, the resemblance was strong enough to understand the mistaken identity. The brief document attached to the photos outlined Jenna Caddrick's habits, manners, routines, interests, and hobbies.

At the other end of the crowded office, Granville Baxter glanced up from the computer screen, looked over the photos, then cleared his throat. "I found Benny Catlin's tour records, but I'm afraid we still have a serious problem facing us—more serious than tracing Benny Catlin in London."

John Caddrick's glare was lethal. "What could possibly be more serious than locating my daughter's kidnapper?"

Bax held up the photograph of Noah Armstrong. "This."

"What *about* it?"

The Time Tours executive paused. Then sipped air and looked like he wanted to bolt for the nearest exit. Ronisha Azzan wasn't sure just what the bad news would be, but she was already *quite* certain she wasn't going to like it.

Granville Baxter didn't disappoint her.

"Well, senator, you see . . ." He held up a snapshot. "This photograph of your daughter's kidnapper . . . This isn't Benny Catlin."

Chapter Two

Of all the historians, criminologists, and reporters fortunate enough to win spots on the Ripper Watch team, none was more determined to obtain the truth of the Ripper story than Dominica Nosette. Not one of the other team members had a quarter the professional ruthlessness she possessed in her big toe. The only one who came close was her partner, Guy Pendergast. And Dominica was utterly delighted with Guy, because he had done what no one else had managed since their arrival in London. He had discovered the identity of Jack the Ripper. The mysterious doctor mentoring the irretrievably mad James Maybrick was the guiding genius of the two-man team known to history as the Ripper. And Dominica intended to vault herself to fame and fortune on the coattails of their murderous partnership.

"His name is John Lachley," Guy had said breathlessly as they'd slipped out of Spaldergate House with their luggage, determined to break loose of their time guides' stranglehold. "He's a medical doctor, with training in the occult and ties to the East End. Came up out of SoHo, just west of Whitechapel. He's our man, I'll stake my reputation on it. Calls his house Tibor, mind. The same word our mystery Ripper used the night Polly Nichols died." Pendegast chuckled thinly. "And those fuzzy-brained idiots with me were so busy doting on that Irish poet, William Butler Yeats, they missed the clue entirely!"

John Lachley, they had since discovered, had ties to the royal family, as well, through the queen's grandson, Prince Albert Victor Christian Edward. And John Lachley had been born right in Whitechapel itself, in Middlesex Street, which explained the Ripper's familiarity with the streets. He'd gone to charity school, had John Lachley, and acquired his medical education in Scotland. Once known throughout the East End as Johnny Anubis, séance parlour medium and small-time occultist, Dr. John Lachley now lectured on mesmerism and other occult subjects to large audiences drawn from London's finest families. He was a member of the Theosophical Society, a respected physician with a surgery in Cleveland Street, a model subject of the crown in every way.

That much, Dominica Nosette and Guy Pendergast had managed to discover thus far, working on their own without those repressive, overly cautious Time Tours guides curtailing their every move. But why John Lachley was working with James Maybrick to murder East End whores, and what was in the letters Lachley was slowly tracking down, killing the previous owners to keep some dark and clearly critical secret, Dominica had no idea. She intended to find out.

The video she had already obtained of Lachley was worth a literal fortune, video footage showing him in company with the young prince, footage of him meeting the soon-to-be-notorious Aleister Crowley, and with the founders of the Golden Dawn magical order, Mathers and Waite and the rest. Whether or not these occultists were also involved in the conspiracy of the letters, Dominica didn't know. That, too, she intended to discover.

"We're going to win that Carson Historical Video Prize!" she told Guy Pendergast as they set out from the flat they'd rented in SoHo. "Lachley will strike again September 30th. The night of the double event . . ."

"Which means Elizabeth Stride and Catharine Eddowes *must* have possession of the letters he's after!"

"Yes. And Mary Kelly must have another one. Guy . . ." Dominica mused, slanting a glance up at her partner. "How good are you at picking pockets?"

"Picking pockets?" he echoed, brows drifting upward in startlement.

She smiled. "Well, it occurs to me that we could probably unlock the key to this whole thing if we could lay hands on one of those letters. Just long enough to photograph it. Then we slip it back into the pocket you steal it from, long before he kills Stride and Eddowes. All we have to do then is follow him after the double-event murders. Videotape *those*, then collect our Carson Prize. And rather an enormous amount of money," she ended smugly.

Guy Pendergast smiled slowly. "Dominica, my pet, you are brilliant."

"Of course I'm brilliant! I didn't get where I am by being stupid. We'll have to tackle Stride, since Catharine Eddowes is leaving London to head out to Kent, picking hops. It might be interesting to videotape Eddowes out there, working the harvest." She frowned. "You know, it doesn't make sense, that. If she's in possession of something so valuable that Lachley is committing brutal murder to obtain it, you'd think a woman like Catharine Eddowes would try to convert it into cash. She's plagued her own daughter for money so often, the poor thing moves every few weeks around South London, just to keep her mother from tapping her for tuppence. Yet Kate Eddowes walks—*walks*, mind you, in this weather—all the way from London to rural Kent, just to break her back working in wet fields picking hops as a migrant agricultural laborer."

"Maybe," Guy suggested dryly, "she hasn't cashed in on her letter because she can't read it."

Dominica dismissed that as chauvinist nonsense. "Don't be a boor. She was educated in St. John's Charity School, Potter's Field, Tooley Street. And all her friends described her as a scholarly, intense woman. Of course she can read it."

Her partner shrugged. "It was just an idea."

"Well, when we get our hands on whatever Long Liz Stride has, we shall find out, shan't we?"

Guy Pendergast chuckled. "Right."

So they set their faces east and started combing the dismal streets of Whitechapel, looking for one particular Swedish-born prostitute who had barely two weeks left to live.

Victoria Station was jam-packed with Ripperoons.

Skeeter, like most of the others jammed in the station's Commons cheek-by-jowl, felt better for a good night's sleep. Memory of the previous evening's riot at Primary was fading in the face of anticipated news from London. After a century and a half of waiting, the world was finally going to learn who Jack the Ripper really was. *If*, of course, and Skeeter grinned to himself, the Ripper Watch experts in London had figured it out.

Tourists who'd appointed themselves lay experts had gathered from all over Commons, surging into Victoria Station and talking nineteen miles to the minute, consulting Ripper-suspect biographies as they argued the merits of various theories. Skeeter, with Kit Carson at his heels, strolled through the madhouse crowd, eyes sharp for any sign of pickpockets or con artists working the throng. Voices like a mile-long swarm of locusts bounced off the girders high overhead with echoes that hurt the senses, expounding favored Ripper theories and wondering what had become of Senator Caddrick's daughter.

"—witness descriptions don't tally well with one another. I mean, they range from a guy in his thirties with fair skin, sandy hair and light brown mustache to a guy in his forties or fifties, dark hair and mustache, dark eyes and complexion, with a 'foreign' look. Personally, I don't think any of the witnesses saw the real Ripper. Except maybe Israel Schwartz, the Jew who didn't speak English. He saw Elizabeth Stride attacked . . ."

" . . . whole slew of people claimed they were Jack the Ripper, including a manure collector who emigrated to Australia. Fellow got murderously angry when drunk, at least he did if a prostitute approached. Told his son he was the Ripper and intended to confess before he died, but never did. Confess, I mean. He died, no problem. 1912."

"—they bring I.T.C.H. agents in to monitor this mess, the Inter-Temporal Court will shut us all down!"

"I heard it was Lewis Carroll—"

"The author of *Alice in Wonderland*? The *Ripper*? You gotta be kidding! I mean, so what if he liked to photograph naked little girls? That's pretty weird, but it doesn't fit the profile of a man who'd rip women open with an eight-inch knife!"

"No, I don't think it was Aleister Crowley, even if he was a sick puppy. Worshipped anything evil and violent, claimed to be the prophet of the anti-Christ. But as a Ripper suspect, I think the evidence is pretty thin . . ."

"—somebody's going to shoot that bastard, that's

what I think, and Caddrick's got it coming to him, walking onto this station and tear gassing a crowd full of innocent women and kids—"

" . . . convinced the prime minister did it, covering up for the queen's grandson Eddy. Although why he would've married a poor Catholic girl when he was screwing half the women in London, and supposedly several men, as well, is anybody's guess . . ."

"Nuts," somebody else nearby muttered. "We are hip deep in nuts. Sheesh. I need another beer . . ."

And finally, from the loudspeakers overhead: *"Your attention please. Gate Two is due to cycle in three minutes. All departures, be advised . . ."*

Thank God, Skeeter thought. He glanced back at Kit and found the retired scout trailing him half a dozen paces back. Kit rolled his eyes at a mob of sign-carrying loons, chanting the praises of their Immortal Lord Jack and heckling the Time Tours guides trying to organize the outgoing Ripper Watch Tour, then indicated with a gesture, "Okay, hotshot, get busy!"

So he worked the crowd, quartering it leisurely, keeping his gaze sharp. When the immense Britannia finally began its cycle, the roar of voices reached a fever pitch. Wagers rattled like hailstones off every echoing surface in Victoria Station. Skeeter prowled through the surging crowd, alert as a snow leopard and beginning to grow impatient, aware of Kit's presence behind him, watching, judging. He knew his particular brand of prey was out here. His senses twitched, searching for telltale movements, the little signs he knew so well. High overhead, the huge gate dilated slowly open . . . And Skeeter rocked to a halt. His gaze zeroed in, a stooping hawk spotting his next meal. The pickpocket was stalking a man in his fifties whose tanned face, lean build, and expensively casual clothes shouted, *California millionaire.* The pickpocket lifted a fat wallet from the Californian's jacket with a practiced stumble and a hasty apology given and accepted with ease.

Skeeter grinned. *Gotcha!*

The handcuffs he slipped out of his pocket weren't real. He'd picked them up cheap from a station outfitter's bin of discount toys. But they were functional enough for Skeeter's purposes. He slid forward between the Californian and the pickpocket just as the latter slipped the wallet into his *own* jacket. Skeeter tapped the thief on the shoulder. "Hi, there!"

And clicked the cuffs around the guy's wrists before he could blink.

"Hey! What the—"

"Security!" Skeeter bawled, grabbing the guy's jacket lapel. "Got a pickpocket over here! Say, mister," Skeeter got the victim's attention, "this guy just lifted your wallet."

The tourist gasped, hand flying to his extremely empty pocket. "Good God! I've been robbed! Why, you sneaking—"

Security arrived before the irate Californian could take a swing at the struggling pickpocket. "What's going on?" The uniformed security guard sported a bruise down one cheek from the previous day's riot.

"Caught this guy lifting a tourist's wallet," Skeeter explained. "It's in his front jacket pocket. Oh, those cuffs are toys, by the way. Just thought you might want to know."

Skeeter indulged a grin at the look on all three faces, then melted into the crowd, leaving the stunned security officer to deal with the irate tourist and the even more irate pickpocket. He could hear the latter howling his outrage all the way through Victoria Station. Skeeter chuckled. This was almost as much fun as picking pockets, himself. More, maybe. Less risk involved, certainly. He was still chuckling when Kit caught up, grinning fit to crack his face.

"That was impressive. Kids' toys!"

"Yeah, well, sometimes you gotta make do."

"As far as I'm concerned, you won't have to 'make do' with toy handcuffs any longer. You're definitely hired. I was watching close, following your gaze, and I didn't see a thing."

Skeeter's face went hot, but it was a proud flush. He'd done a good job and Kit knew it. High overhead, the returning tour started pouring through the open gate. A Time Tours guide rushed down the stairs, well in advance of the tourists, clutching a heavy pouch. Waiting newsies mobbed him.

"Who is it—?"

"—that a videotape?"

"Has the Ripper Watch Team solved—?"

The grim-faced guide vanished into the Time Tours ticket office and slammed the door, leaving the newsies screaming at sound-proofed glass.

"You know," Skeeter mused, "that guy didn't act like an excited courier carrying the news of the decade, did he?"

"No," Kit agreed, expression thoughtful.

A moment later, the rest of the tour reached Commons floor and word spread like racing wildfire: *Two killers!*

"James Maybrick, after all—"

"Complete unknown! Some doctor, nobody has the faintest idea who—"

"Working *together*—!"

And hard on the heels of that shock, yet another, potentially fatal to the entire station: *Missing tourist!*

"—shot two up-time baggage handlers to death—"

"—said he vanished over in SoHo—"

"Oh, my God," Skeeter groaned. "*Another* missing person!" And another shocking murder spree for TT-86 to explain to the press and the government agencies and Senator Caddrick.

"Who was he?" a woman dressed as a Roman matriarch demanded at Skeeter's elbow.

"I don't know!"

"Someone said he's a graduate student . . ."

" . . . heard his name was Benny Catlin . . ."

Benny Catlin?

That name rang alarm bells in Skeeter's memory. Lots of them. Big, fat, warped ones. Benny Catlin was the name on all that luggage Skeeter'd hauled through the Britannia Gate, last time out. What was a graduate student doing with that much luggage? Skeeter hadn't met a grad student yet with enough money to haul five enormous steamer trunks through *any* gate, much less the Britannia. And that trunk Skeeter had almost knocked off the platform had belonged to Benny Catlin, too. Which meant the white-faced, muttonchopped, short little jerk who'd started screaming at him was their missing man. And a double murderer.

He narrowed his eyes, wondering just what Benny Catlin had stowed in all that luggage. And whether or not the tourist responsible for Skeeter losing his job as baggage porter might look anything like the mysterious doctor in the Ripper Watch video. The thought unsettled him. Not that an up-timer might've committed the murders. That theory had been kicked around so many times, it was old news. But Skeeter might have carried through the murderer's own luggage, had maybe talked to Jack the Ripper, himself, without realizing it.

And *that* was a decidedly uneasy thought. That a serial killer as seriously depraved as the Ripper could pass through society looking and behaving like a completely normal person, while inside . . . Skeeter shivered. And was damned glad he hadn't stayed in London, after all, which he'd planned to do before Ianira's disappearance. If he'd stayed, he'd doubtless have been pressed into searching for the missing Benny Catlin. And hunting

Jack the Ripper was not Skeeter's idea of a sane way to pass the time. He'd stick to stalking pickpockets and small-time grifters. Those, at least, he could understand.

He didn't want to understand serial killers.

Not ever.

"Skeeter?"

Kit's gaze was centered squarely on him, brows twitching downward in concern.

"Yeah?"

"What's wrong?"

"I think I saw Catlin, the day the gate opened last week."

"Really? What do you remember about him?"

Skeeter described Catlin, then added, "He had too much luggage for a grad student. Five big steamer trunks. Expensive ones."

"He's not the guy whose steamer trunk almost went off the platform, is he?" Kit asked abruptly, eyes narrowed.

Skeeter blinked in surprise. Then rubbed the back of his neck, embarrassed. "Uh, yeah. I think so. That was the name on the luggage tag. And he was white as any ghost, trying to keep it from falling."

"I think," Kit said in a tight, dangerous voice, "we'd better tell Ronisha Azzan about this, because it looks to me like Catlin may well have been one of the *Ansar Majlis* goons on Armstrong's payroll. I find myself wondering what—or who—was in that trunk. And I'll bet Ronisha Azzan will, too."

"Aw, nuts . . . Kit, I heard she was meeting with Senator Caddrick again this morning, trying to figure out where his kid went. And if he sees me, he's gonna remember I assaulted him, back at Primary. *That* kind of attention, I don't need."

"Nonsense," Kit said firmly. "Nobody's going to jail the guy who figured out where his kid's kidnappers went."

Skeeter had a terrible feeling he would find himself dragged down the Britannia Gate eight days from now as part of the search teams, after all. He wondered briefly if a bullet would've been waiting for *him,* if he'd stayed to haul those heavy steamer trunks to Catlin's hotel? Skeeter sighed, then ran a hand through his hair. Why was it, going legit had turned into the hardest thing he'd ever tried to do? And considering his background, that was saying a lot.

"Well," he muttered, "I guess I'll just have to play it by ear, won't I?"

"That's the spirit!" Kit grinned. "Come on, Skeeter. Let's go find you a security squawky someplace, then maybe by the time we've done that, Ronnie's followup meeting with the senator will be over?"

Skeeter managed a weak grin of gratitude. "Okay. Thanks."

Wondering if he knew what he was doing, he followed Kit Carson's lead. *Just go with Kit,* he told himself, and tried not to think too closely about where the grizzled old scout would end up leading him. He was *quite* sure he did not want to find out.

Mary Jane Kelly was afraid of the man she'd come to visit. Black magic and demon worship and an appetite for the unholy . . .

Marie Jeannette, as she'd been born, knew the whispers were not just hideous rumour, either, they were terrifying fact. He'd told her so, himself, on his many visits to the high-class West End house where she'd worked at the time, the one she'd been thrown out of shortly afterward for excessive drinking, a habit she'd picked up after becoming this particular gentleman's favorite.

"A whore," he'd smiled down into her eyes, "is my ideal of the perfect unholy woman. A sower of immorality, a merchant of sin. A perfect vessel for wreaking the destruction of prudish social convention and absurd, medieval morals. Don't you agree, my dear?"

Whatever the customer wants, had been her initial response to his blazing eyes and strange appetites. The fear had come later, when he whispered between savage thrusts, mouth half full of her left breast, "The Second Coming will bring a Great Year to its close . . . and the powers of hell will destroy all the weak and foolish lunacy Christians call goodness. And I . . ." he murmured darkly as he gave her a particularly hard pounding, excitement glittering in his eyes, "I worship those powers of hell. I shall rule upon this earth when the destruction sweeps away godliness and everything it stands for. I shall be the most powerful of men, preparing the way for the anti-Christ . . . Does this shock you, my dear? Or," he laughed and kissed her hard, "does it *excite* you?"

Of all the men who'd paid to use her body, rich men who'd plied her with furs and beautiful clothes and trips to faraway, exotic places like Paris, East End coster-mongers reeking of gin and dead fish, violent louts who'd blacked her eye, afterwards, and the half-grown boys brought to a certain fancy West End address by their wealthy fathers to learn what to do with a woman, of all those many men, *none* frightened twenty-six-year-old Mary Kelly as deeply as Mr. Aleister Crowley.

But Mary Jane Kelly had been living in fear so deep, she would almost rather have faced Satan, himself, than continue in this terror. So she had brought herself, quaking in her once-fine boots, to Satan's very door-step, praying that Mr. Crowley's ambitions would cause him to find her plight interesting—and that his dark powers would help keep her alive. The butler who answered the door sniffed irritably, but allowed her to step out of the cold wind into a polished, gleaming hall to wait while he took her message to his master.

Moments later, the butler was ushering her into a study whose bookcases were crowded with hundreds of ancient, mouldering books and manuscripts, and whose shelves were lined with items she decided queasily she didn't really wish to look at too closely. The only crucifix in the room was upside down. It hung above a lit, black candle.

"Why, Mary Kelly, it *is* you! I've missed you enormously, my dear!"

Mr. Crowley had not changed. He came around the desk, hands outstretched, and kissed her cheek, surrounded by a black aura of danger that set her quaking in her boots again. She could still remember gulping down whole bottles of gin, brandy, anything she could lay hands on, trying to forget what it had felt like, with this man in her. *What am I doing here, God help me, I haven't any other choice, they'll kill me, else . . . and the baby, too, can't let 'em kill my baby . . .*

Pregnant, utterly penniless, Mary Kelly had nowhere else to turn.

"Sit down, please." He ushered her to a chair, drawing another up close beside her. "What brings you here? Your hands are like ice, Mary, would you like a brandy to warm you?"

"Please, yes . . ." Her voice was shaking as badly as her hands.

He splashed brandy into a snifter, handed it to her, watched her gulp it down.

"What can I do for you, then?"

She lowered the empty glass to her threadbare lap. "I need . . . I'm in terrible trouble, you see, and I thought . . . I thought you might be interested in . . . the reason why."

He tipped his head to one side, eyes merry. "If you're going to tell me I'm the father of whatever brat you might be carrying, I would point out it's been more than seven months, my dear, and you clearly are not seven months gone with child."

Her face flamed. "No, it's not the baby, that's Joseph's, right enough, and he's been good to me. It's this . . ." She dug into her pocket, brought out the grimy sheets of foolscap which Joseph had brought home for her to translate, after buying them from Dark Annie. Poor Joe, he'd thought these hideous little letters would be their ticket to wealth. But Annie was dead, monstrously so, as was the woman *she'd* got them from, and after reading these letters, Mary was terrified that she would be next, she and whoever else had been insane enough to lay hands on one of these sordid little missives.

He glanced at the writing, frowned. "This is in Welsh, is it not?"

She nodded. "My man . . . he bought them, you see, from Annie, when she needed medicines, asked me to read them out for him. There were others . . ." Her voice had begun to shake again. "Annie had them from Polly and now they're both dead! Murdered and cut apart by this madman in Whitechapel!"

Aleister Crowley was staring at her. "My dear," he said gently, "whatever is in these letters?"

In a low, trembling voice, she told him. Word for word, she told him exactly what the letters said. And he saw it as quickly as she had done.

"My God! Eddy? *Collars and Cuffs?* It must be . . ."

She nodded. "Yes. It must be him. And the queen must have ordered all this hushed up, I can't think why else Polly Nichols would have been killed so horribly, or poor Annie Chapman, who was so sick, she could hardly stand up."

Crowley began to laugh, very softly. "Victoria, order this done? Oh, no, my dear, the queen is entirely too *good* to condone what's been done by our friend the Whitechapel fiend. Oh, she's no fool, and if she knew about these," he tapped the letters in Mary's shaking hand, "she might well try to hush it all up. But order someone to cut the owners of the letters to pieces in the streets? No. She would *not* wish for that kind of publicity, for that sort of scrutiny. The police and the press are simply agog over our friend the Whitechapel Murderer. I must say," he chuckled, "quite a reputation, he's given himself, isn't it? This business must be driving the authorities mad. No, Victoria would never be stupid enough to generate that sort of publicity. Take my word for it, Mary dear, someone else is committing these murders. Someone close to Eddy, no doubt. Someone with a great deal to lose, should Eddy's indiscretions become public knowledge." He sat tapping his fingertips against the arm of his chair for long moments. "Well, now, this is quite an intriguing little mystery you've handed me, my dear. One presumes you want money?"

She shook her head, bit her lip. "I . . . I don't want to be . . . next . . ."

"Ah. Of course you don't."

"I've got a baby coming," she got out in a rush, "and a man who wants to marry me, when he gets another job, even though he knows what I've been. Joseph's a good man, wants to take me off the streets, and he didn't know what this horrible little letter was when he bought it, he was just doing Annie a favor, because she was so sick and needed the money for medicine . . ."

He took her trembling hands in his own and patted them, brought them to his lips. Mary shuddered, fighting more terror than she'd ever known in her young life.

"Here, now, no need for such hysteria, my dear. Of course you're frightened, but you've done exactly the right thing, coming to me for protection." He dried her wet face with his hands, brushed her heavy, strawberry-blonde hair back from her brow, planted a kiss there.

"I'll take very good care of you, my dear. Just leave
the letter with me, that's a good girl. I've a fair idea
who might be profiting from these murders, knowing
Eddy as I do, and the way certain men think. Yes, I'll
take very good care of you, my dearest . . ."

He was kissing her, unbuttoning her dress, sliding
his hand up under her skirt.

He gave her two whole crowns, after, worth half a
pound sterling.

Kissed her and told her to buy herself a lot of gin
and a pretty new shawl and not to worry, he would see
to it that she was never molested by whoever was
hunting down Eddy's sordid little letters. When she left
the house, pulling her threadbare shawl tightly about
her shoulders against the cold bite of the wind, Mary
Jane Kelly was trembling far harder than she'd been
when she'd arrived an hour previously. *What've I done,
letting him do that horrible ritual over me, like that,
when he was in me, what in God's name have I done?*

She bit her lip and started for home. Surely, anything
was better than being cut into pieces and having her
insides strewn across the ground? Surely it was? But she
felt dirty and cold and unclean down to her soul, which
she never had felt even when letting the meanest, dirtiest
louts in the East End spend inside her. She brushed
wetness from her eyes and pressed a hand against her
belly, where a child was growing. Whatever else, she had
to think about far more than just herself, now. Which
was why she could have done nothing else, today.

But, oh, God, she was so afraid.

And Mr. Aleister Crowley frightened her only a little
less terribly than the rest.

"Kit!"

Kit Carson glanced around, peering into the nervous
crowds thronging Commons, many of them wondering

in shrill tones what would happen and would their vacations be cancelled and could they get a refund if Senator Caddrick closed down TT-86? He found Robert Li bearing down on him and smiled at his long-time friend.

"Hi, Robert. What's up?"

The antiquarian stared. "*What's up?* You are kidding, aren't you? Kit, are you out of your gate-addled *mind?* Skeeter Jackson, Neo Edo's *house detective?*"

Kit chuckled. "Oh, that. Is that all?"

His friend's expression altered to one of deep pity. "Oh, God, it's true. You have lost your mind."

Kit's lips twitched. "Glad to know you think so highly of me, pal. No, I haven't lost my mind. But you—and just about every other 'eighty-sixer on station—have apparently lost your sense of fair play."

Robert Li blinked, the fair skin of his maternal Scandinavian heritage at odds with features bequeathed him by a paternal Hong Kong Chinese grandfather. "Come again?"

"Skeeter," Kit said gently, ticking off the points on his fingers. "One, that boy never rolled an 'eighty-sixer. *Never.* And if you'd think about it, you'd figure out why. Two, he hasn't been the same ever since that gawd-awful wager of his with Goldie went sour and Marcus ended up in chains down the Porta Romae. Three, Ianira trusted him implicitly. And Ianira Cassondra is no fool." Kit ran a hand through his thinning hair, unable to hide the grief mere thought of Ianira and her missing family brought. "That boy has damn near killed himself looking for them. Lost the only two honest jobs he could find on station doing it, too. And even then, he still didn't go back to picking pockets. The *down-timers* have been feeding him, Robert, because he hasn't had enough cash to buy a hot dog. So what's he been doing? Looking for a job nobody'll give him, tracking down terrorists in Shangri-La's basement, and arresting *thirty-one* small-time crooks in a single week. Without anybody asking him or paying him to do it. So yesterday, when he pulled Rachel Eisenstein out of that disaster at Primary, I decided it was high time somebody around here gave that kid a fair break. He's earned it. Especially with Caddrick likely to press charges for assaulting him, for God's sake. After what Caddrick did, roughing *him* up, that boy is gonna need all the help he can get."

Robert Li closed his mouth. Blinked. "Good God," the antiquarian said softly. Then, slowly, "All right, I'll concede a point when I've been wrong. But you've gotta admit, it's unlikely as hell."

Kit grinned. "Oh, sure it is. And that," he chuckled, "is why I'm having so much fun. What's that you've got with you?" He nodded at the sheet of paper his friend was carrying.

"This? Oh, it's a flier on Jenna Caddrick and that terrorist who grabbed her, Noah Armstrong. Mike Benson's ordered a stationwide hunt, looking for any eyewitnesses who might remember seeing them. I was trying to find you, to ask if you'd seen one of these yet, when I heard the news about you hiring Skeeter."

"No, I haven't seen it." Kit took the flier curiously, glancing at the photos, and ran down the brief descriptions. "I read about Cassie Tyrol. Damned shame."

"What's a shame?" Skeeter's voice asked at Kit's elbow.

He glanced up and took approving note of the security radio he'd sent Skeeter to obtain. "Good, you got the squawky. Cassie Tyrol is what's a shame. She was Senator Caddrick's sister-in-law, poor soul, can you imagine being related to *that*? Have you seen one of these yet?"

Skeeter took the flier curiously. "No." He narrowed his eyes slightly. "Don't know why Caddrick thought

this creep was *me*," he muttered, frowning at the photo
of Armstrong. "Guy looks sorta familiar, though. Not
sure why . . ." The former con artist's frown deepened
slowly. Then, seemingly struck by inspiration, Skeeter
dug into a pocket and came out with an ink pen. He
started drawing over the top of the photograph, startling
Robert Li into leaning forward.

"What in the world are you doing?" the antiquarian
asked.

"Just an idea," Skeeter muttered. He was sketching
in a drooping mustache, sideburns. The pen fairly flew
across the page, sketching in a bandana, a sombrero
pulled low . . .

"My God," Kit whispered, recognizing the face taking
shape. "It's Joey Tyrolin!"

Robert started slightly, swinging his gaze up to meet
Kit's. "Joey—? That drunk pistolero we saw the other
week, headed to Denver? That was *Noah Armstrong?*
We were that close to a murdering terrorist and didn't
even know it?"

Another resemblance clicked in Kit's mind. "Joey
Tyrolin! Skeeter, you genius! By God, I knew I'd hit
on a brilliant idea, hiring you! Jenna Caddrick's aunt's
name was Cassie *Tyrol*. Jocasta Tyrol—Joey Tyrolin!"

Skeeter wasn't smiling, however. In fact, he wasn't
even standing beside them, any longer. He'd bolted
through the crowd. He came back with another flier, one
he'd ripped off the nearest concrete post. Kit had seen
those fliers plastered up everywhere, with photos of the
station's missing down-timers. Skeeter was sketching over
Julius' photo. Skeeter's lips thinned to a grim line as he
drew in long hair pulled back into a bun beneath a wide-
brimmed calico bonnet. Then he held up the altered
sketch of his missing young friend. "And this is the
woman Joey Tyrolin tangled with at the Wild West ticket
kiosk. The one Tyrolin's porter dropped a trunk on. I

worked that gate departure, looking for some trace of Ianira and her family, and dammit, I didn't even recognize that boy!"

Kit remembered the incident clearly. "You're right." He took the altered sketches and scowled down at them. "Miss Caddrick must have used the name Joey Tyrolin on that fake I.D. she bought in New York. And Armstrong simply appropriated the I.D. and her tickets. If Armstrong was in that departures line, you can bet Jenna Caddrick was, too."

"Probably *in* one of the suitcases that porter dropped," Skeeter growled. "What I want to know is, how the *hell* did Julius get tangled up with terrorists? I know that boy. He wouldn't get involved in something like that, not without a damned good reason."

Robert Li said slowly, "Those *Ansar Majlis* leaders you caught are denying it, but it's pretty clear they paid Armstrong to hit Jenna Caddrick. So it's a good bet Armstrong masterminded the hit on Ianira, too. If I remember right, Julius disappeared about the same time her whole family vanished, didn't he? But surely the boy wouldn't have helped the *Ansar Majlis* voluntarily?"

Kit glanced at Skeeter, reading murderous hatred in the younger man's eyes and the set of his jaw. The one-time con artist said through clenched teeth, "If Armstrong blackmailed him with a threat to Ianira's life, he would've done anything that pack of cutthroats demanded. And waited for a chance to slit *their* throats, later."

A chill shivered its way up Kit's spine. This was a side of Skeeter he'd never witnessed, the side that had survived twelfth century Mongolia and the worst childhood any 'eighty-sixer on station could lay claim to. Slowly, Kit nodded agreement. "Yes, I think you're reading this situation very clearly, Skeeter. Julius would've done anything to save Ianira, if Armstrong had kidnapped her as well as Jenna Caddrick. Armstrong's pals in the *Ansar Majlis* might well have been holding the boy prisoner with Marcus and the girls, probably forced him to help them all escape the station. And my bet is, Armstrong sent at least one of his men down the Britannia with the fake I.D. Jenna Caddrick's roommate was supposed to use. Benny Catlin wasn't anything more than a decoy, to make us think her kidnappers had gone to London, when they planned to take her to Denver, all along."

Robert Li swung his gaze from Kit back to Skeeter. "Okay," he grinned suddenly, "I'm convinced! Damned smart move is right, hiring this genius. Question is, what do we do now?"

Kit eyed Skeeter narrowly. "How well do you ride a horse?"

Skeeter Jackson's sudden, lethal grin blazed like a noonday sun. "If it's got hooves, I can ride it."

"In that case, we visit Time Tours, Incorporated. Because your new boss just came out of retirement. It's been a while since I visited Denver."

Robert Li's mouth dropped open. Then the antiquarian started laughing. "Oh, my God! Wait until word gets out! Goldie Morran, for one, may strangle from simple shock. Kit Carson and Skeeter Jackson, *partners in crime?* I just wish I could get away from the studio long enough to go with you!"

Kit clouted him across one shoulder. "The price of being the only I.F.A.R.T.S. agent on station. But there is something you could do . . ."

"Why do I have the feeling I ought to be counting my fingernails and locking my safe?"

Kit grinned. "You wound me. Head over to Connie's, if you don't mind? We've only got six days before the Wild West Gate re-opens, which means we should've started outfitting last week, not to mention all the training Skeeter needs before we step through. I'd head straight to Connie's, but Skeeter and I have to break the news to Ronisha. And the senator."

Skeeter visibly lost color.

"Well, since you put it that way," Robert said hastily, "I'd rather ask Connie for favors than go near Caddrick, any day of the week."

"Thought you'd see it my way. C'mon, Skeeter. The senator's not going to throw you in jail, not when you're the genius who figured out where his little girl disappeared to."

Skeeter swallowed once. "Well, okay."

"C'mon, Jackson. Time's wasting."

Skeeter's grin was a little forced, but it was a brave effort.

Personally, Kit could hardly wait to beard this particular lion. One thing he had very little tolerance for was a cocky politician. Particularly one threatening to shut down *his* station. Senator John Caddrick didn't know it yet, but he'd made the worst enemy of his life. Kit fully intended to enjoy his revenge.

Chapter Three

Ianira Cassondra wasn't sure how long she'd been imprisoned.

The man who'd brought her to this room had kept her drugged for endless days. She knew only that she was somewhere in London, separated from the only people who could help her, and that her life remained in far too much danger from up-time threat to risk returning to Spaldergate House and its Britannia Gate, to seek help from friends on the station. She was as much on her own as she'd been in Athens, married to an inhuman merchant who valued her only for the male children she had been unable to produce. Her first husband had terrified Ianira. But the man who held her captive now . . .

He was mad, this Dr. John Lachley. He was also the ruling half of a killing team the up-time world knew as Jack the Ripper. John Lachley could not come within touching distance of her without Ianira slipping into shock and the most monstrous visions she had ever suffered. When she heard footsteps on the stairs outside her imprisoning bedroom, Ianira broke into a cold sweat and uncontrollable tremors. But the door opened to reveal only the manservant, Charles. He carried a meal tray. "Mrs. Seddons sent up your supper," he said gently, his warm regard filled with pity.

The food would be drugged, of course.

It always was.

"Thank you," Ianira whispered, voice hoarse.

Outside her bedroom window, twilight settled over the rooftops and chimney pots of London. She stilled shaking hands, having waited and planned for this moment, terrified that something would go wrong, now that it had come. Charles set the tray on the little table beside her bed, then settled into a chair to watch her eat. They did not leave her alone at mealtimes, making sure she swallowed the drugged food that kept her witless and utterly helpless in their hands. The manservant and the cook, Mrs. Seddons, had been told Ianira was in deep shock and suffering from delusions. She no longer even tried to speak with them. What John Lachley had done to her after her first attempt to enlist the servants' aid . . .

Ianira shuddered under the bedclothes. There wasn't enough hot water and soap in all of London to wash away what he'd done to her. Afterward, Ianira had planned a different route to freedom. So she sat up, trembling violently, and reached for the tray. Which she promptly dropped, spilling the contents across the carpets with a crash and clatter of broken china and tumbled silver.

Charles lunged to his feet with a dismayed cry, making certain she was unharmed first, then eased her down against the pillows and said, "Let me clear this away and bring another tray for you . . ."

The moment Charles left the room, Ianira lunged out of bed. She flung herself to the window, dragging up the heavy wooden frame, and scrambled out across the sill. Her bedroom was three floors up, but it faced the back of the house, overlooking a dismal, wet garden. The sloping roof of the rear porch broke her fall when she let go, jumping down in her nightdress and nothing else.

She landed with a grunt and a thud, rolled helplessly across slick, wet roofing slates, and grabbed for the metal drain at the edge. She hung for a moment by both hands, bruised and shaken, then dropped the rest of the way to the ground. She fell sprawling into shrubbery and wet grass with a spray of water from the soaked branches. Ianira lay stunned for a long moment, then managed to roll to hands and knees and lifted her head, looking up through wild, fallen hair. She could hear shouts inside the house and the pounding of running footsteps. With a whimper of terror rising in the back of her throat, Ianira came to her feet and ran across the wet grass, limping on a bruised hip.

The garden had to be escaped, whatever the cost. A high wall surrounded it on all sides. So Ianira ran for the front of the house, slipping and stumbling through mud that squelched beneath her bare feet, hiking her nightdress up to her knees. She found a gate and shoved at it, managed to find the latch and wrenched it open. She flung the heavy wooden gate back with a solid whump and ran down a carriage drive, past a small carriage house where she could hear a horse shifting in a wooden stall, kicking the side of its home in rythmic boredom. *A horse . . .*

She didn't know how to ride, but surely a horse could take her farther and faster than she could run on bare, bruised feet? Ianira lunged into the carriage house, groping through near darkness to the stall where the animal snuffled through its feed trough, looking for stray oats. Teeth chattering, Ianira forced herself to calmness, found a lead rope hanging from a peg, and slipped open the stall door. "Hello," she whispered to the startled creature. "Let us go for a ride, we two."

She clipped the lead rope to the horse's halter and led him out past the dark silhouette of Dr. Lachley's carriage. She clambered awkwardly onto the animal's back by means of the carriage's running board. Then she guided him with a soft nudge and whispered words of encouragement, bending low as they clopped through the carriage house door. She turned toward the street—

"There!"

The shout came from the garden behind her.

She thumped muddy heels against the horse's flanks and the startled animal jumped forward, breaking past the front edge of the house at a jogging trot. She clung to the mane and gripped the horse's sides with bare legs, clinging for dear life. A dark shape loomed directly in front of them. Someone shouted and flung something straight at them. The horse screamed and reared, trying to shy away from the sudden threat. Ianira lost her grip and plunged backwards with a ragged scream of her own. She hit the ground with a sickening thud and lay winded, unable to move. The horse clattered away, riderless.

Then he was on top of her, grasping her wrists, checking for broken bones.

Ianira struck out wildly, trying to rake his face with her nails. *"Don't touch me!"*

"She's delirious again, poor thing." John Lachley dug his thumb into the hollow of her throat, silencing her and cutting off her air. Ianira struggled until darkness roared up to swallow her awareness. When she could see and breathe again, he was carrying her up the stairway to her prison once more. She could feel the rough texture of his woolen coat against her cheek, could feel the dampness where he'd just come in from the raw night. Ianira clenched her eyelids down over burning wetness. Another five minutes . . . Had she only been given another five minutes . . .

"You're sure she's taken no injury?" A man had spoken, somewhere behind her captor. She didn't know that voice, tried to stir, was held savagely still against Lachley's chest. She moaned softly as he answered his unknown companion.

"I'll examine the poor thing at once, of course, Crowley. Dreadfully sorry to've brought you slap into this."

"On the contrary," Crowley said with a hint of delight in his voice, "I am amazed and intrigued. Who the devil is she?"

"So far as I've been able to ascertain, a foreigner who fell prey to footpads the moment she set foot on English soil. Poor thing's been raving for over a week, out of her mind with terror and delusions. I've had to sedate her to keep her from doing herself a mischief in her delirium."

"Seems devilishly determined to escape, I'd say."

"Yes," Lachely said dryly, carrying her back into her room. "The footpads were brutalizing her. She hasn't been in her right mind since, poor child. Imagines we're all footpads, intent on finishing what they started. I'm determined to see her through the crisis, learn who she really is, perhaps make some sort of amends for the wretched abuse she's suffered at English hands."

"Rather a striking child, isn't she? Mid-twenties, I'd guess. Has the look of the East about her."

"Indeed," Lachley placed Ianira in her bed once again, "she speaks Greek like an angel. Now, then . . . Ah, Charles, good man. You've brought it."

Ianira struggled to escape the needle. "No, please . . . I will tell no one, please, just let me go . . ."

It was no use. He injected her easily, holding her

down until the drug roared through her veins, leaving her limp and helpless. With the drug came the visions, terrifying, of the women who had died under this man's brutal hands, of the knife in the other man's hands, striking in the darkness, directed by her captor . . . And the ghastly chamber beneath the streets, which reeked of stale blood and decaying flesh . . .

Crowley's voice came from far away. "Poor thing's raving."

"Yes. The way she babbles like that, I can't help wonder if she didn't escape this hideous Whitechapel fiend, only to fall prey to footpads."

"She's no common streetwalker," Crowley's voice said, roaring dimly in her ears.

"No. But how are we to know the Whitechapel murderer won't attack ladies, as well as common slatterns, given the opportunity? She's clearly only just arrived from the docklands, after all, and if she was separated from her family in the crush of the crowd and didn't know how to summon help . . ." Lachley's voice was fading in and out of Ianira's awareness. She managed to open her eyes and found him leaning down over her. Lachley smoothed her hair back from her brow and smiled down into her terrified gaze, promising dire punishment for what she'd attempted, tonight. Ianira shuddered and turned her head away, closing her eyes again over despair. What he would do to her if she tried to warn Crowley that Lachley *was* the Whitechapel murderer . . .

The horror of it was, Crowley wouldn't believe her. No one would.

She sank, helpless and despairing, into darkness.

Ronisha Azzan had already been in the war room for an hour that morning, hard at work on the Jenna Caddrick abduction case, when security escorted the senator up from the Time Tripper Hotel. He arrived flanked by staffers carrying briefcases, intimidating by themselves, but the federal agents were conspicuously absent. That unexpected pleasantness allowed Ronisha to relax a fraction—but only a fraction, because the senator's grey eyes blazed with a look that boded ill for her immediate future, leaving her to wonder if he'd spent a bad night or if he woke up every morning in a foul temper.

Bax arrived on the senator's heels, carrying a sheaf of printouts and a CM disk. If the bags under his eyes were any hint, the Time Tours CEO had definitely spent a bad night, working as hard as Ronisha had. She nodded Bax toward the coffee; he poured himself a deep cup before sliding into a chair at the war room's immense conference table. Ronisha turned her attention to their unwelcome guest. "Good morning, Senator. I hope you slept well?"

Caddrick scowled. "As a matter of fact, a bunch of goddamned maniacs kept me awake all night, in the room under mine. Am I to understand that you actually permit lunatics on this station to worship Jack the Ripper as their personal god?"

Ronisha shrugged. "Last time I checked, we still had freedom of religion, Senator. As long as they don't actively threaten anyone, they can worship whomever they like."

Caddrick flushed. "So you have no intention of protecting the public safety? Or of enforcing public disturbance laws?"

His staffers began scribbing notes.

Ronisha bristled. "I will enforce whatever laws and policies are necessary to keep the peace on this station, Senator. As a number of federal agents have already discovered. Now, since the issue of the Ripper cults is not germane to the business at hand, I suggest we tackle the subject of your daughter's possible where-abouts."

"That suits me!" Caddrick snapped. "And let me make one thing very clear. If you don't produce my little girl, alive and uninjured, I will personally see to it that your career is over! You will never work again, not in the time-touring industry, not anywhere else. And don't think I can't do it. I've destroyed far more important careers than yours!"

An ugly silence fell, into which Granville Baxter, at least, copiously perspired.

Ronisha had been expecting it, of course, but antici-pation of such a threat didn't lessen the impact. The bottom of her stomach turned to solid lead. "Senator," she said softly, refusing to roll belly up at the first tight-ening down of political thumbscrews, "I want you to know that's a mud-ugly road you're walking down. You just take a good look at who's sitting in the station manager's chair right now. Then you think real hard about it. *Real* hard. You are not the only person on this station who can bring out the big guns. The last five politicians of your caliber to tangle with the African-Origin Business Women's Caucus did not fare well at the polls, their next election bid. Not well at all. And since we both share the same goal, finding your daughter and returning her safely to this station, there's no need to head down that particular road, now is there?"

Dust could be heard falling onto the tabletop.

Bax actually looked sick and the senator's staffers turned white as ice.

John Caddrick stared at her for long moments, his expression a shuttered mask, grey eyes narrowed into calculating slits. She did not back down under that cold, thoroughly reptilian gaze. When the mask unfroze just enough for one corner of his mouth to quirk in a sardonic, unpleasant little smile, she knew her warning had been heeded. She'd have to watch her back; but he wouldn't try anything else heavy-handed. Not for a while, yet. And if she could produce one live and kicking kid, maybe not ever. Caddrick might be a thorough-going bastard, but he wasn't stupid.

"I'm glad we understand one another, Senator. Now, I would suggest we study your daughter's profile for clues, hers and her kidnapper's, and track each potential gate they might have used."

"That's the best suggestion you can make, after an entire night to work on this? Next, I suppose, you will magic Jenna out of a silk top hat?" The scorn in his voice relegated Ronisha to the back of the intelligence bus.

Ronisha narrowed her eyes and bit down on her tongue. *You will eat yours one day, Senator, and choke on it raw! I just hope I'm there to watch.* "Right now, we're doing what can be done, regardless of how little you may like it. Since we have not been able to identify either Jenna or her kidnapper from tour records, I suggest we take a look at Jenna's most active interests." She ran down Jenna's dossier. "Historical re-enactment, horseback riding . . . She keeps two horses in a stable on Long Island?"

The senator nodded. "Her aunt pays for them. Paid, rather, before the shootings."

Bax cleared his throat reluctantly and leaned forward, steepling his fingertips. "Well, horsemanship skills would stand her in good stead down Shangri-La's gates. Horses were the primary means of land transport for thousands of years, after all. Jenna's kidnappers will doubtless take advantage of that, since most up-timers know very little about horses. Some of the tour gates, however, are better choices for your daughter's kidnappers than others."

"Meaning?" The senator's scowl boded ill for Bax's future.

The Time Tours executive, however, was made of stern stuff. Holding a job like his, he had to be. "Well, Senator," he cleared his throat again, "Athens in the age of Pericles, for instance, is not a likely choice. Neither Jenna nor her abductors would have the language skills to blend in and disappear, not without help from temporal guides. The majority of Philosopher's Gate tourists are wealthy Greek tycoons, artists, and classics scholars. You've got the same problem with Porta Romae and its destination, Claudian Rome—neither your daughter nor her kidnappers are likely to speak classical Latin. Or Greek or Aramaic or any of the other dozen or so languages spoken in Rome.

"That's not to say they couldn't easily lose pursuers, choosing Rome, they could. But it would create a whole list of problems for them to overcome. Like, how the money works, where to find living space, how to earn a living, obtain food and clothing, avoid all the pitfalls Rome offers the unwary and ignorant visitor."

Caddrick's continued withering glare brought beads of sweat to Bax's forehead, but he kept gamely at it. "According to this profile, your daughter favors more modern history, particularly the periods after the use of gunpowder in personal arms became widespread." He frowned slightly, pursing his lips and tapping them with doubled forefingers, clearly thinking through some chain of surmised options.

"Spanish Colonial South America is closer to her period of interest, but it wouldn't be a good choice for her kidnappers, either. One presumes they'll be armed, which could pose problems for them down the Conquistadores Gate. Under the Spanish colonial system, firearms were tightly restricted to the upper classes. Very few Conquistadores tourists opt for the role of peon, for obvious reasons. Your daughter's kidnappers, however, would have difficulty passing themselves off as Spanish nobility, again because of language difficulties. Most Conquistadores Gate tourists are of Hispanic descent, with the balance taken up mostly by Amer-Indians."

"I don't give a damn about Amer-Indian tourists!" Caddrick snapped. "What about the other gates?"

Bax started down the list. "The Mongolian Gate is out of the question. It hasn't cycled in months. Same with the Colonial Williamsburg Gate. The Anachronism's timing is off, too, and besides, a Society for Creative Anachronism tournament is the last place your daughter's kidnappers would try hiding." When Caddrick gave him a baffled look, Bax explained. "The SCA is a tightly-knit organization of people who recreate the middle ages, complete with jousting, knights battling in homemade armor, trained hunting falcons, you name it. They're very clannish and you have to be a member in very good standing to go on a tournament through the Anachronism Gate. Outsiders wouldn't stand a chance of slipping through undetected."

Senator Caddrick's expression made it clear that he considered tournament-bound medieval knights in homemade armor to be unstable lunatics, fitting in with the rest of Shangri-La Station's environment. Bax made an aborted movement to blot his glistening brow, then plowed steadily through the rest of his list. "The Shogun's Gate into medieval Japan is completely out of the question, of course. The Japanese under the Tokugawa Shogunate actually killed any occidental unfortunate enough to be shipwrecked on Japanese shores. Firearms were outlawed too—any mere peasant could kill a samurai with one, which made them too dangerous to have around. Firearms hadn't been invented yet at the time of Thor's Gate, of course, and the Viking age would also present insurmountable language barriers. Did Jenna speak any foreign languages?"

Before the senator could comment, the Security channel sputtered with static. "Hey, would somebody let us through the mess out here? We need to see Ronisha Azzan, ASAP."

Ronisha stared at the speakers. Skeeter Jackson was the last person she'd expected to hear on a Security channel. She leaned over and punched the intercom that patched her into the security network. "Skeeter? What are you doing on a security squawky?"

"Later! Listen, would you tell these goons down here to let us through? We need to meet with you. I wouldn't interrupt, but it's important. Real important. Kit Carson's with me."

Ronisha scooted her chair back. "I'd better see what this is about," she said a trifle grimly, nodding to the senator and Bax. "Skeeter, I'll meet you at the aerie. Bax, see what you can do with that profile while I'm gone." She dialed Mike Benson's code and told him to let Kit and Skeeter through, then climbed the stairs to the fifth-floor manager's office. Two security agents followed, making her feel a little better about walking into a potential trap set by disgruntled federal marshals. They hadn't taken kindly to her order to lock down their weapons, a precaution she'd taken to safeguard visitors and residents. After what those agents had done with their tear-gas cannisters, she did not want a bunch of uniformed thugs running around with riot guns, stirring a hornet's nest that had already been shaken several times. The last thing they needed was some trigger-happy fed opening fire on somebody like the Angels of Grace Militia.

Trying to shove that ghastly image aside, Ronisha emerged into the glass-walled office just as the elevator from Commons hummed to life. Moments later, Skeeter Jackson and the world's most famous time scout stepped onto the thick carpet. They'd come alone. Kit

Carson was all but bouncing on his toes, eyes alight with a wild kind of exultation. "Hi, Ronnie. Got a minute?"

"Good God, Kit, what *is* it? You know what we're in the middle of, here." She'd never seen the ex-time scout so excited.

"It's Jenna Caddrick's kidnapper. We found him! Skeeter did, that is. I had the good sense to put Skeeter on the payroll as a detective for the Neo Edo—which is why he's got a squawky, since you asked—and the first thing he did was solve the mystery of where Noah Armstrong went."

"*You found Armstrong? Where?* My God, Skeeter, say something!"

La-La Land's most notorious miscreant—Neo Edo's *house detective?*—smiled wryly and handed over a couple of improvised sketches. He'd drawn over the top of a flier with Noah Armstrong's photo. "That's what Armstrong looked like when he went through the Wild West Gate. Dressed as a pistolero named Joey Tyrolin. Pretended to be drunker than a British lord, stumbled around bragging about how he was going to win a shooting competition. Now for the bad news. Our missing down-timer, Julius, went through with him. Posing as a woman and probably under duress. You ought to be able to pull the gate records to find out which name Julius was using. He was dressed as the woman Joey Tyrolin's porter dropped a trunk on." He handed over a second sketch.

She stared from one altered photograph to the other, mind racing back to the events at the Denver Gate's last opening; then pivoted on one stiletto heel and headed for the telephone. "Good work, Skeeter, very good work. Denver opens—" she peered through the windows to the nearest chronometer hanging from the Commons ceiling "—at nine-fifty a.m., six days from now. Be there. You're joining the search team. If I remember right, you've been down the Wild West Gate before and you're good in a scrap. And clearly, you've got more than laundry fuzz between your ears."

Kit said drolly, "Better make that two reservations for Denver, Ronnie. I'm going, too."

Telephone halfway to her ear to arrange for Skeeter's gate pass, Ronisha aborted the motion midair. She stared, mouth coming adrift. Kit and Skeeter started laughing. "Okay," she muttered. "You're going, too." She punched the direct-line intercom to the war room. "Bax, outfit a search team through the Wild West Gate, stat. Skeeter Jackson and Kit Carson have located Noah Armstrong. He's posing as Joey Tyrolin, in company with those kids headed for the Colorado pistol competition. And I've got a sketch up here to match against photos of all the women who went through on that tour. I want you to put a name to one of them. The one Tyrolin's porter dropped a trunk on. You remember the incident? That lady was our missing down-time teenager, Julius. Looks like Armstrong forced the boy to help him escape by threatening Ianira and her family."

Startled sounds came over the speaker, then Bax replied strongly. "I'm on it."

Ronisha closed the open circuit and jabbed a lacquered fingernail down onto one of the phone's memory buttons, linking her to security. "Mike, send somebody to every outfitter on station. Jenna Caddrick's abductors went down the Wild West Gate. They had to pull together an outfit for Denver, so somebody on Shangri-La ought to remember them. Get somebody on it. Several somebodies."

"On the way."

"Skeeter. you and Kit get busy outfitting. I'll join you—where? Connie Logan's is your favorite outfitter's, isn't it, Kit? I'll authorize the expenditures from station coffers. Kit, you're priceless. With a little luck, we may yet keep Shangri-La open for business."

"That is," Kit said dryly, "the basic idea. C'mon, Skeeter. Did I say twenty an hour? Make it fifty."

Skeeter looked like a man in deep shock.

Ronisha sympathized.

Skeeter and Kit, the latter grinning like the devil's own favorite imp, sauntered into the elevator, Kit whistling merrily as the doors slid closed. Ronisha stared after them for a long moment, still nearly speechless, herself; then she was on the telephone again, tracking down every Wild West guide who'd ever worked the gate, for somebody to guide the search team out to the site of that black powder shooting competition.

Six days wasn't much of a head start to plan a time tour, when the so-called tour was a search-and-rescue mission into dangerous country by horseback, on the trail of armed terrorists holding hostages. If he'd had time, Skeeter might have panicked. Fortunately, Skeeter Jackson had plenty of practice in falling slap into unexpected little "situations" and landing more or less on his feet. Nor had he truly panicked in quite a while. At least, not since encountering that enraged gladiator, Lupus Mortiferus.

An hour after leaving the aerie, Connie's staff was busy packing away his new wardrobe and Skeeter was bent over a table in the infirmary, getting a backside full of needles. He'd already received the necessary immunizations once before, of course, having been down the Denver gate on a trip wheedled out of a rich mark. But his records showed a need for several booster shots, so he dutifully reported to the infirmary, where he listened to some tourist complain bitterly about the sting as injection after injection went in. Rachel Eisenstein's voice floated in, calm and unsympathetic. "If you'd followed the instructions in your tour-planning immunization schedule, you could have had this over with weeks ago, one at a time."

"But I'm going to be too sore to sit in a saddle!"

"That is not," Rachel said briskly, "my problem."

Skeeter grinned as unhappy curses, centering mostly around the sadistic bent of doctors in general and women doctors in particular, issued from the cubicle, interspersed with complaints about the waste of paying good money for a tour the price of the Wild West Gate if one had to spend the entire trip as a walking, talking pincushion.

"Tourists," Skeeter grimaced. "You'd think they'd remember to bring their brains along, when they leave home."

"You just said a mouthful," the nurse behind him agreed. "There, that's it. Last one. Six boosters, all guaranteed to keep you from coming down with a full-blown case of what ails you. Get going. Kit's chewing nails, waiting to drag you over to the library."

"Oh, God . . ."

The next six days passed in a blur of frantic activity. Kit Carson put Skeeter through the most rigorous training he'd ever endured. He learned that speaking "Old West Slang" was not as simple as imitating John Wayne movie dialogue, which was what he'd done in the cathouses and gambling dens of Denver on his last trip—major portions of which he preferred not to recall too closely. And loading bullets for black-powder guns, even replica models made of higher quality steel, with closer tolerances, was nowhere near as simple as shoving a cartridge into a six-shooter and pulling the trigger. Not if you wanted to hit what you were shooting at when the six-shooter went bang. And Skeeter had never even heard of "balloon head cartridges." The only thing he really comprehended was that you could get slightly more black powder into them, which was fine by him. More bang for the buck was a great idea, in his opinion, going after the *Ansar Majlis* down time.

He also learned how to reload them. And while he measured bullets and sorted them out by weight and discarded those with any slight flattened spots or surface bumps, Kit taught him Old West Slang. He learned why a man should never bake a bang-tail before bedding-down the remuda and why a gentleman never called a lady a Cypriot. If he did, the lady's husband or father might shoot him over it. Might as well just come right out and call her a whore.

And so it went, until Skeeter thought his brain would burst.

He spent two entire days at the firing range, where Ann Vinh Mulhaney put him through hours of shooting lessons, both live-fire and inside the computer simulator she'd built, a room-sized Hogan's Alley affair with 360-degree rear-projection screens and plenty of real props to use as cover. He spent most of the first day in the computer simulator, working on target acquisition skills and reacting to armed threat and finding out just how many ways one can miss with a firearm at close range under stress. The second day was less fun than the room-sized shooting gallery, but just as instructive. Skeeter could hold his own in a knife fight, but he'd never fired a gun. Ann doled out electronic earmuffs, which allowed her to continue the lecture, while filtering out the sharp, damaging reports of guns discharging the length of the weapons range. "I had to kick a tourist off the line and he wasn't happy about it," she said, dragging him toward an empty lane. "Kit wants you on this firing line all day, Skeeter, which means we've barely got time for adequate weapons selection, load selections, firing procedures, shooting practice, and cleaning lessons."

"Cleaning lessons?" Skeeter blurted, genuinely startled.

Kit nodded impatiently as they joined him at the firing line. "The priming compounds used in 1885's black powder cartridges were corrosive and black powder's residue attracts moisture. There's a reason those old time gun slingers were fanatical about cleaning their weaponry."

"Wouldn't it make more sense for me to carry what I'm familiar with? Like a big Bowie-style knife? I'm pretty good with a fighting knife, but what I know about guns wouldn't fill a teacup."

"We'll see Sven before we leave the weapons range. But we're going up against armed terrorists holding hostages. Believe me, if things get rough down that gate, you'll want the ability to reach out and punch somebody well beyond arm's length."

"What are you carrying?" Skeeter asked, eying the pile of weapons Ann had set out on the shooting bench.

"I've always favored the S and W Double Action Frontier. I lost a light-weight model called a Wesson Favorite in the Silver Plume, Colorado, fire of 1884, just about a year before the time we're going to. *This* one," he held up a revolver, "is in .38-40 and has a six and a half inch barrel. Some folks might call it a horse pistol, because it's almost as big as the pistols from before the War Between the States, and most people carried it in a strap over the saddle horn. I'll wear it on my belt, though."

Kit picked a small handgun from the pile on the bench. "For a hideout, I'll be taking my little five-shot S and W .38 double action. The second model with a three and a quarter inch barrel, for concealability. And for a long gun," he hoisted a rifle, working the action with a sharp metallic clack to demonstrate its mode of operation, "I'll bring a Winchester 73 rifle, in .38-40 caliber, same as the big Smith and Wesson. It won't be good out beyond two hundred yards or so, but my eyes aren't what they used to be, so something like a Sharps would be a waste of time for me. And you don't know enough to bother with one, either."

"Why don't you just put a good scope on it?" Skeeter asked, brows twitching down. Then, answering his own question, "Because it's an anachronism, right?"

Kit chuckled. "Actually, rifle scopes were in use as early as the Civil War, a good twenty years before the Denver Gate's time period. But we won't be taking period-scoped weapons. They had too many problems to bother with them. They were so hard to see through, shooters of the day compared them to peering through a rusty pipe. And they weren't very well sealed, so if you carried one around on a hot, muggy day, the minute the temperature dropped, at night, for instance, moisture would condense inside the scope. Very bad for scopes. And they were fragile. Most of them used black-widow spiderweb silk for cross hairs, which broke very easily, and steel wire cross hairs were more prone to breakage than spider silk."

Ann fished out a couple of ordinary telescoping spyglasses made from brass tubing, just like the ones in old movies about sailing ships, and a couple of pairs of early-style field glasses. "These gather light much more effectively and offer better magnification, too. You should do just fine with the iron sights on the firearms and one of these for distance reconnaisance."

The first gun they armed Skeeter with was one of Ann's Royal Irish Constabulary Webleys. "Unlike the later military issue Webley," Ann said briskly, "which was a clunky monster of a top-break pistol like Kit's Smith and Wessons, the RIC is a good concealment gun, with a solid frame and a loading gate more like the big Colt you'll also carry. It's bigger than Kit's .38, and it shoots a bigger cartridge, which is a distinct advantage for an amateur shooter. You might find it easier to handle because of its size, plus bigger bullets might make up for some of your lack of expertise with handguns."

The Webley had a tiny, stubby little barrel, only two and a quarter inches long, but the thing had plenty of heft when Skeeter accepted it. When he swung it around to see how the gate at the side of the cylinder opened, Ann grunted in exasperation and grabbed his wrist, levering the barrel around so that it faced downrange, not at her midsection.

Skeeter reddened to his undershorts. "Oops. Sorry!"

"*Always* point a firearm downrange. Even if you're absolutely positive it's not loaded. Imagine a laser beam coming out the end of that barrel. Anything that laser touches is at risk for having a hole blown through it, if you have an accidental discharge. Now, then, let's put you through the paces for loading, firing, and unloading."

Skeeter learned how to use that little Royal Irish Constabulary Webley better than he'd ever dreamed he could. Ann was a crackerjack teacher, patient and thorough and very clear in her instructions. After more or less mastering the Webley and overcoming his movie-instilled desire to "throw" bullets by jerking his hand forward, Skeeter graduated to a big six-shot Colt Double Action Army in .38-40 with a four and three quarter inch barrel, which Ann referred to as the "The Thunderer."

"This one uses the same cartridge Kit will be using in his belt revolver and his rifle, so you guys will have at least some ability to interchange ammunition."

"But why the shorter barrel?" Skeeter asked. "Kit's other gun has six and a half inches!"

"So you can draw it faster," Ann explained. "You're not as experienced with this as Kit, so don't argue. You need a weapon you can draw, point, and shoot fast and easy, without needing a lot of drilled-in practice on sight pictures and target acquisition techniques. I'm not going to turn you into a champion marksman, never mind Kit's equal, in the time you have before the gate goes, Skeeter. I'm going to teach you the point-shoulder technique, which ought to work pretty well out to ten yards or so, and you don't need a long barrel to do that. We're not comparing your anatomy, here, we're trying to keep you alive. So a four-inch barrel is what you get, my friend."

Skeeter reddened again and opted to keep his mouth shut.

For a long gun, Skeeter discovered he would be carrying a twelve gauge double-barrel shotgun, which he learned how to use with buckshot. It felt a little— granted, a *very* little—more like shooting a bow, which he knew how to use, than the handguns had. As long as his target was within fifty yards, Skeeter stood some chance of success with the shotgun, if he remembered to cock the hammers first. "I hope," he muttered to himself, after hours of practice with each gun, "we won't have to rely on my marksmanship to get out of this alive."

Kit, who had been steadily punching neat, absurdly tiny groups of holes in his paper targets, glanced over at Skeeter's dismal ones and grimaced. "I hope not, either. Keep practicing."

Skeeter felt a great deal better about the pair of Bowie knives Sven Bailey presented him with, one to wear openly in a sheath and one that was somewhat smaller, like a camp knife, to carry concealed under his shirt. "This is more like it," Skeeter nodded, far more at home with a blade in his hand. "And much better quality than what I grew up using in Yesukai's camp."

"Just try to bring them back undamaged," Sven glowered. The bladed weapons instructor was no taller than the diminuitive projectile weapons instructor, but broader and heavier boned. The epithet "evil gnome" had been hurled Sven's way more than once, although usually not to his face. Sven Bailey was widely acknowledged the most dangerous man on TT-86, which was a considerable accomplishment, given Kit Carson's presence on station.

"I'll take care of them," Skeeter promised with a gulp and a hasty retreat from Sven Bailey's armory.

Skeeter's final lesson of the day, after another intensive round of firing practice, involved properly cleaning a black-powder firearm in the field, using 1885 techniques and equipment. "Clean your firearms after every use," Ann explained as Skeeter learned how to disassemble each of his borrowed weapons, "or you'll end up with a rusted, corroded piece of junk. That can happen fast, in a matter of days."

"What do you use?" Skeeter asked dubiously, eyeing the stack of filthy firearms.

"Soap. Not detergent, mind, but *soap* and water. Modern shooters usually use one of the liquid-formula soaps or even chemical cleaners that don't require water, but you won't have that luxury down the Wild West gate. You'll carry soap flakes or shave thin strips from an ordinary soap bar, dissolve them in hot water, and scrub the disassembled pieces with gun brushes. Then you oil every piece thoroughly to prevent rust. You'll carry a small flask of a modern substitute that looks and feels like sperm-whale oil and works even better, without killing an endangered species." She nodded to the heavy little flask Skeeter held.

Kit grunted softly, scrubbing hard at his disassembled Frontier Double Action with a stiff, soapy brush. "Beats what I've used, on occasion. A lot of shooters in the Old West carried strips of leather wrapped around lumps of lard. It works, but man, oh, man, does it smell."

Skeeter chuckled. "Hot iron, burnt powder, and

rancid pig fat? Yeah, I'll bet it does. Of course," he added wryly, "I did grow up with people whose idea of *haute cuisine* was *tsampa* and *kvess*. *Anything* rancid smells bad, take my word for it. Okay, show me how to shave soap flakes and disassemble these babies."

Once Kit and Ann were satisfied that Skeeter could load, shoot, disassemble, clean the pistols and shotgun, then successfully reassemble them in working order, Ann loaded him down with ammo and cleaning supplies, gunbelts and holsters, all the miscellaneous gear he'd need for carrying the weapons down the Wild West Gate. Then, and only then, did Ann and Kit consent to let him leave the gun range. Reeking of burnt gunpowder and gun oil and reeling on his feet, Skeeter took the elevator up with Kit, who clapped him on the shoulder and told him he was doing fine, just fine, then got out on a different floor and left Skeeter to make it home under his own steam.

The hot shower he crawled into felt marvellous. As water sluiced over his skin, carrying away sweat and the reek of burnt powder, Skeeter discovered he couldn't shake the feeling that something important was eluding him, niggling at the back of his mind, something that didn't quite fit.

He cast back through his memory to the day of the first station riot, the day Ianira Cassondra and her family had vanished without a trace. He finally put his finger on what was bothering him. If Jenna Caddrick's abductors had kidnapped them, who had rescued Marcus and the girls at the daycare center? *Somebody* had shot dead two terrorists attempting to snatch the girls. It just didn't make sense that the *Ansar Majlis* would've killed two of their own, did it? The terrorist leaders he and Kit had nailed were hotly protesting the kidnapping charge, claiming they'd never touched Jenna Caddrick.

Nobody on station believed them, of course, but given what had happened during that first station riot, it was just possible they were telling the truth. What if someone else *was* involved? Someone who'd known those murderous fanatics were planning to kill Ianira and her family? It was certain that *somebody* had broken up the attempted kidnapping at the daycare center—there'd been plenty of terror-stricken witnesses. Where was that somebody now? And who had he been? And if the *Ansar Majlis* hadn't snatched Caddrick's daughter, who had?

Skeeter narrowed his eyes and slicked back wet hair, scrubbing at his hide with soap while he went over the whole thing in his mind again, from the first sign of trouble to the disastrous end of the first station riot. Come to think of it, there'd been *two* people involved in the initial attack on Ianira, neither of whom fit the profile of terrorists carrying out a hit mission. There was that wild-eyed kid who'd shot the construction worker—one of the same crew that had later tried to kill Bergitta—and somebody else, who had knocked Skeeter and Ianira to the floor.

At the time, Skeeter had thought that second person had shoved them out of the way to keep the wild-eyed kid from killing Ianira, but now he wasn't so sure. Killing that construction worker might've been accidental, if the kid had been aiming at Ianira. But maybe that kid had been aiming at the construction worker, instead? Who'd been standing right behind Ianira? If *that* were true, they might *not* be looking at a relatively simple case of kidnappers running with a hostage and setting up a hit against Ianira on their way through the station.

Not at all.

A scowl tugged the edges of Skeeter's mouth down as spray cascaded down his chest. The senator's hired detective hadn't mentioned anything like this in his report. Skeeter narrowed his eyes, trying to recall every detail of that first riot. He'd glimpsed the wild-eyed kid brandishing a black-powder pistol, right about the time someone crashed into Skeeter and Ianira, sweeping them to the floor. And the kid had yelled something, too. The word "no," and a cry of fear, all slurred together like, "No! Ahh—"

Skeeter gasped and swallowed a mouthful of water. Not *"No, ahh—"*

Noah! Noah Armstrong!

Skeeter blinked water out of his eyes, mind whirling in sudden confusion. Noah Armstrong was the terrorist leader who'd grabbed Jenna Caddrick. The *Ansar Majlis* killer who wanted the Lady of Heaven Temples destroyed. But why would a terrorist's hired gun intervene to stop his own hit, when that hit was about to be successfully carried out by his own minions on station? A coil of ice-cold fear slithered its way into the pit of Skeeter's belly despite the hot water cascading down his skin. Just what had they stumbled into the middle of, here?

If Noah Armstrong had been trying to *stop* Ianira Cassondra's murder . . . Then the information the senator had given them about Noah Armstrong and his plot to kidnap Jenna was suspect. Which meant the FBI and the senator's paid detective were wrong, too, dead wrong. He'd have to tell Kit, warn him about what they might be walking into, down the Wild West Gate. But not here, not on station. Not within reach of Senator Caddrick's electronic ears and eyes. Skeeter muttered under his breath and finished his shower. *More trouble we need like a white rhino needs Chinese horn hunters.*

But if Skeeter was right, more trouble had landed squarely in their laps. Even worse, it looked like Skeeter was going to have to get them out of it. And that made for a very long and sleepless night.

Chapter Four

The man travelling under the name Sid Kaederman knew something had gone seriously wrong the moment he stepped into Time Terminal Eighty-Six. While children shrieked and zoomed in and out of line, parents burbled enthusiastically about which gates they planned to tour, bored couriers waited to haul through deliveries of critical supplies, and newlyweds cooed, glued together at lips and palms, Sid Kaederman focused his entire attention on the angry, close-mouthed station security and BATF agents scrutinizing new arrivals and their identification papers.

By the time his own turn for scrutiny came, Sid Kaederman—whose real name and face were a far cry from the ones he currently carried—was sweating blood and planning out in exquisitely barbaric detail exactly what he would do to John Caddrick and his missing offspring when he finally caught up to them. The time terminal's public address system blared nonstop, belting out messages in half-a-dozen different languages until Sid's eardrums ached and his temper approached breakpoint. He bit down and held it, though, not daring to draw attention to himself.

He shuffled forward in a long, snaking line, as thick and variagated as a reticulated python, and cleared various checkpoints: baggage handling, ticket verification to validate his Primary Gate pass, medical stations where his records were scanned in and checked against his identification paperwork. Sid had no real qualms about the quality of his I.D. He could afford the best in the business. It was the other security arrangements that worried him. Adding insult to injurious invasion of his accustomed privacy, Sid Kaederman found himself, along with every other in-bound tourist entering the station, subjected to the most thorough search of luggage and person conducted in the history of TT-86.

Station officials were clearly trying to prevent contraband weaponry or explosive devices from entering the embattled station. Fortunately, Sid possessed a cover story that gave him a perfectly legitimate reason to be armed: a private detective in Senator John Caddrick's employ. He showed his paperwork for the firearms he'd brought along and received his clearances from Time Tours and BATF security, then stalked into TT-86 nursing a silent, volcanic rage.

Shangri-La Station, for all its vaunted fame, was little more than a fancy shopping mall with hotels and bizarrely dressed patrons playing dress up in outlandish costumes. The station itself didn't much impress him, beyond its apparent lunacy of construction, with stairways to nowhere and steel platforms hanging midair for no apparent reason. What got Sid's immediate attention, however, was the *feel* of the station. The mood of Time Terminal Eighty-Six was explosive. If that seething anger had been aimed at the proper target, Sid would've been delighted; his plans called for riots and mayhem directed at specific, carefully chosen groups and individuals. But the meticulously planned fury his operatives were orchestrating against down-timers and time tourism, a campaign of terror and intimidation which formed a critical piece of Sid's long-term plans, was notably distorted on TT-86.

People were angry, all right. Murderously angry.

At exactly the wrong target.

"Who does Caddrick think he is?" a slender woman in expensive Victorian attire demanded, voice as strident as the colors of her costume. "That creep waltzes in here with a pack of armed thugs like he owns the place. Teargasses half of Commons and tries an armed take-over of the whole station . . ."

" . . . keeps it up, somebody's gonna shoot that son of a bitch! And I'll dance on his grave when they do!"

" . . . heard Caddrick can't even leave his hotel room. He's terrified the Angels of Grace will break his neck. And for once, I agree with that bunch of lunatics . . ."

" . . . hear about his fight with Kit Carson? The senator demanded a suite at the Neo Edo. Kit turned him down flat! God, I wish I could've seen his face. Jackass had to settle for the *Time Tripper*, because everybody else was full up for the Ripper Season! I hope Orva puts stinging nettle in his bedsheets . . ."

The running commentary dogged Sid's heels from the precinct surrounding Primary clear through the sprawling insanity of the station, all the way to the lobby of the Time Tripper Hotel, a modest hostelry that clearly catered to tourists on a limited budget. Smiling tightly at the thought of Caddrick's well-earned discomfiture, he placed a call to the senator's room from the lobby's courtesy phone. Ten minutes later, Sid found himself in a tawdry little hotel room littered with empty liquor bottles, facing down the disgruntled senator. John Caddrick's air of calm self-assurance faltered slightly when Sid allowed the steel to show in his gaze. The staff weenie who had escorted Sid up from the lobby hesitated nervously.

"That'll be all," Caddrick snapped.

The man fled. The moment Caddrick's aide closed the door, Sid exploded.

"What the goddamned hell do you think you've been doing?"

Caddrick backed up a pace, eyes flickering in visible dismay. Sid advanced on him. "Are you *trying* to get us all electrocuted? My God, Caddrick, what possessed you to walk in here with *federal marshals*, trying to take over the whole goddamned station?"

"Now, listen just a minute—"

"No, you listen!" Caddrick actually jumped, then closed his mouth, lips thinning as his face lost color. Sid jabbed a finger at the nearest chair. Caddrick thought about arguing, thought better, and sat. Sid stood glaring for a long moment, wrestling his temper under control.

"You are out of your mind, Caddrick, stirring up a hornet's nest like this. Grandstanding for the press will earn you a one way stroll to the gas chamber, if you're not damned careful. And I, for one, am *not* taking that walk with you. Get that very clear, right now! I'm here to contain the damage as best I can. It was bad enough your kid slipped through the net we threw up around New York. But now you've got the *Inter-Temporal Court* diddling in the middle of our business. I heard the station courier sent through placing the call the instant he came through Primary into the up-time lobby. Do you have any *idea* what an investigation by I.T.C.H. means?"

Caddrick had enough intelligence, at least, to lose an additional shade of color. "Yes." He swallowed hard enough to bounce his Adam's apple like a nervous bird. "I do know. That goddamned bitch of a deputy manager—"

"No! Don't lay this one on the station, Caddrick. You're responsible for this mess. Haven't you figured out by now, there are some people you can push and bully and others you have to slip up behind with a silenced gun, if you want to neutralize them? Didn't you even bother to do a little basic personnel research? That deputy station manager you're bleating about is the granddaughter of Coralisha Azzan!"

The senator had the grace to blanch, widening his eyes in alarm.

"Yes, you begin to see just how badly you've stepped in it, don't you? That woman is not going to back down, not for you or God or anybody else. And word out there is," he jerked his thumb toward the station Commons, "you've also managed to piss off Kit Carson. For God's sake, Caddrick, you'd better not buy that drivel about Kit Carson being a washed up has-been, playing hotel manager and hiding from the world. That bastard is one dangerous old man. And he's just as likely as the Inter-Temporal Court to start poking into your affairs, just to get even for threatening his station."

"But—"

"*Shut up, dammit!*" He had to grab his temper in both hands to keep from cracking the idiot across the mouth with the back of his hand. "I *told* you to lay low, Caddrick, *told* you to keep your nose out of this! Playing choked up Daddy for the press cameras up time is one thing. Throwing your weight around TT-86 and threatening an armed takeover of a major time terminal . . . Jeezus H. Christ, Caddrick, I think you've actually started to believe your own biographers! Nobody, not even John Paul Caddrick, is *that* invincible."

"What the hell was I *supposed* to do?" Caddrick snarled. "Sit around with my thumb up my ass while Jenna and that putrid little deviant Armstrong slipped back through this station with their evidence and took it straight to the FBI?"

Sid just looked at him, unable to believe the man's colossal stupidity. "Slip back through the station?" he repeated softly. "Are you out of your mind? No, you have to be in possession of a mind, first, to be out of it. For your information, Armstrong and your misbegotten little girl won't risk setting foot back on this station for the next *year*. Armstrong is nobody's fool, Caddrick. That bastard's given us the slip three times, already. There was never any danger of Armstrong *or* Jenna slipping back through this station with their evidence. Not before we could trace them and shut them up for good. Time was on *our* side, not theirs. But no, you had to stick your big, fat foot right in the middle of the biggest hornet's nest I've ever seen, and smash it for good measure."

"All right!" Caddrick snapped, "you've made your point! But things aren't nearly as grim as you seem to think. We know where Armstrong took Jenna *and* that down-timer bitch, Ianira Cassondra. They went through the Denver Gate. The station's mounting a search and rescue mission, naturally. It leaves in three days. All we have to do is put you on the team. Armstrong and Jenna won't live to testify, not to Kit Carson or anyone else on the search team."

"Kit Carson?" Sid echoed. "What does he have to do with it?"

"Carson," the senator muttered, unwilling to meet Sid's eyes, "took it upon himself to lead the damned search mission."

Sid Kaederman counted twenty. Twice.

"All right," he finally grated out. "What other nasty little surprises do you intend springing on me?" Sid listened in appalled silence as Caddrick related the state of affairs on TT-86. When the senator finally wound down, Sid promised himself to see Caddrick's career down in flames. "What's done is done," he muttered. "And as much as it pains me to say it, I would suggest you throw your excessive weight around the station manager's office one more time, because I don't think there's a chance in hell Kit Carson is going to allow me on that search and rescue mission without threats from you to put me there."

Caddrick glared at him, hatred burning in those famous grey eyes, but he picked up the telephone and dialed. Sid found the hotel room's wet bar, downed a full tumbler of scotch, and waited.

Kit Carson was too busy to watch Primary go through its antics. With only three days until the Denver Gate cycled, he was putting Skeeter through as much cram-session training as possible. Nor did Kit have any intention of being caught near the start of another potential riot. Skeeter Jackson, sweating and swearing where he'd just fallen to the gym floor's protective mat yet again, victim of Kit's smooth Aikido, wiped wet hair out of his eyes with the back of a sweaty arm and glared up at him.

"Hey, boss?"

"Yes?" Kit balanced lightly on the balls of his feet, waiting.

"You *are* gonna let me live long enough to walk through the Wild West Gate, aren't you?"

Kit just grinned, which left Skeeter muttering under his breath again. Kit understood enough basic Mongolian to catch the gist of what he'd just said, if not the specific details. "Good God, Skeeter, where'd you pick up language like that?"

The newly fledged Neo Edo house detective grunted and heaved himself back to his feet. "Pretty little thing named Houlun."

Kit blinked in surprise. "Yesukai's captive bride?"

It was Skeeter's turn to stare. "Good grief. You're the only person besides Nally Mundy who's ever heard of her."

Kit found himself laughing. "I've forgotten more history than Doc Mundy ever knew, bless him. And he would've made a fine time scout, if his health hadn't been so frail. So, Houlun could swear like a sailor, could she?"

Skeeter rolled his eyes. "Oh, man, could she ever. Well, she did have reason to be pissed off. Yesukai kidnapped her right out of her wedding procession to a guy from another clan. I was there when it happened. After I'd learned enough Mongolian to figure out what she screeched at him all the way back to Yakka Clan territory, I turned red for a solid week. I was only eight, after all."

Kit chuckled. "Someday—" and Skeeter's headlong rush toward Kit transformed itself into an abrupt need for the ex-thief to become airborne "—I'd love to hear the whole story."

"*Oof . . .*" Skeeter knew, at least, how to land, which made Kit feel better about the younger man's chances in a fight. He groaned and rolled over onto hands and knees. "No way. I ain't gonna live long enough."

"You're just soft from easy living. Now, let's try it again—"

"Hey, Kit!" Sven Bailey poked his head out of his office. "Phone! Ronisha Azzan. And she doesn't sound happy."

Kit and Skeeter exchanged startled glances.

"Now what?" Skeeter muttered.

"We'll find out. Take five." Kit jogged over to Sven's office, where the bladed-weapons instructor had gone back to sharpening a *gladius*. Kit grabbed the phone left lying on the desk. "Kit Carson."

"We've got trouble."

Echoing Skeeter, Kit said, "Now what?"

"You'd better get up here. Skeeter, too. We're adding somebody to the search team. And you're not going to like it."

"With Denver cycling in three days, I already don't like it. Who?"

Ronisha said very dryly, "A detective. Senator Caddrick's. He just arrived through Primary. He and the senator are in the aerie, demanding to see you."

Hoo, boy . . .

"We'll be there in five." Kit didn't plan on showering first, either; honest sweat never hurt anybody and the senator deserved it, thrusting some up-time detective down their throats, without adequate time to prepare him for down-time work.

"What's Caddrick done now?" Sven asked, glancing up from a whetstone, where he was putting a keen edge on the thrusting tip of his favorite Roman short sword.

"Saddled us with some up-time detective."

"Oh, great. That's all you need."

"You're telling me. I'll see you later. If Caddrick doesn't toss us in jail for telling him what I think of his idea."

Sven snorted. "Yeah, right. Bull Morgan's one thing. *Kit Carson*, not even Caddrick's stupid enough to tangle with."

Rarely—very rarely—world-wide fame had its advantages. Kit grinned, then headed out at a jog. "Skeeter, heads up, we got trouble. We're going to the aerie."

Skeeter, rubbing gingerly at bruises, whipped around. "The *aerie?*"

"Come on, I'll fill you in on the way."

"But, Kit! I smell worse than my last pony at the end of a Mongolian summer!"

Kit's grin blazed. "Good."

Skeeter, bless his quick mind, chortled and fell into step beside him. "Caddrick, huh? Now what?" Kit told him. Skeeter rolled his eyes. "Oh, God, do me a favor, huh? This detective, whoever he is, make *him* spend six whole hours weighing and sorting bullets while learning how not to bake a bang-tail, will you?"

Kit chuckled all the way to the aerie.

Once they arrived, however, all desire to smile fled. Senator John Paul Caddrick was in the middle of a tirade, demanding to know where the search team was, did they think he had nothing better to do than cool his heels, waiting, when there was work to be done and if Ronisha Azzan wanted to keep her job, she'd better produce them in the next sixty seconds or less . . .

"Save your threats," Kit growled as he left the elevator where Skeeter was visibly gulping for courage. "They don't impress me. Now what's this garbage about adding somebody to my search team?"

John Caddrick rounded on him, mouth opening for something doubtless intended to be earthshattering. Then he rocked back on his heels and thought better of it. "As I live and breathe . . . Your manners always were atrocious, Carson."

Kit ignored the insult and came straight to the point. "What's this about saddling me with a detective you want to tag along?"

Caddrick started to reply, then evidently caught a whiff of Kit's gym-clothes perfume, because the senator stepped back a pace, nostrils pinching shut, as Kit advanced. It was a minor psychological victory, forcing the senator to give ground, but it served to put Caddrick slightly off-stride and that was exactly where Kit wanted him. He pressed his momentary advantage.

"You do realize how stupid it is, how dangerously stupid, sending somebody without down-time experience on a mission like this? And with only three days' worth of prep time? We're not heading for New Hollywood, Caddrick. People who don't know what they're doing can get themselves killed all sorts of messy ways in 1885, even *without* chasing armed terrorists."

"I would point out," Caddrick said coldly, "that Wardmann-Wolfe agents are the most experienced in the business. Sid Kaederman has more than impressed me with his credentials. He's the man for this job and I insist he be added to the search team."

Kit flicked his gaze to the man seated behind Caddrick, a serenely unruffled man with dark hair and fair skin who looked to be in his mid-thirties and might have been as much as ten years older. Or younger. He was already dressed for the Denver Gate, in a fancy-cut Eastern gentleman's suit with an embroidered silk vest. He sported a silver-headed cane that doubtless concealed a lethal sword. *Christ, he looks like a riverboat gambler. That's all we need.* Short, compact, probably well muscled under that fancy costume, he had the kind of face that would've looked equally at home in a Wall Street brokerage firm, on a fishing trawler in the North Sea, or cutting through a bank vault with acetylene torch and plastic explosives. His gaze, as he returned Kit's appraising stare, was direct enough, yet hooded and wary as any predator's faced with an unknown opponent.

"Mr. Carson," he said softly, rising with abrupt, easy grace that spoke of superb conditioning, but probably not much martial arts training, "Sid Kaederman's the name."

He offered a hand. Kit shook it, detecting in the process a slight roughening of callus along the pad of his index finger, suggesting long hours of practice on a firing range, using a trigger with grooves cut into it. "Mr. Kaederman. How many temporal gates have you stepped through? And how well can you handle a horse?"

A tiny smile came and went. "I've never been down a time gate, actually. I confine my work to the up-time world. And rarely indulge in vacations. As for horses, I've never had any trouble dominating lesser creatures. I can ride well enough to suit even you."

Kit ignored the veiled insult. "A search-and-rescue into the Rockies of 1885 on the trail of known terrorists with hostages isn't a quick jog down a bridle trail at some dude ranch or urban riding club. And I won't be putting you on the back of a well-trained hack used to beginners. The Old West doesn't bear much resemblance to the up-time urban world where Wardmann-Wolfe agents pick up most of their clients. Just exactly what *does* qualify you for a mission like this? If you don't mind?"

A glint that might have been humor—or something else entirely—appeared in Kaederman's dark eyes. "Apart from anything else, I'm going because my employer will shut down this station if I'm not on the team. Senator Caddrick has made it quite clear that he doesn't trust any effort put forth by this station. More to the point, we're dealing with *Ansar Majlis*. Terrorists, I *do* understand. Very thoroughly."

Caddrick had them over a barrel and Kit knew it. Worse, he knew that Sid Kaederman knew it, too, and was amused. Kit shrugged, conceding defeat in the only way possible. "If you're thrown by your nag the first time it steps on a rattler or hears a puma scream, you're on your own. As team leader, I won't take the time to nursemaid an injured greenhorn back to the Denver gatehouse. If you don't have an acceptable kit thrown together by the time the gate cycles, too bad. You'll either miss the gate or find yourself on your own to furnish it down time, because I won't wait for you to buy or rent items you should've been acquiring days ago."

"I'll do my best not to disappoint." Dry, self-assured, amused once again.

Kit snorted. "Frankly, Kaederman, I don't give a damn whether you disappoint me or not. Do your job or you'll be looking for another one. Senator," he glanced at Caddrick, "since you insist on including Mr. Kaederman on the search and rescue team, you can pay the bill. Send him to Ann Vinh Mulhaney for appropriate historical arms. I'd suggest a Remington suite," he added, glancing at the fancy cut of Kaederman's clothes.

The senator blinked. "A what?"

Caddrick, who had introduced some of the most draconian anti-gun legislation in the history of Western civilization, clearly had no idea what Kit was talking about.

Kit glanced directly at Kaederman. "As a Wardmann-Wolfe detective, you doubtless know how to use modern guns. But you won't have the slightest idea what to carry for 1885."

"Black-powder firearms can't be any more challenging than service-rifle competitions."

Kit raised his brows. "You've done long distance shooting, then? All right. We'll start you out with, say, the Remington Model 1875 single action revolver in .44-40 and a Remington Number Three rifle in .45-70, the Hepburn falling-block model. Tell Ann to put Creedmore sights on it, and if you take the time to learn it, that'll give us a half-mile range if we end up in a long-distance shootout with the *Ansar Majlis*. And put a .41 Remington derringer in your fancy coat pocket, Mr. Kaederman, if you want a hideout gun. Just be careful you don't blow your foot off with it. Those derringers don't have safety mechanisms and the firing pins are longer than the breech faces. Drop one hammer down, it'll blow a .41 caliber hole in your gut. Get Ann to show you how to safely load and unload it. Tell her to bill the senator. Meet me in the station's library first thing after dinner. You've got a lot of research ahead, if you want to go on this mission. Now, if you'll excuse us, Mr. Jackson and I have some unfinished business waiting."

Senator Caddrick sputtered, "Now, wait just a damned minute—"

Kit narrowed his eyes and held Caddrick's gaze coldly. "Those are *my* terms, Senator. You hired him. So don't try to blackmail the station into paying his expenses. Those are *your* problem. Mr. Kaederman," he nodded curtly, "I'll see you at the library, six-thirty sharp. Don't be late."

Skeeter all but tripped over his own feet, rushing into the elevator ahead of Kit. Senator Caddrick was still sputtering. But as the elevator doors slid shut, Sid Kaederman gave Kit a small, satisifed smile and a tiny flick of the fingers at his brow, acknowledging a minor victory in the murderous little game in which they were embroiled. Skeeter Jackson rearranged sweat on his forehead with a glistening forearm. "Sheesh, Kit, you really do like to live dangerously, don't you?"

"Skeeter," he sighed as the elevator carried them down toward Commons, "there's only one thing infinitely worse than running a luxury hotel on a time terminal."

"What's that?"

"Not having a time terminal to run that hotel *on*."

To that, Skeeter had no reply whatsover.

Catharine "Kate" Eddowes generally enjoyed her annual trek out to the fields of Kent to work the harvest. Picking hops wasn't as difficult as some jobs she'd done and the Kentish countryside was almost like a great garden, full of flowers and green fields and fresh, crisp air. Moreover, John Kelly, with whom she had shared a bed more or less continuously for seven years, almost always benefitted from the change to the countryside, where the cleaner air eased his constant cough.

But this year, things were different.

Late September was generally warm and beautiful. But the whole summer had been unseasonably chilly and full of rain. By the time they arrived in Kent, the late September weather was raw. Working sunup to sundown in wet, cold fields, John Kelly's health deteriorated alarmingly.

"It's no use, John," she finally said. "We can't stay the season, this time. You'll catch your death, so you will, and then what'll become of me, luv? I need you, John Kelly."

Tears of defeat and shame caused him to turn aside, but by nightfall, his cough had grown so alarmingly worse, he agreed to abandon the hop harvest, even though it meant giving up money they both needed. They had no choice but return to London, where they could at least find a dry room for Kelly to sleep in at night. It was a long walk from Hunton, Kent back to London, but they hadn't any money for a train, so walk it they did, in the company of another couple they'd met working the same fields.

"We're off for Cheltenham," their newfound friends said as they came to the turning for London, "so we'll say goodbye and luck to you. Kate, look here, I've got a pawn ticket for a flannel shirt up there in London, why don't you take it? It's only for two pence, but the shirt might fit your old man, there, and I'd say he needs a bit of a warm shirt, what with that cough of his."

"Thank you." Catharine accepted the crumpled pawn ticket gratefully. "I worry about John's health, with the cold weather coming and us with no money. It's good to us, you are." She slipped the ticket into one of her pockets, next to the wrinkled letter she'd bought from

Annie Chapman, poor soul, the letter she'd been too terrified to have translated, after what had happened to poor Annie. And Dark Annie had confessed to buying the letters from Polly Nichols, who was also brutally dead.

Maybe the smartest thing would be to get rid of the letter altogether?

Just throw it away or burn it, never even try to have it translated?

As they waved goodbye and set out walking again, taking the fork in the road that would lead them back to London, Catharine stole worried glances at John. His color wasn't good and his breathing was labored. His kidney complaint had flared up again, too, given the number of times he had to stop along the roadside and from the way he rubbed his side and back from time to time, when he thought she wasn't looking. They needed money for a doctor and medicine, just as poor Annie had, and they'd very little left to sell or pawn to obtain it. They'd so counted on the money from the hop harvest to see them through the winter and now there wouldn't be anything in reserve at all, with the coldest months yet to come.

I'll have to find out what's in the letter, Kate realized with a shiver, *I'll have to find who wrote it, if I want my John to live 'til spring. Too bad them coppers won't put up a reward for that Whitechapel murderer what's done in Polly and Annie.* She didn't want to try blackmailing the author of the filthy thing, not after what had become of its previous owners, but she didn't know what else to do.

Well, she told herself, *there are plenty of Welshmen in the East End, so there are, surely one of them can tell me what's in this precious letter of Annie's. Pity John doesn't speak Welsh, then I wouldn't have to worry about sharing the money with whoever translates it for me. Maybe I can pawn the flannel shirt somewhere else and use the money to pay someone to read it out for me in English?*

Her stomach rumbled, as empty as the pocket she reserved for cash when she had any. John Kelly, striding gamely along despite his labored breathing, glanced over and smiled briefly. "Heard that, luv," he chuckled. "Hungry, are we?"

"I could stand a meal," she admitted, aware that he would be just as hungry as she and in greater need of food, what with fighting off two kinds of illness. "Don't fret about it John Kelly, we'll get to town all right, even if we're hungry when we get there, and you always manage to earn a few pence, luv, so we'll have ourselves a hot supper soon enough."

And she could always earn a few pence, herself, if it came to that. She only resorted to selling herself when their circumstances became truly desperate. But whenever he fell ill, they had to have money, and Kate Eddowes was not too proud to earn fourpence any way she could. And her daughter, doubtless prompted by her new husband, had taken to moving about the south end of London with such frequency, Kate often found it difficult to trace the girl and ask for tuppence.

She'd try to find her daughter again when they got to town, first thing after securing a bed at their old lodging house, down to 55 Flower and Dean Street. They'd pawn something to raise the money for food and the bed, then she'd find her little girl and try to get more cash, and if that didn't work, then she'd jolly well find some drunken Welshman who wanted a quick fourpenny knee trembler and trade herself for a translation of Annie Chapman's letter. Once she had that, there'd be plenty of money for John Kelly's medicines and her own gin and as many warm, dry beds as they wanted, for the rest of their lives. And whoever had butchered Polly Nichols and Annie Chapman would find himself dangling from the end of a gallows rope. Kate Eddowes had once made a fair living, writing and selling cheap books of lives at public hangings. She suppressed a wry smile. Wouldn't it be ironic, now, if she ended up making her fortune from a little gallows book about the Whitechapel Murderer?

A fierce sky shimmered like an inverted bowl of beaten bronze. Dust, hot and acrid, bit Skeeter's throat despite the bandanna tied across his lower face. Skeeter shifted his weight in the saddle once again, nursing a blinding headache and a prickle of heat rash under his dirty, grit-filled clothes. The constant shift and sway of his horse under aching thighs reminded Skeeter forcefully how long it'd been since he'd done any sustained riding. He was a good rider. Skeeter had, in a different lifetime, felt at home on anything a saddle could be thrown across. But after years of easy living on Shangri-La Station, he was simply—sadly—out of practice. And thanks to Sid Kaederman's irritating, smug presence, somehow contriving to be constantly underfoot without ever becoming downright intrusive, Skeeter hadn't found even three seconds alone with Kit to air his suspicions about Noah Armstrong.

Why couldn't Armstrong have picked January to go on the lam, rather than July? Heat fell like water down into the narrow draw where their string of ponies clattered and clopped along a so-called trail. *And why couldn't that pack of black-powder enthusiasts have picked a spot closer to civilization for their Wild West shootout?* He and Kit had figured Armstrong would ditch the time tour first chance, heading for someplace crowded. San Francisco, maybe. Chicago or New York, if he really wanted to get lost. Searching an entire continent for Noah Armstrong and his hostages had not been Skeeter's notion of a good time, although he cheerfully would do just that, to catch up to Ianira and her family.

But Armstrong hadn't done that. Travelling in the guise of Joey Tyrolin, drunkard and braggadocio, Armstrong hadn't even ditched the black-powder competition tour. Instead, the terrorist ringleader had ridden up into the mountains with the rest of the eager shooters, presumably with his hostages still under duress. Why Armstrong had stuck to the competition group, not even Kit could figure. And Sid Kaederman, who had boasted so suavely of understanding terrorists, offered no explanation at all, merely shrugging his shoulders.

So Kit and Skeeter and the Wardmann-Wolfe agent followed their trail, which meant they took the train from Denver down to Colorado Springs, then saddled up and headed west toward Pikes Peak for the distant, abandoned mining camp where the competition was underway. Kurt Meinrad, the temporal guide detailed to their mission by Granville Baxter, had rounded up a short train of pack mules to haul their supplies. An hour onto the trail, Sid Kaederman began to shift ceaselessly in his saddle, obviously suffering from the unaccustomed activity. He finally urged his horse up alongside their guide's. "Why did that pack of idiots come clear out here to hold some stupid competition? Why not just stay in Denver? There weren't any gun-control laws in effect yet, so why come out to the middle of nowhere?"

Meinrad, face weathered to old leather by years of guiding time tourists through these mountains, turned easily in his saddle. "They wanted the feel of a real Old West event, which isn't possible in Denver. The city's too grown up, too civilized. Millionaires who made their fortunes in the gold and silver booms have turned Denver into a miniature copy of cities back East, with fancy houses, artwork imported from Europe, and some of the most snobbish society you'll ever meet. *Nouveau riche* are always edgy about proving how superior their cultured manners are and the Denver Four Hundred are among the worst."

Kaederman just grunted and shifted again, trying to get comfortable.

"What they wanted was an abandoned mining town back in the hills, with plenty of old buildings and rusting equipment lying around to be shot at and hidden behind. The trouble is, not many camps are abandoned yet. The big strikes started in the 1850s, at places like Central City, with more coming in the '70s, at Animas Forks and Apex and Leadville. They're all boom towns, full of miners and drunken hopefuls and prostitutes and enterprising merchants making fortunes selling supplies at outrageous prices. You can't hold this kind of competition in a boom town, so we decided on Mount MacIntyre." When Kaederman gave him a baffled look, Meinrad chuckled. "The town's been deserted for years. In fact, the legendary Cripple Creek strike was actually ignored for twelve years, because of Mount MacIntyre."

Skeeter, intrigued despite Kaederman's irritating presence, asked, "How come? Even *I've* heard of Cripple Creek. I can't believe gold-hungry miners would ignore a strike that rich for twelve whole years!"

Meinrad grinned. "Well, a guy name of Chicken Bill claimed he'd struck ore that assayed out at two thousand dollars to the ton—quite a motherload, even for this area. Trouble was, the whole thing was a hoax. Miners flooded in and ripped the countryside to shreds, looking, and all they found was dust and bedrock. Folks got to calling it the Mount Pisgah Hoax, through a mix-up in locales, so when drunken old Bob Womack found ore worth two hundred dollars a ton at Mount

Pisgah back in '78, nobody would believe it. They still don't. It'll be another five years, 1890, before a German count by the name of Pourtales proves Womack right. Then, of course, Cripple Creek becomes a legend, particularly after the fires of '96 burn the whole town to the ground. By 1902, they'll be bringing twenty-five million a year out of Cripple Creek's gold mines, but right now, the whole region is deserted, thanks to the Mount Pisgah Hoax."

Skeeter chuckled. "Which really happened at Mount MacIntyre. Sounds like the perfect place to hold a black-powder competition. And if folks do a little prospecting on the sly, down toward Mount Pisgah, who's going to complain?"

Meinrad laughed. "Certainly not the BATF. They'll get their cut of any nuggets brought home. Anyway, there's enough local color to give our competitors all the Old West they can stomach." He glanced at the unhappy detective, who was shifting uncomfortably in the saddle again. "Don't worry, Kaederman, you'll survive, although your thighs might not thank you for it. You shouldn't develop saddle galls, that only happens when your clothes and your gear don't fit proper, but if you do, you can smear them with a salve I always bring along for the greenhorns." He grinned and tapped his saddle bags. "Antiseptic, antibiotic, and plenty of anesthetic to deaden the pain."

The thought of the insufferable Mr. Kaederman smearing saddle galls in his fancy backside cheered Skeeter no end. Kaederman's performance for the press at their departure had been enough to earn Skeeter's enmity for life, standing there sucking up to that overweening toad, Caddrick, calmly assuring the newsies that he would personally see Jenna Caddrick safely back to her father's care, a job clearly beyond the capabilities of the station's search team.

Skeeter would've given a great deal to jab a straight pin in the man's rump during that so-called press briefing, just to watch him yelp. He already dreaded the hullaballoo waiting for their return. The *next* newsie who stuck a microphone in Skeeter's face and shouted, "Is it true you're running a con-game on the senator, taking advantage of his bereavement?" would get a mouthful of unpleasantness, courtesy of the nearest object not fastened to the floor.

Meanwhile . . .

There were two ways to reach the dud mines at Mount MacIntyre, from Colorado Springs. They could loop around to the north, through Woodland Park Divide then down through Florissant toward Cripple Creek, or they could ride south past Victor, then swing north around the flank of mountains in the way. Either route would take time, but the northern trail was longer, so Meinrad chose the route down past Victor. They'd left the Colorado Springs rail station near midmorning, moving at a steady lope that wouldn't put too great a strain on the horses. By the time the sun was low over the shoulders of the Rockies, Skeeter was bushed, far worse than their tough mountain ponies. The canyon they'd been following finally opened out into a moonscape of blasted, barren hillsides where nothing but scrub grew along deep, eroded gullies. *Gold mining country.*

They straggled along in a stretched-out line, rounding enormous mounds of broken rock and silt left to bake in the hot sun, and came at length to a ridge above a ramshackle town. The mining camp sprawled between piles of tailings, sluice flumes, open-pit mine works, boarded-over mine shafts, and the meanders of a sparkling river which caught the hot sun in diamond flashes. Water rippled and spilled its glittering way over and around immense boulders which had been blasted down from the surrounding mountainsides.

A sharp report cracked on the still air, prompting Skeeter's pony to shift under his thighs. He controlled the uneasy animal with his legs, settling it down to blow restively and champ its bit. A long, dry wooden flume teetered its way a good three-hundred feet down a barren hillside to the valley floor. Down beside it, a cloud of blue-grey smoke puffed out onto the hot afternoon air. The smoke hung above the flume's broken sides for a moment before gradually dissipating. A hundred feet away, another puff of smoke appeared as a second shot was fired from the vicinity of a ramshackle livery stable.

Then a galloping horse burst out of the stable and shot across a broad stretch of open ground at a dead run. The rider, leaning low over his horse's neck, drew smoothly from a right-handed hip holster and fired at the side of the flume. Smoke bellied out and hung on the still air. Dust swirled up from thundering hooves as the rider holstered his six-gun, then reached across to his left hip and pulled a second enormous pistol from a cross-draw. He fired again as the galloping horse shot past the flume. He reholstered at full gallop and raced down to a shack at the edge of the clearing.

The sweating rider pulled up hard on the reins and hauled his mount to a slithering stop. Then he drew from his right-hand holster again and twisted around, firing a shot at the flume over his shoulder. Kicking his horse into motion, he reholstered once more as the animal swept around the shed and galloped back toward the rickety wooden watercourse. Another cross-draw shot from the left-hand hip and the horse raced past the flume to the livery stable. A sharp whistle sounded as the horse galloped back inside, hidden by a cloud of dust.

"Time!" a man's voice rang out from one of the abandoned houses. Then, "Reset! And . . . Next shooter up!"

This time, Skeeter saw a man crouched behind the flume, positioned several yards uphill from the mounted rider's target. The guy at the flume ran downhill and yanked targets from either side of the dilapidated wooden structure, hastily tacking up new ones for the next contestant. He ran back uphill and jumped into a pit which protected him from flying lead. He then drew a revolver and fired into the air. At that signal, another shot rang out from the livery stable.

This time Skeeter saw the puff of dust fly up from the dry, brittle wood as lead struck a target. Then a second galloping horse shot out into the open, the second rider also leaning low. This contestant wore his six-guns butt forward. The rider fired both shots at the flume as his horse, a big paint with brown splotches down its flanks, raced past. Again, the rider galloped to the shed, where he pulled up hard, his single-leather reins hooking down under his belt buckle as he snugged his horse's head back for the sliding stop. He fired the over-the-shoulder shot and reholstered, then urged his mount forward, letting the reins slide forward.

The single leather strap hooked itself under his second, butt-forward pistol, and dragged it out of the holster neat as anything. The gun flipped midair and landed in the dust with a disastrous thunk. The rider froze in dismay for a long, penalizing second. Then he scrambled out of the saddle and retrieved his piece, lunged back into the saddle again with a one-footed dancing hop, and urged his mount around the shed. He had to circle it again, to give himself time to reholster his gun and draw it correctly for the shot on the return gallop.

Skeeter chuckled. "I'll bet that guy's cussing a streak by the time he gets back to the livery stable."

Kit glanced around. "Yes. And if that was a real

shootout, down there, he'd probably be an embarrassed corpse right about now."

Skeeter sobered. "Point taken."

The judge in the abandoned house called, "Time!" and Kurt Meinrad put hands to lips and gave out a loud, drawn-out whistle. Then he yelled, "Halluuuu!" For a moment, all was still in the abandoned mining town; then doors were flung open and abruptly the place swarmed with life. Men in faded, dusty denim work pants and checked shirts or fringed buckskins came out of hiding from a dozen buildings. Women, too, some clad in buckskins like the men, others in long prairie skirts and frontier-rugged dresses, with wide-brimmed bonnets to shade their faces from the fierce sun, came running excitedly from seemingly abandoned structures. Down beside the disused ore flume, the target changer waved up at them and returned Meinrad's vigorous greeting.

"Move out," Meinrad called.

Kit Carson's thump of heels to his pony's sides was almost as weary as Skeeter's own. The retired scout hadn't been in a saddle any more recently than Skeeter had—and while Kit was as lean and tough as old belt leather left too long in the sun, he wasn't getting any younger. The sight of the toughest man Skeeter knew, just as whacked out as he was, cheered Skeeter a little. They rode silently into "town" while the re-enactment shooters assembled in front of the ramshackle livery stable. Someone had refurbished the stalls and corral sufficiently to house several dozen horses, but only a dozen or so were in sight. He spotted drifts of smoke from the chimneys of several tumble-down houses, their windows long since broken out by storms and wild animals.

A thickset man in his thirties, holding a Spencer repeater propped easily across one shoulder, blinked

up at their guide. Skeeter recognized the man vaguely
as one of Time Tours' Denver guides, who spent most
of his career down time. The guide was staring at them
in open puzzlement. "Kurt Meinrad! I didn't figure
they'd send *you* out here! Weren't you supposed to be
on vacation by now? Not that I'm sorry to see you. I
told that courier we needed the best help there was.
You must've been sitting in the Denver gate house,
to get here this fast."

Skeeter swung himself out of the saddle as Meinrad
and Kit, the latter all but unrecognizable under gritty
dust, dismounted. The ground was hard under Skeeter's
boot soles, baked dry by the blazing summer sun. The
town smelt of woodsmoke, sulphurous gun powder, hot
sunlight on dust, and human sweat. Skeeter reeked of
overheated horse.

"Courier?" Kit asked sharply. "What courier? We're
not here because of any courier."

The Time Tours guide with the Spencer glanced at
Kit, then did a classic double-take. "Good God! *Kit
Carson?* No, they certainly wouldn't have sent you to
answer my call for help. What in God's name are *you*
doing here?"

Kit shook his head. "Never mind that now. Why'd
you send out a courier? What kind of trouble did you
need help with?"

"Two murders, is what," the man grunted, spitting
tobacco juice to one side with a brown splat. "Two
stinking murders and four disappearing tourists." When
Skeeter groaned under his breath, the man glanced
from Kit to Skeeter to Sid Kaederman and shot a
worried look at Kurt Meinrad, then held out a meaty
hand to Kit. "Orson Travers. Let's get you settled in
before I give you the details. It's hot as blazes out here
and you men look to need a good, cold drink before
we start poking into this mess."

Kit nodded, clearly impatient with the delay, but acknowledged their need to slap the dust off and slake their thirst and care for their horses. "Pleasure to meet you, Mr. Travers. This is Skeeter Jackson, Neo Edo House Detective. And Mr. Sid Kaederman, private detective with the Wardmann-Wolfe Agency."

"Gentlemen," Orson Travers said gravely. "My drovers'll see to your ponies and settle your pack mules. We'll go up to the saloon and talk things out. I got a funny feeling our trouble's related to whatever you're doing here with two detectives."

So did Skeeter. And from the look on his face, so did Kit. What Sid Kaederman thought, Skeeter didn't care. John Caddrick's pet snoop could jump over the nearest cliff, if he wanted to do something really useful.

"Saloon is up that way," Travers pointed.

Shortly, Skeeter found himself in a mended wooden chair sipping cool water from a chipped enamel cup. Tourists crowded into the ramshackle saloon to listen. Skeeter didn't see a single face in that crowd that could possibly have belonged to Noah Armstrong or Jenna Caddrick, let alone his missing friends. He was seriously worried that he knew exactly who was dead and who was missing.

"All right," Kit said quietly when the last of the tour group had crowded in. "You say you've lost six people. I'm betting your bad news will tie in with ours. We're here on a search and rescue mission. One that will either keep Shangri-La operational or see the station closed down, depending on how well we do our jobs." He studied the whole group closely. "I don't see Joey Tyrolin anywhere. Or Cassie Coventina."

Orson Travers ran a hand across his sweat-soaked face and hair. "No, you won't. That's the trouble I mentioned." Travers grimaced. "There was an ambush, out on the endurance course. Two tourists dead, shot to death by God only knows who. One of their horses, too. And another tourist lit out during the confusion, just skied up with everything he owned. Took his porter with him, the porter *and* his kids, who weren't even supposed to be out here. Bull Morgan and Granville Baxter will have my job," he added glumly, "losing six members of my tour group in one day."

Skeeter hardly dared breathe. Who was dead and who was on the run? The porter with the children could be nobody but Marcus, with Gelasia and Artemisia. Only who was with them? Ianira? Might his friends be safe, after all, running for their lives out in the mountains? But two people were dead—and there'd been six hostages. Quite abruptly, Skeeter needed to know just who had died, up here. He found himself on his feet, voice grating harshly through the dust and weariness. "Show me the bodies."

Travers hesitated. "There's more to this than you realize, Mr. Jackson—"

"*Show me the goddamned bodies!*"

Kit was on his feet, as well. "Easy, Skeeter," he said, voice low. Then, to Travers, "You'd better show us. I take it you didn't send the bodies back with the courier?"

"I thought I'd better wait until the search party got back. I was hoping to find our deserters and send them back together, but the trackers haven't shown up yet, so I sent a rider on ahead to Denver. I wanted him to get there before the gate cycled, but if you didn't run across him, he obviously didn't make it." Travers nodded toward a doorway at the rear of the room. "We embalmed 'em from the medical kits and put 'em in body bags, back in the saloon's storage pantry. It's the most secure place in town. Didn't want the local wildlife getting to them, after all. Our surgeon went with the search team, just in case."

"Paula Booker?" Kit asked sharply.

Travers nodded. "After what happened on the trail, there was no stopping her. Said she could've saved one of 'em, if she'd gotten to him in time. I've never seen a woman so upset in all my born days."

Kit sighed, weariness etched into his grizzled features. "Open it up, please. Let's get this over with."

Skeeter and Kit followed Travers into the next room, leaving Kaederman to bring up the rear. None of the tourists volunteered to go with them. A sickening, sweet stench met them when the heavy door groaned open. A moment later, zippers went down on the body bags and Skeeter found himself staring at two dead men. One was a stranger, thank God. The other . . .

Even expecting the worst, Skeeter lurched, the shock took him so hard. The dusty room, the sun-baked mountains beyond the broken windows, swooped and dove for a long, dizzy instant. Skeeter clutched at the open doorframe. He heard his voice, distant and strange, saying, "I'm gonna break the neck of the bastard who did this . . ."

Julius had been gut-shot. He'd clearly survived the fatal wound long enough to reach camp and Paula Booker, because someone had taken stitches before he'd died. Kit's hand settled on Skeeter's shoulder. "I'm sorry, Skeeter." The scout's voice had filled with a compassion that would've touched him, had the pain not been so sharp and terrible.

"Dammit, Kit! That boy wasn't even seventeen yet!" Skeeter jerked around, half-blind and not wanting Kit to notice. He was set to stride out of the monstrous little room, to get outside, to breathe down some fresh air, when he noticed Sid Kaederman. The detective had come up quietly behind them to peer past their shoulders. Even through Skeeter's blinding grief, Sid Kaederman's sudden deathly stillness brought Skeeter's instincts to full, quivering alert. He'd seen that kind of lethal tension before, in one or two of Yesukai's most deadly warriors, men who would've cheerfully slit a friend's throat for looking crosswise in their direction. The look in Kaederman's eyes set the tiny hairs along Skeeter's nape starkly erect.

Kaederman was staring down at the bodies. And for one unguarded moment, Skeeter glimpsed a look of naked shock in his cold eyes. Skeeter followed Kaederman's gaze and realized he wasn't staring at the murdered down-time teenager, but at the other corpse, a man who'd been shot several times through the back, by the look of the wounds. Kaederman's sudden stillness, the stunned disbelief in his eyes, set inner alarms ringing.

Without warning, Kit had Skeeter by the arm. "Easy, Skeeter, you're awfully white around the mouth. Let's get you outside, get some fresh air into your lungs. I know what a terrible shock this is . . ." The former scout was literally dragging him across the saloon's warped floor, past the gawking tourists, outside into the hot sunlight where the air was fresh and a slight breeze carried away the stink of death. An instant after that, the scout thrust a metal flask into his hand and said a shade too loudly, "Swallow this, Skeeter, it'll help."

Whatever Kit was up to, Skeeter decided to play along, since it had taken them out of Kaederman's immediate presence for the moment. Whatever was in the flask, it scalded the back of his throat. Skeeter swallowed another mouthful as Kit steered him down toward the livery stable, one hand solicitously guiding him by the arm, as though taking a distraught and grieving friends away from curious eyes. When they were far enough from the saloon, Kit muttered, "What the hell did you see in Sid Kaederman's face, Skeeter, that caused you to come out of shock so fast? One second, you were falling apart, ready to bawl, and the next you looked like you were ready to kill Kaederman where he stood."

Skeeter glanced into Kit's hard blue eyes. "That why you hustled me out of there so fast?"

Kit snorted. "Damn straight, I did. Didn't want Kaederman to notice the look on *your* face. Left him staring at the bodies."

"Huh. Well, that's exactly what stopped me in my tracks. The way he was looking at those bodies. Got any idea why the senator's pet bloodhound would go into shock, looking at a dead drover? Because for just a split second, Sid Kaederman was the most stunned man in this entire camp. Like he knew the guy, or something, and didn't expect to find him dead on a pantry floor."

Kit let out a long, low whistle. "I find that mighty interesting, don't you?"

"Interesting? That's not the half of it. There's something screwy about Caddrick's story, all that guff he fed us about Noah Armstrong. Either Caddrick's lying, or somebody fed *him* a line, because I'm starting to think Noah Armstrong didn't kidnap anybody. And maybe he's not a terrorist, at all."

Kit halted mid-stride, his lean and weathered face falling into lines of astonishment. Grimly, Skeeter told him, all of it. About the wild-eyed kid who'd shouted Noah's name. "And I'm willing to bet," Skeeter added, "it was Noah Armstrong who shot the *Ansar Majlis* gunmen in the daycare center, when those bastards tried to grab Ianira's kids. They lit out through the Wild West Gate, came up here, and after somebody murdered Julius, Noah Armstrong went on the run with Marcus and the girls. Only . . . Why was Julius posing as a girl?" That part bothered Skeeter. It didn't fit anywhere.

"I wonder," Kit mused softly, "just who Julius was supposed to be? Why, indeed, pose as a *girl?* Unless, of course, he was acting as a decoy for someone."

"*Jenna Caddrick?*" Skeeter gasped.

"Isn't any other candidate I can see. But why? And if Noah Armstrong isn't *Ansar Majlis,* then who the hell is he? And how did he know there would be an attack on Ianira and her family?"

"I've been asking myself those very same questions," Skeeter muttered. "Along with the name of that wild-eyed kid in the crowd."

"You said he was carrying a black-powder pistol?"

Skeeter nodded.

"It would be very interesting," Kit said, scratching the back of his neck absently, "to know if that gun had once been registered to Carl McDevlin."

Skeeter stared. "You mean—that kid might've *been* Jenna Caddrick? Disguised as a boy?"

Kit's grimace spoke volumes. "She disappeared in the company of Noah Armstrong, whoever he turns out to be. And we know Jenna's a Templar. That gives her a powerful motive to protect Ianira's life. Jenna would certainly be in a position to suspect Ianira's life was in danger, after the attack that killed her aunt and roommate."

Skeeter whistled softly. "I don't like this, Kit. Not one stinking little bit."

"Neither do I," Kit growled, kicking savagely at a dirt clod under his boot toe. It exploded into a shower of dust. "But then, I already didn't like it, and I've never had any reason to trust a single word that came sideways out of John Caddrick's mouth. The question I want answered is what motive Caddrick would have for lying about Noah Armstrong. Surely the FBI would be able to corroborate or disprove his claim that Armstrong is a terrorist?"

Skeeter said uneasily, "Maybe Caddrick *bought* the FBI? It's been done before."

Kit shot him an intense, unreadable glance, then swore in a language Skeeter didn't recognize. "Skeeter, I really hate it when you say things like that. Because I have this terrible feeling you may just be right."

"Great. So what are we going to *do* about it?"

"First," and Kit's face closed into a lean, deadly mask, "we find out just what happened in this camp that left two men dead and Marcus on the run for his life, with his kids. Then, we track down Armstrong and our friends. Before another pack of *Ansar Majlis* killers beats us to it."

As they headed back for the dusty saloon, Skeeter wondered uneasily about yet another mystery: just what Sid Kaederman's role in this lethal mess might be.

Chapter Five

John Lachley laid a sheet of blotter paper gently across the glistening, blood-red ink of the missive he'd just finished, then held the newly penned letter up to the light to read it again, judging the effect. It hadn't been easy, writing in the style of Maybrick's disjointed ramblings. He'd worked very hard to sprinkle the man's irritating Americanisms into the language. But he was proud of the results.

"*Dear Boss . . .*" the letter began.

I keep on hearing the police have caught me but they wont fix me just yet. I have laughed when they look so clever and talk about being on the <u>right</u> track. That joke about Leather Apron gave me real fits. I am down on whores and I shant quit ripping them till I do get buckled. Grand work the last job was. I gave the lady no time to squeal. How can they catch me now. I love my work and want to start again. You will soon hear of me with my funny little games. I saved some of the proper <u>red</u> stuff in a ginger beer bottle over the last job to write with but it went thick like glue and I cant use it. Red ink is fit enough I hope <u>ha. ha.</u> The next job I do I shall clip the ladys ears off and send to the police officers just for jolly wouldn't you. Keep this letter back till I do a bit more wo7rk, then give it out straight. My knife's so nice and sharp I want to get to work right away if I get a chance. Good luck.

> Yours truly,
> Jack the Ripper

Dont mind me giving the trade name.

P.S. Wasn't good enough to post this before I got all the red ink off my hands curse it No luck yet. They say I'm a doctor now. <u>ha ha</u>

John Lachley dated the letter September 25th and blew the final line of red ink dry, then chuckled to himself. He'd instructed Maybrick to bring his diary to London during his last visit, and had read the depraved drivel scrawled in it with avid curiosity. He'd copied the madman's way of writing, including his insane insertions of the words <u>ha ha</u> and other underscored phrases here and there. When Maybrick's diary was discovered in Liverpool, this letter would help to hang him.

Perhaps he'd write out a few more letters and cards, drop them in the post over the next few days? After all, once he'd recovered Eddy's wayward missives from Stride and Eddowes, he would no longer need Maybrick for anything save a weight at the end of a gallows rope. He grinned down at the bloody signature line, intensely proud of the appellation he'd thought up. *Jack the Ripper* . . . Poor James, who referred to himself in his diary as Sir Jim. He'd protest innocence of writing this all the way to the drop. Yes, Lachley smiled, he would write out a few more letters, perhaps scrawl one or two across a newspaper article, something with the word Liverpool in it . . .

A tap at the study door roused him from delightful musings. He hastily slid the letter into his desk drawer and locked it. "Yes? Come!"

His manservant bowed in the doorway. "You asked to be notified when your patient woke, sir."

"Ah, yes, thank you, Charles. I'll see the young lady directly."

"Very good, sir."

Lachley climbed the stairs while planning where to send his traitorous little missive. The editor of the *Daily News*, perhaps, a respectable newspaper with a large circulation and a keen appetite to solve the mystery of the Whitechapel Murderer. Or maybe the Central News Agency. He wished he might see the face of the editor when that letter landed on the gentleman's desk. Chuckling at his own joke, Lachley entered the room of his comely young captive.

"Good afternoon, dear lady!"

The girl was awake, listless from the effects of the drugs he fed her daily. A spark of terror flared in her eyes as he sat beside the bed. He took her hand, felt the chill of her fingers. "Now, then. Let us chat, Miss Ianira."

A shudder, very faint, ran through her.

He patted her hand. "I have seen what you are capable of, my dear. I intend to make excellent use of your skill." He brushed hair back from her brow, stroked her ashen skin. "How pale you are, today. Come now, you must surely see the advantages of a connection with me? I can give you all of London, all of Britain's power and wealth." He stroked her hand again. "I've obtained the license, you know. Special dispensation." He chuckled. "Knowing Eddy really is such a tremendous help. It isn't easy, getting a special license from the dear old C of E. Clergy are such ruddy sticklers for details. However," he smiled brightly, "you will soon be Mrs. John Lachley and I will strew pearls of gratitude at your feet."

A choked sound escaped pale lips. "No . . ."

He frowned. "No? Of course you shall marry me, dear girl. I cannot have you living under my roof, unmarried. People will talk and talk is one thing I cannot afford."

She was struggling to speak. "My husband . . . children . . ."

Astonishment swept through him. "Married? You are *married?*" Then he began to laugh. "Widowed, you mean. I shot your dear husband dead in the street. Put a bullet into his head."

She strained away from him, dark eyes wide with revulsion. "No! Not Jenna . . . *Marcus.*"

Lachley frowned again. "The man I shot was not your husband?"

The girl lay trembling, tears sliding down her face. She had given him only one name to call her by, despite the drugs he'd fed her, refusing against all efforts he'd made thus far to reveal her full name.

"What is your husband's surname, girl?"

She shook her head. "What . . . what is a surname?"

"A last name!" he snapped, growing impatient. "Dammit, I know they use surnames even in Greece!"

"Not Greek . . ." she whispered. "Poor Marcus, sold in Rome . . . He'll be frantic . . ."

She was babbling again, raving out of her head. He gripped her wrists, shook her. "Tell me your last name, girl!"

"Cassondra!" she shrieked the word at him, fighting his hold on her. "I am Ianira, Cassondra of Ephesus!"

"Talk sense! There is no city of Ephesus, just a ruin buried only the ancients know where! How did you come to London?"

"Through the gate . . ."

They were back to that again. The sodding *gate,* whatever the deuce that was. She babbled about it every time he questioned her. Lachley changed his line of attack. "Tell me about the letters. Eddy's letters."

Her eyes closed over a look of utter horror. "Lady, help me . . ."

Losing patience, Lachley poured the drug down her throat, waiting for it to take effect, then put her into a deep trance. She lay without moving, scarcely even breathing beneath the coverlet he straightened over her. "Now, then," he said gently, "tell me about the letters."

Her lips moved. A bare whisper of sound escaped her. "Eight letters . . ."

"Tell me about the eight letters. Who has them?"

"Morgan . . . down in the vaulted room with the tree and the flame that always burns . . ." A shudder tore through her despite the grip of the strong medication. "Polly is dead . . . and poor Annie, who could scarcely breathe . . . Stride carries Eddy's words beneath the knife . . . Kate fears the letter in her pocket, picks hops in the countryside, afraid to touch it . . . and the pretty girl in Miller's Court, she'll die cut into pieces, poor child, for a letter she learned to read in Cardiff . . ."

"*What girl in Miller's Court?*"

Ianira's eyes had closed, however, so deep in the grip of the drug that no amount of slapping would rouse her. Lachley paced the bedroom in agitation. *What girl in Miller's Court?* Annie Chapman hadn't mentioned any such person! He narrowed his eyes, thinking back to that last conversation with the doomed prostitute. They'd been interrupted, he recalled, just as she'd been

telling him who she'd sold the letters to, mentioning
Elizabeth Stride and Catharine Eddowes. He'd thought
she was finished, after giving those two names, but
wondered now if perhaps that interruption had kept
him from learning the name of a third person in
possession of Eddy's incriminating letters?

He swore savagely, wondering what in God's name
to do now.

The bitch must be found, of course, found and
silenced.

She lived in Miller's Court, Ianira had said. He knew
the place from his childhood. Miller's Court was not a
large space, after all. How many girls from Cardiff could
there be, living in that dismal little square? He closed
his eyes against such a monstrous spectre. A Welsh girl,
in possession of Eddy's Welsh letters . . . Had she already
sent a blackmail demand to the palace? Were Eddy's
power and position in mortal peril, after all? Because
Annie Chapman, the stupid bitch, had neglected to
mention a third recipient of her letters?

He drew a deep, calming breath. Surely no blackmail demand had been sent, yet. Eddy would've come
to him in a high state of panic, if one had. Hopefully,
Polly and Annie's grisly fate had frightened the Welsh
tart too deeply to act. Still, she had got to be found
and done away with, the sooner the better. God, would
this nightmare never come to an end? With yet another
woman to trace and destroy, perhaps Lachley ought
not send his damning Ripper letter to the press, after
all? A moment's consideration, however, convinced him
to risk it, anyway. Maybrick would be in London at
the end of the week, so this girl in Miller's Court could
be eliminated on the same night as Stride and Eddowes.
Three women in one weekend was a bit much, true . . .

But he hadn't any real choice.

He spared a glance for the mysterious Ianira, pale

and silent in her bed. "You," he muttered aloud, "must wait a bit. Once this business is done, however, I *will* discover the identity of your husband."

Christ, yet *another* murder to be undertaken.

This mess occasionally bade fair to drive him insane.

The silence in the dusty little Colorado mining town was so utterly complete, Skeeter could hear the distant scream of an eagle somewhere over the sunbaked mountains. The scrape of his chair as he dragged it harshly around and sat down caused several women to jump. Julius' too-young face, waxen with that ghastly, bluish color death brought, floated in his mind's eye, demanding vengeance. The dark look he bent on Sid Kaederman went unnoticed, because the detective was busy glaring at Orson Travers. Clearly, the Time Tours guide had stalled him off until Kit and Skeeter's return. The silence lay so thick, the creak of wooden floorboards as tourists shifted sounded loud as gunshots.

The moment Kit settled into an easy stance beside Skeeter's chair, Sid Kaederman growled, "All right, Travers, you want to tell us just what's been going on?"

"Yes, let's have the details, please," Kit agreed. "This is messier than you can possibly guess."

Orson Travers, an unhappy man made monumentally unhappier by Kit's pronouncement, cleared his throat. "There wasn't any hint of trouble on the way up here. Oh, it was a rowdy enough bunch, lots of high spirits. We packed our gear in by mule from Colorado Springs, whipped the town into shape for the competition, refurbished a couple of houses to bunk down in, built the target stands and laid out the course of fire for the running action events. All that prep work was part of the package tour, using nineteenth-century techniques to build the competition course and refurbish the camp. And we planned the wedding, of course—"

"Wedding?" Kaederman interrupted, startled.

A pretty girl in a muslin gown blushed crimson and leaned against a tall, gangly kid in buckskins. He grinned. "Got ourselves hitched proper, brought a preacher with us and all, held the ceremony over at the trading post last week."

"Oh, it was so wonderful!" his bride put in excitedly. "There were real Indians and mountain men and everything! And the silliest salesman you ever saw, selling ordinary crescent wrenches, called them a new high-tech invention out of Sweden, patented only three years ago. People were paying outrageous prices for them! It was amazing, I'd never seen anything like it, fur trappers and miners buying crescent wrenches!" The blushing bride was clearly determined not to let the tragedy of a double murder mar her honeymoon.

Kit smiled. "Congratulations, I'm sure it was a wedding to remember. Now, *what the hell happened?*" He swung his gaze back to the Time Tours guide.

Travers sighed. "The action and endurance course runs through the hills and gullies around town. The idea is, you stalk and shoot every full round of the course over a period of several hours, to test your endurance and accuracy under pressure. Well, Cassie Coventina, or rather, the kid we *thought* was Cassie Coventina, was moving steadily through it on horseback, just as planned. We put spotters out along the route to act as judges and scorekeepers, but she—I mean he—never made it to the first target. Let me tell you, it was one helluva shock, when Dr. Booker stripped that kid off and we discovered Cassie Coventina was a teenage boy in drag!"

Skeeter bridled. Kit pressed a restraining hand against his shoulder. "Never mind that, Travers, just tell us what happened."

The thickset guide shifted uncomfortably. "Someone

ambushed him. Killed the kid *and* his horse. We found it on the trail, later. Joey Tyrolin claimed he and his porter followed the kid out onto the course. They weren't supposed to be out there, but Tyrolin was always so damn drunk, he pretty much did what he pleased. Guy claimed all he wanted to do was watch. Said he and his porter rode up right after the kid was ambushed. Tyrolin gave chase and killed the attacker—one of the drovers," Travers added unhappily. "A tourist who signed up to work the tour, so he could get a cheaper ticket."

"And Tyrolin killed him?" Kaederman asked softly.

An underlying tone in the man's voice, a tone Skeeter would've sworn was agitated anger despite those curiously chilly eyes, brought Skeeter's hackles up again.

"Oh, yes, Tyrolin killed him. Was bold as brass about admitting it, too. Said the man shot at him when he gave chase, so he fired back. Killed him stone dead. I'd have said it was a case of self-defense, if Tyrolin hadn't bolted out of camp with his porter and those kids, right after. While everybody was rushing around trying to set up an emergency field surgery, they just packed up their gear and rode off. We sent riders after them, of course, and half the tour group volunteered to help search. Not that we let anybody but guides and regular Time Tours drovers out of camp, after what happened with Tyrolin and that tourist. And the kid, poor bastard."

"I don't suppose," Kaederman put in, "you happen to have a photograph of Tyrolin and his porter?" The tension in his voice caught Skeeter's attention once more. Kaederman wanted that picture badly.

"Never mind the photo just now," Kit overrode him. "I presume you dispatched your courier to inform Denver of the double murders? After sending out the search party on Tyrolin's trail?"

"Yes. I'm the only guide left in camp right now. I sent everyone else and half the drovers out after them. Along with Dr. Booker. She insisted on going, in case her surgical skills were needed." Travers sighed. "So that's what happened on our end, but you haven't told us why *you're* up here, looking for Joey Tyrolin, too. Don't tell me he was a wanted criminal, up time?"

Kaederman said coldly, "You might say that. A terrorist, to be exact."

Gasps broke from the tourists. A couple of the women let out tiny shrieks.

Kit said a little wearily, "We've got troubles of our own on station just now. *Big* troubles."

"He's not kidding, either," Skeeter muttered. "Senator John Caddrick's on station. Threatening to shut us down if we don't bring back Joey Tyrolin. Among other things."

"*Caddrick?*" Orson Travers' face washed white.

"Yes," Kit nodded. "And it gets better. Joey Tyrolin's real name is Noah Armstrong. A member of the *Ansar Majlis,* that terrorist cult out of the Middle East. They murdered Cassie Tyrol in New York and kidnapped Caddrick's only child. Not to mention kidnapping Ianira Cassondra and her entire family. Between the Templars and the cult crazies flooding into the station and starting riots, we've had several critical injuries and nine murders. And if we don't find Jenna Caddrick and bring her back safely, her father will shut down Shangri-La for good. The Inter-Temporal Court's been called in, as a last-ditch measure to try and keep the station operational. Mr. Kaederman, here, was hired by the senator to help search for his daughter."

Travers looked like a slight breeze would've knocked him over.

Someone from the back of the crowd whispered, "Oh, my God. And we let the terrorist responsible get away!"

"Yes," Kaederman said with enough frost to freeze every cup of water in the room, "you did. And we're here to find him. Now, does anyone have a photo of Tyrolin and his porter? I want to make a positive identification of that bastard before we ride out after him and his hostages."

"I have a photo," a woman spoke up, pushing her way to the front. "I should have several, in fact." She ignored Kaederman, addressing Kit, instead, which left the Wardmann-Wolfe agent bristling. "Ellen Danvers, Mr. Carson, professional photographer. Hired to do the wedding party. I've been taking pictures steadily with a digital camera. I can bring all the disks for you to study, if you like."

Three minutes later, Skeeter found himself staring at a photograph of Marcus on the miniature screen at the back of Ellen Danvers' digital camera. He was clearly in disguise, but a guy didn't live through what Skeeter'd lived through, trying to rescue his friend from slavery, without getting to know that friend's face well enough to recognize him under any circumstances. The only reason he'd failed to spot Marcus at the gate's opening was Joey Tyrolin's masterful performance, drawing attention away from everything else within a thousand paces.

Ellen Danvers scrolled through shot after shot. "Joey Tyrolin was camera shy, considering how drunk he was all the time. I didn't get many shots of him. In fact, I had to work hard to get any photos of his face at all, and my client specifically asked for candids of the entire competition group." She'd used up dozens of disks taking pictures of just about everything but the horse dung.

"There," Miss Danvers paused the scroll, freezing a frame for them to look at. "That's them. Joey Tyrolin and his porter. And these are the porter's little girls. Beautiful children, both of them." The photographer's gaze was troubled as she glanced up at Kit. "We had no idea they were Ianira Cassondra's daughters, or that the porter was her husband. Are they really hostages?"

Sid Kaederman answered, voice still colder than spiked icicles. "They most certainly are, if they're even still alive. This," he tapped Noah Armstrong's photo, "is one of the most dangerous men in the world. Or rather, one of the most dangerous *people*. Armstrong's an intersexual, neither male nor female, able to assume any disguise he pleases. Armstrong's the cleverest, deadliest bastard I've ever run across. God help those kids, in the clutches of a monster like that."

Skeeter peered sharply at Kaederman, wondering about the level of venom. Was Kaederman that prejudiced against intersexuals? Lots of people were, Skeeter knew, although Kaederman didn't strike him as the type who would hate without reason. He could be playing some other game, however, painting Armstrong as the one thing Skeeter was beginning to suspect he wasn't: a terrorist.

Ellen Danvers, of course, with no reason to suspect Kaederman's motives or honesty, had paled, her expression stricken. "Those poor little girls! Can you find them?"

"We'll give it our best shot," Kit said quietly. "Let's check our gear and rations. I want to ride out within the hour."

Skeeter stayed where he was until Kit and the Wardmann-Wolfe agent had left the room. As the meeting broke up and the tourists milled around outside, trying to help and mostly dithering and getting in everyone's way, Skeeter took Ellen Danvers quietly aside and asked to see her photos again.

"All of them?" she asked.

He nodded, studying each of the shots in turn, looking carefully at every digitally recorded face. "You're sure you took pictures of every single person in the group?" he asked at length.

"Yes, quite sure."

"And there wasn't any way they could've been hiding someone else? In their luggage, say?"

"No, I don't think that would've been possible. Not an adult, anyway. The porter smuggled the children in his trunk, but they're such little things. I can't imagine how anyone could have stuffed an adult into one of those trunks."

"But they took their luggage with them? Steamer trunks, pack horses, all of it?"

Puzzled, she nodded. "Yes. Why?"

Skeeter merely shook his head. "Just a theory. Nothing I want to discuss, yet." He wondered if Kit had noticed, or Kaederman, for that matter, that the one face missing from Ellen Danvers' impressive collection of photos was Jenna Caddrick's? Nor did Ianira Cassondra appear in any of her shots, which struck Skeeter as both ominous and profoundly odd. If neither Jenna nor Ianira had come with Armstrong and Marcus, just where had the two women gone? Were they, in fact, hidden away in the steamer trunks? Or buried somewhere in a shallow grave? Skeeter's gut churned queasily. He didn't want to share those particular thoughts with anyone just yet, not until he could get Kit alone once more. He said only, "Thanks for letting me look through these again."

"Of course. Do you think there's much chance you'll be able to find them?"

Skeeter hesitated. "We'll do the best we can. I'm a good tracker. So's Kit. But they've got a good lead on us and it's a big country, out here. Frankly, I'm not holding out much hope. And I've got more reason than most to find them. Marcus is the closest friend I have in the world."

Ellen Danvers' eyes misted. "I'm sorry, Mr. Jackson."

"Thanks." He handed back the camera. "I'd appreciate it if you didn't mention this conversation."

"Of course." She hesitated. "You don't trust the senator's detective much, do you?"

Skeeter's laugh was as colorless as the burnt sky overhead. "Does it show that much? Would you trust a man working for Senator John Paul Caddrick?"

She bit one lip. "Well, no, not as far as I could throw him, which isn't very far. Good luck, Mr. Jackson. And be careful."

Her concern surprised Skeeter. He hadn't realized ordinary people could care so much. "Thank you, Ms. Danvers. I appreciate that, more than you know."

He left her peering at the screen on her camera, studying the photos, clearly wondering what, exactly, he'd been looking for. Ellen Danvers was a smart lady. He wouldn't be at all surprised if she didn't tumble to it on her own.

If she did, he hoped she kept it quiet as a tomb.

Elizabeth Stride was known throughout the East End for her stormy temper and her explosive relationship with her lover, Michael Kidney—a violent relationship she wasn't particularly ashamed of, any more than she was ashamed of the way she made her living. When Liz's younger lover drank, which was frequently, Michael grew abusive. And when she drank, which was even more often, Long Liz Stride grew belligerent. And when they quarelled, which was nearly every time they drank, Liz usually ended by slamming Michael's door behind her— if he hadn't padlocked her in again to keep her off the streets.

On Wednesday, September 26th, after another violent and drunken row, Long Liz Stride found herself on the streets once more, fuming and furious and looking for a bed at her favorite lodging house, 32 Flower and

Dean Street. The kitchen was filled with more than a dozen women and girls of all ages, most of them cold and frightened and in various stages of drunkenness. All of them whispered about the shocking murders which had struck down so many women just like them since Easter Monday.

"—scared to let a man touch me, I am," one girl of seventeen was whispering miserably, "but I got to eat, 'aven't I? What's a lady to do, when she's got to eat and there ain't no other way to put bread in 'er Lime'ouse Cut, but lift 'er skirts for whatever man'll pay 'er to do it?"

Liz had, until recently, entertained her own ideas about the infamous Whitechapel Murderer, as the newspapers had taken to calling him. She had spent a hard-earned shilling to buy a short, blunt knife to carry in her pocket as protection, after what had happened to Polly Nichols and Annie Chapman. Ever since Dark Annie's murder, Liz had been terrified to do anything about her own letter. But surely, if Annie had been killed because of these letters, the killer would have dragged out of the poor woman the identity of everyone she'd sold the letters to? Logically, a killer looking for those letters would've found that out first thing, then come after anyone who'd bought one. But nearly two weeks had passed and no one had come knocking on her door, so the newspapers must be right and poor Annie had simply fallen victim to a madman, same as poor Polly Nichols, a week before.

Besides, there were those other women killed, Martha Tabram on August Bank Holiday and Emma Smith on Easter Monday, and *they* couldn't have had anything to do with Annie Chapman's letters, which, by her own admission, she'd had from Polly, rest her soul. Still, Liz bought that knife, and she was careful not to approach any potential customers resembling the descriptions of the killer.

As Liz hesitated on the doss house's kitchen threshold, a woman she'd met during her last visit called out a greeting. "Why, Liz," Catharine Long exclaimed, gesturing her to a vacant chair beside the hearth, "I haven't seen you here in three months! Whatever's happened?"

Liz joined her, grateful for the warmth of the coal fire. The weather outside was blustery and wet, cold enough to turn her ungloved fingers red. "Oh, I had words with my man, is all. I'll let him cool his temper for a few days, then he'll see the error of his ways and I'll go back to him, drunken fool."

"But will he take you back, Liz?"

She smiled a little grimly. "Oh, yes, Michael will take me back." She patted her pocket, where several folded sheets of foolscap rested, down beneath that sharp little knife. Surely it must be safe to do something about her little investment now? And with the blackmail money she would obtain, Michael would certainly take her back, temper or no. All she had to do was find a Welshman in one of the ironworks sprawled through the vast shipyards to translate her letter and she would be rich. More than rich enough to tempt any man she wanted.

"Yes," she said again, her slight smile at odds with the atmosphere of terror and misery in the kitchen, "Michael will take me back, Catharine. So tell me the news, it's been an age since I saw you."

"Oh, I'm fine enough, Liz. But these killings . . ." Catharine Long shuddered. "And the police are such hopeless fools. You heard what Sir Charles Warren's done?"

Liz shook her head, not particularly interested in what the head of the Metropolitan police force did. As long as a woman kept moving and didn't try to stand in one place, coppers generally didn't bother her. "No, I haven't heard."

"He's taken every single East End detective off the beat! Assigned them to patrol *west* London. And he's switched about the West End detectives to patrol Whitechapel and Spitalfields and the docklands. Have you ever heard of suchlike? Why, the detectives out there don't even know the street names, let alone the alleyways this madman must be using to escape!"

A woman seated beside them moaned and rocked back and forth. "They don't care about us, so they don't! All they want is to show the ruddy newsmen they've put a few coppers on the street. Not a man Jack of 'em gives a fig for the likes of us. Now if it was fine ladies he were cuttin' up, they'd have a policeman in every house, so they would . . ."

Liz and Catharine Long exchanged a long, silent look. It was only too true, after all. Despite the show of putting extra men on the beat, both women knew they would have to defend themselves. Liz clutched the handle of her knife through her worn skirts and held back a shiver. Perhaps she ought to just burn the letter?

That won't do you any good if he comes after you, she told herself grimly. *Might as well get some money out of it, then leave London, maybe go across to America.*

She'd find someone to translate the sheets of foolscap for her, get out of this hellhole, live decently for a change. Meanwhile, she'd do a bit of charring to earn her keep, maybe offer to clean some of the rooms in the lodging house for a few pence. She might even ask around the Jewish community to see if anyone needed a charwoman for a few days. She'd done a great deal of char work for Jewish businessmen and their plump wives. They knew her to be dependable when she could get the work. And not a lot of charwomen would work for a Jew just now, not with these Whitechapel murders being blamed on a foreigner, same as that Lipski fellow last year, who'd poisoned that poor little girl, barely gone fifteen.

Long Liz didn't care how many people in the East End hated Jews or called them dirty, foreign murderers. Work was work and she certainly didn't mind cleaning houses, if it came to that. Charring was better than selling herself and she'd done that enough times to keep body and soul together, not only here in London, but back in Sweden, too, so what was a little thing like charring for a few Jews? Besides, she wouldn't need menial work much longer, would she? Not with money to be made from Annie Chapman's legacy.

"Say, Catharine," she asked quietly, leaning close to her friend so as not to be overheard, "do you know any Welshmen?"

Her friend gave her a startled glance, then laughed. "Oh, Liz, you are a piece of work! Quarrelled with your man this morning and looking for a replacement tonight! Try the Queen's Head pub, dearie, I've heard there's a Welsh ironworker from the docks with money in his trous, likes to have a drink there of an evening."

Long Liz Stride smiled. "Thank you, Catharine. I believe I will."

By week's end, Elizabeth Stride intended to be a rich woman.

The trail Armstrong had taken out of camp did not lead south, along the shorter route to Colorado Springs and the railway station. Armstrong and Marcus had fled north, the long way up toward Florissant. By nightfall, Skeeter, Kit, and Sid Kaederman, along with their guide, were deep in the Colorado Rockies, following the path the other Time Tours guides had already taken. They camped overnight in a sheltered nook of rock out of the wind, then set out at first light, covering ground rapidly along a trail Skeeter, at least, could've followed blindfolded. He'd hunted with the Yakka Clan often enough to learn what spoor to follow through rough country. "It hasn't rained for a while, at least," Skeeter muttered, studying the fading trail which sporadic wind gusts had partially obliterated in the more open spots. "Fortunately, their trail was protected in low-lying areas like this." He pointed to faded hoofprints. "They were in a tearing hurry, too. The Time Tours guides who came through after them weren't moving nearly as fast as Armstrong and Marcus."

"How do you know that?" Kaederman demanded.

Skeeter shrugged. "I've tracked quarry through broken country before. Look," he dismounted and crouched down alongside the trail, pointing to a mish-mash grouping of hoofprints. "These are the oldest prints. They're nearly a blur from the wind filling them in and the mud's completely dried out. And look how far apart the stride is." He paced off the distance between hoof prints. "They were moving at a fast canter or a slow gallop, depending on the height of their ponies. Given the weight their pack horses are carrying, that's a gruelling pace to keep up. These other prints, the fresher ones from the search party, are a lot closer together. They're trotting, at best. They'll never catch up if Marcus and Armstrong keep up the pace they've been holding, pushing their ponies that fast."

"But they'll wear out their horses in no time!"

"Not if they're smart and careful," Skeeter disagreed. "I've been studying these prints all morning. They slow to a walk periodically to give the horses a breather, probably more for the pack animals' sake than the riding mounts. And I've spotted a couple of places where they dismounted and let the animals

rest and graze. But when they're in the saddle, they're
moving fast. Judging from those photos Ellen Danvers
took, Armstrong can't weigh much more than one-
thirty, one-forty, and Marcus is slender, too. He and
Ianira never had the money to indulge overeating.
Even with the children, he's probably lighter for a
pony to carry than I am and I'm not exactly massive,
myself. Armstrong is obviously no fool. I'd say he
knows exactly what he's doing. As long as they're
careful with the pack animals, or don't care about
abandoning their baggage, they won't founder those
horses. And wherever they're going, they'll get there
a lot sooner than any of us will."

The big question Skeeter *couldn't* answer from
these tracks, however, was whether or not any of the
Time Tours guides or drovers searching ahead of them
might be in the pay of the *Ansar Majlis*. If *he'd* been
part of a terrorist cult dedicated to murdering someone like Marcus and Ianira, he would've sent more
than one hit man through the Wild West Gate. Which
left Skeeter wondering just how many killers they
might yet run into on this trail—or how much use Sid
Kaederman would be, if they did. He kept his eyes
and ears open and hoped they didn't stumble into an
ambush somewhere along the way.

By their third day of hard riding, they'd swung
around the north flank of Pikes Peak and were moving
east toward the rail line again. They had to call a brief
halt when Kaederman's pony pulled up lame. The
detective dismounted stiffly and watched unhappily as
Meinrad showed him how to check his pony's hooves
for stones, lifting each foot in turn to check the soft
pad known as the frog. They were prying loose a sharp
rock from his near forefoot when Skeeter heard it: a
faint, sharp report that echoed off the mountains.
Another distant crack reached them, like a frozen tree

splitting wide open, then a third, followed by a whole volley. The sound fell into an abruptly familiar pattern.

"*Gunfire!*"

Lots of it.

Kit jerked around in the saddle. "Jeezus Christ! There's a war breaking loose out there! Kurt, we don't have time to wait, nursemaid him when you've got that pony's hoof cleared! Skeeter, move it!" Kit clattered off at a gallop just as Skeeter jerked his shotgun out of its scabbard. Skeeter put heels to flanks and sent his mount racing after Kit's. He leaned low over his horse's neck, his double-barrel clutched in one hand like a war spear, and snarled into the teeth of the wind. Even above the thunder of hooves, he could still hear gunfire popping ominously ahead. He couldn't imagine locals producing that much gunfire. But the *Ansar Majlis* easily could. Had the Time Tours guides found Marcus and the girls after all, bringing them back toward camp, only to ride into the fusillade of an ambush?

Kit crouched so close above his horse's neck, he looked like a fluid statue cut from the same flesh as the racing animal. The retired scout surged ahead, splashing through a shallow, rocky creek and switching with consumate skill around outcroppings, tumbled boulders and loose piles of scree. Skeeter's horse slipped and slid through the jumbled heaps of weather-fractured stones, then drew up nose to tail behind Kit's, nostrils distended and running flat out. This was bad country for a full-bore charge. If either nag put a foot wrong at this speed . . .

A sudden silence ahead robbed him of breath. Then the staccato pop of gunfire rattled again in the harsh sunlight, sporadic but closer than before. *Somebody had to reload. Several somebodies. Both sides, maybe.* Which meant there was a chance the *Ansar Majlis* were using period firearms, rather than modern stuff smuggled through the gate. Against black-powder guns, even replica models, his friends might stand a halfway decent chance. Given the sound of that shooting, whoever was under attack was firing back, giving at least as good as they were getting.

Then Kit was reining in and Skeeter pulled up hard to slither to a halt beside him, both horses blowing from the run. Kit held up a warning hand, then pointed down into a narrow little arroyo. Two riderless horses pawed the dusty ground uncertainly, skittish and laying their ears back each time gunfire tore through the hot sunlight. Their riders lay pinned between an outcropping of stone and a jumble of boulders, firing up toward a knife-edge ridgeline that lay to Skeeter and Kit's left. Skeeter dragged his field glasses out of his saddle bag, the brass warm with the scent of hot leather, and peered toward the ridgeline while Kit studied the riders pinned below.

"That's a Time Tours guide," Kit muttered. "And Paula Booker!"

"*Shalig!*" Skeeter snarled under his breath. "There's at least six gunmen up there." He pointed toward the narrow ridgeline. "Counting puffs of smoke, at least six, maybe more."

"*Six?*" Kit shot back, brows diving toward his nose. "That's too many for Armstrong's crew."

"Maybe. How many guys did he plant with those drovers?"

Kit swore. "*Shalig* is right. Let's get around the back side of that ridge, come at them from behind."

They had to abandon the horses halfway up, the slope was so sharp. Skeeter panted for breath and scrambled for handholds, climbing steadily, shotgun gripped awkwardly in one hand. Kurt Meinrad and Sid Kaederman, arriving late, struggled to climb the same slope in their wake. Skeeter gained the top and bellied forward, lying flat so he wouldn't skyline himself and make a visible target above the ridge. Kit slithered out beside him, grunting softly and peering through his own field glasses. Kurt Meinrad arrived just as Kit began surveying the scene below. Skeeter handed the guide his own field glasses and jerked Kaederman down when the idiot just stood there, standing out like a neon sign flashing "shoot me." Skeeter waited in a swivet, using the naked eye to mark spots where gunmen lay hidden in the rocky outcroppings of the ridge. Meinrad gave a sudden grunt.

"Huh. That's no pack of terrorists, Carson."

Kit swung a sharp look on the Time Tours guide. "Oh?"

"That's the Flanagan brothers. With a couple of their low-life pals. Irish railroad men who took to holding up trains after they finished laying track. Small-time thugs, temporal natives. We've had trouble with them before, roughing up a couple of the tours. They like holding up stage coaches, too, and robbing campsites."

"They may be small time, but they've got your guide and Paula Booker pinned down neat as any trap I've ever seen," Kit shot back. "And if they're down-timers, we don't have any guarantee they *can* be killed, even if we shoot amongst 'em."

"Maybe not," Skeeter said, misquoting a favorite mid-twentieth century television show he'd watched endlessly in reruns, "but I'll bet you credits to navy beans I can put the fear of God into 'em."

Before Kit could reply, Skeeter let out a war whoop and charged down the precipitous slope, yelling and cursing in twelfth-century Mongolian and loosing off rounds as fast as he could jam shells into his scattergun. Six astonished faces swung up toward him. Skeeter let fly another round of buckshot and heard Kit scrambling down the slope after him, yelling in some unknown, bloodcurdling language that left Skeeter's hair standing on end. Kit's Model 73 barked with a roar like thunder. Lead whined off rock so close to a Flanagan brother's ear, the man jumped six inches straight up and landed running.

When Kurt Meinrad joined the insane plunge, shooting and shouting on Kit's heels, it was too much for the Flanagans. They all broke and ran, heading for ponies concealed in the brush. A clatter of hooves rattled away in a boiling swirl of dust, then Skeeter slithered to a halt, panting and sweating and wondering if he'd completely lost his mind, pulling a stunt like that. But he hadn't felt this alive since returning to civilization at the age of thirteen—with the possible exception of fighting for his life in the Circus Maximus.

Kit Carson, hair dishevelled, jaw unshaven, pale eyes alight with an unholy look that might've been fury or glee, stalked toward him. "Skeeter, you *lunatic!* What possessed you to pull a bone-headed piece of insanity like that?"

Skeeter grinned. "Got rid of 'em, didn't it?"

Kit's mouth thinned. "Yes. And I could be piling rocks over what was left of you, too."

"Well, hell's bells, Kit, I never yet met a bully who wouldn't back down when confronted."

One corner of Kit's lips twitched. "Next time, wait for instructions."

Skeeter sketched a sloppy salute. "Yessir!"

"Huh. Thank God you were never in the army, Skeeter, you'd have ended in Leavenworth inside a week. All right, let's go find out what that Time Tours guide is doing out here by himself with Paula Booker. Besides playing bait for every outlaw in the territory."

Wordlessly, they headed down into the rocky defile.

Chapter Six

Time Scout in-training Margo Smith was so keyed up she was very nearly shaking as she and her fiancé—freelance time guide Malcolm Moore—eased open the gate beside the International Workingmen's Association. A lively concert was underway, spilling Russian music out into the streets. Malcolm held the gate as Margo slipped into the long alleyway leading back to Dutfield's Yard. The Ripper Watch Team followed silently, carrying miniaturized equipment they would use to film Long Liz Stride's brutal murder. Their satchels were heavy, carrying three times the equipment needed for the previous two murders. This was only the first stop of three the team would make tonight, placing low-light cameras and microphone systems in Dutfield's Yard, on a certain stairway landing in Goulston Street, and in Mitre Square.

While Margo and Malcolm stood guard, the team members placed their tiny cameras, hiding them where they would not be discovered by the police, some at the entrance to the alley and others back in the yard.

Margo glanced every few moments at the windows of the crowded hall, convinced someone would spot them and demand to know what they were doing down here, but no one noticed. It gave Margo an insight into how the Ripper had been able to strike so frequently in the heart of a crowded slum. The people of Whitechapel, like those in many another overpopulated city, turned their attention inward to their own business and feared to pry too directly into the business of neighbors, particularly with a deranged killer walking the streets.

Margo drew a deep breath of relief when the Ripper Watch Team finally finished and she was able to lead them all back to the street once more.

"Very good," Malcolm said quietly, easing the wicker pedestrian gate closed, "that's the first one. Now, Mitre Square is this way."

Malcolm led the way toward the soon-to-be infamous site that Margo and Shahdi Feroz had first visited only two weeks previously. They had noticed, during their study of the killing zone, that the Ripper had left his fourth victim within sight of both a policeman's house and a Jewish synagogue. Tonight, Catharine Eddowes would walk straight into that killing zone, where her life would end violently. Margo shivered in the darkness and thrust away memories of her own mother's brutal murder, concentrating instead on their surroundings and her primary task of guarding the Ripper Scholars from footpads and gangs.

The overwhelming sense of Whitechapel by night was a region of utter darkness punctuated randomly by brightly lit pubs which drew residents like moths. Their attraction was due as much, Margo suspected, to the cheerfulness of the light and the sense of safety it gave, as to the gin and ale. They walked down entire city blocks without passing a single working gas lamp, skirted past alleyways and side streets which loomed like black caverns in the night, inhabited by God alone knew what. Sounds came drifting to them, scuffles and muffled arguments. Children lurked underfoot by the hundreds, crowding into doorways and open landings of stairwells, their eyes following the Ripper Watch team with hungry intent.

Pubs were packed with rough workmen and drab women carrying hungry-eyed children, all swilling alcohol and talking uproariously, faces puffed and reddened from drink. Outside the pubs, women walked endlessly up and down, pausing only briefly in the doorways, drifting from one pub to another soliciting customers at the Britannia, the Princess Alice, The City Darts and the Alma, at King Stores and the infamous Ten Bells, Mary Kelly's favorite haunt for plying her trade.

Stepping out onto Commercial Road was a shock, by comparison. From where they stood on the corner, all the way down to Mile End highway, stretched a raucous hive of bright-lit pubs, shops with dim gaslights still flickering, street preachers surrounded by heckling crowds, a waxworks displaying reproductions of the latest Whitechapel murder victims—children with pennies clutched in grubby fingers struggling to gain admittance—a suit salesman pitching the quality of his wares to a crowd of avid listeners, and drifts of sailors up from the docks, swilling gin and ogling the women. Despite the lateness of the hour, the Saturday night street stunned Margo with its noise and throngs of merrymakers, intent on forgetting the horror stalking the lightless roads nearby.

One of the Watch Team's experts, Dr. Shahdi Feroz, studied the street carefully as they pushed their way west, toward the border with The City of London and Mitre Square. Margo edged closer to her. "Is it usual for people to pretend like nothing's happening?"

Shahdi flicked her gaze up to meet Margo's. A slight vertical line appeared between her brows. "It is not surprising. It has been two weeks since the last killing, after all. People with no choice but to stay in this place persuade themselves the terror is over, or at least they drink and pretend it is. You have noticed the darker streets are nearly empty?"

"Yes, I was just thinking about that. Frightened people are drawn to the light and bustle." She nodded down the roaring thoroughfare. "I guess they're hoping to find safety in numbers. Not that it will do any good."

"For most, it will. Very few of these people will be up and about between one and two A.M., when the murders will occur. And even the prostitutes are trying to be cautious," she motioned with one slim, Persian hand, "staying near the lighted pubs or Saint Botolph's Church."

Margo shivered. "Not even buying a knife will help poor Liz."

"No."

They pushed past the end of Commercial Road, gaining Adgate, and turned off for Mitre Square. Once again Margo and Malcolm stood watch at each of the two ways into the secluded little square, while the Ripper Watch Team rigged their miniaturized equipment behind a temporary construction fence which closed off one interior corner of the square. Catharine Eddowes would die just outside that fence. Margo watched closely through the dark alleyway known as Church Passage, which ran beneath an overhanging building, turning the little lane into a tunnel between Mitre Square and the street beyond. Rough workingmen could be heard laughing and singing at pubs. Women's voices drifted past, some openly brazen, accosting potential customers. Others were hushed with fear as they whispered about the killer, wondering what to do to protect themselves and their families.

Most of the women in the East End weren't prostitutes, any more than most of the men were pickpockets and thieves; but these women had no way of knowing the killer loose amongst them wouldn't be attacking "honest women." They were all frightened, as unaware as the police of the psychology that drove psychotic serial killers like James Maybrick and his unknown accomplice. Who that man was, the team hoped to learn tonight. They also hoped to discover which of the killers was the rabid anti-Semite.

As soon as the equipment was in place, Malcolm led the way once more, moving north and east again, across Houndsditch and past Middlesex Street, over to Goulston Street and the landing of the Wentworth Model Buildings. The tenement was noisily occupied, which made the installation hazardous. Malcolm slipped up the dark staircase past the landing and stood guard above while Inspector Conroy Melvyn worked alone to fix the tiny, button-sized camera and transmitter in the upper corner of the landing. A raucous burst of voices from above sent both the up-time police inspector and Malcolm plunging back down to street level, sweating profusely.

"Got it," Melvyn gasped out, voice shaking slightly.

"I would suggest we leave the area at once," Malcolm said urgently, glancing back as several men and women burst from the staircase, locked in a bitter argument that threatened to turn violent momentarily.

"Agreed," Melvyn nodded, heading back for Middlesex Street at a brisk walk.

A clock from one of the many breweries in the district, Margo wasn't sure which one, tolled the hour. Midnight. An hour before the first murder, plus another forty minutes until the second one. Moving in utter silence, the Ripper Watch Team headed for Leadenhall

Street and the Bank of England, where their carriage would be waiting to take them back to Spaldergate. Margo glanced once over her shoulder into the dark maze of alleys that formed the Ripper's killing ground and held back a shudder.

Jack the Ripper had already posted his first letter to the editor.

Tomorrow morning, the *Daily News* would publish it.

Skeeter reached the bottom of the bone-dry gully slightly behind Kit. Before either of them could call a greeting, Paula gave a glad cry. She came hurtling out from behind a sheltering boulder and threw herself straight into Kit's arms. "Oh, God, Kit Carson! I've never been so happy to see anybody in my whole life! And Skeeter Jackson!"

"What's happened?" Kit asked tersely, fishing for a clean bandanna. Paula dried her eyes with it, gulping to control tears of sheer relief at her rescue.

The Time Tours guide with the surgeon answered through clenched teeth. "Bastards jumped us from cover, when Paula's horse threw a shoe. I was trying to reshoe the nag when they started shooting."

"Then you haven't caught up with Joey Tyrolin, yet?" Kit asked sharply.

Paula shook her head. "No. And we won't, either. Mr. Samuelson and I were bringing back the bad news."

"Too right," Samuelson growled. "Little bastard and his porter *emigrated* on us! They jumped a train before we could catch up and headed east. The drovers and other guides are trying to trace them, but they bought a ticket for Chicago, so they could jump off anywhere between here and Illinois. Or keep going, switch trains in Chicago and head for the East Coast."

Skeeter kicked disgustedly at a clod of dirt. "Great. Now what, Kit?"

The grizzled scout shoved his hat back and wiped sweat from his brow. "We hold a council of war."

Skeeter certainly didn't have any better ideas.

Dominica Nosette was so excited she could scarcely stand still. *At last!* John Lachley and James Maybrick together on the same street! The night was windy, full of rainshowers and sudden gusts that whipped Dominica's skirts against her ankles and rattled her bonnet around her ears, but Dominica scarcely noticed. Her tiny video camera rode next to her ear, mounted underneath the concealing brim of her bonnet. The lens recorded everything in front of her, whichever way Dominica turned her head, and the camera was specially fitted with low-light and infrared technology to record video signal in even the darkest alleyways. An infrared light source in the fake fruit fastened to her bonnet illuminated a wide fan in front of her, switched on whenever she pressed the plunger inside her pocket. She'd been holding it down steadily for the past five minutes, eyes riveted to the two men who conferred briefly under a grimy street lamp, one of the few scattered through the East End. The directional microphone in her bonnet picked up their low-voiced conversation and broadcast it to her earplug.

"The woman lives in this house," Lachley's voice said. "Eddowes is her name, Kate Eddowes, a dirty whore."

Maybrick's voice, breathless with sick excitement, answered. "I want her, John, I want to rip her . . ."

"Not until I have my letters."

"Of course . . ."

Dominica finally knew what was contained in the letters John Lachley sought. She and her partner had managed to make a photocopy of Long Liz Stride's priceless missive, telling her precisely why John Lachley was stalking these women to death. The queen's grandson, the firstborn son of the Prince of Wales, in the direct line of succession, had been indiscreet. Highly indiscreet. With a male prostitute, no less. If proof of that indiscretion fell into the wrong hands, Eddy would be ruined, possibly even jailed. And John Lachley's career as Eddy's spiritual advisor would come to a disastrous end. Classic motive and response. Except, of course, that Lachley was a psychopath and was using another psychopath as a weapon to rid himself of all witnesses.

Poor Kate Eddowes. She and her lover had returned to London on Friday from Kent and the hop harvest, a return Dominica and Guy had videotaped.

"I'll get a room over at the casual ward, Shoe Lane, luv," Eddowes had told Kelly. "We won't be apart long. You rest, now, and see to that cough."

Dominica had followed her down to Shoe Lane, capturing for posterity her fateful conversation with the casual ward's superintendent. "Oh, I'll get money, right enough. I know the Whitechapel murderer, I do. I'll collect that reward being offered by the newspapers!"

But if Kate Eddowes knew, she'd done nothing about it, contacting neither the police nor the newspapermen who were offering rewards of up to a hundred pounds— a literal fortune to someone like Catharine Eddowes— for information on the Ripper. She avoided constables, shunned reporters, and walked the streets as always, drinking what she earned and staring into shadows, clearly trying to drink her way through her terror or perhaps trying to drink her way to enough courage to finally act. Dominica thought pityingly that she was doubtless too frightened to come straight out and say, "Look, here, I've got a letter from the queen's grandson in my pocket and I think he's your killer . . ."

Prince Albert Victor was, of course, safely away in Scotland with his grandmother, just now, providing him with an ironclad alibi for the murders of Stride and

Eddowes. Dominica doubted the prince even knew what Lachley was doing, although he might guess. Perhaps that was why he'd fled to Scotland, leaving his spiritual advisor behind in London.

When the night of September 30th arrived, Dominica and Guy followed Lachley from his home in Cleveland Street, then lost him for more than an hour in the teeming streets of Wapping. "Where the deuce did he get to?" Guy Pendergast muttered as darkness descended over London's rooftops.

"Where the devil does he always get to? Wherever it is, I intend to find out!"

"To do that, pet, we'll have to find him again. Of course, we can always pick him up at Dutfield's Yard."

"I plan to videotape much more of his activities this evening than that! We'll go to Catharine's doss house," Dominica decided. "Surely he'll show up there?" And that was exactly where they caught up to him, in the company of James Maybrick, at long, bloody last.

"We'll find Eddowes, first, if we can," Lachley muttered, his voice whispering electronically in Dominica's ear. "She's too bloody dangerous to leave wandering the streets any longer."

Lachley and Maybrick set out, stopping at public house after public house, searching for the doomed Kate Eddowes. Dominica, of course, knew exactly where Eddowes was—at least, where she'd be at eight o'clock, or thereabouts. Lachley wandered, by chance, directly into her path just in time to see events unfold in Aldgate High Street. He watched in open-mouthed disbelief and rising fury as two police constables incarcerated the woman he had waited two entire *weeks* to kill.

Catharine Eddowes was drunk. So drunk she could hardly stand up. Wailing like a fire engine and giggling, one would've thought her a girl of twelve. The sight of a forty-six-year-old prostitute whooping her way into

Bishopsgate Police Station, carrying a letter in her pocket that could destroy everything Lachley had worked for, had *murdered* for, very nearly put the man over the edge. He stood across the street from the police station, hidden in shadows, soaking wet from the gusting rain, and closed his gloved hands into fists so tight, his hands trembled. The look of murderous rage in his face left Dominica momentarily shaken. When he stepped close to Maybrick, the words he hissed at his accomplice sent a shiver up her back.

"They can't keep her there forever, God curse her! And if she shows them that letter, I'll set fire to the whole bloody police station, blow up the bleeding gas main under it!" He jerked his black cloth cap down further over his brow, all but concealing his face, even from Dominica's low-light camera. "We'll find Stride, follow her as we did the others, wait until she's drunk, then I'll approach her and secure my letters. You can have her, afterwards."

"Yes . . ."

"You remember the code, James, that we agreed upon, should anyone come upon us while we're about our business?"

"Yes, yes," Maybrick said, his voice a trifle impatient now, "if you see someone, you'll cry *Lipski!* and I'll do the same if I spot anyone."

Lipski . . . The name of a poisoner who'd triggered a wave of anti-Semitic hatred in these streets the previous year. That hatred was sickeningly alive and well in the wake of the Ripper's murders. John Lachley and James Maybrick were deliberately fanning the flames of anti-Semitism, throwing the police even further off their trail, by using a word like Lipski as a coded warning. Anyone hearing that particular name would automatically assume it was aimed at a foreign Jewish murderer, rather than a warning between conspirators.

Bishopsgate Police Station, carrying a letter in her pocket that could destroy everything Lachley had worked for, had *murdered* for, very nearly put the man over the edge. He stood across the street from the police station, hidden in shadows, soaking wet from the gusting rain, and closed his gloved hands into fists so tight, his hands trembled. The look of murderous rage in his face left Dominica momentarily shaken. When he stepped close to Maybrick, the words he hissed at his accomplice sent a shiver up her back.

"They can't keep her there forever, God curse her! And if she shows them that letter, I'll set fire to the whole bloody police station, blow up the bleeding gas main under it!" He jerked his black cloth cap down further over his brow, all but concealing his face, even from Dominica's low-light camera. "We'll find Stride, follow her as we did the others, wait until she's drunk, then I'll approach her and secure my letters. You can have her, afterwards."

"Yes . . ."

"You remember the code, James, that we agreed upon, should anyone come upon us while we're about our business?"

"Yes, yes," Maybrick said, his voice a trifle impatient now, "if you see someone, you'll cry *Lipski!* and I'll do the same if I spot anyone."

Lipski . . . The name of a poisoner who'd triggered a wave of anti-Semitic hatred in these streets the previous year. That hatred was sickeningly alive and well in the wake of the Ripper's murders. John Lachley and James Maybrick were deliberately fanning the flames of anti-Semitism, throwing the police even further off their trail, by using a word like Lipski as a coded warning. Anyone hearing that particular name would automatically assume it was aimed at a foreign Jewish murderer, rather than a warning between conspirators.

Eddowes. Dominica doubted the prince even knew what Lachley was doing, although he might guess. Perhaps that was why he'd fled to Scotland, leaving his spiritual advisor behind in London.

When the night of September 30th arrived, Dominica and Guy followed Lachley from his home in Cleveland Street, then lost him for more than an hour in the teeming streets of Wapping. "Where the deuce did he get to?" Guy Pendergast muttered as darkness descended over London's rooftops.

"Where the devil does he always get to? Wherever it is, I intend to find out!"

"To do that, pet, we'll have to find him again. Of course, we can always pick him up at Dutfield's Yard."

"I plan to videotape much more of his activities this evening than that! We'll go to Catharine's doss house," Dominica decided. "Surely he'll show up there?" And that was exactly where they caught up to him, in the company of James Maybrick, at long, bloody last.

"We'll find Eddowes, first, if we can," Lachley muttered, his voice whispering electronically in Dominica's ear. "She's too bloody dangerous to leave wandering the streets any longer."

Lachley and Maybrick set out, stopping at public house after public house, searching for the doomed Kate Eddowes. Dominica, of course, knew exactly where Eddowes was—at least, where she'd be at eight o'clock, or thereabouts. Lachley wandered, by chance, directly into her path just in time to see events unfold in Aldgate High Street. He watched in open-mouthed disbelief and rising fury as two police constables incarcerated the woman he had waited two entire *weeks* to kill.

Catharine Eddowes was drunk. So drunk she could hardly stand up. Wailing like a fire engine and giggling, one would've thought her a girl of twelve. The sight of a forty-six-year-old prostitute whooping her way into all over the station, that jackass Benny Catlin missing in London—"

"Benny Catlin?" Paula echoed, staring. "You mean that nice young kid is *missing*?"

Kit jerked his gaze up. "You *know* Benny Catlin?"

Paula blinked, started by the sudden intensity of the stares levelled at her. "Well, yes. I mean, it isn't every day I give a whisker-job to a girl."

Kit's lower jaw came adrift.

Sid Kaederman actually grasped her arm. "*What?*"

"Take your hand off me!" Paula snapped, yanking herself loose.

Kaederman flushed and apologized. She shrugged her shoulder, rubbing her bicep, then asked Kit, "I take it you didn't you know Benny Catlin was a girl? She told me she wanted to disguise her gender, which was a big disadvantage in London. It's not that unusual, actually, I've just never done a whisker job on a girl that pretty."

"My God!" Skeeter matched the face in the senator's photo to one in his memory and came up with an unpleasant, inescapable conclusion. "*Benny Catlin is Jenna!*"

Sid Kaederman swore in tones that caused several horses to lay back their ears. "God *damn* it! Armstrong duped us again! That stinking little bastard ordered his men to take her to *London . . .*"

"Yeah," Skeeter agreed, "but how did they get tickets? The Britannia's been sold out for nearly a year!"

"Jenna and her roommate must've bought Britannia tickets from that up-time scalper," Kit said slowly. "A year ago, when they first planned to go down time. There would've been plenty of Ripper Tour tickets floating around the black market, a year ago."

Skeeter groaned, "The senator said she wanted to

film history. She must've planned to videotape the Ripper terror."

"Yes. And landed right in the middle of the *Ansar Majlis* terror, instead." Kit scrubbed at his lower face with one sweat-begrimed hand. "We have to get back to TT-86. We'll sleep here tonight, set out first thing in the morning. I'm afraid we'll be riding hard, to make it back to Denver in time to catch the gate. Can you keep up?" He glanced from Paula to Kaederman.

Paula Booker thinned her lips. "I'll cope. The last thing I want to do is stay *here*. I've had about as much vacation as I can stand, this year."

Kit turned his attention to Kaederman. "I'd suggest you try pain pills for those muscle cramps, or we'll leave you behind."

"I'll take the pills," Kaederman growled. "And when this is over, I am never setting foot down another gate in my life! I hate it!"

"Suits me," Skeeter muttered.

Kit's hard-eyed gaze met Skeeter's. "Well, Jackson, looks like you'll be going to London, after all."

"Great," Skeeter groused. "Jack the Ripper *and* the *Ansar Majlis*. Just my cup of tea. Anybody want to place a bet on what the senator has to say about all this?"

He didn't have a single taker.

Chapter Seven

The stalk was in James Maybrick's blood, hot fire that only the red stuff of a life pouring out across his hands could quench. The wild night, with its gusting rainshowers and biting cold winds, spoke to the demons raging in his soul. It called them forth, hungering and slavering, until they ran barefooted through the flames of his own private hell. *She shall pay! By God, the bitch shall pay, her and her whoremaster both! All London knows my work, now, and she trembles with fear when people speak of Sir Jim's deeds. Soon, I will pay her the same as I gave the others, whores all . . . and my knife will drink the bitch's blood, as well . . . Maybe I'll take her before I rip her open . . . take her while her whoremaster watches, then rip them both, God damn them!*

James Maybrick held in his mind the face of his beautiful, stupid wife, who had whored herself again and again with that fool Brierly. He summoned up the memory of the terror he'd inflicted on that prostitute in Manchester, the even more delicious terror of Polly Nichols and Annie Chapman here in London, painted that same wild-eyed fear across his wife's vapid face . . . and smiled as he watched his mentor close in on the common streetwalker chosen as Maybrick's next victim. Maybrick's blood pounded in anticipation.

The potent medicine Lachley gave him each time he visited London left James absolutely invincible, stronger and more sure of himself than he'd felt in his entire fifty years of life. He laughed behind his moustaches, laughed at the notion of Abberline and those bumbling idiots in the Metropolitan Police Department actually *catching* anyone, let alone Sir Jim and his personal god. So many constables and fine inspectors, wasting their time searching for a foreign Jew to hang!

The game delighted him. That leather apron left in the basin beside Annie Chapman had been a most diverting clue. It had sent the idiots of Whitechapel's H Division chasing after the wrong sort of man. They'd actually arrested a fellow over that lovely apron, so they had! A dirty Jewish boot finisher they'd desperately wanted to be guilty.

Too bad he'd had an alibi, an unshakeable one, at that. Not that they'd have believed him guilty for long, when other filthy whores had to be punished, had to be ripped with his shining knife. No, they wouldn't have held Mr. Pizer forever, certainly not past tonight. Tomorrow, all London would quake in its shoes at the work he would perform, he and John Lachley. A clever cotton merchant from Liverpool and a doctor of occult medicine from London's own SoHo, playing them all for the fools they were . . .

Rain spattered down from dirty skies, black and cold as last winter's ashes. The whore they'd been following for almost two hours, now, was a filthy foreigner. Lachley had told Maybrick about her. She frequently went begging at the Swedish parish church, spinning lies about a nonexistent husband and children. She'd supposedly lost them ten years previously, when the saloon steamer *Princess Alice* had collided with the steamship *Bywell Castle* in the Thames, killing nearly seven hundred people. Lachley's inquiries, quiet but thorough, had revealed that the bitch's real English husband had died of heart failure only four years previously, in 1884, not in the famous steamship collision. Children, she had apparently never had.

The one thing about Liz Stride that fretted Maybrick was her nephew, or rather, the late John Stride's nephew, who was a member of the bloody Metropolitan Police Force, of all things. But that didn't worry James too much. Clearly, the nephew couldn't care overly much for his aunt, not if Liz Stride were living in Whitechapel, charring for Jews and mending their garments for them, selling her body to whatever man would have her. He must remember to leave some nasty little clue on the streets, tonight, pointing the finger of suspicion at the foreign Jews again, he really must. He'd remembered to bring his chalk, this time, too.

But he couldn't write out any messages until his knife had drunk its fill.

After witnessing Catharine Eddowes' arrest for public drunkenness, they spent hours searching pubs for Stride and finally caught up to her shortly before eleven P.M. on Settles Street, at the Bricklayer's Arms Public House. Alarmingly, they found her in the company of a short, well-dressed man she laughingly called Llewellyn. *A Welshman!* Maybrick darted a glance at Lachley, who watched the couple narrowly from the shadows.

The whore and her Welshman stood in the doorway of the pub, waiting for the driving rain to slacken. Her customer was eager enough for it, kissing her and carrying on like some low sailor, rather than the respectable tradesman he clearly was, probably some arse of a merchant up from Cardiff on business, slumming in the East End where a man could have whatever he wanted for the price of a glass of cheap gin.

Two workmen, also taking refuge from the rain, ordered ale and watched the antics in the doorway, clearly bemused. One nudged the other. "Hey, Liz, why don't you bring your fella in and 'ave a drink, eh?" The tall woman glanced around, laughter shaking her strong-boned face, then whispered something to her customer. The man shook his head, intent on pawing at her bosom under her drab coat. The man who'd invited them in snorted knowingly. His friend called over the noise of laughing, swearing, singing voices, "Better watch out, Liz, that's Leather Apron trying to get round you!"

Laughter greeted this assessment, since the man clearly was not an Eastern European Jew. He was obviously too new to town even to understand the reference. James Maybrick smiled into his own ale glass, delighted. *Leather Apron, now there's a lovely joke, indeed! Little do they know Leather Apron's sitting right here, watching, waiting for that bastard to finish, so Sir Jim can have his own chance at her.* Not that Sir Jim would actually taste her dirty wares. That wasn't what he was here for. Sir Jim could take a whore anytime he wanted, just by bedding his wife.

Shortly after eleven, Liz Stride and her importunate Welshman left the Bricklayer's Arms, heading out into the rainy night for a tryst in a dark stairwell on Goulston Street. From his place of concealment at the foot of that stairwell, Maybrick could hear her asking the man to read a letter for her, one she had in her pocket.

"Read a letter for you?" he gasped out, clearly giving her the business while she asked her question. "Are you daft?"

or Czech . . . They came from halfway across Europe
to this miserable little meeting hall where upwards of
two hundred working-class louts and their women
crammed themselves in to give plays and musical
concerts, all of them hideously amateur, not to mention
the radical meetings that attracted troublemakers from
all over the East End. Maybrick detested them, agitators
with wild notions about the manumission of the
labouring classes. Why, they and their kind would bring
down the Empire, so they would, them and their dirty
whores, the ruination of decent British morals . . .

Elizabeth Stride, as foreign a bitch as the workers
in the lively hall opposite, was taking her time, back
there in Dutfield's Yard. Was the sailor reading out the
letter for her? Maybrick caressed his knife. He didn't
give a damn about the sailor, although he would have
to die, too, if he'd translated Dr. Lachley's letter for
the dirty screw. Christ, they were taking their time
about it! He eased his pocket watch out, peering at
the crystal face in the dim light filtering out through the
Workers' Club windows opposite. Bloody near twelve-
thirty A.M.! He was cold and tired and wet, had spent
five miserable hours on a train today, just getting here
from Liverpool, and they'd had to walk across the
whole bloody East End since his arrival.

Get on with it! He snapped shut his watch with a
savage motion, thrust it back into his waistcoat pocket.
Impatience was making him edgy. Once already
tonight, he'd primed himself to strike, only to have the
chance snatched away, thanks to Catharine Eddowes'
drunkenness. By the time Stride finally emerged, James
Maybrick was ready to do a violence worse than anything
he'd unleashed to date. By God, the moment Lachley
had his letter, he would knock the bitch into that
alleyway, throttle her, then slash and slash until the
fury was finally spent . . .

"Sorry about the note in your pocket, darlin'," the sailor was saying as they stepped out of the black little alleyway. "I can read me own name, just about, but not anything else. Never went to any school."

"Oh, it isn't your fault," she said, voice peevish. Clearly, she was no happier about this customer's lack than the previous one's. "I'm beginning to think there's not a Welshman in all of Britain can read his own language!"

The sailor laughed. "Give me a kiss, then. I'd better be off and find me mates, they'll wonder where I've got to."

If Maybrick hadn't been so feverishly furious to strike, he'd have laughed aloud. Poor, dirty whore, had a letter in her pocket worth a king's ransom—literally— and she couldn't find a soul to read it to her. The sailor gave her a lusty kiss, then strode off toward Poplar and the docks. Maybrick stepped forward, seething with impatience, only to curse under his breath when a young man in a dark coat and deerstalker hat left the Workman's Club, carrying a newspaper-wrapped parcel some six inches high and eighteen inches long. He was moving fast, eyes clearly not yet adjusted to the darkness beyond the club, because he very nearly ran her down.

"Oh, I am sorry!" he exclaimed, steadying her on her feet. His accent marked him as a foreigner.

"Give me a fright, you did," she gasped, managing a smile for him.

"You are not hurt, then?"

"No, I'm fine, honest. I don't suppose you'd know anybody hereabout who reads Welsh?"

The young man looked startled, but shook his head. "No, I'm afraid I do not. I am Hungarian, have not been long in England."

"Oh. Well, maybe you might walk me back to my

rooms, eh? It's not far and I'm that nervous, with this madman walking about the streets . . ."

"Of course, madam."

He escorted her across the street, straight toward Maybrick's hiding place. Maybrick all but crushed the handle of his knife under his fist and shrank back into the darkness of the doorway he stood in. God above, would this lousy whore never spend two minutes alone? If she made it all the way back to her doss house with the blasted Hungarian, they'd never have a chance at her! Then *another* set of footsteps coming along the pavement sent Maybrick even deeper into the shadows. *Holy Christ, it's a bloody police constable!* Pulse thundering, he stood paralyzed, watching the constable approach Stride and her Hungarian. The constable frowned at her, moustaches twitching. "'Ere, now, move along, Liz, none of your dirty business along 'ere."

Liz Stride drew herself up, drunk and beginning to show the effects of her own night's frustration. "I never asked this gentleman a thing like that! He nearly knocked me down, coming out that door." The Hungarian doffed his hat nervously and muttered something about getting home, then fled down Berner Street in the opposite direction from the constable. The policeman shrugged and moved on, leaving Stride to mutter a curse after him.

"Well, at least I got enough for the doss house. Bloke might not've been able to read, but he had money in his trous, sure enough." She sighed, then headed back across Berner Street, clearly intent on giving up her quest for the night.

And finally, God, *finally*, she was alone.

Across the street, John Lachley moved in fast, stepping out of his concealment and hurrying toward her. "Madam? I say, madam, I couldn't help overhearing you just now." He was speaking in a very low voice, but Maybrick, senses twitching, heard every breath drawn, every syllable uttered. "You said you were looking for someone who reads Welsh?"

Liz Stride paused, taken by surprise. "Welsh? Why, yes, I am."

He doffed his rough black cap, gave her a mock bow. "I'm Welsh, as it happens. What were you looking to have read?"

Eagerness flooded across her face and she reached toward her pocket, then she paused, sudden wariness stealing across her features. "You couldn't help overhearing?" she repeated nervously. "How long have you been watching me?"

"Why, madam, not long at all. Here, do you want me to read this letter out for you or don't you?"

She backed away from him, toward the alleyway to Dutfield's Yard. "I never said it was a letter."

Anger flushed Lachley's face. He was as impatient as Maybrick, maybe more so, having waited two full weeks for this moment, while Maybrick had been busy with his work in Liverpool and the children and a household to run. "Of course it's a letter! What else would it be? Oh, for God's sake, just hand the bloody thing over!"

"I've got to go, have a friend waiting for me at the pub down the street, there . . ."

She started to step away and Lachley's temper snapped. He grabbed her by the arm, flung her back toward the alley. "Give me the letter, you stinking whore!" When she tried to break free, Lachley slammed her to the muddy ground. A tiny scream broke loose from her throat, then two more. She was trying to scramble to her feet, digging for something in her pocket. Maybrick, pulse racing, reached for his knife, started out into the open, then heard footsteps coming and swore under his breath. He fumbled out his pipe instead, lit it with shaking hands just as Lachley glanced up.

"*Lipski!*" The warning burst from Lachley, galvanizing the short, dark little man approaching. Already in the act of crossing the street to avoid the altercation at the gate, the heavily bearded man, obviously Jewish from the prayer shawl visible under his coat, started walking much faster. Maybrick went after him, so furious at yet another interruption he was ready to slash anything and anyone who got in his way. The Jew broke into a run and Maybrick pelted after him, chasing the interloper all the way down to the railway arch. He finally realized that Lachley would be back at Dutfield's Yard, securing his letter. Chasing a damned interfering Jew wasn't why he was out here tonight, wasn't why he'd spent the whole stinking night in the cold rain.

Maybrick turned and hurried back to the alleyway, where Lachley had finally snatched his letter from the whore's pocket. He'd forced her back against the gate, one hand across her mouth, his arm pressed against her throat, cutting off her air and trapping her against the gate. Murderous rage had twisted Lachley's face—and mortal terror had twisted hers. Her eyes rolled as Maybrick approached, hope flaring wildly.

"Not in the street!" Maybrick hissed as he came closer. "That bloody constable might come back any moment! Get her into Dutfield's Yard . . ."

Keeping her safely throttled, they dragged Elizabeth Stride back into the blackness, down the eighteen feet of blind alleyway and along the wall in the yard beyond. She fought them with every scrap of strength in her brawny frame, giving them a dreadful time, subduing her. Lachley, wheezing and panting, finally threw her against the brick wall and pinned her with one arm across her chest, bruising her while his hands closed around her throat; Maybrick held a gloved hand clamped across her mouth while Lachley strangled her, to keep her screams from alerting the crowd in the hall just above their heads.

"I want her!" Maybrick hissed.

"When I've bloody well finished!" Fury cracked through Lachley's voice. She was struggling, but more feebly now, losing consciousness. Maybrick had his knife out, shaking with need. At length the struggles ceased, her life fading away with a harsh rattle in her throat; then Lachley was shoving her down into the mud. "Got to make it look like she was back here for the sex," he was muttering, voice a bare whisper. Maybrick could hear the doctor searching her pockets. "Ahh . . . that's grand, a packet of Cachous . . ."

Ahh, indeed . . . Maybrick smiled. Pills used by smokers to sweeten the breath. When the constables found her, they would think she'd taken them out to chew before servicing her customer, never dreaming she'd been strangled to death and cut open for the letter Lachley was stuffing into his coat pocket. On the heels of that thought, Lachley swore. "Christ! The bitch had a knife in her pocket!" He came up holding a short, wicked little blade Maybrick could just make out in the near blackness. "Bloody bitch! All right," the doctor hissed at last, "she's yours! Make it fast!"

"Give me her knife!" Maybrick gasped, wanting to do her with her own blade. Lachley handed it over and Maybrick crouched down, delighting in the shock against his hand as he slashed through the throat. He reached for her skirts, wanting to rip at her gut—

And the gate at the end of the alleyway rattled open.

A horse's hooves struck the bricks sharply, heading straight toward them. Maybrick stood up so fast, he went dizzy. Lachley grabbed his arm, dragged him deeper into the yard, back toward the stable. Maybrick's heart thudded, heavy and hard and terrified. Hot blood trickled down his hands, which shook wildly out of control as the pony cart clattered right into the yard with them.

Dear God, we're going to hang for this goddamned slut!

The pony nearly trod on the bitch's body. The animal snorted and shied at the last moment, obviously having caught the scent of blood, and tried to avoid the bundle on the ground.

"What's got into you?" a man's voice muttered, heavily accented. "What did I do with that whip? Eh, is there something on the ground?" They could hear the man scraping and probing downward into the blackness. "Who's this? Are you drunk? Get up, you're blocking the way." Then, voice suddenly uncertain. "Maybe she's ill." He jumped down from his cart, hurried back down the alleyway. "I must fetch help, get a lantern, it is black as pitch in here . . ."

Oh, my God, he's leaving!

"Quick!" Lachley's voice hissed into his ear.

Maybrick needed no second prompting. His legs shook violently as they made their escape, silent on their rubberized servants' shoes. Thank God Lachley had thought of using them when this business began, they'd have been overheard leaving the yard for certain, without them. He still couldn't quite believe they were going to make their escape. He shoved both knives into his coat pockets as they hurried down Berner Street, while the cart driver entered the noisy Working Men's Club behind them.

"What is it, Diemschutz?" a man's voice floated to them.

"A woman, collapsed in the Yard. Get a lantern . . ."

The man's name burned in Maybrick's mind. *Diemschutz!* Another stinking *Jew!* He would hunt the bastard down, so he would! Slit his goddamned throat, how dare he interrupt like that? He'd had no time to do more than cut her throat, curse it!

"Keep your hands in your pockets," Lachley hissed. "They're covered with blood. We'll have to get underground as fast as possible."

"But I didn't get to rip her!"

Fury blazed in his mentor's eyes. *"I don't give a bloody damn what you didn't get to do!* You sodding maniac, we were damn near caught! And the whole East End is going to be crawling with constables inside a quarter of an hour!" Lachley's cheeks had gone ashen.

"I know we were almost caught, blast it!" Maybrick hissed, gut churning with frustrated rage. "But we *weren't,* were we? And the bloody buggers won't be looking for *us,* they'll be looking for a lone man. A stinking foreign Jew, walking by himself!"

Lachley's breaths slowed perceptibly. His jaw, knotted with anger, gradually relaxed. "Right. All right, then, we walk along together. Just a couple of jolly mates, 'aving a bit of a bobble on a Saturday night, out for a quick one down to boozer."

Maybrick blinked in surprise. "Good God. You really *have* lived in these streets before, haven't you? I didn't quite believe . . ."

"Of course I have, idiot!" Lachley hissed, moving down the pavement at a more leisurely pace. "How the bloody hell do you think I know the sewers so well?"

"Oh, I hadn't thought of that, really . . ."

"Just shut up, James, for God's sake, just *shut the bloody hell up!"*

He considered arguing, but one look into Lachley's eyes told Maybrick that his mentor was in no mood for trouble, not even from him. He walked along in broody silence, the blood on his hands drying into a sticky mess. When they passed a gutter with a broad puddle, he paused and glanced both directions down the street, then crouched and rinsed off his hands and his whore's knife. Her blade was sticky with its owner's lifeblood. His hands were still unsteady as he shook the muddy water off and thrust the prostitute's knife back into his other coat pocket, opposite his own, longer-bladed weapon. He shoved his hands into his pockets to hide the bloodstains on his white cuffs.

"I want to get right out of Whitechapel," Lachley muttered, moving steadily west. "Forget about your rooms in Middlesex Street. If there's an inquiry, if that bloody Jew on Berner Street identifies us to the constables, I want to be out of Metropolitan Police jurisdiction, fast."

They were already in Commercial Road, walking steadily west toward the point where Commercial Road took a sharp bend toward the north to become Commercial Street. Once past Middlesex Street and the Minories, along Aldgate, they would be in the jurisdiction of The City of London, with its own Lord Mayor, its own city officials and—ah, yes, Maybrick smiled, clever Lachley!—its own constabulary. As they passed a nasty little alley, they nearly stumbled over a drunk, who lay snoring in the gutter. Lachley paused, cast a swift glance around, then stooped and pulled the drunken sailor deeper into the alley.

"Well, don't just stand there! That miserable Jew can describe these clothes!"

Lachley was stripping off his dark coat, peeling off the sailor's jacket and grimy shirt. "Here, put this shirt on, your cuffs are bloody."

The idea of putting on a filthy sailor's unwashed shirt did not appeal to James Maybrick. But neither did the gallows. He stripped off his shirt in haste, switching his blood-stained one for the sailor's. Lachley had appropriated the man's jacket for himself, dropping his own coat over Maybrick's arm. Maybrick slithered into it, then dumped his coat, the sleeves spattered with Stride's blood, across the drunk's naked torso. When they stepped back into the light, Lachley wore a grey cap instead of the black one he'd left behind, a salt-and-pepper grey jacket, too loose for him, and a red kerchief knotted around his neck, nautical fashion.

"You don't look the same man at all," Maybrick said softly, studying Lachley with a critical mein. Then, wistful and frustrated, "You don't suppose those sodding constables at Bishopsgate have let that drunken bitch Eddowes out yet?"

Lachley stared at him, then gave out a short, hard bark of laughter. "Great God, you do enjoy danger-ous living, don't you? One wife in London, another wife *and* a bloody mistress in Liverpool, every week you swallow enough arsenic to poison all Bethnal Green, and now you want to stop at the police station and ask if the nice whore they arrested for imperson-ating a fire engine has sobered up enough to go home!"

"What I want," Maybrick growled, "is what I didn't get with the whore in Dutfield's Yard."

Lachley, equilibrium restored by their semi-miraculous getaway and a change of disguise, laughed again, harsh and wild as the rain-lashed night. "All right, damn your eyes, we'll just go along and see! The fastest route from here," he peered at their surroundings, "would be down Houndsditch from Aldgate."

As they were currently in Aldgate High Street, it was a matter of perhaps two minutes' walk to reach Aldgate proper, then they swung sharply northward up the long reach of Houndsditch, moving away from the Minories to the south. The clock on a distant brewery up in Brick Lane chimed the half hour. One thirty A.M. and his blood was high, the terror of having nearly been caught now transformed into a feral sort of euphoria. Pure excitement flowed through his veins, hot and electrically charged, as though he'd just taken a dose of his arsenic. Sir Jim was invincible, by God! All he asked was to get his hands on that other bitch he'd been promised. He'd cut her with all the wildly charged strength in him, rip her to pieces and leave some jolly little rhyme for the City Division's bumbling fools to puzzle over. His brother Michael, who could rhyme like anything, sat in his lovely rooms over in St. James's writing songs the whole sodding country was singing. If Michael could do it, so could he. He'd think up a right saucy little rhyme to tantalize the police, maybe stir up more trouble with the Jews. Yes, a truly fine way to cap off the evening . . .

As they approached Duke Street, a short, auburn haired woman emerged from that narrow thoroughfare, moving with angry strides and muttering to herself. A dark green chintz skirt with three flounces picked up the light from a distant gas lamp, revealing yellow flowers of some kind in the cloth. Her black coat had once been very fine, with imitation fur at the collars, cuffs, and pockets. A black straw bonnet trimmed with green and black velvet and black beads was tilted rakishly on her hair. The woman was strikingly familiar, Maybrick couldn't immediately think why.

" . . . lousy bastard," she was growling to herself, not having seen them yet, "give you two whole florins, I will, he says, if you can get me to spend! How was I to know he was so sodding impotent, he hadn't managed it in a whole year . . . Half a damned hour wasted on him and not tuppence to show for it! I've got to find somebody who can read that blasted letter of Annie's, that's what, get some real money out of it. The newspapers will give me a reward, that's what I told the superintendent of the casual ward, and I meant it, by God! If I could just get a reward, now, maybe I could take John to a regular hospital, not a workhouse infirmary . . ."

Lachley closed his hand around Maybrick's wrist, halting him. Recognition struck like a rolling clap of thunder. *Catharine Eddowes!* Wild exultation blasted straight through him. Lachley hissed, "I'll lure her down to Mitre Square, in City jurisdiction . . ."

Yes, yes, get on with it! His hand already ached where he gripped his own long-bladed knife. Maybrick faded back into the shadows, leaving Lachley to approach the angry prostitute, whom they'd last seen so drunk she could scarcely stand up. Clearly, the evening's stay in jail had sobered her up nicely. *Good!* Her terror would be worse, cold sober.

"'Ello, luv," Lachley said with the voice of a rough sailor, a voice that matched his stolen jacket and cap and neckerchief. "You're a right comfy sight, so y'are, for a bloke wot's far from 'ome."

Catharine Eddowes paused, having to look up a long way into Lachley's face. She was barely five feet tall, nearly seven inches shorter than the man smiling down at her. "Why, hello. You're out late, ducks, the pubs have all closed. I know," she said with a wry smile, "because I wanted a drink tonight and couldn't get one."

"Well, now, I can't say as I could 'elp you to get boozey, but a body don't need gin to 'ave a good time, now does a body?" Lachley dug into his pocket, came out with a shining coin. "Just you 'ave a butcher's at this, eh? Sixpence, shiny an' new."

Catherine's eyes focused sharply on the coin Lachley held up between gloved thumb and forefinger. Then she smiled and moved closer to him, rested a hand on his chest. "Well, now, that's a pretty sixpence. What might a lady have to do, to share it?"

Further along Duke Street, where lights blazed in a local meeting hall known as the Imperial Club, three men emerged into the wet night, glancing toward Lachley and Eddowes. They moved off in the opposite direction, giving the woman and her obvious customer their privacy. James Maybrick watched them go and smiled in the darkness from his hiding place on Houndsditch.

"Let's take a bit of a stroll, shall we?" Lachley suggested, following the men who'd just left the Imperial Club, but moving at a far more leisurely pace to give the talkative trio plenty of time to lose themselves in the streets ahead. "Find us someplace nice an' comfy to share?"

Her low laughter delighted Maybrick. The song she started singing left him laughing softly to himself. The silly screw had perhaps ten minutes left to live, at best, and here she was, walking arm in arm with the man who was going to kill her, singing as though she hadn't a care in the world. Maybrick laughed again.

Soon enough, she *wouldn't* have.

After two solid weeks in a saddle, short of sleep and in dire need of a shower, Kit Carson was in no shape for a face-to-face with Senator John Caddrick and half the newsies in the northern hemisphere. But he didn't have much choice. They were waiting as soon as he stepped into the station through the Wild West Gate. Guides bringing back Julius and the murdered tourist followed on his heels. Screams and a roar of voices broke out, a solid wall of noise.

"Jenna!" Senator Caddrick's voice cut through the chaos. The senator was bolting past the ropes . . . *"Jenna!"* A Time Tours employee caught the senator and held him back. His expression twisted through a whole range of emotions.

"Senator Caddrick," Kit told the ashen politician, "it isn't your daughter. Neither of them is."

Visibly shaken, Caddrick, gasped out, "Not my

daughter? Then where is she? Why isn't she with you?" Sudden fury crackled in the senator's eyes. He shook off the hands holding him back and advanced menacingly. "What are you doing back if you haven't found her? Explain this immediately!"

"She isn't with us because we didn't find her."

Newsies were crowding against the lounge's velvet-rope barriers, shouting questions. Barricades fell with a crash, spilling newsies into the chaos as the returning tour reeled back into the station. Skeeter Jackson, gaunt from hard riding, came through the open gate just ahead of Sid Kaederman and Paula Booker. A steady stream of returning tourists and guides began to pour through the gate as Senator Caddrick dragged his gaze from the body bags to his exhausted detective and back to Kit's face. "Didn't find her? Why not?"

"Because we have excellent reason to believe your daughter never left TT-86 through the Denver Gate at all. I'd rather not say more until we've spoken in private." Kit glanced toward shocked Time Tours employees. "Could someone notify Ronisha Azzan we need a meeting with her? Thanks. No, I'm sorry, there will be no further comments at this time."

He waded against the tide of shouting newsies and shaken tourists, heading for the aerie, then decided he didn't want to risk the kind of fireworks that would explode if he took the entire search team with him. So he shoved his way through the chaos in Frontier Town and muttered, "Paula, get out of here. Kaederman, go with Skeeter to Connie Logan's. Start outfitting for the Britannia."

"Right, boss!"

"You got it, Kit."

Skeeter peeled off so fast, news crews were left stammering in the vacuum. Paula took advantage of their surprise to haul Sid Kaederman away in his wake.

"What's going on?" Caddrick demanded.

"I'll brief you at the station manager's office," Kit growled.

"But—"

Kit left him standing in the midst of an unholy, shrieking mob of newsies. The senator, trailing reporters like a school of noisy fish, caught up and stalked along in thin-lipped silence. At the aerie's elevator access, Kit threw a body check to hold out the crowd on their heels and mashed the button for the top floor. The elevator rose swiftly toward uncertain sanctuary. When the doors slid open, Kit discovered just how uncertain that sanctuary was. Along one glass wall, lined up like so many gargoyles, sat three stone-faced men and women from the Inter-Temporal Court of the Hague, their uniforms glittering with brass officialdom. Like it or not, I.T.CH.'s grand inquisitors had arrived.

Kit held back a sigh and entered the glass-walled office anyway. The I.T.C.H. agents were stiff in their spotless uniforms, while Ronisha Azzan stood in cool elegance behind Bull Morgan's immense desk, which left Kit feeling even dirtier, grittier, and wearier than before. He rearranged grime on the back of his neck, then stalked over to the nearest chair and promptly folded up into it. Tired as he was—and stolid as the Grand Inquisitors were—Kit didn't miss the slight shuffle in chairs as his pungent perfume, the accumulation of fourteen days on a horse, wafted across the office.

"Welcome home, Kit," Ronisha Azzan greeted him quietly. "If I could have your report, please?"

Kit told the Deputy Station Manager what they'd found in the mining camp, bringing everyone up to date in a few brief sentences. When he finished, utter silence held the glass-walled aerie. Senator John Caddrick's expression was a study in lightning-fast realizations: shock, dismay, anxiety, and oddly, triumph. Then Caddrick's face went slowly purple as anger— or something approximating it—won out over the other emotions. *"Benny Catlin?* Do you mean to tell me you've wasted two entire *weeks* chasing the wrong tourist? When my daughter has been lost down your godforsaken Britannia Gate this whole time?"

"It wasn't wasted!" Kit snapped. "We know a great deal more than we did two weeks ago. One of our residents was *murdered,* down the Denver gate! That boy hadn't even turned seventeen, Caddrick, and he took a bullet *meant for your daughter!"*

Caddrick had enough sense, at least, to shut up. He sat breathing hard for long moments. Ronisha Azzan sat back in her chair, looking abruptly tired and grey around the lips and nostrils. Kit sympathized. He felt grey all over. Ronisha shoved herself to her feet and poured out three stiff scotch-and-sodas. Caddrick's hand was shaking as he lifted his drink, nearly sloshing it down his expensive suit jacket. Kit drained his own glass at one gulp. "Thanks, Ronnie. God, I needed that. So . . . What we're trying to determine now is our best chance of tracing Benny Catlin in London. Dr. Paula Booker is probably the best bet we've got for identifying Jenna, since she's the surgeon who gave Jenna a new face."

"I want to see this doctor," Caddrick growled. "I want to know how my little girl was when she came through this station, who was holding her prisoner, why the surgeon didn't report any of this—"

"Dr. Booker didn't report it for the simple reason there was nothing to report. Your daughter came in voluntarily, alone, claiming to be a grad student. Paula gave her a set of false whiskers, surgically implanted. The very next day, Paula left for her own vacation down time. You're damned lucky, Senator, to have any witness at all. When we caught up to Dr. Booker, trying to trace Armstrong and his prisoners, she and her guide had been bushwhacked by a gang of local bandits. If we hadn't come along, Paula might well have been murdered in cold blood."

Caddrick glared at him, his mouth tightened into a thin white line. "Live witnesses won't do any good if Jenna's already dead in London! For your information, Carson, my daughter was nearly killed her first night there. Twice! Then she disappeared, leaving two dead men behind her. And now you tell me you've got two *more* men murdered in cold blood down the Denver Gate? Not to mention a known international terrorist who escapes with three hostages—and you don't even bother to *follow?* My God, mister, of all the careless, irresponsible—"

"That is enough!" Kit Carson had the lungs to be heard when necessary.

Caddrick slammed the scotch glass down, knuckles white. "Don't you dare use that tone with me—"

"Gentlemen!" Ronisha bellowed, towering over both of them. "Senator! You will remain civil or you will leave this meeting! Is that understood? Kit Carson has just risked his life, not to mention two weeks of unpaid time away from his business, looking for your little girl. In my book, you owe Mr. Carson a very serious apology! As well as whatever humble thanks you can muster up as a parent. You ought to be dancing for joy he's discovered as much as he has, considering what he was up against, out there!"

Caddrick clearly didn't intend to dance for anybody, much less for joy. He sat glaring at Ronisha for a long, dangerous instant, then glowered at Kit, obviously waiting for further explanations. Kit considered walking out, then considered unemployment and life as suffered up time. Speaking coldly, he said, "Suppose you tell me just what I was supposed to do, Senator? Spend the next five years combing the North American continent for Armstrong? When we had a positive lead on your daughter's whereabouts? The Time Tours guides we left in Colorado are still searching for Armstrong and his hostages, will be for months to come, down the Wild West Gate. But *this* search and rescue mission was charged with finding your little girl. And that's exactly what it's going to do. Find your daughter. In London. Ronnie, what's the news from Spaldergate House?"

Ronisha sighed. "We know Benny Catlin was involved in two fatal shootings, leaving two baggage handlers dead and a carriage driver wounded. Malcolm's been searching, of course, but no one in London has any inkling that Benny Catlin is Jenna Caddrick."

Kit grunted. "Sounds to me like Jenna's managed to escape, which means our searchers will have to split up to locate Jenna and whoever took her through the gate. I pity the searchers. They'll have a helluva time, covering London for two separate targets with a three-week lead on them."

"*They?*" Caddrick echoed. "What do you mean, *they?* You're the team leader, Carson! I insist you continue to lead this mission!"

"I can't," Kit said bluntly, rubbing sweat and grit from his brow. "And it's got nothing to do with your lack of gratitude or my pressing business interests, so forget the protests. I already exist in September of 1888. I'd shadow myself and die instantly if I attempted to enter London during the next four months. Someone else has to head up search and rescue operations there. I'd suggest Skeeter Jackson, working closely with Malcolm Moore. Skeeter's already—"

"Now, wait just a minute! I've done some checking on this Jackson. Not only is he the same little creep who assaulted me at Primary, I've heard more than enough to know I don't want a con-man and thief heading up the search for my little girl!"

Kit silently counted ten. "Skeeter Jackson is not conning anybody, Senator. I hired him as my own hotel house detective and believe me, it takes a helluva lot of trust to hire somebody for that job. As for the so-called assault . . ." Kit swallowed the words poised on the tip of his tongue. "Just be forewarned. If you press assault charges against him, I'll be damned sure he countercharges you with criminal battery."

John Caddrick's entire face went white.

Even the I.T.C.H. inquisitors shifted in their chairs.

When Caddrick started to sputter, Kit overrode him. "Forget it, unless you really want the fight of the century on your hands. We've got photographic evidence of the whole incident, Senator. I, for one, will *not* allow a personal vendetta against Mr. Jackson to cripple this search mission. There's too much riding on the outcome. Skeeter's more than proven himself. Virtually every breakthrough in this case has been made by Skeeter Jackson, whereas *your* detective is virtually useless. I told you Sid Kaederman wasn't qualified for a down-time mission, whereas Skeeter's already experienced down the Britannia Gate. And he'll be working with Malcolm Moore, who specializes in London tours. Jackson and Moore head up the London mission, whether you like it or not, Senator. Unless, of course, you *want* your little girl killed?"

Senator John Caddrick's normally florrid jowls faded to the color of old wax. He opened his lips several times, but no sound came out at all. He glanced once at the I.T.C.H. inquisitors, then swallowed and sat motionless in his chair for long moments. The only sound in the room was the whir of the air-conditioning fans. Caddrick finally managed a faint, "All right. I don't see that I have much choice." His voice strengthened into a low growl.

"But I will not be browbeaten and threatened, is that clear?"

If he stayed, Kit knew he would say something the entire station regretted. So he stood up, heading for the elevator. "Quite. Now, if you'll excuse me, we have a lot of work to do before the Britannia opens again. And frankly, I need a shower and a shave before I do any of it. And a cold beer."

Kit stalked into the elevator before Caddrick could protest.

On his way down toward the howling mob of newsies, he thought bleakly of Margo, already in London, and of poor Julius, no older than his granddaughter, who lay dead with a bullet in his gut. Kit wondered with a chill just how many of the searchers on this hunt were likely to come out alive?

Chapter Eight

Dominica Nosette was cold and wet where she stood shivering in the darkness. Rain was falling again, as dirty as the grimy brick walls along Whitechapel's narrow streets. Sudden gusts sent torrents skating across the cobblestones like rats scurrying for shelter. Soot ran black in the gutters where the occasional gaslight illuminated swirls and foul-smelling rivers of refuse on their way to the sewers. It was a hideous night to be alive, a worse one to die in.

Dominica had seen far too much death this night to have stomach for any more. She prided herself on a tough professionalism, a hard core of indifference under layers of thick callus that had made her one of the most ruthless and successful photojournalists in the business. Watching the death of Polly Nichols on video from the vault beneath Spaldergate House in Battersea had been very much like watching an ordinary movie. It was easy to disconnect the reality of it and watch dispassionately, even though it had been frustrating for her professional sensibilities. She would've obtained far better video footage by filming the whole thing on site, using more creative camera angles, better audio equipment.

Elizabeth Stride's murder in Dutfield's Yard had been harder to witness, with the immediacy of sight and smell and sound and the knowledge that only the complete blackness of the closed-in yard and the concealing half-walls of a disused stable stood between her camera lens and the man crouched over Stride with a gutting knife, nearly severing her head with a few powerful slashes. But even there, it had been only a murder, after all. At least Stride had been dead when the knife struck, strangled by that other lunatic, Lachley.

But Catharine Eddowes . . .

Tough as she was, Dominica did not relish the death waiting in this square for poor Kate Eddowes. Mitre Square resembled a miniature amphitheatre in brick. Along one edge ran a solid, three-story brick structure comprised of vacant cottages, jutting out like a peninsula perpendicular to Mitre Street just beyond. Along the short, squat end of this peninsular "cottage" ran a tiny, short jog of road and pavement giving access to the square. The pavement zagged back in a loose Z-shape from the Mitre Street access, with the Sir John Cass School running slap up against the vacant cottages. The resulting interior corner, like the crook of an elbow, was isolated, with a broad pavement that stood nearly three times wider than a normal walkway.

Beside the school rose a tall warehouse belonging to Kearly and Tongue. Opposite, facing the warehouse and school, stood another Kearly and Tongue warehouse, the Orange Market along King Street, and a house belonging to Police Constable Pearse. Along Duke Street, the fourth border of the square, stood the Great Synagogue. Narrow, lightless Church Passage—a covered alleyway—led into the square from Duke Street, past the southern edge of the synagogue.

The tiny "square" thus formed, a secluded island cut off from the busier streets surrounding it, was where Lachley and Maybrick would lead their second victim of the night. There was a sickening symmetry, Dominica realized, to their revolting anti-Semitism. They were murdering Eddowes within view of a synagogue. And given their narrow escape from Dutfield's Yard, these men possessed a terrifying confidence, to kill her within plain view of a policeman's home not half an hour after nearly being caught dead to rights. That alone shook Dominica as she and Guy Pendergast fled Dutfield's Yard before Mr. Diemschutz could bring help. She and her partner sped along side streets, running to get ahead of the murderous Ripper duo, literally racing the whole distance to Mitre Square to get into position for the best vantage point to film Eddowes' death.

In front of the school, a waist-high iron railing partitioned off half the available pavement. Because of minor work being done, a much higher temporary fence had been erected along the line of that railing, effectively cutting the broad pavement in half and sealing off the entire corner of the elbow. It was behind this temporary fencing Dominca and Guy chose to conceal themselves, less than six feet from the spot where Catharine Eddowes was slated to die.

Five minutes after they went into hiding, Constable Watkins appeared in Church Passage, doing his rounds and peering dutifully into the square. And not two minutes after Watkins retreated down Church Passage again, John Lachley appeared, escorting the unsuspecting Catharine Eddowes. Dominica held her breath, trembling slightly in the cold, wet air. Lachley and Eddowes paused within whispering distance of Dominica's hiding place, while James Maybrick slipped up silently behind them, knife already out of his pocket.

Dominica knew what was coming. But the shock left

her trembling when John Lachley smashed Catharine Eddowes to the pavement, strangling her right in front of them. The woman struggled, flailing her arms and kicking helplessly, while Lachley snarled into her face and crushed her throat under his hands. Kate Eddowes finally went limp, arms falling lifelessly to the pavement at her sides. Lachley rifled her pockets for his letter even as the slavering Maybrick struck with his knife, too impatient to wait any longer.

And it was that, watching the infuriated and massively frustrated Maybrick, which finally broke through Dominica's tough professionalism and left her trembling and sick behind the high, temporary schoolyard fence. This was no make-believe movie, no documentary on ordinary little murders. Not even the impersonal blowing apart of a solider by an artillery round. This was a frenzy of psychopathic hatred, a man who was no longer fully human, slashing at an innocent woman's face, cutting an inverted "M" straight through the flesh of her eyelids, hacking off ears, nearly severing the head from its neck. And when he jerked up her skirts . . .

Dominica couldn't watch, squeezed shut her eyes and swallowed hot bile, tried hopelessly to force away the image of him snatching out Catharine's intestines, tossing them across her shoulder, cutting part of them loose and arranging them beside her. *Don't gag, don't heave, they'll hear you, oh, dear, God, the smell* . . . Guy Pendergast's hand was bruising her shoulder, the fingers digging in and flexing as he, too, fought to remain silent during the ghastly ritual Maybrick and Lachley were enacting beyond the fence. She could hear low voices, almost whispers, and didn't want to distinguish individual words.

When at last their footfalls moved away, she opened her eyes. She tried not to look at the mangled shape lying huddled in front of the empty cottages. Dominica was violently atremble, dizzy and light-headed. She wasn't sure she'd be able to take a single step without collapsing. "They're gone," Guy whispered directly against her ear, to prevent the sound from carrying. She nodded. *Time to leave. Get the hell out of here, Dominica, because Police Constable Watkins is going to walk into the Square down Church Passage in about two minutes, discover the body and raise all bloody hell . . . come on, legs, move it!*

She'd taken one step, no more, when racing footfalls thudded back into the Square. Her vision greyed out for just an instant and only Guy Pendergast's grip kept her on her feet. Maybrick had jogged back to the body, was hacking at it again, tearing away part of her apron and wrapping up something . . . oh, Christ, something he'd cut out of her, he was carrying part of her insides away with him . . .

"James!" An all-but-silent hiss of fury broke through the shock. It was Lachley, white-faced. "Get the hell away from her! Come on, man, before a copper strolls in here. They do a patrol past the Square every few minutes and they're bloody well *due!*"

"Forgot my dinner," Maybrick said calmly.

If Guy hadn't been behind her, propping her up, Dominica might well have fallen against the fence, giving them both away. The pistols she and her partner had concealed in their pockets were utterly useless against these two. The men out there arguing over the remains of Catharine Eddowes literally could not be killed, not by anyone from up time. Maybrick wouldn't die until 1889, of arsenic poisoning, and until Mary Kelly was murdered more than a month from now, neither of these men could be so much as harmed.

But Dominica certainly could be.

"If you want to make off with her kidney and uterus,

fine!" Lachley snapped. "But I'll be damned if I go walking along with you while you carry them! I'll meet you back at Lower Tibor, as usual."

The two halves of the team that comprised Jack the Ripper split up, Lachley pale with anger, Maybrick flushed and euphoric. Lachley uttered one short curse, then strode off through the broad opening to Mitre Street, vanishing to the southwest, walking fast. Maybrick thrust his bloody prize under his coat, shoving the knife into a deep pocket. Something dark fell out as he pulled his gloved hand free again. It landed with a dull sound against Eddowes' mangled body. Something small, made of leather . . . Dominica had to stifle the wild, hysterical impulse to laugh as Maybrick strode jauntily down Mitre Street, following Lachley's route at a more leisurely pace. Maybrick had dropped a red leather cigarette case, the one experts had puzzled over for a century and a half. It was far too expensive for a destitute woman like Catharine Eddowes to have been carrying. She'd have pawned it for cash in a heartbeat. It lay, now, amidst the contents of her rifled pockets, which Maybrick had set out neatly beside her body.

Then Maybrick's footfalls died away and they had scant seconds in which to make their own escape, before the momentary arrival of PC Watkins stirred this whole neighborhood to a frenzy. There were only two ways out of Mitre Square and the constable would be arriving through Church Passage. They had no choice but to follow on the heels of the killers.

"Well, come on, then," Guy hissed, dragging her toward the exit to their hiding place. "You're the one who wanted to follow those damned lunatics!" His anger stung her pride fully awake. She jerked away from his supporting grasp and stalked out from behind the temporary fencing. After what she'd been through tonight, Maybrick had better not give her the slip!

Concentrating fiercely on Carson Historical Video Prizes and million-dollar movie advances, Dominica Nosette eased past the pitiful remains of Catharine Eddowes and set out down Mitre Street. *I can still find out how they pull that disappearing act, in the middle of a crowded city . . .*

As they slipped down Mitre Street, a police whistle rose shrilly behind them.

Maybrick's bloody legacy had just been discovered.

Skeeter supposed he should've seen it coming, at least where Goldie Morran was concerned. But he was so tired and still so shaken by Julius' murder, he didn't, not until it hit. The Duchess of Dross spotted him through her shop windows and shot out the door like a javelin going for the gold. "Skeeter! Just the person I've been looking for!"

He stopped dead, about as eager to talk to Goldie as he was to spend the night in Senator Caddrick's hotel room. "What do you want, Goldie?"

"A bit of . . . mmm . . . professional advice."

Skeeter's glance came up sharply. "*You* want advice from *me*?"

Purple-tinted hair glinted evilly; so did her faintly sharp teeth. "Why, yes, Skeeter. You do have a certain amount of useful knowledge tucked away in that bony head of yours."

"Really? And what makes you think I'd go out of my way to accept a cup of coffee from you, never mind give you advice?"

She glanced around nervously, wet her lips. "Well . . . Since you ask, it concerns a mutual acquaintance."

Skeeter narrowed his eyes. "I've been helping Kit Carson arrest most of our mutual acquaintances, Goldie. Going to bribe me to look the other way when one of your cronies comes through? Forget it. Besides, you must've heard? I'm leaving through the Britannia in a couple of days. I'm busy."

For just an instant, real anger flickered through her eyes. "I'm talking about Jenna Caddrick!" she hissed, voice carefully modulated not to carry.

"What about her?"

"Not here. Too many ears."

"Huh." With I.T.C.H. crawling all over the station, never mind Caddrick and his staff goons and all those disgruntled federal marshals, that was no lie. "All right. Where?"

"My shop. In back. It's sound-proofed."

Figures. "As long as you make it quick. I've got about a thousand hours of library work ahead of me before I go to bed tonight."

She sniffed autocratically and led the way into a shop completely devoid of customers. Tourists, wary of the violence that kept breaking out, were staying in their hotel rooms unless a gate was actually cycling, abandoning Commons to the loons and the protestors, all of which had hit station entrepreneurs hard in the cashbox. Goldie hung up the "Out to Tea" sign—a ruse to gain privacy, since mere tea never passed Goldie Morran's lips—then turned the lock. She led the way into the back, past a solid steel door that clearly served to secure her vault. It thumped as she closed it.

The large room beyond was divided, one part lined with small, metallic drawers floor to ceiling, labelled neatly as to semi-precious contents. The balance formed a cozy corner where she'd rigged a sitting room of sorts with a comfy sofa, a table stacked with trade magazines, a small wet bar, and a beautiful porcelain birdcage. Skeeter did a classic double-take. Inside sat two birds which very few people now alive had ever seen outside a museum's stuffed collection. Lovely grey with bright splashes of yellow and white and orange, the breeding pair of Carolina parakeets chirped cheerfully above the sound of quiet music.

He wondered how many viable eggs she'd sold to smugglers already.

"Now," she said briskly, "let's get down to business. Would you care for anything?" She was opening a scotch bottle.

Skeeter was parched, but shook his head. He had his standards. "What have you got to say, Goldie? That you didn't tell Security when they came calling?"

She smiled slightly. "My, my, testy, aren't we?" She poured a drink, neat, and sipped delicately, then came around the end of the bar to settle into her sofa, waving Skeeter to a seat. "I need your help with possible . . . legal entanglements that don't necessarily need to come to light."

Skeeter remained standing and just looked at her.

Something in his expression caused her to sit up straighter. "You do recall, Skeeter, I did save your life once. Lupus Mortiferus would've chopped you into mince if I hadn't interfered. You owe me."

Dammit, she was right. For once. He did owe her, despite the savagery they'd done one another during that idiotic, near-fatal wager. "All right, Goldie. I'm listening."

"I didn't tell Security about this, for reasons you'll understand in a moment. That tourist who went missing in London, Benny Catlin? He came in here to exchange some currency just a few minutes before the Britannia cycled. He was a very nice young man. Quiet, a little scatter-brained, it seemed. It was idiotically easy, really. And if Benny Catlin had been an ordinary graduate student instead of Jenna Caddrick . . ."

"Christ, Goldie, what did you do?" He was afraid he already knew.

Goldie didn't disappoint him. "I, er, passed some

counterfeit bank notes. Someone stiffed *me* with them, returning from a Britannia tour. Which should tell you how good they are. I didn't give her *all* counterfeit notes," she added hastily, "but enough that if Jenna Caddrick has been spending them, well . . . She's been down the Britannia long enough, now, it could get her into serious trouble if they're detected. They're good fakes, quite good, but I didn't intend for anyone to spend months down the Britannia with them. I mean, nobody expected Benny Catlin to go missing—"

"Or turn up as Senator Caddrick's kidnapped daughter!"

Goldie flushed.

"God, the messes you scheme yourself into . . ." He was tempted to tell her she could just scheme herself right back out again; but he wanted to know the rest. "So just what do you want me to do about it?"

Again, she wet her lips. "Well, you see, it occurred to me that Jenna Caddrick might be missing because she's been, well, jailed. For counterfeiting. I mean, if she got away from her abductors the way everybody's saying, that would certainly explain why nobody's been able to trace her. Searchers wouldn't think of looking in a Victorian prison, after all, for a terrorist's hostage. Probably not even the terrorists would think of that."

Reluctantly, Skeeter had to admit she had a point. "So you want me to check all the London jails, looking for a woman disguised as a man, arrange a prison break, then sneak her out through Spaldergate while whoever's trying to murder her isn't looking, then convince her not to press charges against you for passing her counterfeit banknotes in the first place? Jeez, Goldie, you don't ask much."

"It isn't just getting her out of jail," Goldie said quickly. "I mean, there would be a considerable, ah, sum of money involved to compensate her. For legal expenses in London. Inconvenience experienced. That sort of thing."

"You want me to *bribe* her? My God, Goldie! We're not talking about some addled half-wit tourist, here! Do you honestly think you can bribe your way out of this with *Senator Caddrick's kid?*"

"Well, it's worth a try! I'll pay you, too," Goldie added venomously. "Don't worry about that. Cash advance for half my offer, with the balance on delivery of one live and kicking, close-mouthed kid!"

"I don't want your money, Goldie. If I do find Jenna Caddrick, maybe I'll pass along your message. Then again, maybe I won't. If you did get her tossed into some Victorian hellhole of a jail, just pray real hard she doesn't have the same capacity for holding a grudge her father does."

He left her sitting, mouth ajar, and heard a forlorn chirp from the caged parakeets as he swung the vault door open and stalked out. He was tempted to head for the nearest bathroom just to wash his hands. Instead, he headed for Kit Carson's office. Kit needed to know about this. As he headed down through Urbs Romae and Victoria Station toward Edo Castletown, having to push his way through a crowd of chanting protestors, it occurred to Skeeter that Jenna Caddrick might not even *be* in London any longer. Particularly not if she'd discovered her money was no good. Hiding in London would be expensive, which meant she was likely running short of funds already.

Caddrick's story was even more full of holes now than it had been before. If Jenna Caddrick had been a hostage, she wouldn't have simply waltzed into Paula Booker's surgery *or* Goldie Morran's shop unaccompanied, looking to alter her face and change currency. But Benny Catlin had done just that, then had climbed the five flights of stairs to the Britannia platform and chewed Skeeter's backside over a steamer trunk that had very nearly skidded over the edge. There hadn't been anyone up there with Benny Catlin. Nobody holding a metaphoric gun to Jenna Caddrick's head. She was on her own, in London. The guys she'd shot and killed must have been London counterparts of the bastard who'd murdered Julius. Who'd been doubling for her, as a decoy. And since it was clear that Armstrong was helping Marcus and the girls, Jenna Caddrick must be helping Ianira Cassondra . . .

Skeeter actually went so dizzy, he staggered, rocking to a halt so fast, the protestor behind him ran slap into his back. Skeeter caught his balance, ignoring a flurry of angry mutters from the sign-carrying loon, and stood there with his eyes narrowed to slits, thoughts racing, then groped for the nearest wrought iron bench and collapsed onto it, shaking.

"My God," Skeeter whispered aloud. *"Ianira was in the trunk!"* No wonder Jenna Caddrick had been so badly shaken! He shut his eyes for long moments, trying to blot out the image of that trunk sliding off, falling the long, fatal way to the Commons floor . . . Then shoved himself to his feet and stalked through the jostling horde of lunatics rampaging through Victoria Station, carrying signs and howling out protests he barely heard, furious with himself for not tumbling to it sooner. "Kit'll have my badge, overlooking a clue that big," he muttered under his breath.

When Skeeter reached the Neo Edo Hotel, he found Kit in his palatial office, bent over his computer. Skeeter paused just long enough to kick off his shoes before stepping onto the pristine *tatami* rice mats. "Where's Kaederman?" Skeeter asked tersely, searching the corners of Kit's office with an uneasy gaze. "I thought he was coming up here."

Kit glanced up. "Kaederman," he said flatly, "went to bed. That man is the laziest detective I've ever met."

"How'd we luck out? At least he's nowhere around to hear the news."

"What news?" Kit leaned forward, eyes abruptly glittering.

"Ianira's in London. She went through in a steamer trunk. One of Benny Catlin's. I'm sure of it. You remember that pile-up of luggage at the platform, when one of the trunks nearly slid off."

"Yes, you mentioned it belonged to Benny Cat— Oh." Kit could out-swear Yesukai the Valiant. Then he grimaced. "Skeeter, you had no way of knowing, not at the time."

"Maybe not," he muttered, pacing from the enormous desk to the withered landscape garden of raked sand and carefully placed stones to the wall of television monitors which kept Kit abreast of events all over Shangri-La Station. "But if I hadn't been so damn muddled, I'd have figured it out a lot sooner. And the trail wouldn't be so cold!"

"Well, beating yourself up over this won't do Ianira any good," Kit pointed out gently. "At least we have a pretty good indication Ianira was alive, inside that trunk, given Jenna's reaction. I begin to wonder if *anyone* from the *Ansar Majlis* was with that girl when she went through the Britannia," Kit mused. "Other than a couple of hit men who died messily? And since she went through on her own, that really makes me wonder where Marcus and Armstrong went after hopping their train in Colorado. Once Armstrong eliminated the man who shot Julius, they certainly lost no time hightailing it out of there." Kit frowned slowly as he sat back in his chair. "Unless," he mused, "they weren't running *away* at all."

Skeeter halted his pacing. "Huh?"

"Maybe . . ." Kit tapped steepled fingertips against his lips. "Just maybe, they were running *to* something."

Skeeter stared, trying to figure out what he was driving at. "Running *to* something? What? Where? There's nothing in 1885 they'd *want* to go to!"

"No. Not in 1885. But in *1888* . . ."

Skeeter felt his eyes widen. *"London?"*

"Makes sense. A lot of sense. Hide out for three years, make damned sure nobody's on their trail, cross the Atlantic to meet Jenna and Ianira when they come through the Britannia. Armstrong could easily have set up a base of operations in London, complete with false identity, a good occupation lined up, so money's coming in steadily. They could hide out for months, years, if necessary. With damned little chance of the *Ansar Majlis* ever finding them."

"Or anybody else, for that matter," Skeeter added bitterly.

"A definite plus, when one's marked for murder. And they'll have the children to think of," Kit added gently. "Surely you can see that?"

He could. All too clearly. "So you think we shouldn't look for them, after all?"

"No, I didn't say that. Shangri-La Station's still in mortal danger. And something tells me none of our fugitives will be safe until we get to the bottom of this. Too many pieces of this puzzle are still missing. Like that guy who killed Julius, for one. He was certainly no down-time Arabian *jihad* fighter. So who hired him? The *Ansar Majlis?* Hiring a paid killer isn't their style. Crazies like the *Ansar Majlis* do their own killing. So, if not them, who?"

Skeeter didn't like the road Kit was walking down.

"Yes, you do see it, don't you? I'm getting very itchy about the safety of this search team. If someone *besides* the *Ansar Majlis* is trying to kill Jenna, then merely looking for her could be as dangerous as finding her. The question is," Kit mused softly, "how, exactly, to begin the search once you get to London? I'd rather not risk Paula's life any more than necessary, but she ought to go along, to make a positive identification."

Skeeter snorted. "That part's easy."

Kit blinked. "Oh?"

He told Kit about Goldie's counterfeit banknotes. Kit whistled softly.

"So, you'll start by looking for angry merchants who've been ripped off? Hmm . . . It might work. There was a fairly large trade in counterfeit banknotes and coins, especially near the waterfront, where the fakes could be passed to unwary newcomers, people unfamiliar with English currency, but it's certainly the best lead we've got so far." Kit's grin was sudden, blinding, and terrifying. "Grand idea, Skeeter. Let's have you pose as a Pinkerton agent. Say you're after a Yank from New York, who's been counterfeiting money in the States, tell our angry London merchants you think he's moved his operation to London. We'll get Connie to whip up Pinkerton identification papers for you."

"Good grief. First a house detective for the Neo Edo, now a Pinkerton agent? Who'd a-thunk it? *Me,* a private eye!"

"And a pretty good one, so far," Kit grinned. "Get over to Connie's. I'll call her, give her a head's up. You'd better collect a few of those counterfeits from Goldie, too, so you'll have samples with you in London, as part of your cover story. And Skeeter . . ."

"Yeah?"

Kit's smile was positively evil. "Let's not tell Sid about this?"

Skeeter started to laugh; then felt a chill, instead, straight down his spine.

Margo was not keen to watch the murders of Stride and Eddowes. Rather than join the Ripper Watch Team in the Vault, she changed clothing, requested a cup of hot tea from one of the Spaldergate House maids, and curled up beside the fire in the parlour. There she stayed, sitting on the floor in front of the hearth, chin on knees, watching the flames dance across the coals. Malcolm came in shortly after two A.M., looking for her. He paused in the doorway.

"There you are. Well, it's over, down there. Maybrick turns out to be the one who chalked the graffiti in Goulston Street. And you'll never guess who we caught on tape? Those idiot reporters, Dominica Nosette and Guy Pendergast. They're following Maybrick and Lachley. Shadowed Maybrick to Goulston Street and photographed the graffiti after he left, then started trailing him once more."

"Great. We should've staked out the murder sites, ourselves, and waited to nab those idiots."

"Perhaps, but the chance is gone now. We've sent out Stoddard and Tanglewood to try to locate them, but they'll be long gone before either man can get close, I'm afraid." Malcolm crossed the parlour toward her, navigating his way around heavy furniture and tables full of bric-a-brac. "Whatever have you been doing, sitting here alone in the dark?"

"Trying not to think about what's going on in Whitechapel."

He settled on the carpeted floor beside her and wrapped an arm around her shoulders. "You're trembling."

"I'm cold," she muttered. Then, betraying the lie, "You don't think I'm too weak for this job, do you? Because I can't watch?"

Malcolm sighed. "There's a fairly large difference between running slap into something you're not expecting and going out of your way to watch something grisly, particularly when others are on the job to do it, instead. No, I don't think you're too weak, Margo. You extricated several people from that street brawl at the examination of Polly Nichols' remains, didn't you? Doug Tanglewood said he'd never been more thoroughly frightened in his life, yet you pulled them safely away, even Pavel Kostenka, when that lout was intent on beating him senseless."

"That wasn't so hard," Margo shivered. "I just charged in and did the first thing that came to mind. He wasn't expecting Aikido, anyway."

"Then you did precisely what a budding time scout should do," Malcolm murmured, stroking her hair gently. "Between the Ripper Watch and searching for our missing tourist, I haven't had the time to say how proud of you I've been. You've nothing to be ashamed of, nothing at all."

She bit her lip, wondering if now was a good time to talk about the past, which had been troubling her ever since she'd come to London. Her mother's descent into prostitution had been Margo's shameful secret for a long time, one she'd feared at first would drive Malcolm away; but she'd had time to think about it and wondered now if she'd misjudged him, unfairly assigning to him the same prejudices she'd encountered in Minnesota. He knew about her being raped by a gang of fifteenth-century Portuguese, after all, and still wanted to marry her. Surely he wouldn't mind what her mother had done to make ends meet, if he didn't mind the other?

Malcolm lifted her face, his expression deeply concerned. "What *is* it, Margo?"

She leaned against his shoulder and told him. All of it. Her father's drinking. Her mother's desperation to pay the bills, when her father spent his paycheck and her mother's both, buying the booze. What her mother had done . . . and what her father had done, when he'd found out. "I never meant to say anything, because it would kill Kit, to learn how his little girl died. But I thought you ought to know. Before you married me."

"Oh, Margo . . ." His voice shook. "I wish to God I could go back and undo it all. No wonder you fight the world so hard. You've had to, just to survive . . ." He brushed his thumb across her cheek, across her unsteady lips. "You're so beautiful, so full of courage, it makes my heart stop. If your father hadn't died in prison, they'd have to hang me for him."

Margo's mouth twisted. "They don't hang people anymore, Malcolm."

Then he was holding her close and nothing else in the universe mattered.

Dominica watched in astonishment as James Maybrick unlocked the door of a filthy hovel in Wapping and disappeared inside. Gas light appeared briefly through the windows and a ferocious barking erupted, then subsided just as abruptly. A moment later, the gas went out, leaving the house dark again.

"What on earth?" she wondered aloud, startled. "What d'you suppose should we do now?" she whispered.

"I'm going 'round the back, see if I can get a look inside."

"Be careful!"

Dominica waited impatiently while her partner vanished into the inky blackness. Rain spat at her, cold and miserable. She huddled deeper into her coat and shifted from one foot to the other, trying to keep warm. She'd been waiting for perhaps five minutes when snarls and savage barking erupted again from the house. A single gunshot split the wet night.

"Guy!" Dominica ran across the street, just in time for the front door to be thrown wide. Guy snatched her wrist and pulled her inside. "Come on! There isn't a moment to lose!"

"What—"

"Shh!"

He dragged her through the dark house into a central, windowless room where a gaslight burned low. A massive black dog sprawled across the bare wooden floorboards, dead in a puddle of spreading blood; Guy had shot it through the skull. In the center of the floor rested a heavy trap door, which Guy pulled up cautiously. Beneath, they found steps leading down into a cellar. "He's nowhere in the house," Guy whispered urgently. "He had to go through here. There's nowhere else he could have gone."

Dominica dragged out her own pistol, aware that she was trembling violently.

"There's no lantern," she muttered, eying the black hole uneasily.

"He had one. Must have. It's pitch black, down there, but we'll hear him at the very least, follow the sound."

Yes, she thought, *and he'll hear us, as well.* But they'd come this far and she wasn't giving up on the story of the century so easily. She gripped her pistol with damp fingers and followed Guy into the cellar, which proved to be no cellar at all, but rather a tunnel through the sewers beneath Wapping. *So this is how he did it! Simply popped home to Wapping and vanished beneath the streets!* Then, faint with distance, they heard it: the splash of footfalls through the filth in the tunnels. She and Guy, pausing at the base of the stairs, exchanged glances. Then Dominica hiked up her skirts and waded cautiously forward.

She was *going* to get that Carson prize. And all that lovely money, which her video would fetch in the up-time world. Dominica Nosette intended to be the world's most famous photojournalist ever. And nothing was going to stop her.

Chapter Nine

John Lachley had just finished burning Elizabeth Stride's letter in the flames of his altar beneath the streets when a woman's high, ragged scream echoed out in the sewer. A man's angry snarl and a volley of gunshots roared through the tunnels, followed by a thud of colliding bodies, a grunt and sudden masculine cry of pain. Then James Maybrick's voice, maniacal: *"Lipski!"*

Over and over again, *"Lipski! Lipski! . . . Lipski LipskiLipski . . ."*

The ragged chant jerked Lachley across the room and out through the open iron doorway. The Liverpudlian was on his knees in the muddy water, his lantern thrown aside, hacking and stabbing at a motionless form. The thing lying on the sewer floor had, before Maybrick's violent assault, been a man. Blood had spurted and sprayed across Maybrick's face and chest. It dripped and spattered down his chin and hair from the arterial bleeding Lachley had warned him against when stalking the prostitutes. But a more terrible sound, by far, than the slam of Maybrick's knife into dead flesh came to Lachely's ears: running footsteps, receding into the blackness, unsteady and desperate.

The woman who had screamed.

Lachley left Maybrick to his grisly pleasure and raced after her. He had to stop her. Had to silence her. *Whoever* she was. It didn't matter a damn *who*, he had to catch her. She was slipping on the wet bricks ahead. Scrabbling up to run again. Blind and deaf and crashing into walls in the darkness. He could hear the scream of her breath. Shallow. Ragged. Wild. Could hear the scratch of her shoes. The splash of puddles under her staggering feet. Could smell the terror. Thick. Sexual. Delicious.

When he caught her, she screamed. Fought him. Writhed and clawed at his hands, his face. He backhanded her into the bricks. Caught a fist in her hair. Forced her head back. Found the death grip at her throat . . . And ghostly red light flickered in his eyes, eerie and startling. Lachley reeled back a step, bringing up one arm defensively. Her head moved and the light vanished. Then a gunshot split the darkness. The bullet whined off bricks behind him. Lachley backhanded her again, fist clenched. The gun discharged, blinding him. They struggled for the weapon and she fired until the gun clicked, empty. He struck her a third time, knocking her to the floor, this time. She splashed into the muck at his feet and lay still. A faint moan escaped her. Lachley caught her under the arms, grasped her jaw, tilted her head—

And the flicker of dull red light came again.

Badly startled, he searched along her neck, up toward her ear, and touched slick, alien cords of some kind, something glassy, an odd tube of some kind, what felt like tiny wires . . . *What the bloody devil?*

He gave a practiced heave and tossed her across one

shoulder. Her head trailed down his back, arms loose, unjointed. Lachley strode back through the darkness, guided by the light pouring from Lower Tibor's open door. Maybrick was still hacking at the dead man.

"James!"

When the sharp sound of his voice failed to break the maniac's slavering frenzy, Lachley shoved him off balance with a booted foot. Maybrick sprawled sideways, splashing into the water, then snarled like an animal, knife flashing at the ready.

"*James! Put the sodding knife down! He's dead!*"

The cotton merchant blinked slowly and, as the wildness faded gradually from his eyes, he focused on Lachley's face. "Sorry," he whispered, voice shaking, "I'm sorry, doctor, didn't realize . . ."

"You did well, James, killing that bastard. Drag him inside, now, and we'll see who our visitors might be."

"Yes, of course." He hauled the dead man up by the arms, dragging the body out of the filthy water, and pulled him into Lower Tibor.

"Leave him by the door, James, and find his sodding gun." Lachley dumped the unconscious woman across his work table and bound her wrists efficiently with a twist of rope. He found a cup and calmly poured out a dose of the drug he always gave Maybrick when they returned after a successful hunt through Whitechapel. "Ah, you found the pistol. Very good. Put it there. Now, James, you're shaking, badly in need of your medication. Here, swallow this down. Then take off your coat and the rest of those clothes. Burn them, you're covered in blood."

Maybrick drank the powerful drug without question, then stripped off the blood-caked garments and dropped them on the altar for burning. Lachley heard water splashing as he cleaned himself up at the tiny basin. Satisfied that his mad cotton merchant was under proper control once more, Lachley turned his attention to the mutilated body lying beside the door. He opened the coat, torn and hacked through in two dozen places, searched the pockets, emptied the contents of his waistcoat and trouser pockets, as well. Then frowned slowly at what he found. Crouched beside a perfectly ordinary corpse, John Lachley found himself confronted with objects he could not comprehend.

The man's pockets contained a handful of shillings, florins, a few half crowns, plus a wad of bank notes, a surprisingly large number of them. Nearly two hundred pounds, in fact. But the other items . . . He found a stiff, rectangular card of some sort, made of a substance Lachley had never encountered. Neither paper nor wood nor metal, it was nevertheless shiny and brightly colored, with a series of dark stripes down the back, formed of some other unknown substance which could not be scratched off easily with a fingernail. It reminded him of gutta-percha, obtained from the milky sap of a tree native to Malaysia, which like latex hardened on exposure to the air, forming a stiff substance somewhat like this, useful in cements, insulations, and so on. This card was not gutta-percha, however; attempting to dissolve it with oil of turpentine and naptha had no effect whatever, which proved it to be some other substance. Nor was it caoutchouc, which was not even as strong as gutta-percha and certainly nothing like as strong as this substance. Frowning, he put the little card aside and studied the other mysterious object he'd found, a tiny cylinder covered with a soft, spongy substance, with trailing wires coming out of it, coated with something slick and flexible. The wires plugged into a compact, heavy box. This was made of some other unknown substance, its feel similar to the stiff card, yet completely different, bent into a virtually seamless shape with tiny buttons and a hinged lid. This boasted a transparent cover of something that was not glass. In fiddling with the buttons, he pressed one that caused a faint, whirring sound to emerge from the box. Startled, he mashed other buttons, trying to get the sound to stop . . .

And James Maybrick's voice spoke from inside!

He dropped the thing with a shocked yell, toppled straight over onto his backside and stared at the box which lay there talking to him, like some parlour medium's trick with ventriloquism or the tiniest Victrola phonograph imaginable; but there was no one here except Maybrick and himself, and Maybrick stood on the other side of the room, gaping, mouth dropped wide to hear his own voice coming from a box the size of Lachley's hand. Lachley could not imagine anyone making a phonograph *this* small.

"What is it?" Maybrick's voice shook violently.

"I don't know!" Lachley picked up the box and shook it gently. Maybrick's voice kept talking. Then he heard another voice and recognized with a jolt of shock what he was hearing. *"James! Get the hell away from her! Come on, man, before a copper strolls in here. They do a patrol past the Square every few minutes and they're bloody well due!"* This was followed by Maybrick's calm, prosaic, *"Forgot my dinner . . ."* and his own furious, *"If you want to make off with her kidney and uterus, fine! But I'll be damned if I go walking along with you while you carry it! I'll meet you back at Lower Tibor, as usual."*

He stared, open-mouthed now, himself. This little box had somehow captured their conversation of one hour previously, when they'd stood over the gutted remains of Catharine Eddowes. "It *is* like a phonograph or a miniaturized telephone," he whispered, awestruck, "one that *records* voices, rather than transmitting them across a wire! My God, how is this accomplished?

Where is the mouthpiece? Both a telephone and a phonograph's recorder have a mouthpiece to capture the voice and transmit it, but there's nothing except these little wires and this tiny thing at the end. And what powers it?"

"They must be police!" Maybrick gasped out, shaking with furious terror. "Filthy coppers, following us, they're onto us—"

"London coppers do not have devices like this!"

"Then who are they?"

Lachley stared from Maybrick to the dead man and back, considered the box in his hand and the unconscious woman, stared at Maybrick again. Under other circumstances, the tableau they presented might have struck him as enormously funny: a naked man with blood in his hair, dripping water down his face and chest, a corpse in possession of a talking box, and a woman with bound hands lying sprawled across his work table. "I've no idea who they are," Lachley said at last, pushing himself to his feet and fiddling with the box until the voices stopped. "But I intend to find out. Get dressed James, you're bollock naked. And rinse the blood out of your hair before it dries to a clotted mess."

The madman ran a hand through sticky, thinning hair and grimaced, then bent over the basin again and washed his balding head clean. He recovered the clothes he'd worn on the train down from Liverpool and dressed himself silently. The drug was beginning to take hold, thank God, leaving him calmer and quieter. Lachley searched the unconscious woman, finding even stranger things secreted about her person than he had on the man. He had no idea what to make of the tiny, lenslike device hidden in her bonnet, nor could he comprehend the other device, which emitted the dull red light he'd seen in the dark sewer. Footsteps roused him from his frowning reverie. Maybrick had come to stand behind him.

"What's that?" he asked quietly, pointing to the little tube the light came from.

"I've no idea. It emits a pale, red-colored light."

"I don't see anything."

Lachley shone it at his eyes. "There, see it?"

"No."

Even when the cotton merchant stared directly into the device, he could not see the dim reddish light that was plainly visible to Lachley. Curiouser and curiouser . . . The lens-like affair and light emitter were connected via slick-coated wires to a heavy, very dense gadget hidden under the woman's coat. It resembled the voice recorder only in the sense that both were housed in compact boxes of some unknown material. Her device had metal parts, however, buttons and levers, and a strangely textured surface along one side that resembled a dark window, but there was nothing to see through it. In fact, it wasn't even transparent, the way the hinged lid of the voice recorder was.

Lachley found another of the stiff, strange cards in her pockets, along with a surprising amount of cash, a tiny mirror and other personal grooming implements, and a variety of oddments to which he could ascribe no purpose whatever. Her clothing was perfectly ordinary stuff: a cheap if substantial coat, heavy woolen skirt and bodice, worn over petticoats and combinations. Knitted stockings, stout and well-made shoes for walking. A heavy chemise under the bodice . . .

And under *that*, a garment the likes of which he'd never seen. Straps and smooth cups of some stretchy black substance, fastened snugly around her breasts, clearly meant to support her anatomy in a fashion superior to any female garments he'd ever seen, and he'd had enough sisters, growing up, plus several hundred female patients who visited his surgery, to know whereof he spoke. "What the devil is it made of? It isn't latex rubber, yet it's very *like* rubber, and exceptionally well crafted."

"C'n I rip her?" Maybrick's voice came from nearby, dulled by the drug, sleepy.

"No, James. She's mine." He glanced around to find the drugged merchant swaying on his feet. "Come here, James, you'd best lie down and rest." He dragged the unconscious, half-naked woman to one side, making room on the long work bench for Maybrick to stretch out. Ignoring the woman for several minutes, Lachley concentrated on taking Maybrick into a deep trance to erase any possibility of Maybrick's mentioning him or the bizarre devices they'd found tonight, when he returned home and scribbled out his diary entries.

"When will you be able to return to London, James?" he murmured.

"Not sure . . . long time . . . business . . ."

"Dammit, we have to find the Welsh woman in Miller's Court and eliminate her," Lachley muttered, "the sooner the better. Very well, James, the next time you return to London, you will locate a woman in Miller's Court for me, one who speaks Welsh. She is the woman you will kill next."

Maybrick's drugged face changed, coming alive with a hunger Lachley recognized very well, now. "I want to rip her . . . I'll slash her face, the faithless whore, cut off her breasts, kiss them when I've cut them off . . ."

"Later, James! You may do all of that, the next time you return to London." Maybrick's eyes were closing again, his breaths deepening. "Later . . ."

"Sleep, James," Lachley muttered. "When you wake, you will return to Liverpool. You will have no memory of me at all, not until I send you a telegram. Only then will you recall my name, this place. Sleep, James, and dream of ripping the whore in Miller's Court . . ."

The drugged merchant slept.

That nasty little chore out of the way, Lachley returned his attention to the woman at the other end of his work bench. It was time his mysterious prisoner woke up. He needed to question her, but she would not be likely to cooperate with the men who'd killed her companion. The dead man probably wasn't her husband, given the absence of any wedding ring on her hands, but they were clearly connected somehow, so he would have to take steps to ensure her compliance. He prepared another draught of the drug he'd given Maybrick, then roused her with water splashed into her face and gentle slaps across the cheeks.

"Wake up, now . . ."

She stirred, moaned softly. Gaslight glinted along her dark blond hair and fair complexion. She was a pretty little thing, with wide and frightened blue eyes that gradually opened. For a long moment, confusion held those eyes perfectly senseless. Then memory stirred sharply and an indrawn shriek broke loose. She focused on him, cowered away, tried to get her hands under her, and belatedly discovered the ropes on her wrists.

"Hold still," Lachley told her, "before you fall off the edge of the bench."

A tiny whimper broke free. He lifted her head and felt tremors ripping through her as he pressed the rim of the cup to her lips. "Drink this."

"No . . . please . . ."

"Drink it!" She struggled feebly, no match for his strength. With the simple expediency of pinching shut her nostrils, he forced the drug down her throat. She coughed, gagged, then swallowed it. Lachley stroked her hair gently. "There, that wasn't so bad. Don't bother to fight me, pet, you're not going anywhere. I haven't poisoned you," he added with a wry smile.

She trembled, biting a lip, and tried to hide her face. "Please, don't kill me . . ."

"Kill you? Oh, no, my dear, I've far more interesting things in mind for you." The shuddering gulp of air she dragged down left him chuckling. "Now, then, my dear, the drug I've just given you will make you very sleepy. By the way, would you mind terribly telling me your name?" She lay trapped against him, shaking, and didn't answer. He drew a fingertip down her wet cheek. "All right, then, we'll wait a bit, until the drug's taken hold. Terribly sorry about your friend, you know. James was quite beyond himself this evening." The woman's tears came faster and her breaths went ragged. Curiosity prompted his next question. "Was he your lover?"

She shook her head. "No."

"Your brother, perhaps?"

"No . . ."

"What, then?"

"B-business partner." Her eyelids had begun to droop.

"What sort of business, my dear?"

"Journalists . . ." A faint sigh of sound.

Lachley frowned. *Journalists? Penny-dreadful journalists?* What was the world coming to, when women presumed to enter a sordid profession like newspaper muckraking? The entire world was unravelling these days, with women demanding suffrage and entering medical training at university, becoming doctors, for God's sake, setting themselves up with typewriting machines as secretaries, a fine and estimable man's profession. Women would turn the job of personal secretary into a mockery, offering their sexual services, no doubt, breaking up the homes and marriages of perfectly respectable businessmen. Society was disintegrating and *women* were largely at fault. "What newspaper do you work for? Or do you write for some absurd women's magazine?"

"Newspaper . . ." Her eyes had closed completely. *"London New Times."*

New Times? He'd never heard of it. Hardly surprising, though, new penny dreadfuls hit the market every month, competing for readership and advertisements. "What were you doing in the sewer?"

"Following you . . ."

A chill chased down his back. Well, of course she'd been following him, how else would she and her partner have found their way down here?

"What did you come here for?"

A tiny, fleeting smile. "Going to win the Carson Prizec . . . in historical photojournalism . . . nobody else had the guts to try it, following the Ripper . . ."

For a long moment, Lachley stood dumbstruck. The *Ripper?* She knew of the letter he'd sent out? The one the Central News Agency had not yet made public? He'd expected the newspaper to print the Dear Boss letter immediately, but the dratted editor had clearly held it back and might well have sent it to the police. Perhaps she'd seen the letter at the Central News Agency office, spying for her own publication? Then the rest of what she'd said sank in. *Historical photojournalism?* He'd never heard of such a profession, any more than he'd ever heard of a Carson Prize, whatever that was. Clearly, winning it was important enough to risk her life for it. "Historical photojournalism?" he echoed blankly. "Are you a photographer, then?"

Perhaps that device she'd been carrying was some sort of camera?

"Oh, yes, a very good photographer. Dominica Nosette, most famous photographer in the world . . ."

Lachley indulged a wry smile, at that. He'd never heard of the bloody bitch.

"Videotape's going to make me rich," she sighed. "Fools on the Ripper Watch Team, all those famous criminologists and historians, they don't know anything . . . too cowardly to try what I did."

Ripper Watch Team? This sounded deuced ominous. "What did you try?" he asked softly.

Another fleeting smile. "Hid in Dutfield's Yard, of course, waited for you to bring Liz Stride there. And we hid again in Mitre Square, behind that high fence. They put their hidden cameras up and filmed it from the vault, but you can't get a decent story hiding in a cellar halfway across London. You have to get right out where he's going to strike next . . ."

The room spun as the implications of her babbling story sank in. *She'd known exactly where to hide! Had known where to watch them kill Stride and Eddowes! Had known in advance!* It wasn't possible, how could anyone know where he and Maybrick were going to be, when they hadn't known, themselves, where they would encounter the prostitutes? They hadn't even realized Catharine Eddowes had been released from Bishopsgate Police Station, not until they'd run across her on Duke Street. Yet *others* knew, she'd said, had put up cameras in advance, to photograph him and Maybrick . . . others who sat in a vault of some sort halfway across London . . .

John Lachley seized her chin, shaking her hard. "Explain! *How did you know where I would be?*"

She blinked slowly. "Everybody knows. Ripper's a famous case. Most famous murder mystery in the last two centuries . . . and I'm going to solve it, *have* solved it! When I go back to the station, to my own time, I'll be famous, and rich, I've got videotapes of Jack the Ripper . . . both of them . . . who'd have guessed it was two men?"

Lachley stood shaking. She was babbling, out of her head. Had to be . . .

"All those idiots," she was murmuring, "thinking it

was Prince Eddy or his tutor, or that barrister who drowned himself or Sir William Gull. They've been arguing over who it was for the last hundred-fifty years . . . even thought it might've been some time traveller using the Britannia Gate . . ."

John Lachley stared at the raving woman, seriously considering whether she had taken leave of her senses or if he had taken leave of his. Time traveller? A *century and a half*, arguing over his identity? She wasn't a journalist, she was an escapee from a lunatic asylum somewhere on the fringes of London . . .

Then something she'd said hit home.

The gate! Ianira, the woman who had known so much about him, had babbled endlessly about a mysterious gate. Was she, too, some sort of traveller in time, who had come to hunt him? He reeled at the implications. His gaze rested on the heavy box he'd taken from her coat, with its trailing wires and tubes and cylinders hidden in her bonnet, and frowned. He picked it up, then shook the woman. "Look at this." Her eyelids fluttered for a moment before opening. "Tell me what this is."

"My camera. Digital videocamera, best in the business . . ."

*Video*camera? Latin for *I see*?

"Show me how it operates!" He loosened the ropes on her wrists, braced her in a sitting position and leaned her against him. She fumbled the camera into her lap and fiddled with controls. "See? This is what I recorded tonight." She tried to hold the camera up, but couldn't lift her arms. He took it from her—and let out a yell. The strangely textured surface along one side was *moving*. Pictures flickered across it, in color, showing Maybrick bent over Catharine Eddowes, hacking her to pieces . . .

Dear God! How the devil could such a tiny little box

have captured them in pictures like this, color pictures, *moving* pictures? He pressed the controls she had manipulated and the box whirred softly, the pictures flashing with such speed he couldn't follow the motion. People racing backwards, colors flashing and rippling across the surface, a blur of sight and confusion. When he fumbled at the controls again, hands shaking, the motion slowed abruptly. He found himself staring at a place straight out of nightmare. Vast open rooms, with whole buildings inside, hundreds of tiny people moving about the floor and climbing staircases made of metal, insanely colored lights glowing in strange shapes. "What is this place?" he demanded, voice shaking.

She blinked slowly and focused on the camera he held. "Shangri-La Station," she murmured. "The time terminal . . ."

Lachley drew a whole series of deep breaths, gulping down the damp air, gradually steadied his shaking nerves. "You," he said slowly, enunciating each word with care, "are from my future?"

"Had to come down time, through the gate, to catch the Ripper, to photograph him . . ."

He didn't really believe it, didn't want to believe it, such things were fantasy, the maunderings of popular authors like that Frenchman Jules Verne. Yet he was holding a camera that no craftsman in the British Empire could possibly have constructed, made of things Lachley had never seen or heard of, and the bitch was drugged, *couldn't* be lying, not with what he'd given her. Excitement stirred to life, with tantalizing glimpses of a world which could offer him more power than anything he'd dreamed possible. "Eddy," he whispered, "tell me about Eddy. Prince Albert Victor. When does he become king?"

"Poor Prince Eddy," she sighed, eyes closing again. "Only four more years . . . so young . . . 1892 . . ."

Lachley began to tremble in a wild excitement. *Four years?* Eddy would be crowned king in only four more years? Dear God, what was going to happen, that would kill both Queen Victoria and the Prince of Wales? Bertie was healthy as an ox and Victoria, herself, likely to live for another decade. "What happens?" he demanded, breathless now, "What happens in 1892?"

"Influenza. Epidemic of '91–'92. Poor Eddy, he'd just been engaged to be married, named Duke of Clarence, whole life ahead of him, and he's killed by influenza. Victoria was heartbroken, his parents inconsolable . . ."

The room lurched under his feet, swaying and whirling in mad circles. *Dead of influenza? Never crowned?* It couldn't be, he'd worked too hard, invested *everything*, spent five weeks in hell, tracking down Eddy's God-cursed letters to protect him, to ensure the ascension to the throne. Had done murder after stinking murder to keep Eddy safe, so he could become king, to ensure himself the power Lachley craved, the safety of wealth and control over the political future of an empire . . .

And Eddy was to be killed by a *stupid influenza epidemic?*

Lachley began to laugh, the sound wild and high, echoing off the bricks of the vaulted ceiling. He gripped the impossible camera in both hands and laughed until the sound choked him, until he could gasp out, "How do you get back? To your own time?"

"Through the gate," his drugged victim answered in a sleepy, reasonable tone.

"Gate? What gate? Where?" He was still laughing, the sound of it edged with mania, a mind giving way under the stresses.

"The Britannia Gate. In Battersea, Spaldergate House. But it doesn't open for days, not until the second of October, only opens every eight days . . ." Her head was lolling. "Won't go through it, though, not 'til

Mary Kelly's murdered on November ninth. . . I'll take my videotapes back, then, I'm sure to win the Kit Carson Prize . . ."

Another spate of laughter broke loose. Mary Kelly? She must be the bitch in Miller's Court. What the bloody hell did he care about a scheming little whore with a letter written by a dullard who wouldn't even survive to wear the crown? Oh, God, it was too funny, here he stood in a satanic sanctuary devoted to the accrual of political and psychic power, with a dead time traveller on the floor, a drugged maniac on his work bench, and a babbling journalist planning to photograph a murder he no longer had any earthly reason to commit, with a total of *four* whores dead and cut to pieces for no reason whatever, and the decaying head of an adolescent Nancy-boy glaring at him from across the room and laughing at his shattered dreams . . .

Only this woman had brought him a glimpse of something new, something which fired his imagination even more passionately than Eddy's prospects had done. A whole, immense new world to explore, in which to control little minds and live as a king, himself. He laughed again and stroked the woman's hair. Thoughts of Eddy fell away like flakes of rust from fine Damascus steel. Dominica, the self-important photojournalist, had done him a greater favor than she dreamed, tracking him through London's sewers.

He left her tied to the great iron hook on his sacred oak tree, drugged into a stupor, and deposited the equally stupified James Maybrick on the floor of the sewer outside, then locked the door to Lower Tibor and began walking through the dark tunnels beneath London, laughing softly and wondering what he ought to wear when he carried Dominica through the Britannia Gate two days from now, dying of the wounds he would inflict shortly before arriving in Battersea?

❖   ❖   ❖

Sometime early in the morning hours, Ianira Cassondra woke to gibbering terror. Dr. John Lachley had crashed into her bedroom, rousing her from drugged sleep with slaps, bruising her arms and shaking her. "Tell me about the gate!" he demanded, cracking his hand across her face. "Wake up, girl, and tell me about the gate! And the station! Where are you from?"

Ianira shrank away from him, weeping and trembling. "I came through the Britannia Gate! From the station! Please . . ."

"What station? What's it called?"

"Shangri-La," she whispered, her bruised face aching where he'd struck her. Her wrists, crushed in his hard hands, were slowly purpling under his grip. "Time Terminal Eighty-Six—"

"*Eighty-Six*? My God, are there so many of them? Tell me about your world, woman!"

She shook her head, desperate and confused. "I live on the station. I am not permitted to leave, for I am a down-timer—"

"A *what*?" His face, looming so close above her own, had twisted into an unholy mask of madness. She shrank back into the pillows, but he jerked her up again, roughly. "Explain!"

"I was born in Ephesus!" she cried. "Came to the station through the Philospher's Gate! From Athens . . ."

He went very still, staring down at her. Voice quiet, now, he said, "Tell me again where you were born. And when."

"In Ephesus," she whispered. "We did not reckon the years in the same way, but the Philosopher's Gate opens into what the up-time world calls 448 B.C., in the time of Pericles . . ." She trailed off at the look of naked shock in his eyes.

"My God," he whispered. "It's true, then. Of course

you kept saying you were born in Ephesus, when the city doesn't exist any longer."

Ianira blinked up at him, terrified and confused. Clearly, he believed her. Why, she couldn't imagine. Something had obviously happened tonight . . . Ianira's eyes widened. The Ripper Watch! He must have encountered someone from the Ripper Watch tonight, must've seen something that had left him convinced of the reality of time travel. John Lachley's wild eyes focused slowly on her bruised face. He smiled, stroking her hair possessively. "My dear, tell me about the people trying to kill you."

She tried to explain about the up-time world's Lady of Heaven Temples, the *Ansar Majlis* terrorists who had sworn to destroy the Templars and her family, about Jenna's murderous father and the men he'd sent to butcher his own daughter.

"Then you are quite important," Lachley mused. "Far more important than that brainless bitch I left in Lower Tibor. A woman journalist, whoever heard of such a thing?" Ianira closed her eyes to shut out horror. He'd not only encountered members of the Ripper Watch Team, he'd kidnapped them. "Yes," he was murmuring, "I do believe you're far more important than Miss Nosette. Very well, my course is clear. I'd better do that bloody lecture tomorrow night, curse it, to lull suspicion. I shan't risk drawing attention to myself over those wretched murders on the eve of stepping into the future!" He shook her again. "Tell me about the gate. What time it opens. That Nosette woman said something about Spaldergate House, in Battersea."

"I don't know what it looks like," Ianira quavered, straining away from him. "They smuggled me out of the station in a steamer trunk. I know the gate opens in the garden behind the house, but I don't know what time. It is in the evening, always, every eight days."

"Ah. Miss Nosette can tell me precisely when, before I dispose of her. Very well, my dear," he pressed a kiss to her brow. "I do believe," he said quietly, "you had best be moved for safekeeping. I don't wish to risk having you escape, my pet. Eddy has proven himself worthless as dross, but you, my dear, will take me into a place of power beyond anything I imagined."

She gasped, staring up into his mad grey eyes. "You can't go to the station!"

He laughed softly. "Nonsense. I'm John Lachley, I can do anything. The police haven't a clue that I've helped butcher four destitute whores in the East End, controlling Maybrick's pathetic little mind. Miss Nosette tells me your world has puzzled over my identity for a century and a half. If I can accomplish that in London, with no more than I've had to work with, I will become a god on your station!" He smiled at her through dark, insane eyes. "And you, my pet, will be my goddess . . ."

She fought him when he drugged her again.

And wept hopelessly when he carried her down the stairs, wrapped in a cloak, carrying her toward the nightmarish room she had seen in visions, the brick room beneath the streets where he had carried out at least one murder and had planned so many others. Somehow, she must find a way to stop this madman before he reached the station. Down-time men whose minds were sound and whole sometimes went mad when they first entered a time terminal and confronted the shocking realities of the up-time world. What John Lachley would do, once he reached TT-86 . . .

She faded into unconsciousness, still trying to discover some way to stop him.

Jenna tried to ignore the ugly roar of voices in the street just outside their little house, but there was no escaping the angry sound of brawling out there. The bells of Christ Church, Spitalfields, sounded bleak and hopeless this morning, calling worshippers to a rainy Sunday service, while the grim news flashed like wildfire from house to house: two women butchered within half an hour of one another, confounding the police of two separate jurisdictions and shocking the entire city of London, this time, not just the East End. And that at a time when most residents here had believed themselves beyond further shock.

Noah had gone out to buy fresh-caught herrings for their breakfast, refusing to let Jenna set foot into the angry mob outside. Jenna was determined to cook breakfast today, however, so she bent over the monstrous, coal-fired stove in the kitchen, trying to take in Marcus' instructions on how to operate it, when Noah Armstrong rocketed into the house.

"I've got a lead," the detective said without preamble, dumping a wrapped packet of fish onto the kitchen table with a thump.

Jenna and Marcus jerked around. "What lead?" Jenna demanded breathlessly.

"There's to be a lecture tomorrow night at the Egyptian Hall, on Theosophy and the occult sciences. The speaker's a doctor, claims to be a mesmeric physician. I ran across a man talking about him when I was coming back from the costermonger's. It seems the doctor who's giving the lecture came up from Whitechapel, was born in Middlesex Street, turned to mediumism and the occult. I don't know if this is our man, but the doctor who attacked you, Jenna, reacted violently to whatever Ianira said in trance. So maybe he had occult connections. We're certainly running out of leads, trying to trace ordinary doctors. And with the Ripper terror coming to a boil out there, I'm not sure it's entirely safe just now, asking about physicians and surgeons. The police are looking for a doctor connected to the Ripper, after all, and poor Dr. Mindel has barricaded himself into the house, terrified of the mobs. Frankly, I think it's worth a shot, going to see this Lachley fellow."

Jenna's mouth had dried out like thistle-down, all the liquid in her body rushing to her palms, which she wiped unsteadily on her trousers. "Yes. I agree. I'm coming with you, Noah." The detective started to protest. "No, hear me out! I can identify him faster than you can. If he's giving a lecture, there'll be a crowd, which means I can watch without him noticing me. If he's the right man, we can trace him to where he lives, maybe even find Ianira there."

Noah's lips thinned. Clearly the detective wanted to argue. Then a sigh broke loose. "You're right, dammit. But I don't like putting you in harm's way for any reason."

"I'll go armed," Jenna muttered. "For bear."

"I, too, will go," Marcus interjected. "Mrs. Mindel has offered to watch the girls if I ever need to leave them alone. Ianira is my wife. I *will* go to search for her."

Again, the detective clearly considered arguing, then gave in. "All right," Noah groused. "If things do get sticky, another gun hand will be welcome. God knows, you learned quickly enough when I gave you those shooting lessons after that mess in Colorado."

"You taught me well," Marcus said quietly. "I have not forgotten how to use the revolver I bought in Chicago."

Noah nodded. "We'll *all* go armed. And we'll need better clothes than these. The Egyptian Hall is a respectable place. If we show up in East End castoffs, they might not even let us through the door."

Jenna frowned. "The only good suit I've got is what I was wearing the night the gate opened. It's got bloodstains all over it. The last thing I want to do is show my face in public with blood on my clothes. Somebody'll take me for Jack the Ripper. I had decent stuff in my luggage, but I had to abandon all my baggage at the Picadilly Hotel."

"The lecture's not until tomorrow night, so there's plenty of time to pick up new clothes. For all of us, if it comes to that. Fortunately, it's market day in Petticoat Lane, so there'll be plenty of new suits to pick and choose from."

Jenna nodded. "Good. I'll get my money belt out. I changed a lot of currency at the station. We can use that to pay for everything."

"Very well. Let's get over to Petticoat Lane, before the best bargains are gone."

Wordlessly, they set out to buy yet another set of disguises.

Chapter Ten

Margo had never placed a wire tap before.

Watching Inspector Conroy Melvyn work that morning in near darkness, her admiration for the up-time Scotland Yard detective's skill soared. He placed the tap into the telephone lines leading into the Home Office in a very short time, then rejoined her on the pavement. "Got it," he grinned. "Now when the queen telephones the Home Office this afternoon from Scotland, expressing shock over the double murders, we'll get a recording of it."

"That's great!" Margo grinned, wondering how much money the residuals for up-time broadcast of the historic phone call might land in her bank account. "What's next?" Whatever it was, it wouldn't be nearly as hair-raising as recovering their hidden equipment from the murder sites had been. Thank God the Victorian police hadn't yet carried the forensic science of crime-scene evidence very far. Not only had they failed to put a quarantine on the murder scenes, they'd allowed surgeons and coroners to disturb the bodies, wash away the blood, and Sir Charles Warren had even erased the chalked graffiti over on Goulston Street after Maybrick had slashed it across a stairwell landing. Margo could almost understand the reasoning behind the erasure, given the anti-Semitic slur Maybrick had written and the already explosive mood of the East End. To their credit, the City police had argued about it, hotly, finally forced to give in to the Metropolitan police decision to erase it before it could be seen or even photographed, since Goulston Street lay in Metropolitan Police jurisdiction.

"What next, indeed?" Inspector Melvyn mused scratching his chin thoughtfully. "I think, my dear, I'd like to be on hand at the Central News Agency when the Saucy Jack postcard arrives."

"Do you want to try videotaping Michael Kidney when he shows up at the Leman Police Station, accusing the PC on duty for his lover's murder?" Margo sympathized with the man. Poor Michael Kidney. He really had loved Elizabeth Stride, despite their stormy relationship.

"Might be a bit of a risk," the inspector frowned.

"More risky than recovering that equipment from Mitre Square?" Margo laughed nervously. "Or tapping the Home Office telephone lines?"

The inspector grinned. "Well, now you mention it . . ."

"All right, we'll try to get a video of Mr. Kidney. I'll change into East End togs before we go."

"Right."

They set out at a brisk walk for Spaldergate House. Malcolm was already in the East End, with Pavel Kostenka and Shahdi Feroz and Doug Tanglewood, studying the crowd dynamics on the streets. Margo shivered, remembering the explosive riot the day Polly Nichols' mutilations had been discovered, and was selfishly glad Malcolm had assigned her to Conroy Melvyn, rather than the Whitechapel group.

The sun rose while they walked westward down Whitehall where, tomorrow morning, a decapitated, legless, armless woman's torso would be discovered in a vaulted cellar beneath the New Scotland Yard building, still under construction. Tonight, Malcolm and Conroy Melvyn would try to place miniaturized camera equipment in the cellar to see if they could catch the perpetrator of the so-called Whitehall torso mystery and settle once and for all whether that anonymous victim had also fallen prey to the Ripper's knife.

As they walked westward, early morning paper criers were already on the streets, hawking the morning's shocking news. Church bells tolled from St. Paul's Cathedral, from Westminster Abbey and churches Margo didn't even know the names of, the sounds of the bells deep and sonorous and inexpressibly lonely in the early light. They paused and bought copies of the papers, listening to the gentlemen who gathered on street corners, men who spoke in hushed, angry tones about the horror in Mitre Square, taping the conversations with hidden microphones and the miniaturized cameras in their scouting logs.

"The *Financial News* is offering a three-hundred-pound reward for this fiend's capture," one gentleman muttered as they passed.

"The Lord Mayor's offering five hundred pounds," another said, his heavily-jowled face flushed with anger. "The government jolly well should've done so ages ago, before six women were cut to pieces, four of them in as many weeks! That Lusk fellow, with the Whitechapel Vigilance Committee, asked just yesterday for a reward to be offered, officially, by the government. And they turned him down! Now we've two more women dead . . ."

"Sir Alfred Kirby telephoned me to say he planned to offer one hundred pounds sterling and fifty militia men to help apprehend the beast, asked if I would volunteer. My wife had a fainting spell at the notion of me hunting such a madman, wouldn't hear of it . . ."

"—said he'd heard a chap named Thomas Coram found a bloodstained knife in Whitechapel Road. Ruddy thing was nine inches long! You could put a knife like that straight through a woman, God help the poor creatures. Sir Charles Warren's at his wit's end, trying to investigate, what with the City Police demanding cooperation and frothing at evidence destroyed . . ."

Conroy Melvyn murmured, "Poor Sir Charles. I feel for the chap, I do. Trying to tackle a thing like the Ripper killings, without the faintest notion of psychopathic serial-killer profiling or decent forensic science. This case breaks his career. I shouldn't want to try investigating such a thing in *my* jurisdiction, I can tell you that."

"I wonder what the coroner will do at the inquest for Elizabeth Stride?"

He shook his head grimly. "Not enough, clearly. Still, I intend to be in Cable Street when the inquest opens. Vestry Hall will be jam-packed, right enough."

Margo sighed. *Another* inquest. With descriptions of wounds and witness testimony . . . She'd almost rather be with Malcolm in the explosive East End, than trapped in a room full of shouting reporters after the gruesome details of murder and mutilation. "You know, one thing has me puzzled," she said at length. "Someone wrote an entry in the Swedish Church Parish Register that Elizabeth Stride had been murdered by Jack the Ripper. They dated the entry September thirtieth, the morning she was killed. Yet the name Jack the Ripper wasn't released publicly until today, October the first."

"I know," Melvyn sighed. "Pity we can't be everywhere, isn't it? But even with a team of us working and you lot of guides helping, we can't solve *every* mystery connected with the Ripper."

"Maybe someone who worked at the Central News Agency, who'd seen the Dear Boss letter, wrote it?"

"Or someone backdated the entry by a day," the police inspector mused. "But we'll never know, eh? What drives me batty is not identifying this bloke working with Maybrick. We've come up empty handed at every turn, trying to trace the blighter."

"Well, somebody's got to know him. Dominica Nosette and Guy Pendergast figured out who he is, I'm willing to bet on it. Whatever William Butler Yeats and his friend said, that night at the Carlton Club, Pendergast figured out who the mystery doctor was."

"Or maybe he just saw the bloody chap and followed him," Melvyn muttered, flushing with embarrassment over the affair. The police inspector had not taken it well, that a reporter had given him the slip while he'd been focused on a famous poet.

"Maybe. That might mean he could have an occult connection, if he was there on the night of the Theosophical meeting. Or even if he wasn't there, because Malcolm said you were discussing Celtic religions and other stuff that would interest someone like Yeats."

"Bloody hell . . ." The inspector's footsteps faltered as a look of surprise crossed his face.

"What?" Margo asked. "What did I say?"

"Perhaps nothing. Perhaps everything." The policeman was staring at the newspaper they'd just bought. "It's this." He tapped the newspaper, then opened it hastily, skimming one finger down the newsprint columns. "There was a lecture notice on the front page . . ." he muttered. "Jumped out at me just as you spoke about Celtic religions. There! Got it."

He held the newspaper open so she could see the article.

"Dr. John Lachley," Margo read out loud. "SoHo scholar of the occult, mesmeric physician . . ." Her eyes widened. She clutched at the policeman's sleeve. "He keeps a surgery in Cleveland Street, *in a house he calls Tibor.*"

Conroy Melvyn stared at her, mouth coming adrift. "My God! The same place our chap told Maybrick to meet him!" Then he frowned. "Cleveland Street, though? That's a bit of a distance to walk, with blood-stains on one's sleeves. Still, it's a ruddy good clue. Good job, eh what? Jolly well done, Miss Smith!"

She grinned. "You saw the article, not me."

"Which I would have failed to notice if you hadn't been reminding me of what I'd heard that night in the Carlton Club. I say, let's get back to Spaldergate post haste. I can hardly wait to spring the news on the rest of the team!"

Margo laughed. "Me, either. And wait until Malcolm hears!"

"Mr. Moore," Conroy Melvyn said, stepping to the kerb and hailing a hansom, "will quite likely insist on attending tonight's lecture."

"Hah! You couldn't keep him away with wild horses. Me, either!"

"Well said. Now, then . . . Battersea, cabbie," he said, handing Margo up into the cab which had drawn to a halt beside them, "Octavia Street. And no tricks, my good man, I've consulted Mogg's for the fare!"

"'ere, now, guv'nor," the cabbie protested, "I'm an honest man, so I am!"

Margo settled in with a grin. She'd learned the hard way to consult Mogg's map of cab fares, to avoid being cheated blind by the cabbies. Then they were rolling down Victoria Embankment at a rush, headed West for Battersea Park and an unexpected break in the Ripper case. She couldn't take full credit for the discovery, but glowed nonetheless. Just wait until Malcolm heard! And Kit!

Maybe she was cut out for this job, after all!

By the following evening, Jenna had been transformed, as had Noah and Marcus, by the acquisition of decent quality gentlemen's clothing, the sort a middle-class businessman might wear. They left the girls in the care of Mrs. Mindel, making certain that Dr. Mindel was armed and knew how to use a revolver, in case of trouble from the mobs, then walked to Threadneedle Street, the financial district in the heart of The City, to find a cab. It was impossible to hire a hansom cab anywhere in Spitalfields—not only were the residents too poor to afford the fares, cabbies were leery of robbery from East End gangs. They finally found a cab rank near the Bank of England and hired the conveyance at the front of the line. Jenna crowded in with Marcus and Noah for a jolting ride up to Picadilly and shivered at the memory of her last visit to those environs. She'd very nearly died, that night in Picadilly. *No sense dwelling on it,* she told herself firmly. *Even if I am looking for the man who shot me in cold blood.* She couldn't quite suppress a shiver, however, and earned a long, worried look from Noah, which she returned with a forced smile. When the cab finally halted, Jenna climbed down on shaking legs, hoping no one recognized her as the individual who'd jumped from a window in the Picadilly Hotel after a bloody shootout. It was one thing, hiding in anonymous Spitalfields. It was far more frightening, coming into a part of London where she'd nearly been murdered—twice.

"There's the Egyptian Hall," Noah said quietly.

The building was tall, its face decorated by elaborate stonework, including a winged scarab above a tall, rectangular window which was crowned by an ornate pediment. A sign above the door proclaimed the premises to be the Egyptian Hall, museum and meeting room. Down the street, on Picadilly's south side, she could see the immense facade of Fortnum and Mason's famous store, and down the other way, the imposing edifice which housed the Royal Institute of Painters in Water Colours. Along the north side stood the Burlington Arcade, bustling with fashionable shoppers going home for the evening. Shopkeepers were busy closing up for the night; the building loomed above them, dark and forbidding in its shadows next to Burlington House Mansion. Jenna swallowed nervously as fine carriages rattled past, drawn by well-groomed, shining horses flinging their hooves out smartly. Wealthy gentlemen strolled the pavements. Silver-headed canes gleamed in the twilight, silk top hats nodded like mobile chimney stacks, and heavy gold watches and fobs glinted as their owners checked the time. The ladies on their arms wore thick silks and fur-trimmed coats over swaying bustles; ostrich and egret feathers drooped from exquisite hats and fur muffs in fox, mink, and black sable protected their hands from the cold air. In this exquisitely upscale area, Jenna felt very downscale, drab and vulnerable in her middle-class wool and fake mutton chops.

Then Noah was leading them into the Egyptian Hall, buying tickets to the lecture and the exhibits. Signs explained the origins of the collections, which had belonged to naturalist and antiquarian William Bullock, who had built the hall in 1812. Faded photographs of General Tom Thumb, the American dwarf who had come here for a wildly popular exhibit, hung on the wall near the entrance. Other gentlemen were arriving for the talk, accompanied by a few intrepid and curious ladies. A sign with the subject of the evening's lecture directed them to the meeting room, where they found a fair crowd gathered. Voices washed through Jenna's awareness as she peered anxiously at faces, but she saw no one resembling the man who'd tried to murder her outside the Royal Opera. She consulted the thick, silver-plated pocket watch she'd purchased earlier in the afternoon, and frowned. The lecture was due to begin at any moment . . .

"Where the deuce is Lachley?" a man just behind her complained. " 'Tisn't like him to be late!"

"Perhaps," another man's voice drawled, "he's pre-occupied with that ravishing creature he took in, the other week? If I'd rescued a girl that lovely and had taken her into my home, I might be a bit distracted, as well!"

"Is it immoral liaisons you're insinuating, Crowley? Of Dr. Lachley?" The speaker's voice held a thick Irish lilt, tinged with anger.

Jenna turned to find several gentlemen watching the two speakers. The first speaker, Crowley, shrugged. "Men will be men, after all. I don't doubt the good doctor's intentions in trying to help the poor creature. But what a comely little thing she was, even if she was half crazed. It would be a simple enough, after all, to take advantage of a lady in such distress."

The other man, in his twenties, perhaps, with a fire-eaten look to his eyes, glared at Crowley. "You, sir, are contemptible! In Dublin, you would be publicly shamed for such slanderous sentiments!"

"Easy, Yeats," another young man muttered. "Crowley's infamous for baiting people with his depraved ideas. Ignore him. We do."

Crowley's eyes glinted with amusement. "Only a fool ignores the devil, sir."

The young man shrugged. "You may bill yourself as the prophet of the anti-Christ, Mr. Crowley, but you're no devil. Unless, of course, it's you ripping up these poor souls in the East End? Hardly your style, I should think. Reading a black mass over them is more in your line."

Several listening gentlemen gasped aloud, faces paling in shock, but Crowley merely smiled. "Perhaps you might join me, next time? No? Pity. Ah . . . Here's Lachley, at last."

Jenna turned quickly toward the front of the meeting room . . . and lurched. For a long, terrifying moment, the entire room circled like a washing machine on spin cycle. She knew the man who'd appeared, who stepped up to the tall lectern. The last time she'd seen him, he'd levelled a pistol at her head and pulled the trigger. Her mind reeled, partly with the implications of the conversation they'd just overheard. *If that's Lachley and Lachley's holding a young lady in his house, she can't be anyone but Ianira Cassondra!*

Dr. John Lachely was in a high state of agitation, Jenna realized as the spinning room steadied down. His color ran high and his dark eyes glinted with a touch of madness that left the fine hairs along Jenna's neck and arms standing erect. She clutched at Noah's arm. "*It's him!*"

The detective gave her a sharp stare, then gripped Marcus by the arm and forcibly held him back. Ianira's husband had started forward, fists clenched. "Not here!" Noah cautioned sharply. "We'll sit through the lecture. Then we'll follow him home."

Marcus, his own eyes a trifle wild, glared at Noah; then he glanced at the room full of eyewitnesses and subsided. "Very well," Marcus growled under his breath. "But if he has hurt her, I will kill him!"

"I'll help you," Jenna muttered. "I owe that bastard a bullet through the skull!"

"Keep your voice down!" Noah hissed. "And take a seat, for God's sake, the lecture's starting."

Jenna found herself in a chair next to the young Irishman with the fire-eaten eyes, Mr. Yeats. The name was familiar, somehow, from long ago, she couldn't quite place where or why. Yeats sat glaring across the aisle at Crowley, who listened calmly to the opening of the lecture and ignored the Irishman's furious stare. Jenna sat wrapped in her own feverish thoughts, hardly paying attention to what Lachley said, and only stirred when Yeats' friend, the other dark-haired Irishman, muttered, "What on earth can be wrong with him? I've never heard such ramblings. He doesn't make proper sense, half the time."

Yeats murmured, "I'm sure I don't know. I've never seen Dr. Lachley in such a state."

Jenna frowned and concentrated more fully on what Lachley was saying.

" . . . the Classical writers were notorious for confusing all things Celto-Gaelic with all things Germanic. I have been to Germany, to Hungary and places north. The taking of trophy skulls . . . drinking from them . . . rites of blood on oak trees . . ." Lachley's eyes were wild, his hands shaking visibly on the edges of the podium. He drew back from some hideous thought with evident difficulty and cleared his throat. "These sacrifices, yes, ancient Roman writers consistently erred. Attributed human sacrifice to ancient Celts, when such rites should more appropriately be laid at the feet of their savage and bloodthirsty northern neighbors. These Germanic tribes gave Caesar enormous difficulty, it is to be remembered. And Germanic rites and customs of the Viking period, it should be noted, included such barbaric practices as the blood eagle. A man would cut out a living victim's lungs and drape them across his back like an eagle's wings . . ."

Several women in the audience emitted cries of horror. Up at the lectern, Lachley's eyes, shining and wild with a sort of unholy pleasure, widened slightly at the shocked sounds coming from his audience. He calmed himself a little, settling into a more lucid frame of mind. "I beg pardon, ladies, but the subject is a most indelicate one. So, I cannot help but conclude that classical sources for Celtic barbarism and human sacrifice *must* be suspect. Their traditional enemies, the Romans, wished most profoundly to rule the Celts and thus cannot be trusted to have painted them with anything approaching honesty.

"The Celtic peoples therefore have been seriously maligned for the past two thousand years. They have been held up to the world by their Roman enemies as barbarians who would slaughter an innocent victim, simply to read the oracles in his death throes. Maligned and slandered, the Celts have ever since been painted villainously, when their history and many accomplishments in law and the arts prove that their rightful place in history is among the most civilized and learned peoples of the world. Their ancient magical wisdom was very nearly destroyed by systematic genocide waged against the Celts' intellectual class by their conquerors.

"This wisdom has now been recovered through the wood-carved ogham script, from hundreds of 'library sticks' bundled to form whole books, hidden away in Irish attics and cellars, and is revealed in its astonishing depth and power. This magical legacy of the Celtic peoples will certainly prove to the world at large that we, as Theosophists and students of the psychic sciences, owe a profound debt to the original inhabitants of the British Isles. We who look to the occult for spiritual guidance walk in the footsteps of true greatness and surely shall rule the world for centuries to come!"

Lachley was trembling at the podium, eyes glowing with a hideous passion that left Jenna queasy and cold. He surveyed his audience, then gave a mocking little bow. "Thank you, this concludes my lecture for the evening."

The applause was thunderous, the entire hall surging to its feet in a spontaneous ovation. Dr. John Lachley bathed in the glory of the moment, bowing and stepping back from the lectern, raising his hands in a show of humility which he was clearly far from feeling. His smile was almost manic as he stepped down and shook hands with luminaries from society and the arts, bowed over the hands of great society matrons and ladies of more dubious reputation, mystics and mediums who had come to hear him speak on the popular subject of Celtic occultism, allowed himself to be congratulated by journalists who wished to interview him . . .

Jenna felt sick, trapped in the same room with him. "Noah, we have to find out where he lives."

At her side, the young Irishman named Yeats gave a start and turned toward her. "Are you ill, sir?" he asked at once. "Dr. Lachley keeps a surgery in Cleveland Street, of course, but I daresay I wouldn't go near it. The man's raving, tonight. I've never seen him in such a state."

Jenna took a risk. "Do you know anything about the girl that man Crowley was talking about?"

Yeats frowned, his intense eyes turning frosty. "No. And I don't care to discuss filth with you, sir."

Noah spoke up. "You misunderstand. Our friend, here," he nodded toward Marcus, "is searching for his wife. She was the victim of foul play. This gentleman," the detective nodded toward Jenna, "was escorting her from the docks the night of her arrival in London and was set upon, shot nearly to death. We are merely hoping that Dr. Lachley may help us. We've reason to believe he witnessed the lady's abduction. Cleveland Street, you said? Thank you, sir. We'll meet the good doctor there, no need to bother him now, while he's busy with the lecture audience."

Noah hustled them out of the hall, rushing Jenna and Marcus through the darkened museum, its collection of oddities and antiquities looming like something out of a horror flick. They finally reached the street. Picadilly was brightly lit, jammed with carriages as the fashionable and wealthy of London took to the streets in search of diverting entertainment. "We'll have to reach his house before he returns," Noah said grimly. "She must be there. We'll break in and carry her out by force if the servants object. Hurry, there's a cab rank further along."

Please, let this work, Jenna prayed. *And let Ianira be all right . . .*

After three weeks in Dr. Lachley's mad care, Jenna didn't see how she could be.

Malcolm Moore enjoyed dressing to the nines, particularly when Margo was able to dress the part as his lady companion. She looked stunning in watered silk the color of pale lilacs, with several yards of skirt trailing down over a swaying bustle and her fiery hair augmented by a hairpiece from Connie Logan, which allowed her to imitate the upswept coiffeurs popular with stylish ladies.

"My dear," he murmured as he handed her down from the gatehouse carriage to the pavement of Picadilly, "I shall be the envy of every gentleman who sees you."

She blushed. "Nonsense, sir," she said, glancing toward Shahdi Feroz.

Behind them, Inspector Conroy Melvyn was handing down the Ripper scholar, whose exotic beauty was so striking, she captured the attention of several passing gentlemen; but Dr. Feroz held far less appeal for Malcolm than Margo's fresh enthusiasm and sparkling, lively green eyes. "Nevertheless," he offered his arm, escorting her toward the Egyptian Hall, which stood opposite Bond Street's terminus, where their carriage had dropped them, "you are quite a fetching sight. Inspector," he turned to the policeman, "Madame Feroz, the lecture awaits."

"Well," Margo smiled, glancing at Shahdi Feroz as they crossed Picadilly through heavy carriage traffic, "it is a relief from East End rags, isn't it?"

Dr. Feroz chuckled. "Indeed, Miss Smith. A welcome relief."

The police inspector grinned as Malcolm purchased tickets for the lecture. He and Melvyn escorted the ladies inside, where a sizeable crowd had already gathered. Frock-coated gentlemen and elegant ladies murmured pleasantries while they waited for the speaker to put in appearance. Malcolm steered the way toward a far corner, where he and Margo could watch newcomers while remaining unobserved, themselves. Conroy Melvyn and Shahdi Feroz strolled through the room, circulating through the crowd, speaking to such luminaries as Madame Blavatsky and filming the event through concealed cameras. They had been waiting for perhaps six or seven minutes when Margo clutched at Malcolm's arm, denting his fine woolen sleeve with her nails. *"Look!"* She was staring toward the entrance, where three gentlemen had just appeared. "My God, *it's Marcus!*"

He frowned. "Surely you're mistaken?" One of the trio did, indeed, look very much like Ianira Cassondra's missing husband. Yet there was too much grey in his hair and he'd aged in other ways, with a deep-set look of fear and frustration etched into his features. Then Malcolm noticed the mutton-chopped gentleman at his side and stiffened. "Great Scott! That may or may not be Marcus, but the chap with him is most certainly Benny Catlin!"

"It is, too, Marcus," she insisted stubbornly. "If

somebody were trying to kill me and my whole family, I might've gone grey overnight, too! But what's he doing in London with Benny Catlin? And who's that guy with them?"

"You do have your camera running, don't you?" Malcolm whispered, referring to the tiny digital video-camera hidden beneath Margo's elegant bustle, its wire snaking up her back to a miniature lens concealed in her brooch.

"I turned it on while we were still in the carriage." When Malcolm started to move closer, she grasped his arm. "*No!*"

He glanced down, surprised.

"If Marcus spots you, wanna bet he'll bolt? He could've called on friends for help while he was still on the station, but he didn't. After everything that's happened, he'll be too terrified, Malcolm, to trust anyone."

"Anyone except Benny Catlin," Malcolm growled. "I'd like to know the reason for that."

"So would I. If they're in London, want to bet Ianira and the girls are, too?"

"No bets," Malcolm shook his head. "But how the deuce did they slip through the Britannia without tickets?"

"That Time Tours driver who was shot, up at the Picadilly Hotel, said Benny Catlin smuggled a woman through in his luggage. We've been assuming she was another student who couldn't get a ticket, or maybe that she and Benny were actually reporters. But what if that woman was Ianira Cassondra? And maybe Marcus and the girls were in some of the other trunks and got out before the police opened the luggage?"

"However they got here," Malcolm said quietly, "the main question is why they would come with two gentlemen they hardly know. It doesn't look to me like Marcus is here against his will."

"No, it doesn't look that way to me, either."

"Oh, bother!" Malcolm said abruptly, noticing another newcomer. "That's all we need, tonight!"

"What?"

"Those gentlemen who just came in? Mr. William Butler Yeats and Mr. Bevin O'Downett. Poets over from Dublin. I know them both, slightly. Met them at the Carlton Club the night Guy Pendergast and Dominica Nosette vanished. Mr. O'Downett and I have scraped acquaintance before. I certainly don't want them to recognize me and draw attention while Marcus and Catlin are standing right there!"

"Then sit down," Margo said reasonably. "You're less conspicuous in a chair than you are head-and-shoulders above me."

Malcolm seated himself with alacrity, turning slightly in the chair so that he sat with his back to the group near the door. It was frustrating, having to sit there, unable to see what was happening, but Margo's eyes were sharp and she was recording the entire evening. She murmured, "Looks like Mr. Yeats is getting into an argument with somebody."

Malcolm risked a quick glance. "Aleister Crowley. Good God, and there's Robert Donston Stevenson. Is the entire occult community of London here tonight?"

"Wouldn't surprise me," Margo muttered. "Not to mention a real convention of Ripper suspects." Then she dug fingers into his shoulder. "Look!" She was staring raptly toward the front of the room. The speaker had just arrived to take the lectern.

Malcolm gasped, staring at Jack the Ripper. "*My God!*" he whispered, voice hushed. "It *is* him!"

"Don't look now," Margo hissed, "but Benny Catlin looks like he just saw a ghost!"

Malcolm glanced around cautiously, just in time to see the unknown gentleman with Catlin grasp Marcus

by the arm, holding him back forcibly. The ex-slave's
fists were clenched. A look of murderous rage had
swept his face.

"What the devil is going on?" Malcolm wondered.
"Why would Marcus be so angry with . . . Oh, dear
God." He saw the possibility in a sudden tightening
of his gut.

"Oh, no," Margo protested, voice cracking slightly.
"Not Ianira?"

At the front of the room, Dr. John Lachley began
his lecture. Margo sat down hastily as the rest of the
assembly settled into chairs. Malcolm scarcely took in
what Lachley was saying, as his mind was racing down
unpleasant corridors of conjecture. How had Marcus
and Ianira run afoul of Jack the Ripper? They must be
living somewhere in the East End. Yet Ianira was not
among the Ripper victims, all of whom were frightfully
well known.

Perhaps he'd killed her and they'd discovered the
body, maybe buried her themselves, rather than risk the
public scrutiny of a police investigation? Or perhaps—
and he swallowed hard, at the thought—perhaps the
Whitehall torso, due to be discovered on October 3rd,
was Ianira? He tried to shut out such a vision, even in
imagination, but he couldn't think what other reason
Marcus might have for wanting to murder Jack the
Ripper.

A swift glance toward Margo prompted him to settle
his arm about her shoulders. She was crying, silently,
wiping away the tears with trembling hands. Clearly, her
thoughts had wandered down the same hideous corridors
his had just done. She looked up and tried to smile, then
her face crumpled and she covered it with both hands,
trying to compose herself. Malcolm clenched his jaw and
stared coldly at Dr. John Lachley, loathing him with a
far more personal hatred than he could ever have

mustered for a mere psychotic serial killer. If this man had truly destroyed Ianira Cassondra . . .

With a bleakness like death, Malcolm realized there wasn't a great deal anyone could do about it. Jack the Ripper could not be killed. Not until Mary Kelly had died, if then. It gradually occurred to Malcolm to wonder why Dominica Nosette and Guy Pendergast weren't here. Surely the reporters would've tried to film such a historic lecture, given by the Ripper? Blast those two! They'd trailed Maybrick last night, wandering into camera range at all three key sites: Dutfield's Yard, Mitre Square, and Goulston Street. Had they met with misfortune in the process of tailing Maybrick and Lachley?

He narrowed his gaze, wondering abruptly why Dr. Lachley seemed so manic, up at the podium. Perhaps he was always a disjointed, rambling speaker? A glance at the crowd suggested otherwise. Several listeners looked puzzled, even concerned as they watched Lachley, who was literally trembling behind the lectern. A few were whispering among themselves, clearly wondering about it.

Mysteries on top of mysteries . . .

Lachley ended the lecture abruptly, a wild look in his eyes as the audience applauded, giving him a standing ovation that was, perhaps, out of line with the quality of his oration, but which was a strong testament to the popularity and power of the Celtic revival sweeping through nineteenth-century British society. Malcolm surged to his feet, as well, trying to keep Lachley in sight as the man stepped down into the crowd, shaking hands. Malcolm caught sight of Shahdi Feroz speaking briefly with Lachley and knew a moment's worry for her safety, despite Conroy Melvyn's presence at her side, then glanced back to where Marcus and the others sat . . . and swore aloud.

"Bloody hell! They've gone!"

"What?"

"Marcus and Catlin! They've gone!"

Malcolm shoved his way impatiently through the audience, trying to reach the door. Margo struggled gamely behind him. Malcolm reached the street well before she did, but Catlin and his group were nowhere in sight. Margo, out of breath from running in her form-fitting watered silk, skidded to a halt beside him. "I'm sorry!" she wailed. "I was too short to see over everybody's heads and didn't notice them leave!"

He stood breathing hard for a moment, wrestling his anger under control, then said, "Let's get back inside, blast it! The least we can do is trace Lachley!"

"Malcolm, it isn't your fault."

"No, but it is, too. We were charged with locating Catlin as well as tasked with identifying the Ripper. And the future of the station is far more seriously affected by Catlin's disappearance than any of our work verifying the Ripper's identity."

"I know," she said in a small voice. "At least we know Catlin's alive, now," she said with grim determination, "which is better news than we thought we might end up with, after following that horrible blood trail across London. You know," she said suddenly, frowning in concentration, "if Benny Catlin and Marcus have it in for John Lachley, they might try to ambush him at his house."

Malcolm shot her a startled glance. "Good God, Margo. You're onto something, there."

"So what do we do about it?"

He frowned. "We collect Madame Feroz and Chief Inspector Melvyn, before we do anything. Then perhaps we'd best follow Lachley home? If Catlin and Marcus *are* there, they'll be in far greater danger than Lachley will, because *he* jolly well can't be killed."

Margo's face, already pinched with worry, drained

white in a single heartbeat. "Malcolm, we have to find them!"

"Get back inside, warn Madame Feroz and Inspector Melvyn that we may need to leave in a hurry. The Spaldergate carriage isn't due to collect us for another thirty minutes. I'll find some sort of transport to hire, so we can follow Lachley."

"Right." She hurried into the Egyptian Hall, lifting her skirts to make running easier. Malcolm swore under his breath, then headed down Picadilly in search of a cab that would hold all four of them. He worked very hard to dispel the vision of what would happen if Marcus tangled with Jack the Ripper. He had a sinking feeling that neither Dominica Nosette nor Guy Pendergast would ever be seen again. He didn't want that happening to anyone he called friend. If he'd thought he could persuade Margo to return to Spaldergate, he'd have packed her off immediately. But he knew only too well the futility of trying, so he set his jaw and vowed to do what he could to ensure that no more of his charges ended up missing or dead.

So far, in this lethal little game they played, Jack the Ripper had won every round.

Jenna stood in the shadows beside the garden wall behind Dr. John Lachley's house in Cleveland Street, clutching the Beale's revolver she'd brought with her from New York, and waited in a swivet for Noah to reappear. The detective had forced a window casement at the rear of the house and was searching quietly for any trace of Ianira Cassondra. Across the street, Marcus waited to give the alarm, should Lachley arrive before Noah finished the search.

Come on, she breathed silently, *what's taking so long?* She expected Dr. Lachley to return at any moment, expected to hear a scuffle break out inside, terrified that Lachley's manservant, whom they'd spotted in the front parlour, would hear Noah's footsteps and go to investigate. *If he's got a telephone in there, he might even summon the police!* That's all they'd need, to be arrested by London's constabulary for thievery of a respected physician's home.

When Marcus' whistle of warning came, Jenna's heart thundered into her throat. She melted back into the high, walled garden as a carriage rattled and clattered into the drive, coach lanterns gleaming in the darkness. Jenna trembled as she flattened against the inside of the wall, pistol clutched in one fist. *He's back! Oh, God, he's back and Noah's still inside!* She heard Lachley's voice, giving instructions to his coachman to stable the horse, then the carriage-entrance door opened and closed with a rattle and thump and Lachley was inside. She waited, not even breathing, for the shouts to erupt as Noah was discovered . . .

"Hsst! Come on, kid! Let's move!"

She swallowed a scream and nearly went to the ground as Noah materialized from the darkness of the garden. "Noah!"

The detective grasped her arm and led her rapidly through the gate, which they eased closed, then jogged down the carriage drive, slipping past the open stable door. They reached Cleveland Street without being spotted and headed for Marcus. Jenna glanced over her shoulder toward Lachley's home, where lights were coming up in various windows, as Noah began to speak, voice lowered to a whisper. "It's quite clear Ianira was held in an upstairs room for some time. Not only are there toiletries for a lady and clothing of Ianira's size, there are long, dark hairs matching Ianira's, caught in the hairbrush. She is not, however, in the house now. He's moved her. Where, we must discover."

Jenna's heart sank. Marcus' face ran pale in the light

from a distant gas lamp. Then Jenna started. "Look! He's coming out again."

They glanced around quickly, even as Noah herded them all into the darkness of a neighboring yard. Lachley had, indeed, emerged through the carriage drive entrance. Dressed in rough clothes, with an old felt hat pulled low over his brow, hiding his face in shadow, he set out on foot, walking swiftly down Cleveland Street, then turned and headed toward the distant river.

The moment he vanished from view, Noah darted across the road. Jenna and Marcus exchanged glances, then ran after the detective at top speed. They passed a carriage where two gentlemen were involved in a domestic dispute with their wives over a stray muff, then moved steadily eastward, leaving behind the fashionable districts. They came out on a street Jenna recognized as Drury Lane, the same street Noah had carried her down the night Lachley had shot her.

They followed Drury Lane for its entire length and burst out eventually onto the Strand, where they plunged into a maelstrom of shoving, shouting men and boys on Fleet Street. Gradually, they angled toward Bishopsgate and the East End. Jenna wasn't used to so much walking and struggled gamely to keep up, crossing busy Commercial Street into the heart of Whitechapel, then moving south down Brick Lane, past breweries that left the air smelling of spilt beer, past brick-making factories where giant kilns glowed hellishly in the darkness, fire-curing bricks by the millions. They headed down toward Flower and Dean Street, where women strolled the streets mostly alone, a few walking in pairs or small clusters, their eyes bright with fear and misery, soliciting rough-dressed men who emerged from pubs and gin palaces and gambling hells.

Past Flower and Dean, Lachley took them into a narrow alleyway between ramshackle doss houses. A

stink of urine rose like a miasma. Jenna closed her hand
around the butt of her pistol, which she'd thrust deep into
her coat pocket. They moved steadily down the narrow
way, boots squelching in mud and God alone knew what
else. Jenna certainly didn't want to know. Halfway along,
Lachley interrupted a streetwalker and her customer in
the midst of the transaction for which she was being
paid. Mercifully, Jenna caught only a glimpse of white
thighs under the woman's hiked up skirts as Lachley
shoved past, with curses flung after him.

"Sod off, y'bloody feather plucker, or I'll shove me
beetle crusher up yer Kyber Parse!"

To which Lachley flung back, "Don't threaten me,
y'stroppy brass nail!"

Fortunately, the angry prostitute was far too occupied—
and so was her client—to offer any real trouble, not even
when Noah plunged past, leading the pursuit. Lachley
stalked steadily southward, toward the distant river,
down past garment factories where gaslights burned
to illuminate rows of sewing machines. Tailors and
sweat-shop seamstresses worked in such factories for
twelve and sixteen-hour shifts, six days a week, churning
out ready-made clothing for an empire. Jenna thanked
God they hadn't been forced to take up such work to
keep from starving.

*What's a respectable doctor like John Lachley doing
skulking around the East End? Unless . . .* Jenna blinked
in sudden, startled conjecture. *Unless he's Jack the
Ripper! Oh, my God, the facts fit! Poor Ianira! Is she
even still alive?*

They barrelled through a crowd of men gathered on
a street corner, talking loudly about what ought to be
done about the maniac stalking women on these streets.
"Sorry," Noah doffed his hat as angry protests rose on
all sides, "don't want any bother, we're on the trail of
a missing lady . . ."

"Ah, gwan, y'sozzled face-ache," one of the angry men flung after them, "better keep goin' clappers or I'm like to put me bunch o' fives in yer mince!"

As Jenna shoved her way through in Noah's wake, one of the other men muttered, "Button it, Albert, an' lay off the gin, you're drunk as a boiled owl. It's clear they got trouble, all right, Gawd 'elp if it's this bleedin' Ripper again . . ." A block further on, a Salvation Army quartet blared away into the damp night while a frowsy woman with three children half-hidden in her skirts listened intently to the singers. The music sounded like a spiritualized rewrite of an old drinking song, "What Can You Do with a Drunken Sailor?" but included the unlikely refrain, "Anybody here like a sneaking Judas?"

Further along, a shouting match broke out between two very drunken sailors and the badly dressed women who accompanied them. One of the girls, who couldn't have been above thirteen years of age, was pulling a long swig from a gin bottle. Jenna wanted to avert her gaze as they rushed past, but she'd seen worse since arriving in the East End—and was afraid she'd see far worse, yet, before this night ended.

As Noah took them around a corner, an angry roar of voices erupted behind them. Jenna glanced back to see an immense crowd of men burst from a side street and utterly engulf the sailors, their hired girls, and the Salvation Army quartet. They were shouting about the Ripper, making demands and ugly threats that left Jenna intensely grateful they'd missed being swept up with the rioters. She turned and hurried after Noah. Lachley, still oblivious to their pursuit, led them down into Wapping where they encountered two neatly dressed, earnest young men with American accents. The Americans were speaking with a group of women and ragged children.

"No, ladies, the golden tablets of Moroni don't set

aside the Bible, not at all. They are only Christ's revelation of His word in the New World, translated by His prophet Joseph Smith. Here, let me read from this pamphlet, it will help explain the new gospel . . ."

They passed the Mormons, still moving south, and walked all the way to Pennington Street, where enormous brick warehouses lined the road. Jenna could smell the stink of the river. Just beyond the warehouses lay the great London Docks, with the enormous Western Basin closest to them now. The smaller and older St. Katharine's Docks lay to their immediate west, cut into the reeking earth of Wapping, so that streets ended abruptly at the waterside, with immense ships pulled up like cars parked along the kerb. Lachley ignored the docks and led them east, deeper into Wapping. *Did he take her on board a ship?* Jenna wondered. *What would be the point? Unless he's leaving England?* Fear skittered through her nerves.

They left Pennington Street three blocks further along, winding back into filthy, crowded alleyways north of the warehouses. Sailors thronged the streets, shoving their way roughly into stinking pubs and gambling dens, brawling in the middle of the road, singing boistrously in as many as five languages within two blocks' distance. Hollow-cheeked, dull-eyed children sat along the kerb, begging for a few pence. And still Lachley led them back into the maze, past groups of furtive men who eyed them, considered it, then thought better after weighing the odds.

And finally, at one of the sagging, broken-windowed houses along a street where gaslights were as rare as police constables and chickens' teeth, Lachley finally stopped. He unlocked a door and vanished into a tumbledown brick house with filthy, broken glass windows. These were dark. The house was silent, seemingly deserted. Jenna glanced at Noah, then Marcus. "What now?"

Noah was frowning thoughtfully at the door. "If we annouce ourselves, it might provoke him into panic-stricken, drastic action. I don't want to give him time for that."

The detective tested the door gently, then backed up and smashed his booted foot against the heavy panel. The lock splintered on the second try. Jenna dragged her pistol out of her pocket and rushed in on Noah's heels. Marcus brought up the rear. They found a cheerless room empty of anything save bits of refuse and appalling drifts of filth along the floor. A swift search, downstairs and up, revealed only one inhabitant: an enormous black hound chained in a room near the back of the house. The dog had been dead for a couple of days, judging from the stench. Beside the hideous, putrifying corpse lay a rug someone had turned back. And under the rug could be seen the outlines of a trap door.

"Right," Noah said briskly, pulling up the trap.

Marcus helped lift the planks while Jenna gulped back nausea. Stone steps, damp brick walls, the smell and splash of water . . . They could hear Lachley's footsteps receding quickly and Jenna caught a faint flicker of light at the bottom of the hole, which vanished a moment later. Noah glanced up into Jenna's eyes. The gun in Noah's hand looked like part of the detective's arm, an organic piece that had grown there, like the fine hairs on the back of Noah's wrist and the chipped nails that tipped short, strong fingers. "I'd feel better if you stayed here."

"I ain't no weed," she muttered, quoting the girl who delivered their milk every morning. "And if you tell me to stay here, well, then, same t'you, wiv brass knobs on . . ."

Noah frowned. "You're picking up the slang pretty well, aren't you? But that doesn't make you a match for a thing like Lachley. He's a bloody dangerous bastard. Stay behind me."

"No argument, there," she muttered.

Marcus found a stub of candle in a battered tin holder beside the bed and a wooden box with matches, printed with the trade name Lucifers. Marcus lit the candle and handed it to Noah, who led the way down the narrow stone steps. Marcus pocketed the matches and Jenna edged down the steps next, leaving Marcus to bring up rear guard. The stink of decay and filthy water clouted her nostrils well before her feet touched the wet floor below. There was no cellar, as Jenna had been expecting. They were standing in a brick tunnel, its arched roof clotted with cobwebs and stained with poisonous patches of mold and lichen. Water trickled and dripped in the distance.

"What kind of place is this?" Jenna breathed.

"Sewer tunnel, I'd guess," Noah answered, the whisper harsh and strained. "Lachley knows his way around, that's clear." They couldn't see Lachley's lantern, but his footsteps came with a faint echo from further along the sewer tunnel. Jenna stared into the pitchy darkness, then swallowed as Noah set out with soft-footed stealth. She cast a doubtful glance at Marcus, whose eyes were tortured. But they hadn't much choice. Jenna clutched her revolver, the grip solid and reassuring against her palm, and eased forward, trying to walk without her footsteps splashing. Jenna strained to catch the faintest echo of sound in the clammy darkness, but heard only the distant rush of water and Lachley's sharp, clattering footsteps far ahead. The sound ran away down the tunnels, leaving Jenna biting her lip.

"Hsst!"

At that sharp sound from Noah, Jenna froze. Her lungs rasped in the silence and her heart slammed against her ribs. Sweat, cold and dank as the putrid air, clung to hair and skin and eyelashes. She listened . . .

"Bloody bitch!" A man's voice echoed through the sewers, fierce with some nameless rage that left the tiny hairs along Jenna's nape and arms starkly erect. Her fingers tightened of their own volition around the butt of her gun. A bloodcurdling scream, high and ragged, pierced the blackness. A woman's scream . . .

The woman was sobbing out, "Don't kill me, please, I won't tell anyone you're the Ripper, please, just let me go home!" The woman's voice, clearly British, shook on a wild note of despair.

"That is not Ianira," Marcus breathed.

"What time does the gate go?" Lachley's voice . . .

"I don't know!"

"What time was it when you came through, then?"

A choked-off cry of pain floated through the sewer tunnels. "About—about eight o'clock, I think . . . it was just dusk . . . oh, God, please . . . *no!*"

She screamed again, high, ragged. The sound cut off hideously. Jenna stood trembling, torn between the need to stay hidden and the need to rush forward, to stop whatever ghastly torture was underway. A moment later another sound drifted through the sewers, a sound Jenna couldn't identify at first. Heavy, rhythmic thumps, a grating, scraping sound, like someone hacking apart a cow's carcass. Jenna covered her mouth with the back of one shaking hand. Then they heard footfalls and a heavy thump that echoed like a door closing.

Someone was moving through the sewers toward them, splashing quickly through the water. For a long, horrible moment, Jenna thought he was coming back toward them. Noah blew out the candle, plunging them into a terrifying darkness. Lachley's footsteps approached to within a frightful distance, accompanied by a lantern's dim glow, then faded once more, moving away down another route and disappearing back into the maze of sewer tunnels.

Jenna discovered that she was shaking violently. Minutes crawled past in the utter blackness of the stinking sewer while doubt and fear banged around the inside of her skull like screaming, imprisoned monkeys. The echoes of Lachley's footsteps had long since faded, but still they didn't move, scarcely daring to breathe. At last, Noah shifted. The detective whispered, "Marcus, let's have a lucifer, please." A match flared and Marcus relit the candle.

Light sprang up, yellow and warm and glorious, revealing ashen faces. Jenna swallowed hard, hands trembling visibly. "Wherever he was torturing that poor woman, it's not far."

"He closed a door of some kind," Noah mused. "Perhaps another trap door. We'll try to find it and see if he's hidden Ianira down here with his other captive."

A cross-tunnel intersected their own. Noah turned left, opposite the direction Lachley had taken. Jenna cast worried glances back over her shoulder every few seconds, terrified the monstrous killer behind them would turn and come back, having heard their footsteps. Her hand sweat on the grip of her pistol despite the chill in the foetid air. Jenna knew her gun was useless against Jack the Ripper. He *couldn't* be killed tonight, not before Mary Kelly died, more than a month in the future. But it was all she had and just holding it made her feel slightly less panic-stricken.

"Well, blow me for a game of soldiers . . ." Noah muttered.

The low-voiced exclamation brought Jenna around. "What is it?"

"An iron door! Locked tight as a drum."

The low door had been set back into an alcove. Clearly, John Lachley had come from behind that door.

Jenna tested it, searched for a lock, realized that without a key, they would never get in. The hinge-pins were on the inside, so they couldn't even lift the door off. "What we need is a key."

"We'll have to make do with a lockpick," Noah muttered. "I've cultivated the habit of carrying a set, during the past three years. With your father's killers on our trail, we've occasionally needed a fast entrance into a hiding place. Fortunately," the detective fished into a coat pocket, coming out with a set of burglar's tools and crouching before the door, slipping them expertly into the keyhole, "Victorian locks are generally large, clumsy, and easy to open." Marcus held the candle close to the lock, giving Noah the best light available. The lockpicks scraped and scratched inside the iron door, then something grated and clicked.

"Got it!"

The sudden silence was thick with tension.

The heavy door swung noiselessly open, which spoke of constant oiling and maintenance in this damp environment. Surprisingly, the room beyond was not dark. Gas jets in the floor lit a scene from someone's private version of hell. Jenna's skin crawled as she stepped across the threshold, following Noah. She choked the instant she was inside. The sickly odor of rotting meat struck her like a physical blow. The stench permeated the air, foul and thick. When she saw what lay on the floor, Jenna realized with a shock of horror what the stink actually was.

"Oh, my God!"

Somebody had spilled a great deal of blood in this room. And pieces of at least two fresh corpses had been stacked up beside the door like cordwood. Arms, legs, gobbets she couldn't readily identify. And two severed heads, a dark-haired man's and a blonde-haired woman's. They rested on a work bench which stretched beneath cupboards along one long wall, sightless eyes staring at the door, faces set in ghastly expressions of terror and agony. White robes hung from a hook set into the bricks. Dark brown stains were visible across the sleeves and front. A stone pedestal that looked very much like an altar stood in the middle of the room. On top was another severed head, its flesh and hair still rotting off the bones. From what little remained, it looked like it had once belonged to a young boy, a teenager. An enormous tree trunk, with many of its major branches intact, took up at least half the space. Iron brackets and bands held the tree together where it had been sawn apart to get it into the room. Ianira, hands bound above her head, hung naked from an iron hook set into one enormous branch, limp and unconscious, her ribcage barely lifting with her shallow breaths. Gas jets at the base of the tree shone across her skin.

"Oh, sweet Mother Mary . . ." Noah whispered, voice harsh.

Marcus had already whipped off his coat, was lifting Ianira down and wrapping her nude body gently in its folds. Jenna, keeping her jaw tightly clenched, found a knife on the work table and used it to slice through the ropes on Ianira's wrists. Marcus was smoothing hair back from his wife's brow, trying to rouse her.

"She's been drugged," Noah said tersely. "I can smell the chloroform."

"Bastard!" Marcus snarled. "I will put a bullet through him!"

Noah said tersely, "Just now, our business is getting the hell out of here before the maniac who owns this place comes back."

The detective stepped to the door and peered into the darkness while Jenna pressed one hand against her mouth, struggling desperately not to throw up. The blonde woman must have been the one who'd screamed.

And they'd just stood there, listening, while he hacked her apart . . . She bolted past Noah into the darkness of the sewer tunnel and threw up in the murky water against the far wall. The slight current washed the mess away, even as she shuddered and choked again. Noah bent over her shoulder. "You all right?" the detective asked worriedly.

She nodded, and finally managed to straighten up. "Sorry," she whispered, wiping her mouth. "Couldn't help it."

"God, no," the detective managed through clenched teeth. Noah looked very near to being ill, as well. Marcus carried his wife out of the stinking chamber. Noah closed the door and fiddled with the lock again. "Think I'll leave it the way we found it. Let him sweat, wondering how a drugged victim got out of a locked room. Ought to bother the hell out of him."

"If it's all the same to you," Jenna said through chattering teeth, "I'd just as soon not go back through his house in Wapping. I don't want to meet him coming back, not for anything in this world."

Noah's glance was keen. "I couldn't agree more." The detective peered both ways down the tunnel through narrowed eyes. "We must be near the river. We weren't all that far from London Docks when we climbed down those steps. With the distance and direction we came, the Thames must be close by, off that way." Noah pointed at the wall behind them. "Western Basin's probably off that direction, so I'd say we need to go that way." Noah nodded down the tunnel opposite the direction they'd come.

"Let's go, then," Marcus said quietly. "We need to get Ianira to safety and have Doctor Mindel look at her."

It was a silent and tense group that set out through the maze of sewer tunnels beneath the East End's filthy streets, searching for a way out.

Chapter Eleven

John Lachley carried Dominica Nosette's hacked up torso a long way through the sewer tunnels. The bundle he'd slung over one shoulder was heavy and he paused frequently to shift it, but Lachley never considered simply dumping it and turning back. He wanted to leave her somewhere appropriate and had tumbled to just the perfect spot. When he finally reached the place, he paused, listening to the rumble of carriage traffic through a grating overhead, then smiled and turned off into a freshly-broken opening in the sewer. The vaulted space in which he found himself was destined to become part of the cellar of New Scotland Yard. The police headquarters, still under construction, was directly overhead.

Lachley smiled to himself and dumped the butchered remains of his pathetic little journalist where workmen would find her, then tipped his cloth hat. "Ta, luv." He grinned, using the voice of his childhood. "I'm obliged, Miss Nosette, that I am."

Then he set out the way he'd come, whistling jauntily

to himself. The tunnels he followed to reach Tibor snaked and twisted in multiple directions, following gas mains and sewage flows and underground streams bricked over, odd corners and chambers formed out of the remnant cellars of sixteenth and seventeenth, even eighteenth century warehouses and wharfside pubs, all connected like gladiator tunnels beneath an ancient fighting arena. As he walked, he planned exactly what he would do when he carried Ianira to Spaldergate House.

He'd kept the identification papers and cards he'd found in Miss Nosette's possession, as well as those from the recently deceased Mr. Pendergast's pockets. Lachley was quite confident that no one would notice the switch in a dark garden. He would rush in, carrying Ianira, claim to be Pendergast and babble out some story about being attacked by the Ripper, then simply carry her through into the station. He could hardly wait to see what the station was really like. With Ianira in his power, there was no limit to what he could do in such a place.

When he reached Lower Tibor, John Lachley was in exceedingly high spirits.

He set his lantern down with a faint splash. The iron key from his pocket grated in the lock, which clicked open. He slid the key back into his coat, then stooped to retrieve his lantern. The door opened silently at his touch, swinging back on its well-oiled hinges. Light from the perpetual flames burning in the gas jets at the altar welcomed him home again . . .

And John Lachley froze halfway through the door. She was gone.

He literally could not take it in, could not comprehend the emptiness his senses told him existed in the room. He had left her hanging from the iron hook in the great branch above the altar, the hook he'd dangled Morgan from, the night that miserable little sod had

died, had left her hanging as naked as he'd left the
boy, bound and drugged senseless. There was no humanly
possible way she could have freed herself from the
ropes and the iron hook, much less escape from a brick
vault with only one door in or out. And that iron door
had been firmly locked, the lock not forced in any way
he could see. Yet she was undeniably gone.

Nothing in this chamber could have provided hiding
space for a child, let alone a full-grown woman. He
stood there with his hand uplifted against the cold iron
of the open door, gaze jerking from shelf to cabinet
to altar and up to the massive tree trunk and back to
the shelves again. *How had she gotten out?* The key
in his pocket was not a standard iron skeleton key. It
would've taken a master locksmith to slip this lock. Or
a duplicate key. Or an extremely talented thief. Had
someone broken in here, then, and carried her off?
Who?

He could not conceive of a master locksmith having
sufficient motive to pick his way through a maze of sewer
tunnels until stumbling across this one particular alcove,
to open a locked iron door. It simply wasn't *reasonable*.
Common locksmiths didn't have the imagination to
attempt such a thing! And why would a thief have
ventured here? There'd been nothing in that entire
house in Wapping worth stealing, if a thief had come
down that way. A duplicate key, then? That was even
more absurd than the other possible explanations. Take
a wax impression, create a mould, cast a key, all in a
single hour's time, with the owner of this door likely to
return at any moment, irate and possibly murderous?

The longer he pursued a sane explanation, the faster
sanity ran through his fingers like the dirty water under
his feet. Lachley's drugged captive simply could not
have gotten out. But she had. And Lachley's greatest
refuge, the result of years of labour and intensive

study—his very *life* if this place were connected with the deaths of the whores—everything he had built was now threatened, because the bitch had *gotten out!*

The explosion jolted the very bedrock of his sanity.

Fury was an expanding fireball inside him, an anarchist's bomb, a Fenian detonation that sent him plunging across the room, hands so violently unsteady he dropped the lantern with a crash of broken glass and spreading lamp oil. He searched places too small for a mouse to hide, but found no trace of her. A knife had been moved from his workbench and used by *someone* to cut through the ropes on her wrists, ropes he found abandoned on the floor. Someone must have followed him down, picked the lock while he was out.

Lachley swore savagely. He had been so careful, confound it, so bloody careful . . . Had someone recognized him, after all? Recognized the heavily moustachioed man in seedy clothes as the thin and seething boy he'd once been in these streets? Lachley had barely gone twenty when he'd last walked Wapping and Whitechapel, passing himself off as parlour mediumist Johnny Anubis. But who else *could* it have been, if not some god-cursed tea leaf who'd grass on his own loving wife, if a reward might be involved?

He halfway expected to find all of Scotland Yard crouched in the tunnel beyond the open door to Tibor, billycocks at the ready. What he found was a black expanse of dripping brick tunnel, silent and cold as a tomb, just as he'd left it. Lachley stood motionless, gazing at the ruin of his sanctuary, breathing hard and trying to think what he should do. Going home might be fatal. Whether an East Ender had recognized him as Jack the Ripper or the girl's husband had trailed him down here, whoever had taken Ianira had discovered enough to hang Lachley from the nearest gallows. He had to get out of London. Before the police *did* trace him. Well, the gate into the future would open near dusk tomorrow evening, which meant he had to elude capture for only twenty-four hours.

Dominica Nosette's severed head stared blindly at him from his work bench, unable to tell him its secrets. He'd have to take the head with him, he realized slowly. Tell them he'd been trying to locate his partner and had found her hacked to pieces in the sewers, that he'd been able to recover only her decapitated skull. Yes, that's what he would do to gain admittance to the gate, he'd shock them all with her bloody head, then step through while they bleated about what ought to be done.

Moving with calm deliberation, Lachley found a wooden box beneath the work bench and dumped out the implements inside, then replaced them with Miss Nosette's head. He packed away a few other items he'd want along, shoving them into a leather satchel, mind racing. *Can't bloody well go home, I might find the coppers waiting for me. I'll have to stop at the bank tomorrow, secure funds to buy some decent clothing. Best not withdraw too much, don't want to tip my hand that I'm leaving. Better sleep the night in a hotel room or better yet, a doss house. Fewer questions to answer, that way, arriving without luggage . . .*

Decision made, Lachley stripped off his bloodstained clothing and shoes, changed into spare garments he kept on hand for just such emergencies, then carried his satchel and wooden case outside, locking the door to Tibor one last time. He'd never dreamed the day would come he'd leave the sanctuary for all time. But his fate was sealed and his plans were made. He would get onto that station, come hell or high water or the damned souls of all eternity, trying to bar the way.

He literally had nowhere else to go.

❖   ❖   ❖

Malcolm had been to Cleveland Street before, with wealthy tourists who wanted to visit the famous art studios, hoping to buy canvases or commission fine souvenir portraits. He'd never guided tourists to the street's other, more infamous destinations, of course, although a number of zipper jockey tours did, in fact, include stops at Cleveland Street's homosexual brothels. Malcolm found it somewhat ironic that Jack the Ripper had chosen to live sandwiched between London's higher and lower arts and wondered if John Lachley's unstable personality had been affected by the proximity of the brothels.

They had trailed Lachley's carriage halfway across London, following at a discreet distance. When Lachley pulled into a drive and halted, Malcolm asked the cabbie to pull up to the kerb a full block short of Lachley's home. "I think it would be wiser to leave the ladies here and scout this out on foot, Mr. Melvyn."

"But—" Margo protested.

"No. I will not unnecessarily risk either you or Dr. Feroz." He spoke in a whisper to prevent the driver from overhearing, and would brook no argument. "We came here to discover why Marcus is trailing him, not to put either of you ladies in the path of Jack the Ripper. And there's Marcus now, across the street there." He pointed to the dark hedge sheltering the ex-slave from view of Lachley's house. Marcus watched Lachley enter his home by the side entrance and gave out a warning call, a clear and piercing bird's trill in the gathering dusk and gloom. "Want to bet his friends are inside, searching the house?" Margo pouted and favored him with one of her famous stationary flounces, refusing to honor his friendly wager with an answer, but gave him no further trouble. "Driver," Malcolm said a little more loudly, "please be kind enough to wait here with the ladies while we determine whether or not our acquaintance is at home."

"Right, guv'nor."

Conroy Melvyn joined Malcolm on the pavement. "D'you want to go right up and talk to your friend?" the inspector asked quietly, nodding slightly toward Marcus.

"It is tempting, as Marcus appears to be alone."

"What's your plan, then?"

Malcolm was about to reply when someone left Dr. Lachley's house at a brisk walk. Poorly dressed, he would have looked more at home in Whitechapel than Cleveland Street. Whoever the man was, he was headed straight toward them. Malcolm's eyes widened when he realized who it was. "Bloody hell," Malcolm hissed, "it's *Lachley*." He turned at once to the carriage, leaning inside to murmur with the ladies as Lachley approached. Conroy Melvyn also turned to the carriage and said for Lachley's benefit, "Confound it, ladies, we shall be quite late! We haven't time to return and fetch your muff! If you'd wanted it, you should have secured it before calling for the carriage!"

Lachley strode past without a second glance.

Malcolm peered over his shoulder and caught a glimpse of Marcus, who had been joined by Benny Catlin and the other man from the Egyptian Hall. They trailed Lachley straight past the carriage, Marcus and the others passing literally within touching distance. Margo was wailing, "But I must have my muff, Geoffrey, I simply must! Oh, you beastly man, I cannot face Lady Hampton without it, after that dreadful creature showed me up last Saturday with her ermine . . ."

The moment Marcus and his companions had passed, Malcolm handed both ladies down. "We dare not follow in the carriage," he murmured, securing coin to pay the driver. "I fear you ladies are not dressed for hiking, but there's no help for it."

Margo said cheerfully, "I'll worry about blisters on my heels after I've got 'em."

The driver was shaking his head, mystified, as he drove off. Malcolm set out briskly, feeling some affinity for the tail end of a freight train as they whipped through the streets in pursuit. Lachley, far ahead, was moving rapidly. Both Margo and Dr. Feroz had difficulty keeping up. Their fashionably tight skirts and heeled shoes forced them to trot along with mincing little steps.

"Where the devil is he heading?" Inspector Melvyn wondered aloud as they moved steadily eastward, angling down toward the river. "It's the wrong night for another Ripper strike."

"Maybe he's hunting for Mary Kelly?" Margo suggested.

"Without Maybrick? Deuced unlikely, I should think. He kills to a pattern."

"Perhaps," Shahdi Feroz mused, "he works alone to locate the women, then strikes with Maybrick as his weapon?"

Margo put in suddenly, "Maybe the Whitehall torso *is* one of his victims? Somebody he meets tonight? The torso will be discovered just two days from now, after all."

"Another of these unfortunates in possession of his letters?" Inspector Melvyn frowned. "Blast, I wish we knew what these letters were!"

"You said a mouthful," Margo muttered, struggling to keep up.

As they trailed their double quarry steadily eastward, into increasingly poorer districts, Malcolm's misgivings increased just as steadily. They were dressed to the nines, all of them, and Lachley was leading them straight toward the East End, where gentlemen in fancy dress coats and ladies in silk evening gowns would stand out like beacon fires, inviting attack by footpads. Lachley took them down Drury Lane, echoing another night's anxious search, when they'd trailed Benny Catlin with bloodhounds. Tonight, at least, Catlin was in plain sight. They emerged, as they had that previous night, onto the Strand. Lachley headed down through Fleet Street, moving briskly.

Malcolm plunged into the crowds thronging the jammed pavements, trying to keep the others in sight. As the heart and soul of the British printing industry, Fleet Street was clogged by literally hundreds of newspaper reporters, ink-stained printers' journeymen and apprentices, bootblacks, newsboys scurrying along with stacks of the latest editions piled high, and women of dubious status all jostling elbows as they fought for space in the pubs, comandeered hansom cabs, and paid street urchins to run errands for them—all struggling to outwit one another in the business of keeping the Empire apprised of the latest news. From here, reports of the shocking, double Ripper murders had raced outward by telegraph to claim massive headlines across the length and breadth of the British Isles and far beyond.

From out of pubs with names like Ye Olde Cheshire Cheese wafted the multitudinous smells of cheap sandwiches, greasy fried potatoes, and enough alcohol to inebriate several herds of elephants. Malcolm wondered fleetingly just how many journalists affiliated with newspapers like the prestigious *Times* and the *Star* or penny dreadfuls with lofty-sounding titles like the *Penny Illustrated Paper and Illustrated Times* or the *Illustrated Police News* were combing the East End tonight, looking for leads to the Ripper case? Given the number of men and boys crowding these pavements, only a fraction of those he'd expected to cover the case. Fleet Street *seethed*.

"The ladies can't keep up!" Conroy Melvyn called above the roar of voices and bar songs, the rumble of carriage wheels, and the neighing of several hundred, snorting horses in the street. Margo and Shahdi Feroz were struggling through the thick crowds, falling farther and farther behind. Malcolm craned for a glimpse of Benny Catlin and Marcus. "Blast it, we'll lose them! Margo, we can't afford delays. Hire a cab and take Dr. Feroz back to Spaldergate. Let them know what's happening."

"But—"

"No argument! We haven't time!"

"Oh, all right!" she snapped, cheeks flushed with temper as well as brisk walking. "Come on, Shahdi, let's go home like good little girls!" She stormed off in search of a cab for hire, taking the Ripperologist with her.

"I shall pay for that, presently," Malcolm sighed, hurrying after their escaping quarry. The Scotland Yard inspector gave him a sympathetic glance as Lachley led them down past Shoreditch into the heart of Whitechapel, moving steadily eastward and skirting his way closer to the river.

"He isn't going anywhere near Miller's Court, is he?" Malcolm muttered.

Before the inspector could reply, a roar of angry voices erupted from the street just ahead. An immense crowd of angry men spilled out into their path, shouting demands for better police patrols, more gas lights, for a reward to be offered by Her Majesty's government for the Ripper's capture . . .

"Hurry!" Malcolm cried, darting forward. He shoved his way into the mass of shouting workmen who were still spilling out onto the street, unable to push his way through. "Mr. Lusk!" someone was shouting at his elbow. "Mr. Lusk, is it true you asked the authorities to offer a reward for information on the Ripper's accomplices?" The man shouting the question held a notebook and a stub of pencil, trying to scribble down information as he was jostled by the swarm of angry

Vigilance Committee members and loiterers swept up in the crowd.

"They told me t'bugger off!" Lusk shouted back, whipping up a roar from the crowd. "Aren't goin' to pay blood money, they said, t'catch nobody!" The head of the Whitechapel Vigilance Committee was furious, justifiably so. As a prominent East End businessman, Lusk had to live and work here, wondering which of his friends or family members might be butchered next, while police officials like Sir Charles Warren sat safe and insulated in their headquarters and stately homes to the west.

Malcolm fought his way past angry tradesmen, struggling to reach the far street corner where Marcus and the others had vanished. Several men flung curses after him when he shouldered past and one beefy lout swung at him, but by the time the punch landed, Malcolm had dodged past. Shouts erupted in his wake, then he was finally through the mass of seething protestors. Conroy Melvyn struggled out on his heels, panting. "Where'd they go?" the inspector gasped.

"I don't know! Dammit, I can't see them anywhere!" Malcolm plunged down the street at a run, heedless of stares, but within three blocks, they had to admit defeat. Marcus and Benny Catlin and the other gentleman trailing John Lachley had vanished into the maze of dark alleyways, swallowed alive by the black gloom which lurked just beyond Whitechapel's major thoroughfares. Malcolm kept hunting, stubbornly, for nearly an hour, while Conroy Melvyn questioned passers-by in search of clues, running into suspicion and close-mouthed wariness again and again. Not even the lure of shining crowns—coins worth more than a month's good wages in these streets—shook loose any information.

"Well," the inspector muttered, pocketing the last

of his crowns, "looks like they've given us the slip, all right. What now, Moore?"

Malcolm grimaced, eying a knot of roughly dressed men loitering near the entrance to the Kings Stores Pub at the corner of Widegate Street and Sandy's Row, a building once famed as Henry the Eighth's arsenal. Several of the loafing roustabouts were buying roasted chestnuts from a poorly dressed woman who'd stationed herself outside the roisterous public house. Several of the men were staring speculatively in their direction. "Much as I hate to admit it," Malcolm muttered, "we'd best return to Spaldergate House. We're attracting entirely too much attention to ourselves. The longer we remain in these streets, the more likely we are to be attacked, particularly dressed as we are. It's getting late and blokes like those won't hesitate for long, looking for easy pickings."

Conroy Melvyn glanced around. "I agree, but where the deuce are we? Ah, yes, there's the Kings Stores. Been there myself, a time or two, when I was still walking a beat. Good God, that must be Mrs. Paumier!"

"Who?" Malcolm asked, glancing over his shoulder as he turned and headed west, moving briskly to put them out of easy striking distance of the men on the corner.

Inspector Melvyn caught up hastily. "Lady who claimed she spoke with a man in a dark coat, carrying a black bag. Chap asked her if she'd heard of a murder in Miller's Court, the morning Miss Kelly was killed. Claimed she had, indeed, and the bloke told her that he knew more about it than she did. She was standing right outside the Kings Stores, selling chestnuts. Pub still trades on the claim that Jack the Ripper was last seen outside its doors."

"I didn't realize that. It's been an age since I visited *our* London." He laid a slight emphasis on the possessive. "I wonder if the lady spoke with our good friend Dr. Lachley or his accomplice from Liverpool?"

"We'll find out, come November the ninth."

"If we survive so long," Malcolm muttered, glancing back. The men from the Kings Stores pub had followed them. "Step lively, we've got company."

The inspector swore under his breath and speeded up. Malcolm homed in on the roar of shouts from the Vigilance Committee's angry street meeting, steering the Ripperologist back into the chaos in an effort to shake off pursuit. They swept off their high top hats, which stood out like signposts, and edged their way through the mob, taking their time and avoiding any further altercations with the shouting vigilantees. By the time they reached the other side, someone had picked Malcolm's pocket, absconding with all his ready cash, but they'd shaken their more dangerous pursuers in the crush.

"Afraid they cleaned me right out, as well," the police inspector said with a grimace of disgust, searching his own pockets. "Got my pocket watch, as well. Looks like we'll have to hoof it, eh?"

"I fear so. I haven't even tuppence left."

Malcolm did not look foward to arriving at Spaldergate with the news that he'd discovered the identity of Jack the Ripper *and* located both Marcus and Benny Catlin, only to loose them all in the chaos of a street meeting. Margo would spit like an Irish wildcat, after he'd dismissed her from the search back on Fleet Street. And the Ripper Watch Team's work was not yet done for the night, which loomed endlessly ahead of them. They still had to stand watch over the Whitehall torso mystery, to determine whether that unfortunate victim could also be laid at Jack the Ripper's doorstep. Malcolm resigned himself to yet another stressful night of short sleep and kept walking.

✧   ✧   ✧

Jenna unlocked the door to the little house in Spital-fields with shaking fingers, then stepped back to give Marcus room to pass. He and Noah carried Ianira upstairs, fumbling for the treads in the darkness while Jenna hunted for the gaslight. Once she'd lit it, they made better progress up the stairs. Noah called down, "I'll change clothes and pick up the girls from the Mindels."

Jenna nodded wearily. Shortly, Noah left the house in disguise as Marcus' sister once again, returning with the children and Dr. Mindel, who hurried upstairs to treat Ianira. Jenna followed, dreading Ianira's return to consciousness. She found Dr. Mindel bent over the *cassondra,* making worried noises, while Artemisia and Gelasia clung to their father in the far corner, eyes wide and frightened as they gazed at their mother for the first time in three years.

"Drugged, you say?" Dr. Mindel muttered, peering under her eyelids. "Such a hideous thing to do to a helpless lady. Her pulse is strong, though, and her breathing is regular. She should sleep quietly until the drug wears off." He rummaged in a satchel and came out with a small jar of salve, which he smoothed onto her wrists where the ropes had roughened her skin. "There is no way to guess how long the dose will last. When she wakes, please come for me."

"Thank you, Dr. Mindel," Noah said quietly. "We will."

The doctor left and Jenna met Noah's gaze. "There isn't much else we can do, is there?"

"No."

Marcus took the children across the narrow hallway to their little room and put them to bed. Noah rested a hand on Jenna's shoulder. "You'd better get some rest, Jenna. You're exhausted and you don't want to risk the baby."

Jenna nodded. There wasn't really anything else anyone could do, except wait for Ianira to regain consciousness and pray she was sane when she did. Jenna left the room blinking back tears and went quietly to bed, where she couldn't get the image of those dismembered bodies out of her mind, or that blonde woman's head sitting on a work table beside a dark-haired man's skull, left lying as casually as last week's empty milk bottles.

She wished she'd paid more attention to the various theories about the Ripper's possible occult connections. Clearly, Dr. John Lachley was a practicing occultist, not just a theorist and scholar. There'd been symbols painted on those hideous brick walls, symbols of occult magic, satanic ritual, God knew what else. Lachley was a renowned physician and lecturer, a member of the Theosophical Society and a man of means, with royal connections. No wonder the police couldn't find Jack the Ripper. They were searching for some depraved East Ender, a foreigner, not a well-respected member of society.

She could all too easily imagine Inspector Abberline's reaction or Sir Charles Warren's if anyone told the police they were up against a madman with ties to the royal family. A man who had perverted all notions of ancient Druidic rites, including the taking of trophy heads. Jenna shuddered, recalling his hideous lecture and the monstrous excitement in his eyes when talking about such things. And she had actually planned to film the Ripper murders! She and Carl, both. What innocents they'd been. Foolish innocents.

The world was full of madmen like John Lachley, killers looking for power, men like John Caddrick, her father. Jack the Ripper had built himself a hideous house beneath the streets, filling it with death. Jenna curled protectively around her abdomen, where Carl's baby was growing, and vowed that her child would never become a victim of the slaughterhouse her father had built. Jenna would see his monstrous construction torn to the ground and her father dead, first. Even if she had to pull the trigger.

Weeping softly in the blackness of a Spitalfields night, Jenna Caddrick listened helplessly to the hushed whispering from Ianira's room across the hall.

As John Lachley's cab rattled its way up the approach to Battersea Bridge, his thoughts rushed and tripped across one another like spawning fish. He was eager to reach the end of the journey and discover what really lay beyond the "gate." Despite the images in the dead woman's fantastical camera, he could not truly imagine the world which had produced such marvels. Anxious and impatient, he tried to steady his hands, but they would not remain decently calm. He gripped more tightly the case hiding Miss Nosette's severed head and craned forward to see how much farther it was to the end of the bridge. *Soon* . . .

God grant him patience, for *soon* could not come quickly enough.

Full dark settled inexorably across London's rooftops and chimneys as the cab jockeyed for position in the long queue of carriages and wagons crossing the river. On the far shore, Lachley could just make out Battersea Park's miniature lake where, on summer days, children chased ducks and swans or floated little armadas of handmade boats. There were no children in the park tonight, nor anyone else, for that matter, save a few modest carriages and the occasional hansom or barouche for hire. Black smoke pouring from Battersea's chimney pots snaked its way upward to merge with the ominous darkness of yet another rainstorm threatening to the east. Low clouds raced all along the southern bank of the river. From their vantage point on Battersea Bridge, lightning flared and flashed across the distant rooftops of Surrey and Bermondsey and damp wind slashed at Lachley's coat and hair through the open carriage, threatening to rip his hat loose. He secured it with an irritable jerk and checked his pocketwatch impatiently. It was now nearly eight and the journalist had guessed the "gate" would go at about eight-fifteen.

The cab finally tilted down the descent from the bridge and swung past the dark dampness of Battersea Park, cutting off in a right-hand turn which took them toward the long, lazy river bend which formed Battersea's western border. Once they reached Octavia Street, it wasn't difficult to suss out which house was Spaldergate. Carriages and hansom cabs lined the kerbs, disgorging elegantly dressed ladies and immaculate gentlemen and their servants, dozens of people arriving for what neighbors must imagine was an elegant dinner party.

He ordered the cabbie to stop well back from the line of arriving carriages and paid the man, waiting until the battered cab had rattled away down the street before moving toward Spaldergate, himself. Hidden in the shadows, he watched the arrivals through narrowed eyes. If people were still returning to the house, the gate couldn't be open yet. He settled his back against a tree trunk, biding his time, more than anxious to step through the gate but forcing himself to wait until the last possible moment. He did not want to risk being detained by the gate's operators. At length, a final carriage arrived, disgorging its passengers, a portly gentleman who was saying to the lady with him, "Hurry up, Abby, we'll miss the gate!"

At last!

Lachley stole softly down the pavement in their wake, then slipped into Spaldergate's side yard and found a wooden gate set into the high wall. Beyond, he discovered a vast and overgrown garden. Lachley eased into a clump of shaggy rhododendrons and peered into the garden, expecting he knew not quite what, a miniature version of a railway station, perhaps, with a gate leading into somewhen else, or perhaps the iron hulk of some inexplicable and infernal machine. The high stone wall ran right round the sprawling garden, its far reaches just visible in the gaslight from lamps spaced evenly along a patterned stone walkway. His brows rose at the extravagance, so many gaslights illuminating a mere garden, and one that was improperly maintained, at that. The walkway ended abruptly at the rear wall, as though some fuedal war lord had erected a fortress keep straight across an ancient Roman highway. Had that bitch Nosette lied? Was there no "gate" after all? No route into the distant future?

Yet something was clearly afoot, for milling about in a state of high agitation were more people than Lachley—in his own state of high-strung, sweating eagerness—could readily count. Upwards of seventy-five, at least, plus piles and haphazard stacks of luggage and porters swarming like angry mosquitoes, as though this garden were St. Pancras Station, that fantastical castle of brick and iron and glass with its bustling thousands. Most of the strange guests in Spaldergate's garden carried parcels or ladies' toiletry and jewel cases, bulging valises, carpet satchels with ironwood grips, all in a colorful and meaningless jumble of haste and nameless excitement.

Lachley felt the sting and ache of jaw muscles rigidly clenched, of teeth too tightly ground together. The confusion of voices scraped against his very nerves, until he had to close his fists to stop himself taking the nearest chattering bitch by the throat and squeezing until his knuckles collided in the center. The need to move, to do something besides huddle in the shrubbery, clawed at him, shrieked until the very substance of his skull vibrated with an agony like broken bones grating together. He reached for his throbbing temples, wanting to clutch at his head and hold the fury forcibly inside the cage of his fingers.

The vibrating pain had become a shriek when he noticed with a distant surprise that others in the garden were doing exactly the same thing. Some actually clapped hands across their ears, as though to shut out an inaudible noise. The unnerving sensation was not his imagination, then, nor the manifestation of multiple stresses on his overwrought nerves. He frowned, trying to comprehend what it might be—

—and a hole of utter, midnight blackness opened in the center of the stone wall, right above the flagstone path. Lachley sucked air down, a sharp gasp. The hair on his arms came straight up and his back muscles tried to shudder and crawl away down his spine, intent on running as far and as fast as possible, with or without the rest of him.

The gate . . .

It pulsed open with a silent thunder, gaping wider, swallowing up more of the garden wall, which simply ceased to exist where that blackness touched it. The edges scintillated in the glow from the gas lamps, shot through with irridescent color, like a film of oil spilled from steamship bilges across Tobacco Basin's darkened waters. The fascination of it drew him, repulsed him, left him trembling violently. What power did these people possess, to open such a thing out of sheer air and solid stone?

Ancient names and half-recalled incantations stumbled through his broken, sliding thoughts, names of power and terror: *Anubis, destroyer of souls, guardian of the underworld's pitchy gates . . . Heimdall of the shattering horn, watching for any*

who dared to cross the glinting rainbow bridge...
Kur, the coiled serpent of the fathomless abyss,
destroyer of the world in flood and thunder...

The outward shudder of the gate's receding edges finally came to a halt and it hung there, silent and terrible, beckoning him forward while his senses screamed to run in the opposite direction and never glance back. Then, as though such a thing were the most ordinary occurance in the world, the men and women in the garden stepped calmly through it, vanishing from sight like a cricket ball whacked solidly with the bat, rushing away to dwindle down to nothing. They were rushing through, hurrying, crowding on one another's heels. How long would the monstrous thing remain open? He took one step toward it, then another and a third, then rushed forward, impatient with his own gibbering terror, determined to step through, to discover for himself what horrors and delights might lie beyond.

Working himself into a state of frenzy, electrically aware of the risk, Lachley pulled Nosette's dismembered head from its carrying case and rushed forward into the puddle of light from the nearest gas lamp. A well-dressed lady in watered silk saw him first. She let go a high, piercing scream. Lachley was abruptly engulfed by a stinging cloud of liveried servants and distraught gentlemen. "I tried to stop her..." Lachley gasped out, waving Miss Nosette's ghastly head about, her streaming blonde tresses clotted with blood. Summoning tears, Lachley gripped a white-faced gentleman by the arm. "She wanted to follow that madman in the East End, to photograph him! By the time I got to her it was too late, he'd cut her to pieces, oh, God, all I could bring away was this... this little bit of her. Poor, stupid Dominica! I just want to go home, please..."

People were shouting, calling for someone. Lachley started toward the gate, not caring to wait. Just behind him, a woman's voice shrilled out, "My God! It's John Lachley!" He jerked around and focused on a woman who stood not ten paces away, a dark-haired woman of extraordinary beauty, who looked vaguely familiar to him. She was staring straight at him, eyes wide in recognition. Scalding hatred rose in his gorge, threatened to peel back his skin and burst out through his fingertips. *She knows me! By God, she'll not stop me!* Lachley whirled and plunged toward the gaping black hole. Behind him, the woman shouted, "*Stop him! That's Jack the Ripper!*"

Screams erupted on his heels . . .

Then he was inside. Falling, rushing foward with dizzy speed. He yelled. Then staggered across a metal grating, into a railing at waist height. He looked up—

John Lachley screamed.

It was a world inverted. Stone for sky, pendulous glowing lights hanging from iron beams and girders, booming voices that echoed and rolled, more terrifying than any thunder, speaking out of the air itself, a maze of twisting confusion that fell away at his feet, at least five full stories below, as though he stood at the top of Big Ben's clock tower or the highest point of St. Paul's arching dome. Wild displays of light in alien colors hurt his eyes.

People moved in crowds far below, like flotsam caught in the eddy of the docklands' swirling waters. Down a rampway, down endless metal steps, down and further down still, the people who had come through the gate ahead of him wound their way toward the distant floor, while a few yards away, suspended on ramps and metal stairs in a mirror image, crowds of nattily dressed men and women pressed their way upwards, toward the very platform where Lachley stood.

At the base of the metal stairs, confusion reigned. A screaming mob shouted questions, inchoate with distance. Men dressed as guards shoved and pressed the crowd back. Lachley realized with a start that a number of those guards were women, women wearing trousers as though they had renounced their sex and thought themselves the equal of any man. Eddies moved sharply through the crowd as a fight broke out, unmistakably riot, brutal as any mob of drunken dock hands demanding pay higher than the handful of shillings a week they deserved . . .

Someone lunged through the gate behind him, shouting his name.

He whirled. The vaguely familiar woman had rushed through with two men, who dove straight at him across the platform. Lachley hurled aside Dominica Nosette's head and drove an elbow into an unprotected gut, then slammed the heel of his hand against a nose, felt bone crunch. Both men went sharply down, barely stirring. The woman's eyes widened as she realized her abrupt danger. She opened her mouth to scream and tried to lunge away from him. Lachley snatched her back by the hair. She fought him with unexpected ferocity. Her nails caught his face and her knee slammed into his thigh with a sharp flare of pain, narrowly missing his groin.

"Bitch!" He slugged her, putting his entire body into the blow. It caught her brutally across the temple. She collapsed, a boneless weight in his grasp. Someone was shouting from the stairs, where several shrieking women stood in ashen shock and one narrow-eyed, dangerous-looking man was rushing right toward him. Lachley couldn't fight the whole bloody station!

He snatched up the unconscious woman as a hostage, heaving her across his shoulder, and plunged down the steps toward the distant floor. He skidded down flight after flight, one hand balancing the inert burden on his shoulder, the other gripping the railing as he slung

himself around corners at each landing. A glance below
revealed several uniformed men charging up from the
floor, trying to cut him off. He snarled aloud, but
Lachley was only a flight-and-a-half up, so he vaulted
across the rail, dropping a full ten feet into the middle
of the rioting crowd. He landed on someone's back and
felt bone crunch under his feet as the man went brutally
down. Lachley stumbled to hands and knees, dropping
his hostage in the melee. Someone kicked him aside,
sent him spinning and rolling under running feet.
Bruised and shaken, Lachley finally skidded into a
momentary pocket of clear space and shoved his way
to his feet. He thrust himself past intervening bodies,
reeled from a punch against his unprotected side,
turned with a snarl and broke the bastard's neck with
a wrenching heave and twist—

Then he was clear of the riot. Lachley found himself
staring at cobblestoned walkways and park benches
and wrought iron lamps, even a pub that reminded
him incongruously of Chelsea. The riot surged
behind him, shoving Lachley straight past a line of
stunned security guards, who were busy to distraction
searching the rioting mob for him. He bolted,
determined to discover some way out of this madhouse.
He needed to find a quiet place to think, to sort out
what to do next. He was very nearly clear of the
chaos when a group of wild-eyed men brandishing
placards rushed at him.

"*Lord Jack!*"

"Lead us, holiest one!"

"Command us! We are your servants!"

Lachley opened his mouth, not entirely sure what
might emerge. Behind him, someone shouted, "There
he is!" He glanced wildly back toward the platform,
where the two men who'd rushed through the gate on
his heels were stumbling down the stairs under escort,

pointing right at him. Lachley whirled on the placard-carrying lunatics, who were plucking at his very coat sleeves in fawning, worshipful attitudes.

"You want to help me? I need shelter, curse it!"

"At once, Lord Jack!" the nearest cried eagerly, tugging at his arm. "Anything you desire! We have awaited your coming . . ."

They surrounded him, rushed him away from the shouting guards who were shoving rioters aside, trying to reach him. Lachley ran with the madmen, insane sycophants who gibbered at him from all sides and hid his face with their hand-scrawled signs. *Am I doomed to rely on madmen all my days?* He'd traded Maybrick's lunacy for a whole crowd of insanity. But sheltering with madmen was preferable to hanging, should the wardens of the gate catch up to him.

His unanticipated escorts brought Lachley eventually to a place that—despite its overwhelming strangeness—appeared to be a hotel of some kind. The men who'd appointed themselves his adoring acolytes rushed Lachley across a brightly lit lobby, where a desk clerk glanced up only briefly, then ushered him straight into what proved to be a lift. They rose with startling speed and quite delightfully, the controls were automated, eliminating the need for a lift operator who would have to be eliminated for witnessing his flight. The lights overhead were strange, far too bright, and he couldn't determine what the translucent panels covering them were fashioned from. Then the doors slipped quietly open with a soft bell chime and he found himself in a luxuriously carpeted corridor. One of the madmen produced a small, stiff card, which he inserted into a metal box on one of the numbered doors. The panel opened to his touch.

Lachley stepped warily inside, finding two neatly

made beds, a strange box with a flat glass front perched on a low table, several odd lamps, ugly artwork framed on white-painted walls, and just to the left of the door, a lavatory fitted with a large mirror and the strangest water closet he'd ever seen.

"Christ, but I need a drink . . ." he muttered, scrubbing at his face with unsteady hands.

"At once, Lord!" The man who had unlocked the room hurried across to a small cabinet, procuring a bottle of amber-colored liquor which he opened and poured while the other madmen crowded inside. Lachley knocked back a surprisingly good whiskey, then considered the men who stood in a huddle near the door, gazing at him with the intensity of utter reverence.

"Who are you?" Lachley demanded.

"Your Sons, Lord Jack. We have long awaited your coming. Command us. We are your chosen."

He narrowed his eyes as he considered the implications of that patently absurd answer. Were all the inhabitants of this world completely insane? No, not all, he frowned, thinking back to those guards at the gate. Lachley wondered what to ask first and finally decided on the simplest question in his mind. "What year is it?"

None of the madmen seemed at all surprised by such a question. The one who'd given him the whiskey said, "By station time, Lord, it is 1910. Beyond Primary . . ."

"Station time?" he echoed, startled.

"Yes, Lord. The station exists well over a century in our past and some thirty years in your future."

Lachley's mind reeled. Sanity slipped and lurched beneath his feet. He groped for it, finding, instead, the bed, which he sank onto simply to prevent a nasty fall. "Do you know the bitch who followed me through the gate?" he asked harshly. "The one I lost in the crowd?"

"Yes, Lord. She's a Ripperologist, one of the Ripper

Watch Team, Dr. Shahdi Feroz. She went to study your great works in London."

Ripperologist? Lachley narrowed his eyes. She'd come to London to study *him?* The journalist had said as much, but he hadn't believed her. The unlamented Miss Nosette would have said anything to persuade Lachley to release her unharmed. Lachley shut his eyes for long moments, trying to place where he'd seen that Feroz woman's face before. The familiar features finally clicked in his mind. The lecture. She'd attended the lecture at the Egyptian Hall. Had spoken with him briefly, afterwards. Lachley frowned. Had she known all along, then? Known that he was responsible for the deaths of the whores in the East End? She must have. Hadn't she cried out that he was Jack the Ripper, back in the garden behind Spaldergate? Lachley narrowed his eyes coldly. That woman's testimony could see him hanged.

"I must find her," he growled. "Find and silence her."

"Do you want a knife, Lord Jack?"

The question jolted him. He blinked in surprise. "A knife?"

"Yes, Lord. To kill the whores on the station, once you have killed Dr. Feroz?"

The leader of the madmen was opening a leather case. He took from it a long, shining blade, nine inches of sharpened steel edge, with a thick wooden handle. The lunatic held it out to Lachley, balancing it across both palms, presenting it like a royal sceptre. He went to one knee, offering the weapon as a token of fealty. "My Lord, we are your humble servants. Take our knife, Lord, and command us."

Lachley picked it up slowly, realizing it was a far better tool than Maybrick's. Better, even, than his Arabian jambala, with its thick, slightly curved steel blade, nearly as wide as his palm. Better even than the scramasax—a weapon much like an American bowie knife with a hook at the end—which he'd used as a sacramental blade in Lower Tibor to take Morgan's trophy head. *This* blade, held out so reverently, was a delight to behold.

Command us, his followers offered, madmen from a hellish, sunless world he did not yet understand. *'Tis better,* the blind poet's words rumbled through Lachley's memory, boulders crashing down a mountainside in a thundering avalanche, *'tis better to reign in hell* . . . John Lachley began to laugh, a sound so dark and wild, it brought a sharp gasp from those worshippers still huddled near the door. The leader, holding out the knife across his palms, met Lachley's gaze and smiled slowly. Glorying in his newfound power, Lachley accepted the knife from his faithful disciple's hands . . . and gave the orders to kill his first victim: the dark-haired, petite, and lovely Dr. Feroz.

Chapter Twelve

Skeeter Jackson had never minded crowds.

But the packed mob in Victoria Station would've been enough to discompose the pope and his entire College of Cardinals. Skeeter hadn't even reached the rope barricade of the departures lounge when waiting newsies swarmed all over him, shouting questions and shoving microphones and cameras into his face with scant regard for damage inflicted.

"Mr. Jackson! Is it true you're leading the search team over the protests of Senator Caddrick—"

"—tell us your plan to locate the senator's missing daughter—"

"—how much they're paying you to risk your life, bringing terrorists to justice—"

Skeeter, lips thinned down to a tight, white line, had never been gladder in his life to reach a departures lounge. He fled past the barrier, gate pass in hand, leaving them to howl in his wake. Paula Booker had taken refuge in one corner, notably seating herself as far as possible from Sid Kaederman. The detective glared sourly at Skeeter and snapped irritably at a Time Tours employee who'd just brought coffee. Skeeter headed the other way, having no desire to renew his acquaintance until absolutely necessary.

"Coffee, Skeeter?" The voice came from the farthest corner of the lounge, startling him. He found Kit Carson leaning against one of the steel beams supporting the long flights of stairs and departures platform.

"Kit! What're you doing here?"

"Seeing you off, of course. Coffee?"

"Oh, man, how I need a cup! Thanks, boss." Skeeter gulped, while scratching his itching thigh surreptitiously and mentally castigating the British for insisting on woolen suits. He wasn't quite allergic, but misery was relative. He should've put on that synthetic bodysuit Connie had offered, which helped reduce the itch, rather than stuffing it into his luggage.

Kit refilled his coffee cup from a thermos flask and said, "There's just time to go over the use of your new scout's log." He handed over a satchel tucked under one arm. "I've been working on it for the last three hours, getting it set up for you."

"My scout's log?" Skeeter echoed, abruptly excited. He dug open the satchel with eager fingers. The computerized device nestled inside was, Skeeter knew, a mandatory piece of equipment for any time scout. "How come you're giving me a scout's log? I'm not a time scout."

"You've always relied on the time cards before, I know. But it occurred to me this morning, this search and rescue mission might just become far more temporally complex than anyone planned. You may well need a more substantial record of when and where you've been, to prevent potential accidents in the future. Don't worry, I'm not taking it out of your pay." The grizzled former scout chuckled, eyes glinting with wicked amusement. "I chalked it up to Senator Caddrick's account."

Skeeter grinned. "Bet he flips when he gets the bill." Skeeter peered curiously at the device. He'd seen time scouts carrying them, of course, but had never managed to lay hands on one, not even in the days when he could've turned a tidy profit snitching a new one and selling it on the black market. He would never have stolen a used one, of course, even if 'eighty-sixers hadn't been off-limits as prey. Ripping off someone's record of their gate travels would've been tantamount to premeditated murder. But he'd wistfully dreamed of the money a new one could bring, had spent many a pleasant hour drooling over the stuff he could buy with that kind of cash.

"Now," Kit was saying, "you haven't been down as many gates as the average tour guide, let alone a time scout, but you've done enough time travelling to cause potential trouble. Particularly since the Wild West Gate and the Britannia can be lethal, if you don't watch which direction you're moving through them. So you'll use this. I've already programmed in the two weeks we spent in Colorado. You'll want to add the time you've spent down other gates, as well. Your first trip to Denver, your previous trip to London, plus the brief minutes you spent there as a Time Tours porter. And your stay in Claudian Rome, of course, finding Marcus and bringing him back. When you get to London, turn the log on immediately and take your first set of readings. Before this search is over, God knows how many time zones or gates you'll have to jump through, particularly if Armstrong has left London for healthier climes."

"Aw, man, don't even suggest it!"

Kit grimaced, rearranging a whole ladderful of weathered lines. "Sorry, that's my job. Now, then, open it up. Like that, yes. You're going to learn how to use this thing in your sleep. Malcolm and Margo can help, they know the drill cold."

"Believe me," Skeeter said fervently, "the last thing I want to risk is shadowing myself." Dying instantly by stepping into a time where he already existed was not Skeeter's idea of a smart career move. "Okay, show me how this thing works."

Kit put him through drills right up to the two-minute warning, when Time Tours guides urged the departing tour to start climbing the stairs reserved for departures, so they would be ready to step through the Britannia the moment the returning tour cleared the gate. Kit gripped his shoulder in a friendly fashion. "You're doing very well, Skeeter. You catch on fast." The retired scout chuckled. "Margo took much longer, her first few tries, but she by God knows it now. You won't need an ATLS, but it wouldn't hurt to have her and Malcolm show you theirs, run you through the process of taking star fixes and geomagnetic readings when you get to London. Keep the log running as you step through the gate, so you won't forget to turn it on."

Skeeter fiddled with controls, then closed up the log and slid it into the trademark satchel Kit had been the first to design. "I'll check in with Malcolm right away. Thanks, boss."

Kit held out a hand and Skeeter shook it solemnly.

"Good luck, Skeeter," Kit said quietly. "Try not to get yourself—or anyone else—killed on this mission."

Skeeter held his gaze solemnly. "I'll do my best."

"I know you will. Scoot, then. Send word periodically with the returning guides, so we'll know what's happening."

"Right." Skeeter gulped the rest of his lukewarm coffee, then hurried for the stairs, giving Paula a high-sign. Kaederman was still sipping coffee. Caddrick's pet snoop finally began the long climb as Skeeter rounded the first landing and started up the second flight. Baggage handlers were already fiendishly at work on the high platform. In a dizzying moment of *déjà vu,* Skeeter halfway expected to see Benny Catlin barrelling through the piles of steamer trunks and portmanteaus. Then the gate rumbled open with a skull-splitting backlash of subharmonics and the returning tour staggered through, jabbering animatedly.

"—that poor woman, decapitated, they found nothing but her torso!"

"—left the body in the cellar tunnels beneath the new Scotland Yard building—"

"The Ripper Watch team said Jack the Ripper left the body there, himself! Poor Miss Nosette, if only she'd stayed with the Ripper Watch Team instead of striking out on her own, like that—"

Skeeter edged closer to the front of the platform, aware of his conspicuous place at the head of the departing tour. The press corps had trained cameras on him from five stories down. The gate was nearly clear, tourists down to a trickle and baggage handlers staggering through under heavy loads, when a wild-eyed man Skeeter vaguely recognized plunged through the gate. Whoever he was, the guy let out a bloodcurdling yell and went rigid, staring down into Commons. Then Skeeter noticed what was clutched in his hand and stiffened in shock. *A decapitated head!* A woman's head, severed with what must've been an axe. The grisly thing swung by the hair from the man's white-knuckled grip. Screams erupted from the women near Skeeter just as he recognized the dead woman: Dominica Nosette, the Ripper Watch photographer. Then two men Skeeter didn't know rushed through the open gate, with Dr. Feroz on their heels. The Ripperologist was shouting, "There he is! It's Dr. Lachley! Stop him!"

The man at the platform railing spun around—and

attacked with single-minded fury, flinging the severed head aside. He hit both men like a pile driver; they went down hard and didn't stir. Then Lachley grabbed Dr. Feroz. She fought back, even as Skeeter shoved his way toward them, past screaming women and shocked Time Tours guides and baggage handlers, who stood with mouths gaping. "Don't just stand there!" Skeeter shouted. "*Stop him!*"

Lachley cast one wild-eyed glance in their direction, then slugged Dr. Feroz so hard her head snapped around. He threw her across one shoulder and bolted down the stairs for the Commons floor. Skeeter lunged after him—and one of the men Lachley had knocked down came to his knees right in Skeeter's path. Skeeter sprawled and they both crashed to the platform floor. A pile of luggage upended and fell straight off the edge. Screams erupted somewhere far below. Then Skeeter grunted and heaved himself up to look. The luggage had crashed to the floor, knocking half-a-dozen people flat. A panic-stricken riot was spreading through the crowd. Dr. Lachley was almost to the floor, running hard, with Shahdi Feroz dangling over one shoulder like a broken doll.

"Skeeter!" Paula Booker was shouting his name. He glanced back and saw the departing tour rushing through the gate. The Britannia had already begun to shrink back in on itself. A Time Tours guide had bent to help the injured. Paula was waiting at the very edge of the gate. "Hurry, Skeeter! The gate's going! Kaederman's already through!"

Whoever Dr. Lachley might prove to be—and Skeeter had a sinking sensation he might just be Jack the Ripper—Skeeter wasn't about to miss this gate and give Sid Kaederman eight solid days to search for Jenna Caddrick by himself. Skeeter plunged into the shrinking gate, grabbing Paula by the wrist on his way through. They skidded into the dark garden behind Spaldergate House and landed smack in the center of utter chaos. Time Tours guides were racing toward the gate and hysterical women were sobbing. Porters stumbled through into the garden, literally shoved through the rapidly closing gate by station-side Time Tours employees. One of the women was screaming, "My luggage! He knocked off my luggage! I must have my medicine!" Another, less sympathetically, was howling about her jewelry, presumably strewn all over the Commons floor.

"What's going on?" Skeeter demanded of a passing Time Tours guide, who completely ignored him. A tourist nearby gasped, "They said it was Jack the Ripper! He's crashed the Britannia!"

Paula gasped. "What?"

"That man who came through! That was Jack the Ripper! Burst into the garden, shouting something about one of the Ripper Watch reporters, said the Ripper had cut her to pieces . . ."

A final porter struggled through the rapidly closing gate, dragging five steamer trunks hastily roped together, then the Britannia shrank to a point of darkness and vanished, leaving only a tangle of vines and shrubbery along the high garden wall. For better or worse, TT-86 was sealed up tight as a drum. With Jack the Ripper inside.

"Skeeter?" a familiar voice jerked his attention back around. "Skeeter Jackson? What on God's green earth are you doing in London?"

Skeeter blinked up at Malcolm Moore, who had burst into the Spaldergate garden at a dead run. Margo, hot on his heels, slithered to a halt as lightning flared overhead, deepening smudged purple shadows under her eyes. "Skeeter?" she gasped. "And Paula Booker? What's going on? What are you doing here?"

"Uh . . ." Skeeter said helpfully. He struggled to pull his scattered thoughts together. "Was that really Jack the Ripper?" He gestured vaguely toward the now-vanished Britannia Gate. "Crashing the gate?"

Malcolm's lips thinned to near invisibility. "I'm afraid so, yes. Dr. Feroz recognized him and gave chase with some of the guides—"

"I've got bad news, then," Skeeter muttered. "He overpowered 'em. And took off with Dr. Feroz. Knocked her cold and hauled her down the stairs. The gate was going, or I'd have chased them down."

Malcolm's mouth worked for a long second before any sound emerged. *"My God!"* he finally erupted, voice cracking in unmodulated fury. *"What in hell could be more important than letting Jack the Ripper escape into TT-86?"*

Skeeter blinked. Then said unhappily, "Finding a pack of terrorists who kidnapped Senator John Caddrick's little girl and hauled her through the Britannia. She was in disguise. As Benny Catlin."

Malcolm's anger faded faster than an image from an unplugged television. The guide stood blinking for a full sixty seconds, then whispered, "Oh, dear God . . ."

"You said it. We gotta talk. Somewhere quiet." Women were still sobbing hysterically over the severed head the Ripper had hurled at the departing tour, lamenting their lost baggage and the cash they'd left in their trunks, cash they needed for the trip.

"Yes, the sooner the better," Malcolm said thinly. "Margo, my dear, please ask Mr. Gilbert to meet us in his study. With a very large decanter of bourbon."

Margo shot toward the house, threading her way nimbly through wailing tourists and staggering porters. Malcolm asked, "How many men have you brought to search, Skeeter?"

"All the porters who came through are on search

detail if we need 'em. Dr. Booker's come through to help make an identification. She gave Caddrick's kid a new face. Benny Catlin's. And there's a detective you're just gonna love. Caddrick hired him."

Paula Booker peered through the crowd anxiously. "I'd better find Mr. Kaederman. We don't want him slipping off on his own."

Malcolm followed her progress with his gaze, then turned to Skeeter, waiting expectantly. "Long story," Skeeter sighed. "Very long."

"Then the sooner we're inside, the sooner you can begin telling it." Malcolm ushered him through the chaos in the garden, steering him past the back door, which one of the servants had chocked open, leading him to another door farther on. They entered Spaldergate through a scrupulously maintained conservatory replete with hothouse flowers and overly green smells. From there, they followed a carpeted corridor toward the front of the house, bypassing the bulk of the arriving tour. Darkened, silent rooms closed away from public view for the night lay just off the hall, while the parlour, at the front of the house on the ground floor—rather than the more traditional first-floor arrangement found in London town houses—blazed with light. The whole front of the house was filling up with distraught refugees from the shaken tour.

Malcolm turned off the corridor well before they reached the parlour, entering a decidedly masculine room dominated by hundreds of leather-bound books and the unmistakable scent of beeswax and turpentine, used to polish the mahogany furniture. Margo had reached the room before them and stood in the corner, pouring bourbon from a decanter. A film of coal dust dulled every white surface to grey, despite scrupulous cleaning by the house staff. The feel of smooth wood under Skeeter's hand, the thick, rich carpet, and the

mustiness of the air were all familiar from his previous
visit. Like half-remembered ghosts, they filtered through
his awareness while Malcolm headed for the bourbon.
Margo handed over generously filled tumblers and
Skeeter gratefully upended one.

"Thanks. God, I needed that." He refilled the tumbler
and sipped more judiciously, this time. Paula Booker
found her way into the room, lamentably in the company of Sid Kaederman, who thrust out his hand for
the bourbon as though Margo were a mere servant.
Margo handed him a tumbler, eying him curiously.
Kaederman gulped, ignoring Margo and fixing his
attention squarely on Malcolm Moore. Skeeter noticed
that Kaederman's hand was slightly unsteady as he
drained his drink. Skeeter decided he'd better make
the introductions.

"Mr. Sid Kaederman is a detective, hired by Senator Caddrick to search for his daughter. Malcolm
Moore is a freelance temporal guide in charge of the
Ripper Watch arrangements. Margo Smith is a trainee
time scout and is assisting the Ripper Watch Team,
as well."

Kaederman shot Margo a surprised glance, then said,
"Would someone care to explain how the hell you people
let a thing like Jack the Ripper get into your station?
Don't you put any security around your goddamned
gates?"

Malcolm bristled. "It is not my gate, Mr. Kaederman.
Time Tours has charge of the Britannia and I do not
work for Time Tours. Neither does Miss Smith. Now,
then, Mr. Jackson, will you kindly explain your remarks
about Senator Caddrick's missing child?"

Marshall Gilbert appeared in the doorway before
anyone else could comment. "What in the world can
possibly be so urgent—" He rocked to a halt. "*Skeeter
Jackson?* And Paula Booker? What on earth—?"

Skeeter smiled wanly. "Evening, Mr. Gilbert. Hope you don't have plans for tonight."

The gatekeeper frowned. "I don't believe I care for the sound of this. What's happened?"

"Benny Catlin, is what." Skeeter sank into in a leather-covered chair, took a long pull at his bourbon, then explained what had happened and why they were here. Sid Kaederman and Paula Booker sat opposite Skeeter, listening to his terse explanation. "So, after we got back from Colorado," Skeeter finished up, "Senator Caddrick threatened again to shut the whole station down if we don't find his daughter and this terrorist, Noah Armstrong." Skeeter passed around photographs. "And after what he did to Bull Morgan, with all that cockamamie crap he used to throw Bull in jail, we're taking him damned seriously."

"Good God!" Malcolm gasped, staring at the photos. "That *is* Benny Catlin! We saw him just last night! And this Armstrong chap was with him."

"You saw them?" Skeeter sat forward quickly.

"*Where?*" Kaederman had surged to his feet.

"At the Egyptian Hall. They were attending a lecture by the man we identified as Jack the Ripper. In fact, they were following him, for reasons we have yet to ascertain, although I suspect it has something to do with Ianira Cassondra. We trailed them right across London into the East End, but a street meeting jammed our way and we lost them in the crush."

While Skeeter's imagination betrayed him with monstrous visions of what Jack the Ripper would do to Ianira Cassondra, Sid Kaederman bellowed, "*You lost them?* My God! What a bunch of incompetant jackasses! I don't care what that interfering old bastard Carson said, I'm taking over this search operation—"

"Like hell you are!" Skeeter snapped. "Last time I checked, nobody had appointed you God."

"You insufferable little—! How dare you talk to me that way! I've a good mind—"

"*Enough!*"

Coal dust settled in the aftermath of Malcolm Moore's bellow. Malcolm pinned Kaederman with his gaze. "You will please be good enough to refrain from further outbursts, Mr. Kaederman. And we can do without the barbed remarks, Mr. Jackson."

"Huh. You weren't stuck for two weeks in Colorado with this pompous—"

"*Enough!*"

"Oh, all right," Skeeter muttered. "Shutting up." He sprawled deeper into his chair, wishing to God he'd never agreed to come in the first place.

"That's better. Now, then. We'll take this one at a time, gentlemen." Malcolm glanced at Kaederman, who returned his gaze coldly.

"Where are you going to search?" Kaederman demanded. "And just how, exactly, did you manage to lose track of Miss Caddrick and her abductor?"

"As you have not been to the East End, do not presume to judge conditions there. Street meetings are always disruptive and frequently violent. The Ripper murders have sparked riots and serious violence, particularly against foreigners, for the past three weeks. We were caught right in the thick of one. It cut us off from Dr. Lachley and the group following him. Including your terrorist and Miss Caddrick. Not to mention Marcus, Ianira Cassondra's husband. We suspect Ianira is somehow involved, because Marcus had to be restrained from attacking Lachley during the lecture."

Skeeter caught a glimpse of Margo opening her mouth to ask something, then she thought better of it and scooted back in her chair again, brow furrowed slightly. From her corner, she levelled a slow, suspicious gaze at Kaederman. *Good.* With luck, she'd just picked up on the inconsistency in Kaederman's story. Namely, that Jenna Caddrick wouldn't be running around London voluntarily with Armstrong if she were his prisoner. Until Skeeter could get rid of Kaederman, he wouldn't be able to tell Margo and Malcolm the real story—or, at least, his suspicions.

Skeeter caught Malcolm's eye. "Yes, Ianira's involved, I'll stake my reputation on it. She was inside a steamer trunk I carried through, one of Benny Catlin's. Catlin chewed my ass when it nearly fell off the departures platform. Cost me a job with Time Tours."

Malcolm's mouth twitched. "Pardon the frankness, but that's no great loss." Malcolm was famous for his long-standing feud with Time Tours, which he held accountable for the suicide of a long-ago employer. "Well, this is quite a sticky wicket you've handed us, Skeeter."

While Skeeter was wondering what, precisely, a sticky wicket *was*, Kaederman said, "Is that all you've got to say? When are you going to get off your damn dandified butt and *do* something about it?"

Malcolm shot an intent stare at Caddrick's detective. "Mr. Kaederman, there are ladies present. Kindly refrain from vulgarities."

"You're kidding?"

"No, I am not, sir. You will please refrain from swearing in the presence of ladies. Unless you wish to provoke some gentleman on the streets into correcting your manners forcibly? You are investigating a kidnapping. And the London outside those windows," he nodded toward heavy damask curtains falling thick as honey down the long windowpanes to close out the rising storm, "is nothing like the London of our own time. You cannot safely behave as though you were in New York or even up-time London, not if you wish to escape serious injury. Now, you have raised the question we all must answer: What to do next. I feel constrained to point out that neither you nor Mr. Jackson nor Dr. Booker is particularly qualified to search Victorian London. I daresay the baggage porters have more experience down the Britannia than any of you."

Paula said hastily, "Leave me out, please. I had enough searching in Denver to last a lifetime. I agreed to come along because I can provide a positive ID on Miss Caddrick. And Kit thought it would be a good idea to have two surgeons in residence at Spaldergate, with the team going up against armed terrorists."

Malcolm's expression made it clear that he questioned the wisdom of sending through such an inept team, but he merely said, "You say Armstrong went through the Wild West Gate? I suppose he must have arrived in London conventionally enough, by steamship from New York to Liverpool or London, bringing Marcus and the children with him. They'll have had ample time to set up a hideout anywhere in the city, which means they'll be devilishly difficult to trace. On the other hand, we know that Miss Caddrick was wounded—"

"*What?*" Kaederman lunged out of his chair a second time.

Malcolm blinked. "I thought you'd been thoroughly briefed?"

The detective thinned his lips. "That particular detail was left out."

"I see. Well, the dog we used to trace Benny Catlin followed a blood trail away from the Royal Opera House. Not a great deal of blood, but clearly Benny Catlin's. Or rather, Miss Caddrick's. We don't know how seriously she was injured in the fight at the Opera, but we saw her just two days ago, quite recovered, so the wound was clearly not a life-threatening one. We'd been searching the hospitals and workhouse infirmaries without turning up anything, so I would suggest we now broaden the search to private physicians. We'll begin by contacting all the private doctors and surgeons in the region of the Strand, then spread out in sectors from there, trying to trace where Miss Caddrick received treatment for her injury. The baggage handlers can assist with that."

"You've got to be joking?" Sid protested. "That could take months!"

Malcolm favored him with a mild look. "Indeed. Your time might be well spent compiling lists of names and addresses to contact."

Margo leaned forward. "If they've set up house-keeping somewhere in London, they're likely to need a staff, even if it's a small one."

"Not necessarily. Servants gossip. Armstrong won't want to risk that."

Margo looked abashed. "I hadn't thought of that."

Malcolm smiled wanly. "You aren't accustomed to servants, yet, my dear. It's entirely possible Armstrong has chosen to hide in the East End, as the least likely place anyone would search. Conditions in Bethnal Green or Spitalfields, for instance, aren't quite as desperate as they are in, say, Stepney, Whitechapel, or Wapping, never mind Poplar and Limehouse. And Marcus' accent would blend in rather well with the European immigrants in Spitalfields. Whereas it would be quite remarkable in more homogenously English districts, even those as relatively poverty stricken as SoHo or Cheapside. Consider their position for a moment. Armstrong's group includes at least one Yankee gentlemen, or rather, a young lady posing as one, which is dangerous, in itself, plus a man with a decidedly Latin accent, two small children, and attendant guards. That would be extraordinarily memorable in the better London neighborhoods. Enough so, were *I* running from up-time legal authorities, I wouldn't risk that sort of attention."

"Okay," Skeeter nodded, "that makes sense. So we comb the East End, same as half the cops and reporters in London. And check out all the doctors." He wished Kaederman would leave, so he could tell Malcolm the rest of the story. "When do we start?"

"I suggest you begin by settling into rooms and unpacking your cases. Then you and I, Mr. Jackson, will spend a long evening at the Vault's computers, planning the search and assigning personnel to various sections of the city. Mr. Kaederman, you shall begin by working on your list of physicians."

"The sooner I get these goddamned wool pants off, the better."

Margo chuckled. "Better not say that, Mr. Kaederman. Not around here."

"Say what?" Kaederman asked, blinking in confusion.

"In London, the word 'pants' refers to underwear. Call them trousers, unless you want the locals to laugh at you."

The look Kaederman shot her told Skeeter he planned to stay as far from the locals as humanly possible. Which suited Skeeter just fine. The Wardmann-Wolfe agent muttered, "If that's all, I'm tucking it in for the night." He stalked out. Paula pleaded weariness and also left.

"You know," Malcolm remarked to no one in particular, "I'd say that chap doesn't enjoy time travel."

"You don't know the half of it. That man is a major pain in *everybody's* backside. Now that he's gone, though, there's a few little things you need to know . . ."

Malcolm's glance revealed a surprising amount of dread.

Skeeter sighed. "This is the part where this mess gets really complicated. Although I think Margo's already tumbled to part of it."

Margo sat forward, eyes blazing with green fire. "You mean, if Jenna Caddrick's a prisoner, what was she doing at the lecture with Noah Armstrong? Running around London, free as a bird?"

"Exactly."

Malcolm shot his fiancée a startled glance. "I hadn't considered that. Yes, that does complicate things a bit."

Skeeter nodded. "You may not know it, but I was right beside Ianira when she was kidnapped. Armstrong knocked Ianira flat, swept her and me straight to the floor, just as Jenna Caddrick burst out of the crowd and shot a terrorist behind us. An armed one, about to murder Ianira. I started wondering why Armstrong would've knocked her out of an assassin's way, if he was trying to kill her, then I realized the kid who'd shot that terrorist couldn't be anybody but Jenna, herself. They hustled Ianira out of danger and pulled Marcus and the girls out of another terrorist hit at the daycare center. Then Armstrong and Julius took Marcus and the girls down the Wild West Gate—"

"And Jenna came here," Margo finished. "With Ianira."

"Right. And the hit men who went through the Wild West Gate killed Julius, thinking he was Jenna Caddrick."

Margo sat up very straight. "Then the men Benny Catlin killed were *hatchet men*? The one she shot at the Picadilly Hotel and the one who chased her all the way to the Royal Opera?"

"It certainly seems probable," Malcolm frowned. "But what game is Kaederman playing?"

"That," Skeeter answered softly, "is what I intend to find out. Somebody's lying. Either Kaederman is or the senator is."

"Or both," Margo muttered.

"Or both. So we've not only got to find Armstrong and Miss Caddrick, but we don't dare let Kaederman know, if we do locate them. Not 'til we know more about his game and why he's playing it."

"Skeeter," Malcolm sighed, "you have a distressing knack for handing out problems it would take Sherlock Holmes, himself, to untangle."

Skeeter grinned and dug out Goldie Morran's counterfeit banknotes and his Pinkerton badge. "Maybe so, but this time, I've got an ace or two up my sleeve . . ."

Kit Carson had narrowly avoided death hundreds of times during his career as a time scout. But no one had ever tried to crush him by shoving luggage off a five-story platform. The man who'd crashed the Britannia scored a first in Kit's life. Kit saw the big cases slither over the edge of the platform, slither and topple and fall straight toward him, where he stood trapped in the middle of a sardine-packed crowd.

He did the only thing he could. *"Look out!"*

Then shoved aside three women, knocked down two reporters, and lunged sideways, himself, trying to get as many of them as possible out of the way. People screamed and bolted, trampling one another in a rising panic. Then he was down, sprawled flat under running feet, as the enormous steamer trunks revolved in a slow-motion tumble . . .

Steel struck sparks when the first trunk smashed into the lobby floor. Catches burst and contents exploded as the other four trunks and a deadly rain of portmanteaus cannoned into the wild crowd. One of the smaller cases bounced, cracking down one whole side, then rebounded like a grenade into a hapless tourist just above Kit. The blow struck the man's arm so hard, all that broke loose was a sick gasp.

A woman in high heels ran straight across Kit's back, digging divots through his ribs. Kit dragged himself under the rope barricades into the departures lounge, away from the outward rush of fleeing spectators. He'd no more than pulled himself under the nearest

staircase when the man who'd crashed the Britannia
leaped over the railing, landing atop the hapless tourist
with the shattered arm. The man went down with a
scream. The gate crasher staggered, going down under
the weight of the woman slung over his shoulder, then
someone slammed against him and he dropped his
hostage. The woman slithered, unconscious, to the floor
as the gate crasher disappeared under the feet of the
wild throng.

Kit scrambled out from under the stairs, running
toward the abandoned hostage, who lay ominously still.
He checked gently for broken bones and tested the
pulse at her throat, unable to reach her wrist under
its tight Victorian sleeve. She lay crumpled on her
stomach, long dark hair falling in disarray across her
face, obscuring her features. Kit was afraid to move
her until he was certain there were no broken bones.
Very gently, he eased her hair back . . . and gasped
sharply. *Shahdi Feroz!* What was the Ripperologist
doing back in TT-86, weeks too early? She'd followed
the gate crasher through, leading the efforts to capture
him. Kit didn't care for the ominous implications.

A nasty bruise was swelling and purpling along her
temple. She needed medical attention. Kit searched the
confusion of screaming, running tourists. Half-a-dozen
fistfights were in progress and a medi-van was just
arriving at the edge of the riot zone.

"Medical!" The roar of the seething melee swallowed
his shout as though he'd barely whispered. The only
people who heard were a handful of vultures who'd
descended on the spilled luggage, carting off cash and
valuables. The nearest looter glanced up, looked right
at him, then ran for cover, pockets stuffed with spoils.
Kit cursed roundly. He'd have to go find someone.

Kit bolted through the chaos, heading toward the
arriving medi-vans. He reached the nearest and flagged

down a team. "Medical! Dr. Shahdi Feroz is back there, unconscious. The gate crasher knocked her out."

The emergency technician said, "Sorry, we're under a triage emergency. We're transporting critical cases first. There's already been one outright murder. Someone snapped a tourist's neck like kindling." The technician was stooping to work feverishly over a tourist whose broken leg lay at a ghastly angle, with bone protruding from the skin and blood spurting from a severed artery. The tech had tightened down a tourniquet and was trying to stabilize the break enough to transport for surgery.

"Do what you have to," Kit shot back, "but somebody'll want to talk to her ASAP, ask her why she came running through the gate after that maniac, and why he tried to snatch her."

The tech shot him a startled glance, finished strapping the leg brace over the tourniquet, then grabbed his squawky while others lifted the tourist into the back of a medi-van. "We need an assist, pronto, with Dr. Shahdi Feroz. Station manager's gonna want her story the minute she's awake. She's near—" the tech asked with a glance and Kit pointed "—the gate platform stairs."

The radio crackled. "Roger, we've got somebody on it."

"Thanks," Kit nodded.

He was pushing his way back toward Dr. Feroz when the entire station shook to the thunder of emergency sirens. Kit jerked to a stunned halt as the pattern of the maddened wail registered. *"Code Seven Red! Repeat, Code Seven Red!* Clear the Commons! All visitors to Shangri-La Station, clear the Commons immediately! Visitors are hereby restricted to hotel rooms for their own safety. Station residents, please assist security in clearing Commons. Repeat, Code Seven Red, Zone Three . . ."

"*Code Seven Red?*" Kit gasped.

That particular code hadn't been invoked in the entire history of Shangri-La Station. And Zone Three was right outside the infirmary, in Little Agora. Kit bolted, heading for the trouble zone, intent on finding out what had just broken loose inside the station. He met the answer at the door to the infirmary. Ann Vinh Mulhaney, bleeding badly, was being rushed toward surgery by station security. A gash ran down her shoulder, shallow enough, thank God, not to prove instantly fatal, but her collar bone had been laid bare by the slashing attack. She held one of her Irish Royal Constabulary Webley pistols in a white-knuckled death grip. From the look in her eyes, it would take an act of God to pry it loose again.

Rachel appeared at a dead run. "Get her onto a gurney!" she ordered, ripping open the remains of Ann's blouse to apply direct pressure with both hands. "Compresses, stat!"

A nurse ran for the supply cabinet.

Ann Vinh Mulhaney's lips were moving as the gurney rushed past Kit, on a direct course for surgery. "Bastard was on me before I knew he was there. Almost got my stomach. Dropped to the floor to get out from under his knife. Pulled my Webley, shot at him. Missed, God *damn* the son of a bitch . . ."

The Code Seven Red made abrupt, horrifying sense. Kit knew, without anyone having to confirm it, who their gate crasher had been and why Shahdi Feroz had bolted into the station on his heels. Kit shut his eyes for a long, horrified moment.

Jack the Ripper.

Loose on Shangri-La Commons.

And with Mary Kelly still very much alive in London of 1888, it was high odds he couldn't even be killed. History could not be changed. Jolly Jack had to survive long enough to cut that poor girl into mangled pieces.

Kit began to curse, starting in English and moving through Portuguese, German, Latin, Old Norse, and every other language he'd ever learned. If the petite weapons instructor hadn't been so well trained, if she hadn't been the kind of woman who went armed everywhere but bed . . .

Station sirens slashed through the infirmary once more.

"Code Seven Red, Zone Five! Repeat, Code Seven Red, Zone Five! All resident time scouts and guides, report to station security immediately for emergency duty. Clear the Commons at once, this station is hereby under martial law. Code Seven Red, Zone Five . . ."

Kit bolted toward the door, glancing at the television in the infirmary lobby, tuned to Channel Three, which was permanently hooked into the Commons' extensive security-camera system. Station security, pest control, even BATF agents herded terrified and angry tourists toward their hotels, using riot batons to push them along when necessary.

"Caddrick is gonna eat this up like a hog in heaven," Kit groaned, abandoning the television and heading out the door at a dead run. He had barely cleared the entryway when it came again. *"Code Seven Red! Zone Six!* All Shangri-La shop owners, lock down and secure your areas. Any visitors not clear of the Commons in three minutes will be arrested on sight. Repeat, Code Seven Red, Zone Six . . ."

Security rushed past carrying a woman with long, dark hair. She'd been gashed from navel to groin. A badly shaken security officer was holding her abdomen closed, keeping direct pressure on with hands gloved in blood, while two others carried her. Kit started rounding up shaken, confused tourists. "Clear the Commons!" he roared above the wailing sirens. "Get to a hotel!"

"But we're in the Neo Edo!"

"I don't care if you're camping out in the basement!
Get to the nearest hotel and stay there!" He herded
them toward the Time Tripper, which was closest. They
could sort out who was supposed to be where later,
after the innocents had been gotten out of harm's way.
Within five minutes, Commons was nearly clear,
echoingly empty. Scores of tourists huddled in shop
entryways and restaurants, ashen and trapped, unable
to reach their hotels. Security and Pest Control officers,
even BATF, rushed through the station, driving remnant
crowds toward safety. At the edge of Little Agora, Kit
could just see two more ashen, grey-lipped security
officers carrying the bloodied remains of yet another
petite woman with long, dark hair. This one hadn't
survived. Her throat had been slashed to the bone, her
abdomen ripped and gashed.

Kit cursed long and harshly, driving his last charges
into the Time Tripper's crowded lobby, then headed
for the nearest security team to offer his services for
the manhunt. Wally Klontz' radio crackled just as Kit
jogged up.

"We need a medical team in Valhalla, stat! Massive
coronary at the Langskip Cafe."

"On it!" a harried voice responded.

"What can I do?" Kit asked as Wally sent a team
of Pest Control officers bolting toward the emergency.

"Kit, thank God. Try to find someone from the
Council of Seven, get the down-timers organized. We
need a station-wide manhunt. Jack the Goddamned
Ripper crashed the Britannia and the Ripper Cults
have gone mad, attacking every petite, dark-haired
woman on station."

Kit's eyes widened. "My God! They're trying to kill
Shahdi Feroz."

"What?"

"Shahdi Feroz! She came through the Britannia after the Ripper. He tried to kidnap her, but dropped her in the riot. I left her lying unconscious at the departures lounge, waiting for medical treatment."

Wally Klontz keyed his radio. "Alert, Signal Eight-Delta, repeat, Signal Eight-Delta, missing person, Dr. Shahdi Feroz. Expedite, condition red. We need a location on Dr. Feroz, stat. She's the Ripper's target."

The radio crackled and sputtered, then someone said, "Roger, Signal Eight-Delta, Shahdi Feroz."

Kit said tersely, "I'm heading back to Victoria Station to look for her."

Wally nodded as his radio crackled again. Kit broke into a run as Wally flagged down a pair of BATF agents. Commons had never been so echoingly deserted. A score or more of injuries, an outright murder during the Britannia riot, and three women slashed by the Ripper cults, sparking three Code Seven Reds in damn near as many minutes . . . How many more people would die before they could stop this maniac and his worshippers? *If* they could stop him? John Caddrick would have a field day with this, curse him. And God alone knew what those damned I.T.C.H. agents would do, faced with fresh disaster. Shangri-La Station needed a miracle.

Kit was very much afraid they'd just run out of grace.

Chapter Thirteen

Ianira Cassondra woke slowly from a long, blurred
nightmare to the sound of rumbling wagons, bright
voices speaking incomprehensible English, and the
laughter of small children at play. She stirred beneath
warm quilts and turned her head toward the sounds,
deeply confused. The presence which had waited like
a monstrous, ravening wolf, swooping down across her
each time she had awakened from drugged stupor,
was gone without a trace. For long moments she
could not bring herself to believe that, even when
her eyelids fluttered open to reveal a shabby, well-
scrubbed room she had never seen before.

Someone moved close beside her and she focused
her gaze slowly on a familiar face. She knew him at
once, but the change in those familiar, beloved
features shocked her speechless. Marcus' face was
lined, his hair greying at the temples, and a terror
of long standing burned hot in his eyes. His smile
was radiant as the sunlight, however, as he took her
hand. "You are home, Ianira. Safe."

She lifted a trembling hand, touching his face, finding wetness under her fingertips. "How—?"

"We followed him. He gave a lecture and we followed him when he went beneath the streets. We found you after he had gone, took you out of his horrible little room and brought you home. We're in London, beloved, in Spitalfields, hiding with Noah and Jenna. The girls are safe with us."

She began to cry, from sheer relief and the release of pent-up terror. Marcus held her close and she clutched him tightly, revelling in the touch of his hands and lips. "I tried to escape," she whispered, "but he caught me. Kept me drugged. Marcus, he wanted to use me, to gain power . . ."

"He is mad," Marcus said roughly.

"Yes. He is the Ripper."

Marcus' arms tightened protectively. "You will never see him again. This, I swear."

When the first storm of emotion had finally passed, Ianira tipped her head back and gazed into her husband's wet eyes. "I want to see our children, husband."

Marcus hesitated

Ianira touched the grey in his hair. "Tell me."

"We had no choice," he began, voice agonized. "They came after us, in Colorado. Julius . . ." He faltered. "Julius died, beloved. Their gunman murdered him. Noah and I took the girls away, ran for the train and fled east."

The grey in his hair, the lines that had aged his face, his reluctance to call the girls made abrupt sense. "You did not return to the station," she whispered, shaken. "It has been three years for you, hasn't it?"

He nodded. "Please forgive me . . ."

She could not stop the tears, but lifted a trembling hand and placed it across his lips. "No, there is nothing to forgive. I have seen what war does to people.

Ephesus was fighting for her independence. Was not my marriage to an Athenian part of that war, with me as a sacrifice? You and I have been caught in another war, Marcus. We are under attack from these men who seek Jenna's life. They use madmen like the *Ansar Majlis* to destroy and terrorize. In such a war, losing three years of your company, three years from my children's lives is nothing. Nothing at all, compared to losing *you*."

The terror faded from his eyes, replaced by a flood of tears. He kissed her gently, as though she were made of fragile alabaster, and smoothed back her hair where long strands clung to damp cheeks. Then he went to the door and called in their children. Artemisia had grown into a tall, beautiful girl of seven, with wide, dark eyes and a curiously adult air of watchfulness and restraint. Gelasia clung to her sister's hand, eyes bright and inquisitive as she studied Ianira.

Little Gelasia spoke first. "Are you really my mamma?"

Ianira's throat closed and Artemisia said in a voice tinged with distinct British tones, "Of course she is, don't you remember?" Then Misia rushed across the room, flinging herself into Ianira's arms. "I missed you, Mamma!"

"Oh, my darling . . ."

Little Gelasia was more than willing to accept the return of a mother into her life, snuggling up to Ianira and telling her solemnly about her new doll and the lessons Noah had been giving them. "I can read!" she said proudly. "Papa and Noah taught me!"

"You have always been a clever girl," Ianira smiled. "You and Misia, both." She ruffled her older daughter's hair affectionately. "What do you study, Misia?"

"English and Greek and Latin," she answered promptly, "with Papa, and history and mathematics and geography with Noah and Jenna." A shy smile came and went. "And we study the future, too. Noah has a little computer, like a time scout's log, so we will understand science and technology when we go home to the station."

Home to the station . . .

"You miss the station?" Ianira asked softly.

Artemisia nodded. "Sometimes. I miss the school and the television and the music. And I miss Uncle Skeeter. Do you remember when we fed the big pterodactyl and the bucket of fish spilled down his shirt? I can just remember that. We laughed and laughed."

"We all miss Uncle Skeeter," Ianira agreed. "When it is safe again, we will go home."

Artemisia's eyes told Ianira that her daughter remembered the violence of their last day on the station only too clearly. "Yes, Mamma. When it is safe again. If the bad men come here, I will help Noah and Jenna and Papa kill them."

Ianira shivered. Another casualty of war: innocence.

"Then we must hope," Ianira said gently, "that the bad men never come, because I will never let anyone harm my beautiful little girls."

As she hugged her daughters close, Ianira could sense danger beyond the walls of their house in Spitalfields. It was not the same danger she had felt in John Lachley's presence. This was a cold, implacable danger which threatened from the future, from the world beyond the station's Primary Gate. Somewhere nearby, the killers who had sought Jenna's life in New York and their own lives on the station were searching for them in the dismal, rain-drenched streets of London.

Skeeter was up at the crack of dawn and on the street very shortly afterward, with Margo as a guide. They left Spaldergate House in company with a mass of Time Tours baggage handlers, groomsmen from the stables, even a couple of the housemaids, all detailed to the search team.

"We'll spread out through SoHo first," Margo briefed them in the dimly lit stable. "We'll search street by street, combing the clothiers shops. We're looking for a merchant or merchants who've been robbed with counterfeit banknotes. Strike up casual conversations, see what you can turn up. If you stumble onto a hot lead, get word to Skeeter and me. I'll be wearing an earpiece under my hat, so you can signal me by radio." She handed around miniaturized transmitters, which vanished into coat pockets. "I'd advise taking umbrellas, since it looks like more rain. And here are the photos Mr. Gilbert reproduced last night." She handed out thick, card-backed "tin-type" prints of Noah Armstrong, Marcus, and "Benny Catlin" as they'd appeared at the lecture, taken from Margo's scout log. "Any questions? All right, then, let's move."

A Time Tours carriage drove Skeeter and Margo to Regent Street, an ultrafashionable thoroughfare lined with ritzy tailors' establishments, fine bootmakers' shops, ladies' milliners, every sort of fashionable emporium a Londoner might want to visit. At this hour, Regent Street was very nearly silent, the shops deserted and the streets clear of traffic. "We won't actually be searching Regent Street," Margo told Skeeter, carefully holding her skirts and long umbrella aside as Skeeter handed her down to the pavement. "But Regent Street forms the western border of SoHo, which is jam-packed with the kind of shops middle-class businessmen frequent. These," she waved the tip of her umbrella toward the expensive establishments along Regent Street, "won't even open for a couple of hours, but SoHo gets up with the birds, same as its clientele."

She was right about that. As Skeeter escorted her

eastward, activity and noise picked up sharply. Delivery wagons groaned through the streets, their heavy drays straining against harness and collar, heads thrust forward and hooves ringing against the cobbles with the sharp sound of iron on stone. Shop keepers rattled open doors, jangling tiny brass bells against the glass, while clerks arranged window displays to their liking and called greetings to the draymen or dickered over prices and freight charges with delivery men. Shop girls, neat as pins in their starched dresses and aprons, bustled to greet early customers. A tantalizing drift from a bakery's open door set Skeeter's mouth to watering.

"Let's start there," Margo decided, nodding toward a respectable looking shop advertising gentlemen's suiting off the rack.

Skeeter held the door, escorting Margo inside. A middle-aged clerk in a well-made if inexpensive suit greeted them. "Good morning. How may I assist you?"

Margo gave the clerk a surprisingly cool smile, causing Skeeter to glance more sharply at her. "Good morning," she inclined her head politely. "My name is Smythe, sir, and this is Mr. Jackson, of America. We're hoping you might be of some assistance in a rather difficult situation. Mr. Jackson is a Pinkerton man, a sort of private police agency. He's come to London on the trail of a counterfeiter, a man who's deprived me of a considerable sum of money I could ill afford to lose."

"Counterfeiter?" Genuine alarm showed in the clerk's guileless eyes. "D'you mean to say we've a counterfeiter working in SoHo?"

Skeeter produced a sample of Goldie's fake banknotes. "These are some of the forgeries recovered from Miss Smythe, here. I have reason to believe the men producing these banknotes are passing them somewhere in SoHo. This young lady is not the only vicitm they have damaged. I've traced this gang from Colorado to New York to London and I mean to locate them, sir."

The clerk's eyes had widened in sympathetic surprise. "I should hope so! I'll check the cash drawer at once!" The clerk searched carefully, but located none of Goldie's fake banknotes, nor could he recall having seen any of the gentlemen in the photographs Skeeter produced. The clerk frowned over them, shaking his head. "No, sir, I'm afraid I don't recognize any of them. But I'll certainly be on my guard and I shall inform my employer immediately to be wary of any fivers and ten-pound notes we receive."

"My card," Skeeter handed over the first of several dozen Spaldergate's staff had run off for him the previous night, "if anything should turn up."

"Deeply obliged, sir," the clerk said earnestly, "for the warning. I'll keep your card right here in the cash drawer."

Skeeter tipped his hat as Margo thanked the clerk, then they headed for the next shop. And the one after that, moving from street to street, until Skeeter's feet ached and his throat burned and the skies poured miserable, sooty rain down their collars. He and Margo hastily opened thick umbrellas against the downpour and checked the time on Skeeter's pocket watch.

"One o'clock. No wonder my feet are killing me."

"And my stomach's about to have a close encounter with my spine," Margo said ruefully. "Let's find something to eat, then keep searching."

The afternoon was no more profitable than the morning had been, just wetter. By the time Margo admitted they'd struck out, the sun was already below the rooftops and the chilly evening wind was biting through Skeeter's overcoat.

"I'm afraid there's not much more we can do today," Margo sighed.

"Maybe someone else found something?"

"They would've contacted us," she said with a slight shake of her head. "Let's get back to Spaldergate. We'll cross check with everyone else and come up with a new plan of attack for tomorrow."

"My feet aren't even going to speak to me by tomorrow," Skeeter groaned, flagging down a ratty-looking hansom cab.

The two-wheeled, open carriage slithered to a halt at the kerbside. "Battersea," Margo called up as Skeeter handed her into the cab, "and I've consulted Mogg's!"

"Why, I'd never cheat a lady, miss!"

The cabbie flicked his reins and they set out at a jolting trot.

"What's Mogg's?" Skeeter asked, hanging onto his seat and struggling with his stubborn umbrella.

"Mogg's maps." She pulled a little booklet from her handbag and passed it over. "Study it carefully. It lists the fares for every conceivable route through the city. Otherwise, cabbies will cheat you blind."

"I'll remember that," Skeeter said as the horse jolted around a corner and swung smartly into heavy traffic, nearly colliding with two carriages and a drayman's wagon and eliciting rude commentaries from cabbies they narrowly avoided while rounding a traffic circus Skeeter didn't recognize. "If we survive so long. Man, not even New York traffic is this nuts!"

Margo just grimaced and held on.

True to Margo's prediction, nobody else had found a trace of counterfeit banknotes, nor had anyone located a witness who could identify Armstrong, Catlin, or Marcus. Skeeter was feeling massively discouraged when he eased his aching, blistered feet into a basin of hot water in his bedroom. Maybe they hadn't bought their clothes in SoHo? Or maybe they'd lucked out and used genuine banknotes when making the purchase?

What else would they have to buy, which could be paid for with Goldie's counterfeit banknotes? Food, of course, and coal for the cookstove and fireplace. But they weren't likely to pay for any of *that* with five- and ten-pound banknotes.

"Well," he mused aloud, "they have to live somewhere, don't they?" Had they brought enough cash between them to buy a house or were they reduced to renting? Probably the latter, unless Armstrong had found lucrative employment somewhere. According to Goldie's records, she hadn't changed enough currency for "Benny Catlin" to buy a London house, not even a really ratty one. But if they were renting, they might well use larger denominations to make the payments. "I wonder how somebody goes about renting a house in London?"

He asked that question at dinner, since Kaederman had announced his intention of taking all his meals in his room. Malcolm toyed thoughtfully with a spoonful of turtle soup—the mock variety, since no one in Spaldergate House would buy sea turtle, even if the creatures wouldn't be endangered for another century. As he pushed around bits of mock turtle meat, Malcolm's brow furrowed slightly.

"We hadn't pursued that avenue of inquiry, Skeeter, because finding one man in all of London by knocking up every leasing agency in the city is an even longer shot than checking infirmaries and hospital wards. But we're not looking for Benny Catlin on his own, any longer, we're looking for a rather conspicuous group, aren't we? Yes, we might do well, at that, searching for some trace of such a group. One leases a house through a variety of means, generally via agencies which maintain lists of properties to let. Quite a few such agencies also have telephones, these days. We could put someone on it from Spaldergate while the rest of us continue to search along other lines. And there will certainly be agencies we shall have to check in person."

Miss Tansy, Spaldergate's capable administrative assistant, offered to compile a list. "I'll begin telephoning when the agencies open tomorrow."

"Thanks," Skeeter said, flashing her a grateful smile.

When he finally crawled into bed, he dreamed of endless shopfronts, their windows streaming with sooty grey rain, and of endless, babbling voices and blurred faces reflecting only puzzled bafflement as he posed question after question. When Skeeter finally woke, aching and tired with the unfair exhaustion that comes of too many stressful dreams, he roused into consciousness with an immediate awareness of a renewed throbbing from his feet, a gradual awareness of watery light and the spatter of rain falling against his window, and the unhappy knowledge that he would have to coax his swollen and protesting feet through several more miles of London's maze-like collection of storefronts. He sighed, eased gingerly out of bed, and got ready for another day of searching.

Surely there had to be an easier way to go legit?

Shahdi Feroz knew she was lucky when she woke up on the Commons floor. She was alive. Frankly, she hadn't expected to wake up again. She tried to move and bit her lips over a gasp of pain, then opted for lying very still, instead. A station riot had erupted as far as her swollen right eye could see. Given the shocking bruises she could feel the length of her body, Shahdi suspected panic stricken tourists had stepped on her, multiple times. John Lachley's single, if somewhat devastating, right cross to her temple couldn't begin to account for her stiff, unresponsive limbs and aching back muscles.

At the moment, she could only give profound and

shaken thanks that John Lachley had dropped her at all. What he would've done to her . . . She shuddered, recalling the sight of Dominica Nosette's severed head clutched in his hand. Poor, stupid reporter. The rest of her lay in the basement of New Scotland Yard on Whitehall; they'd watched Lachley drop off the mutilated torso and bid her a flippant farewell, via the camera hidden at the construction site. Shahdi was gingerly flexing her fingers, trying to decide whether or not her body would accept being pushed to hands and knees, when someone literally dragged her to her feet. Blinding light caught her square in the eyes and the world erupted into a chaos of shouting voices.

"Dr. Feroz—"

"—comment—"

"—really Jack the Ripper—"

"—how could you allow that monster—"

She stumbled and swayed sharply, and would've fallen again if she hadn't collided with someone far taller and heavier than herself. The man grasped her by the shoulders, keeping her on her feet, then a new voice thundered into her awareness.

"By God, you're going to answer for this!"

Before she could even blink her vision clear, Shahdi was dragged forward, tottering off balance, literally hauled through the chaos by a man whose grip added another layer of bruises. Still half-stunned from Lachley's blow, she couldn't even offer a struggle for the first hundred paces. By the time her head was clear enough to realize she'd just been assaulted—again—and had been kidnapped by some new maniac, there wasn't a security officer in sight.

Shahdi dug in her heels. "Let go of me!"

She wasn't sure whose face she expected to swing furiously into focus.

Senator John Caddrick hadn't even made her list of possibilities. She gasped, then wrenched her arm free. "Who do you think you are? Take your hands off me at once!"

"Oh, no you don't!" Caddrick snarled, dragging her forward again. "You and I have an appointment with federal authorities. I want some answers!"

She twisted free once more, ready for combat. "Touch me again and I will have you jailed for assault and battery!"

Before Caddrick could reply—or grab her wrist again—a howling mob of reporters descended, screaming questions and thrusting cameras and microphones into their faces. From somewhere out of the confusion, a uniformed BATF agent appeared.

"Thank God! You found her!" the agent cried, speaking briefly into her radio. "Secure from Signal Eight-Delta, I have Dr. Feroz, unharmed."

"Roger, bring her in."

"Dr. Feroz, please come with me immediately. Your life is in danger."

Another security patrol rushed toward them, flanking Shahdi and pushing back reporters with a certain callousness that shocked her.

"What's going on?" Caddrick demanded.

"Dr. Feroz is being taken into protective custody. The Ripper cults have targeted her for murder."

While she tried to take in the implications of that shocking statement, the security agents hustled Shahdi through the station, leaving Caddrick and the reporters to trail after them, shouting questions nobody answered. They literally dragged Shahdi through the doorway into security headquarters, with the senator and fifty screaming newsies on their heels. The lobby was in chaos. Agents scrambled past them, swearing and shoving reporters aside with scant regard for broken equipment. Telephones shrilled for attention between deafening hoots from the station's emergency sirens. Dispatchers shouted instructions into radios, scribbled information from the reports crackling over the speakers.

John Caddrick stood staring at the confusion, then strode toward the main desk, mouth thinned to near invisibility. Shahdi was escorted past the uncertain haven of the dispatcher's desk where a harried woman was shouting into a radio. A moment later, Shahdi found herself in a nearly empty corridor lined with closed doors. "This way, Dr. Feroz," her escort said, steering her around a corner. They cannoned straight into someone at least two feet taller than Shahdi was. She staggered and fell against the wall, then found herself staring up at Ronisha Azzan, Shangri-La's Deputy Station Manager.

"Dr. Feroz?" Ronisha Azzan blinked. "Thank God, I was told you'd been located. Come with me, please. I was just coming down to meet you."

Behind the tall deputy station manager, a squat, fire-plug shape was storming down the corridor like a torpedo fired at a battleship. Shahdi blinked in surprise. Bull Morgan was out of jail. Caddrick rounded the corner at just that moment, then stood sputtering. "What's he doing out of jail?"

The squat station manager growled, "What the hell is he doing here?" reminding Shahdi of an angry pit bull.

Caddrick flushed, nostrils flaring with barely controlled anger as he stared up at the tall deputy station manager beside Bull Morgan. "Azzan, I will have your head for this! Letting a known criminal out of jail before—"

Bull Morgan shouldered him aside. "Get out of my security headquarters. You're obstructing an emergency operation during a declared state of martial law. Leave right now or pick out your cell in the detention block. The one I've been using is free."

"How dare you—"

The security agents who'd escorted Shahdi to safety produced handcuffs and startlingly effective grins. The nearest said with a chuckle, "Mr. Morgan never bluffs, Senator. And neither does the BATF."

Caddrick sputtered for an instant longer, then turned on his heel and strode away. Bull bit the end of a cigar he'd magicked out of a pocket. "Better give that schmuck an escort back to his hotel. God knows, we don't want anything happening to him out there."

Security pelted after him as Bull appropriated his deputy manager's radio. *"Benson!* Report, goddammit!" He strode off before Shahdi could hear the reply. Ronisha Azzan stalked after him, drawing Shahdi along.

"Ms. Azzan," she said, wincing as the rapid pace jolted her bruises, "I don't know what a Code Seven Red is, but I do know Jack the Ripper is loose on this station and right now, I know more about Dr. John Lachley than anyone else on TT-86. I'd like to help."

The tall deputy manager nodded her thanks. "Doctor, you just got yourself a job."

Moments later, she was at ground zero of the biggest crisis in the history of time tourism, wondering what on earth she was going to tell the harried, white-faced security officers looking to her for answers.

By the end of his first week in London, Skeeter Jackson had begun to think Jenna Caddrick and Noah Armstrong had made their own clothes. Or that Noah had bought their entire wardrobe in the States and brought it over by ship. Hundreds of tailors' shops and ready-made clothing stores, scattered throughout SoHo, had yielded not so much as a trace of the missing senator's daughter and her companions. Even the inquiry into leasing agents had drawn a blank. None of the agents they consulted had found any counterfeit banknotes, nor could they identify the photos Skeeter and the other searchers circulated.

At Malcolm's suggestion, they turned their attention to the East End, a far more dangerous territory to search. Teams consisted of three searchers minimum, for safety's sake. Also at Malcolm's suggestion, Sid Kaederman remained at Spaldergate, supervising the teams fielded to question private physicians and surgeons; the actual questioning was done by Spaldergate staff and Time Tours porters.

Skeeter's first run into the East End was supervised by two seasoned pros: Malcolm and Margo, who wanted to be sure he knew the ropes before turning him loose with a couple of groomsmen. Whitechapel, with its dismal, dirty streets and its stench of rotting refuse in the gutters, was open for business well before Skeeter arrived, less than an hour past dawn.

Immense wagonloads of freight groaned their cumbersome way down Houndsditch, Aldgate High Street, and Commercial Street. Heavy drays with chipped, ponderous hooves and shabby coats of hair growing in thick for winter, strained against worn leather harness and collars. The big draft horses carted vast tonnages of export goods to the docks for shipment across the face of the world, and brought out staggering amounts of raw lumber and bales of cotton arriving from foreign shores, huge bundles of animal hides and fur for the leather and garment industries, ingots of pig iron and copper and tin for the smelting plants and iron works which belched their stinking smoke into Whitechapel's skies. The high whine and rasp of industrial saws poured from open factory windows, like clouds of enraged wasps spilling furiously from a nest shaken by a foolish little boy.

And everywhere, the people: dirty to the pores with coal smoke and industrial grime no amount of scrubbing with harsh lye soap could remove. Women in frowsy dresses ran bakeshops, trundled basketloads of fish and flowers, plied meat cleavers against stained butchers' blocks in grimy little storefronts whose back rooms often hid the misery and desperation of illegal abortions. Men hauled butchered carcasses over their shoulders or gutted fish in stinking open-air markets where feral cats and fat, sleek rats fought for discarded offal and fish heads.

Other men hauled handcarts piled high with bricks and building stone or carried grinding wheels on frayed leather harnesses, calling out in roughened voices, "Knives to grind!" as they wandered from shop to doorstep. Boys ran urgent errands, clutching baskets of vegetables and heavy stacks of newspapers, or trundled rickety wheelbarrows spilling over with piles of red, coarse brick dust which they sold in little sackfuls. One boy jogged along with a ferret in his arms, leading a bright-eyed spaniel on a worn leather leash.

"Good grief, is that a pet ferret?" Skeeter turned to stare.

Malcolm followed his glance. "Not a pet. That boy's a rat-catcher. 'You maun have a ferret, to catch a rat,'" he added in what sounded suspiciously like a quotation. "He'll spend the day over in the better parts of town, de-ratting some rich woman's house. The ferret chases them out and the spaniel kills the sneaky little beasts."

"And the boy gets paid a small fortune by some hysterical housewife," Skeeter guessed.

Margo shook her head. "More likely by some frantic housekeeper who doesn't want to lose her place because rats have broken into the cellar or littered in the best linens."

"There is that," Skeeter admitted as the boy dodged

past, heading west. Then he spotted a long, shallow wooden trough where girls appeared to be dunking handfuls of dried leaves into stinking dye. "What in the world are they doing?"

"Dying tea leaves," Malcolm said drolly.

"*Dying* them? What for?"

Margo chuckled. "There's fortunes to made in the tea recycling business. Housekeepers in wealthy households sell used tea leaves for a tidy sum, then girls in the tea trade dye the leaves so they look new and sell them in the poorer parts of town."

"Remind me not to buy tea anywhere around here. What's in that stuff they're using? It smells horrible."

"Don't ask," Malcolm said repressively.

"You don't want to know what's in the food around here, either," Margo added. "They keep passing laws against putting in the worst stuff. Like brick dust in sausages, as filler."

"Remind me to skip lunch. And I'm not a squeamish eater." A guy couldn't spend five years in Yesukai the Valiant's tent and stay finicky, not if he wanted to survive. But he'd never eaten brick dust—of that, at least, he was morally certain. They passed the Ten Bells, a public house strategically poised on the corner of roaring Commercial Street and Fournier, within sight of the gleaming white spire of Christchurch, Spitalfields. Rough-dressed men loitered near the entrance, eyeing tired women who walked slowly past, returning the interested stares with calculating glances. A shabby woman selling roasted chestnuts beside the door paid the prostitutes no attention, reserving her efforts for paying customers. One woman who'd stopped to rest against the pub's wall was driven away by a nearby constable.

"Move on, there, or I'll take you in, so I will!"

The woman's reply was not precisely in English,

baffling Skeeter with a sharp spate of incomprehensible syllables, but she moved farther down the street. Skeeter scratched his neck. "What was that all about?"

Malcolm said quietly, "They aren't allowed to pick a spot and solicit. They have to keep moving. Women walk from pub to pub, or simply circle a building like Saint Botolph's Church, known locally as the 'prostitutes' church,' for the women walking in dreary circles around it, hours at a time. They often stake out little territories without ever stopping long enough to get themselves arrested. Mary Kelly patrols the area around the Ten Bells pub, there. Rumor is, she's very jealous of her beat. Of course, that may just be sour grapes from the other women. She's very pretty and vivacious. She likes to sing and the men like her."

Margo put in, "Women like poor Liz Stride would've hated her for it."

Skeeter had seen enough pictures of Long Liz to know she'd been a mannish, horse-faced Swede, missing half her teeth, poor creature. Word was, her lover had been utterly devastated by her death. "Well," Skeeter cleared his throat, "where do we start? I hadn't realized the East End was so big."

"Huh, this is nothing," Margo put in. "You ought to see the docklands. They stretch out to forever."

Malcolm cast a jaundiced eye at his fiancée. "I fear Mr. Jackson will have ample opportunity to tour the docklands before this business is done. Now that you've seen something of Whitechapel, Mr. Jackson, and have a feel for the territory, I would suggest we repair to Middlesex Street. If they're supplying their wardrobe from the East End, it's the likest spot to search."

"I'm following you," Skeeter said ruefully.

Malcolm led the way past Christchurch, which rose in startling white purity from the grime, and walked briskly down to Fashion Street, then cut over to

Middlesex, a long block to the west. The Sunday cloth fair which had given the street its famous nickname was conspicuously absent, but shops selling ready-mades of a cheap cut, mostly stitched from mill-ends cloth, were open for business. Malcolm pushed open the door of the nearest, leaving Skeeter and Margo to follow. As the door swung shut with a solid thump, a well-scrubbed shop girl in a worn dress eyed them, taking in their fine clothes with a dubious, narrow-eyed stare.

"Wot you 'ere for?" she asked suspiciously. "You never come round 'ere t'buy togs, not the likes of you, wiv yer fancy city suiting."

Malcolm doffed his hat. "Good morning, miss. No, indeed, you're very sharp. We're hoping you might be able to help us. We're looking for someone."

"I ain't like to grass on nobody, I ain't," she muttered.

Malcolm produced a shining shilling and said casually, "The gentlemen we're looking for are foreigners, miss, foreign swindlers and thieves. They have cheated this young lady of a substantial sum of money by passing counterfeit banknotes and they have robbed me of quite a sum the same way, passing their filthy money at a game of cards last week."

Margo spoke up in a voice Skeeter scarcely recognized. "Give me a fiver, 'e did, miss, said 'e 'adn't got nuffink smaller, an' I give 'im near four quid change for it, when it weren't worth the paper the cheeky blagger printed it on 'is own self."

The girl's eyes widened, her suspicion dwindling under the twin onslaughts of Margo's East-End voice and alarmingly serious complaint. Skeeter stepped forward with one of Goldie's sample banknotes. "My name is Jackson, ma'am, from America. I've trailed these criminals all the way from New York, where they were counterfeiting dollars. This is one of their forgeries." He handed over the banknote and let her peer curiously at it, then produced the photographs. "Have you seen any of these men?"

The shopgirl took the heavy cardstock photos and gazed at them carefully, shuffling through them. "No," she said slowly, "never clapped me minces on any blokes wot stood for these 'ere likenesses. But I'll look sharp, so I will. Some tea leaf passed me a bad fiver, I'd just about as well shut me doors an' walk the streets or starve." She handed the photos and the fake banknote back with a grim, angry look in her eyes. "Mark me, I'll keep a sharp butcher's out, so I will."

Malcolm handed her a small white card. "If you do see them, here is where you can reach me." He handed over the shilling, as well, which she pocketed hastily, along with Malcolm's card. He put his hat on again, tipping the brim. "Good day, miss."

They tried the next shop on Middlesex Street, then the one after that and the next in line, with Malcolm sometimes initiating the questions and occasionally Skeeter stepping in to fill that role. They had reached the end of the lane, having covered every shop in Middlesex Street, when a voice rose behind them.

"Mister Moore, sir! Wait a bit, mister!"

They looked around to see the first girl they'd questioned, running breathlessly toward them. They waited, hope suddenly an electrifying presence in their midst. The girl reached them and gasped out, "Cor, but I'm glad you 'adn't gone yet! Mistress just come into the shop, y'see, it's 'er shop, like, and I told 'er what you said. She thinks she knows of 'em, mister."

Skeeter exchanged startled glances with Margo as Malcolm said, "By all means, let us speak with your employer."

A moment later, they were showing the photographs to a stout, sallow-cheeked woman with white hair and poor teeth. "That's 'im, I don't doubt," the woman said, pointing to Noah Armstrong's photograph. "Of a Sunday, when the market's in the street, me sister-in-law sets up a stall just outside, there. Sold a fistful of suits, Sunday last, to a bloke wot give 'er a fiver. An' it weren't worth no more'n me shoelaces, come the time she went off t'spend it. I remember the bloke, as I was set up next ter Sally an' she were that excited, she were, t'get a fiver when she needed the money so desperate. Like to put 'er in the work'ouse, bastard did, 'an 'er a war widow wivout no 'usband nor child t'look after 'er in 'er age. It's me own profits, small as they are, wot's paid 'er rent an' put food in 'er Limehouse this week past."

"Do you remember anything about him that might help us locate him? Did he say anything about where he was staying?"

"That 'e didn't, or I'd 'ave sent a copper after 'im."

"My dear lady," Malcolm said, producing two five-pound notes from his wallet, "you have been of incalculable service. Please see that your sister-in-law's losses are replaced."

The old woman's eyes shot wide at the sight of so much money. She took the banknotes with a shaking hand, turned them over and over, staring at them. Wetness spilled over and traced down both cheeks as she closed wrinkled hands around the money. The crackle of crisp paper was loud in Skeeter's ears. Voice trembling, she said to her shopgirl, "Go an' fetch Sally, luv, tell 'er God sent a right proper angel t'look out for us. God bless you, mister."

The girl's eyes were bright, as well. She dropped a brief curtsey and ran out the back way. A door thumped, marking her exit, then Malcolm tipped his hat. "Good day, madam. Thank you again. If you hear anything else, your girl has my card."

They left her clutching the money to her bosom.

The moment the door swung shut behind Skeeter, Malcolm said, "They are here, then, as surmised. It remains to locate their hiding place. It occurs to me that they cannot be staying anywhere in the immediate area, or the shopkeepers hereabouts would have recognized them as neighbors."

"Well, they have to eat, don't they?" Skeeter pointed out.

Malcolm's eyes glinted. "Which means they must procure victuals from a chandler."

"Remember what you said, Malcolm?" Margo said thoughtfully. "If you were going to hide in the East End and knew you would be marked as a foreigner, you'd find a place with a high concentration of immigrants, so you wouldn't stand out so much. Like Spitalfields and Bethnal Green. Let's try the Chandler's Shops up there."

"Indeed," Malcolm glanced north. "A capital idea. Let us begin at Spitalfields Market, shall we?"

They walked rapidly north and jogged west to Bishopsgate, which they followed north again through the bustle and crowds of carts and groaning freight wagons and strolling vendors calling their wares. The market, when they arrived, was a vast confusion of Cockney voices singing out in rhyming patter that echoed with a roar of alien sound.

Fresh flowers spilled a heady perfume into the wet morning air, thousands of blossoms tied in dripping bunches. Flower girls piled them high into heavy baskets and trays for sale in better climes. Fresh vegetables heaped in mounds lent a more sober note to the riot of hothouse flowers. Fishwives haggled over the price of mussels and eels and ragged urchins bartered for coarse-ground flour while their harried mothers counted out pennies for bricks of tea.

"If we can't find a trace of them here," Malcolm

shouted above the roar, "I shall be very much surprised. Mr. Jackson, why don't you take the right-hand side of the market. Miss Smith, try the left-hand way and I shall tackle the middle."

They split up and Skeeter approached the first stall, where a sweating woman in her fifties manhandled huge rounds of cheese, hacking off wedges for sale. He gave her the pitch, holding up a shilling to catch her attention.

"Ain't seen 'em," she said shortly, pocketing Skeeter's money.

He tried again at the next stall, where re-dyed tea sold briskly. The negative response cost him another shilling and several elbows in his ribs from customers anxious to buy a brick of tea for tuppence. He moved on to a flower vendor who gave him a suspicious glare over the nodding heads of pure white daisies, their centers yellower than the sun over Spitalfields' grey sky. The woman shook her head impatiently and pocketed the coin. Skeeter glanced around, searching for Margo and Malcolm, making their grim, determined way through the stalls. He turned back with a sigh and tried the next vendor, where slabs of fatty bacon hung from meathooks.

"Why d'you ask about 'em?" the man behind the counter demanded sourly, eyes narrowed as he peered at the photographs.

"We believe they're counterfeiters. They've cheated a young lady who runs a shop up in Bethnal Green, gave her a counterfeit banknote that nearly landed her in the workhouse, unable to pay her bills. I've followed them all the way from America, where they printed dollars instead of pound notes." The man hesitated, giving Skeeter cause to hope. He fished out a glittering half crown coin. "I realize you don't like to grass on anyone," Skeeter said, holding up the coin, "but these men are

cheating women who can't afford the loss. An elderly
war widow in Middlesex Street lost five pounds to them."

The man's jaw muscles bunched. He spat to one
side, then tapped the photograph of Marcus. "I seen
'im, lots o' times. Lives wiv 'is sister and some chap
who come over from America. And a pair of sweet little
girls, God 'elp 'em, wiv a father like that. Comes 'ere
regular, like, t'buy bacon an' flour, 'e does, along wiv
'is sister."

Skeeter handed over the half crown and produced
a full sovereign, glittering gold in the light. "Where
do they live?"

The man jerked his head to the east. "Be'ind Christchurch, someplace along Fournier Street, is all I know."

"Thank you," Skeeter said quietly, handing over the
sovereign and retrieving his photographs. "More than
you can know."

He hurried through the mob, finding Malcolm near
the end of his own row. The guide wore an expression
of frustration. Skeeter waved him over. "Malcolm! I've
got a solid lead! Behind Christchurch, on Fournier!"

Malcolm's eyes came violently alive. "By damn,
Jackson, good work! Where's Miss Smith?"

They found Margo deep in conversation with a
woman selling flour by the scoop. Malcolm caught her
eye, but she lifted a hand, so they waited. When the
woman finished talking, Margo handed her a whole
sovereign and turned toward them, cheeks glowing with
excitement.

"You've found them, too?" Malcolm said without
preamble.

"Yes! Fournier Street, seventh house on the right.
Mr. Anastagio," she tapped Marcus' photo, "and his
sister and their friend, Mr. Dillon, from America."

"All I got was Fournier Street," Skeeter admitted
wryly.

"Cockney women," Margo chuckled, "love a good gossip. Especially when there's money in it. Let's go beard Mr. Anastagio in his den," she added, eyes bright with excitement.

"By all means," Malcolm agreed, heading out of the crowded market. "And let us pray that Mr. Dillon and Miss Anastagio do nothing rash before we convince them we are Marcus' friends."

Skeeter's heart was triphammering as they turned into Fournier Street and passed poor but well-scrubbed houses where stout women called to one another in Yiddish. At the seventh house on the right, they found shuttered windows and a closed door, but flowers grew in pots along the steps and smoke curled upwards from the chimney. Inside, Skeeter could hear the squeal and laughter of children's voices. His throat tightened. Artemisia's voice . . . teasing her sister . . . Malcolm and Margo waited expectantly, gazes locked on him. Skeeter nodded once, then climbed the stone steps and knocked on the door.

The voices inside cut off sharply, then footsteps hurried their way. Margo joined Skeeter on the top step, just as an unknown voice called out, "Who is it?"

Margo glanced at Skeeter, winking, then raised her voice to carry through the door. "Eh, luv, you got a dog?"

"What?"

"I ast, 'ave you got a dog? There's a bitch wot's littered pups on yer front steps."

The door opened quickly and Skeeter found himself staring at "Benny Catlin"—Jenna Caddrick in the flesh, wearing woolen trousers and a heavy flannel shirt. Wide eyes swept down, looking automatically for the mythical puppies. Suspicion and wild terror leaped into Jenna's eyes and she tried to slam the door in their faces. Margo shoved her foot against it and said, "It's no use running, Miss Caddrick. We're here to help."

At that instant, a childish voice squealed from the dim interior.

"Uncle Skeeter!"

An instant later, Artemisia had flown into his arms. Skeeter buried his face in her thick hair to hide the tears.

Chapter Fourteen

Kit Carson arrived at the security office complex with a mob of screaming reporters on his heels. As Kit fled through the doors, someone in a BATF uniform looked around at the howling noise. "Oh, God, who let *them* in?"

Irritated time scouts joined forces with security personnel to bodily shove the horde of newsies back out the door. Several cameras and more than one face failed to survive the process. A cordon of armed guards was hastily thrown into place in front of the doors, pulled from off-duty shifts called in for riot control and search teams.

"What can I do to help?" Kit asked the nearest harried desk jockey, who was manning five phones at once and handing out search assignments. The officer glanced up and three phones shrilled at the same time. She lunged for the nearest, listened, jotted notes, grabbed the next one without bothering to hang up the first. Then swore and grabbed a microphone.

"*Code Seven Red! Zone Nine!* All visitors on station

are hereby ordered to seek the nearest available shelter. Repeat, Code Seven Red, Zone Nine!"

Somebody else was snarling, "I don't care who the hell you are, get off this channel! We're in a state of emergency, here . . ."

Kit ground his teeth and waited for somebody to tell him how he could help. He was still waiting when Bull Morgan, slightly thinner than the last time Kit had laid eyes on him, arrived. Bull had already managed to scrape up a cigar someplace, despite the fact he couldn't have been out of his own jail more than five minutes. The station manager was busy masticating the end of it into a pulpy, wet mess that indicated his current level of stress. Kit wondered who'd had the audacity to unlock his cell door. Ronisha Azzan, no doubt. With Jack the Ripper loose on station, she very well might have thrown the federal marshals into jail, just to keep them out of everyone's hair.

Bull caught Kit's eye and waved him over. "Kit, I need someone to hustle downstairs to the weapons ranges and open up the arsenals, Ann's and Sven's, both. We don't have enough arms for our security officers. And I want a couple dozen Found Ones deputized as security to search the subbasements. You know the Found Ones, and they trust you. Give 'em weapons from Sven's lockers, they'll know how to use bladed weapons. And if we had some clubs . . ."

"What about those 1880's style baseball and cricket bats the outfitters stock?"

"Good idea. Get 'em. Every Ripper cult on station has gone nuts, killing women. We need all the help we can get, stopping this mess."

"I'll organize the men in the Found Ones, put together sweep teams."

"Make damned sure the women stay out of harm's

way. Especially the dark-haired, petite ones, who look like Dr. Feroz."

"Has anyone seen her?"

Bull twitched the unlit cigar to the other side of his mouth. "She's back with Ronnie, right now, telling us what she knows about this maniac. If he wasn't totally insane before he got here, chances are, he is now. Even the most balanced down-timers go a little bit nuts when they first arrive on station."

The coldness in the pit of Kit's belly deepened. At least the Ripperologist was safe.

"Kit, why don't you join the briefing Dr. Feroz is giving our sweep teams before you organize the Found Ones. You can pass along what she has to say. The briefing is back in Mike's office."

Kit found Shahdi Feroz speaking tersely to a group of security officers, Pest Control units, and BATF. Even the I.T.C.H. agents had put in appearance, listening intently and recording notes of their own.

The Ripperologist was just answering a question. "Yes, that would fit the pattern of a psychotic serial killer. They usually kill to a pattern. If you can unravel the pattern, you can go a long way toward stopping the killer. Unfortunately, in John Lachley's case, it is not so simple. He was killing women in possession of letters which he was desperate to recover. What sort of letters, we still do not know. Clearly, he didn't come to Shangri-La Station looking for them, which suggests he has abandoned whatever plans he'd made, which these letters threatened. I believe he has come forward in time looking for bigger game. Power is what lures him. He rose from obscure beginnings in the East End and pursued a medical degree as a means to greater power. Occult scholarship was another tool he used. Aleister Crowley studied under him and Lachley succeeded in positioning himself as personal advisor to the queen's grandson, Prince Eddy."

A nearby scout muttered, "Now there's a scary thought. The man who bills himself as the prophet of the anti-Christ, studying Satanic ritual under Jack the Ripper."

"What about the Ripper cults?" a BATF agent asked worriedly.

Dr. Feroz thinned her mouth. "That is part of the bad news. Lachley has already begun to wield immense power through the Ripper cults. We must deprive him of his new worshippers, quickly. Isolate him in a time he does not yet understand, while he is still vulnerable to technology which baffles him."

One of the I.T.C.H. agents spoke up. "You can isolate him all you like," the woman said coldly, "but it won't do any good if he can't be killed."

The Ripperologist surprised Kit—and everyone else—with her answer. "We have no guarantee he cannot be killed. After all, Jack the Ripper was two men. It is entirely possible James Maybrick will act alone in the murder of Mary Kelly. The girl looks enough like his adulterous wife to send the man into a frenzy. In crime scene photographs taken the day of her murder, there are initials visible in blood on the walls, an F and an M, suggesting the name Florie Maybrick.

And Catharine Eddowes, poor woman, had an M carved through her eyelids, another clue to Maybrick's identity, had the police realized it. With Lachley out of the picture, Maybrick is on his own, without a mentor to guide or goad him into repeated murders. If one studies Maybrick's diary, one finds a startling change of tone and attitude after Mary Kelly's murder. It is almost as though Maybrick had roused from a murderous stupor of some sort, returning to sanity and remorse.

"Importantly, Lachley is a mesmerist of some note. I would not be at all surprised to learn that Lachley had used that skill to gain control of Maybrick, using hypnotic suggestion to bring his hatred of prostitutes boiling over to critical levels, then pointing him at the victims Lachley chose. Without Lachley to reinforce the hypnotic suggestions, Maybrick might well come to his senses after the butchery of Mary Kelly and look back on what he has done with the very shock one reads in the diary. Given all this, with Maybrick quite probably acting alone in the Kelly murder, we *cannot* assume that Lachley is impossible to kill. Not based on the assumption that he must be present for Mary Kelly's death."

Kit was impressed. Maybe there was hope, yet?

Mike Benson spoke up quickly, however. "We're going to play it safe and assume the worst, just the same. I don't want anyone tackling this guy alone. We've cleared Commons, which has robbed Lachley and his worshippers of easily available victims, but his fury will make him dangerously unpredictable. He may well go to ground somewhere. Or he may start breaking down doors, looking for Dr. Feroz or the next best substitute. There may be no way to stop his killing spree, short of evacuating the station."

"You can't be serious!"

"My God, Benson—"

"*Quiet!*" The bellow came from behind Kit's shoulder. He jerked around to find Bull Morgan striding into the briefing room. "I'm *not* evacuating this station, get that clear right now. One, it's impossible to do, not in time. There is no physical way to get everyone on this station through Primary during its next cycle, not to mention trying to herd every man, woman, and child in Shangri-La down to Primary precinct in the next three minutes, just to make the gate opening."

Glances at wrist watches caused a miniature sea of bobbing heads, a flock of guinea hens popping up and down in tall grass. As though on cue, the station announcer came on, the sound muted through the walls: "Your attention please. Primary is due to open in three minutes. Be advised, all station passes through Primary have been revoked for the duration of the station emergency. Remain in your hotel room or your current place of shelter with the door locked. Do not make any attempt to reach Primary . . ."

Bull Morgan waited for the echo to fade, then said grimly, "I've ordered a total lockdown of this station, including cancellation of Primary passes, so he can't slip out with panic-stricken tourists the way he crashed the Britannia. I want everyone on a search team to stay in radio contact. Work in teams of at least three and never lose sight of your teammates. If your team doesn't have a radio, see Mike Benson. That's it people, move out and comb this station like it's never been combed before."

The nearest I.T.C.H. agent collared Bull. "What do you intend to do with Lachley when you find him?"

"Since you ask, I hope to God he can be killed, because I have no intention of taking Jack the Ripper alive and then ending up stuck with him for the rest of his natural life. Up-time law says we can't ship him home and we can't send him to an up-time prison, either, because that same law prevents us from sending any down-timer through Primary. And frankly, there's not a cage I could build on this station that a psychopath couldn't eventually break out of. We're not equipped to hold a thing like that in a cell for the next forty or fifty years."

"What happened to trial by jury?" the I.T.C.H. agent demanded, her glare icy.

Bull Morgan chewed his cigar to shreds. "I'll tell you

what, lady. You answer me this. What happened to four gutted women? And a man with a broken neck, who was unfortunate enough to simply be in Lachley's way? We have a station cram full of potential victims, here, and it's my job to see they don't become statistics. And just in case you've forgotten, down-timers don't *have* any legal rights, the honest and decent ones any more than some psychopathic butcher. And I didn't write *those* laws, either. I'm just stuck enforcing 'em. I'm not real happy about it, but, by God, I *will* protect innocents. This ain't New York, lady, and it ain't the Hague, and you're not in charge. You don't like it, get the hell off my station."

The I.T.C.H. agent gave Bull a combative glare, but she backed down. They might be stuck in the middle of the worst situation any station had ever faced, but Bull Morgan wasn't going down without a fight. Kit felt like cheering.

"Okay," Bull said briskly, "I want sweep teams out, combing the lower levels, and I want every searcher armed with a knife, bare minimum, and a pistol for the up-timers. Ronisha, organize the new teams by zone. And get the word out to teams we've already fielded, same rules. Let's find this bastard before anybody else dies."

A rush of footsteps brought Skeeter up from his crouch, holding Artemisia in one arm. She leaned her head against his shoulder, arms wrapped around his neck as the door was thrown wide. Jenna Caddrick vanished as someone thrust her aside. An instant later, Skeeter found himself staring at the wrong end of an enormous revolver.

"Put her down!"

It was Noah Armstrong, dressed in women's clothing. There was no mistaking the cold, murderous rage in Armstrong's grey eyes. Behind Noah's shoulder, Marcus appeared, ashen. When he caught sight of Skeeter, the former slave's mouth fell open. "*Skeeter?* And Margo! And is that Malcolm? What are you doing in London?"

Skeeter shifted Artemisia to his other arm. "Looking for you, of course. You might tell your friend, there, to put the gun down."

"Noah, these are my friends! From the station!"

Armstrong didn't even blink. "I don't care if they're Santa's elves. Anyone could've followed them here!"

"Sure, anyone could've," Skeeter agreed, "*if* they'd known where we were heading today. Which they didn't. And I'll put Misia down when you put that pistol away. If anybody's got some explaining to do, it's you, Armstrong. And you'd better start talking fast."

Armstrong's eyes narrowed over a cold glint, then backed up and gestured with the barrel of the gun. "Inside. All of you."

As Skeeter stepped past, Marcus said quietly, "They are my friends, Noah. Skeeter risked death in the Circus at Rome to free me from slavery. He is one of the Found Ones, a trusted friend. My children call him uncle. Malcolm is a freelance guide, friend to Kit Carson, and Margo is to marry him. She will be the first woman time scout, when her grandfather has trained her fully. We can trust them, Noah." Marcus turned to Skeeter, then, his face twisting in an expression that hurt to witness. "I am sorry I did not come to you on the station. Please try to understand, Skeeter. We could not risk it, then. Men were trying to kill us and I could not put my children in jeopardy, not to contact anyone."

"I figured that out," Skeeter said softly. "It's all right."

Marcus' eyes gleamed wet for a dangerous moment, then he managed to say fairly steadily, "I am glad you have come. Ianira needs to return to the station. So do our children. We must end this long terror and go home."

"You found her, then?" Margo asked sharply. "Did Lachley have her, after all?"

Surprise lit Marcus' dark eyes and Jenna Caddrick blurted, "How did you guess?" Even Noah Armstrong was momentarily taken aback.

Margo eyed the revolver still levelled at them, then answered Jenna's question with a faint smile. "We went to the lecture at the Egyptian Hall, of course. Malcolm and I did, that is. Skeeter wasn't in London yet. We're guides for the Ripper Watch Team and we'd finally figured out that Dr. Lachley must be Jack the Ripper, so we staked out the lecture—and saw you. We tried to follow when you left, but lost you in the crowd. Where was Ianira? Not in Lachley's house, surely? You left there without her."

Marcus' eyes darkened with grim memory that set Skeeter's skin to crawling. "In the sewers," he said harshly. "He had a place in the sewers, a room where he kept Ianira and other things, pieces of people he had butchered, a terrible place . . ."

"Good God," Malcolm breathed, eyes going wide as realization dawned, "the *sewers*! Of course no one could catch the Ripper. He was using the sewers to escape!"

"To hell with Jack the Ripper!" Armstrong said in a cold, hard voice. "How did you find us?" The revolver still tracked Skeeter's chest.

Footsteps on the stairs distracted everyone but Armstrong, who said sharply, "Get back upstairs!"

An instant later, Ianira rushed past Armstrong and flung both arms around Skeeter's neck, tears streaming, as she hugged him, Misia and all. "Skeeter! You are safe . . . We have missed you!"

She kissed Skeeter's cheek, then hugged Margo and Malcolm in turn, eyes brilliant with the tears streaming down her face. "It is good to have old friends among

us again! But how *did* you find us? Noah and Jenna
have been very careful and our hiding place was well
chosen."

Skeeter handed Artemisia to her father, lips twitching
into a faint smile. "We tracked you through your money,
actually."

"Our *what*?" Jenna gasped.

Skeeter grinned. "Your money. The banknotes you
picked up on station when you exchanged your up-time
currency."

Her brow wrinkled above the ludicrous mutton
chops Paula Booker had given her. "Banknotes? How
in the world could you trace me through banknotes?"

"They're fakes."

Jenna stared, shaken so badly out of her composure
her face ran dead white. Even Armstrong, who had
finally put the revolver away, blanched. Clearly, they
understood the implications of Victorian prison as well
as Skeeter did.

"Believe it or not," Skeeter spoke into the shocked
silence, "Goldie Morran admitted it before I left the
station. She was terrified you'd been arrested in
London for passing counterfeit banknotes, which
would explain why nobody could find Benny Catlin.
The last thing she wants is your father breathing down
her neck, so she came clean, spilled the whole thing
to me. They're not all fake, but she slipped you enough
counterfeits to cause trouble. You bought some suits
with a counterfeit five-pound note and we traced you
through that. Once we knew you were in the East End,
we started showing people your photographs until we'd
tracked you down."

Jenna's ashen face ran ice pale this time and she
swayed sharply, prompting Armstrong to steady her.
"Oh, my God. You didn't? We can't stay here!"

"Perhaps," Malcolm said quietly, "you would be good

enough to explain why not? The only information we have, your father supplied, through his own sources and from the detective he's hired. And we have reason to suspect that gentlemen's credentials, thanks to Skeeter."

Armstrong said brusquely, "Let's go into the parlour. I could use a drink and Jenna had better sit down."

Marcus brushed his daughter's hair back from her brow. "Misia, please go upstairs and finish your lessons with your sister."

"Okay." She kissed her father's cheek as he set her down, then ran to Skeeter and hugged him tightly before clattering up the stairs, hitching her dress up to her knees.

Jenna Caddrick brushed past, moving woodenly into the parlour, followed by Noah Armstrong. Jenna stood near the window, staring silently into the street, while Marcus and Ianira took seats on the worn upholstery of a high-backed sofa with carved mahogany legs and arms. Armstrong followed them into the parlour, stopping near the hearth, where a coal fire blazed cheerfully, then hesitated. "It's clear that Marcus and Ianira trust you. Very well, I'll give you the full story." Armstrong swept off a woman's hairpiece, revealing short, dishevelled brown hair which didn't quite reach the high Victorian collar of Armstrong's dress. Without the wig, it was abruptly difficult to tell whether Armstrong was a young man in woman's clothing or a young woman with short hair. "It's a very long story, but the upshot is, I'm a detective. I was hired to protect these people." Armstrong nodded toward Jenna, Marcus, and Ianira.

"*You're* a detective?" Skeeter blurted, then narrowed his eyes. "Who hired you?"

"Cassie Tyrol."

Skeeter's mouth dropped.

Margo gasped out, *"Cassie Tyrol?"*

"My aunt," Jenna said in a choked voice. "She hired Noah before they murdered her. They would've killed me, too, if Noah hadn't dragged me out of the restaurant. They killed my fiancé, Carl, at my apartment." Her voice began to quake as wetness spilled over from her eyes. "I was talking to him on the phone when they shot him, so I wasn't at the table when they shot Aunt Cassie. I'm . . ." she bit her lip and pressed a hand against her abdomen, protectively. "I'm going to have Carl's baby. It's all I have left. I can't even call on my family for help," she added bitterly, "because it's my *father* who's trying to kill us."

Mouths sagged open, even Malcolm's. The silence was so profound, Skeeter could hear a clock somewhere out in Spitalfields strike the hour, its ghostly notes singing through the cold October air. Then Jenna swayed and Noah Armstrong hurried to help her to the nearest chair, guiding her with a tender look and gentle hands. Clearly, Noah Armstrong was anything but a murderous terrorist. Skeeter found his voice first.

"Miss Caddrick, your father is threatening to shut down the station unless you're brought back."

Shocking hatred blazed from her eyes. "If I could, I'd put a bullet through his skull!" Even as she spoke, fury transmuted into terrible grief. Jenna covered her face with shaking hands and began to cry, raggedly and very messily. Ianira produced a handkerchief and sat down beside her, sliding an arm around her shoulders. Jenna groped for the handkerchief and struggled to regain her composure. "I'm sorry," she whispered through hiccoughs. She finally blotted her cheeks, then looked up, shoulders slumped, face haggard with too much fear and far too little sleep.

Malcolm suggested gently, "Why don't you tell us your story, Miss Caddrick? I suspect Mr. Jackson, here, knows more of it than the rest of us do, but Miss Smith and I know enough to realize that we're facing a very serious threat."

Jenna rubbed reddened eyes with the backs of her hands, clutching Ianira's sodden handkerchief, then drew a deep, unsteady breath. "Yes. I literally don't know how many people have already died because of what we know. Noah and I, that is. And now Marcus and Ianira." She drew a second watery breath and met Malcolm's gaze. "Guess I ought to start with proper introductions? This is Noah Armstrong, a private detective with the Wardmann-Wolfe Agency."

Skeeter swung a sharp stare at Armstrong. "*You're* a Wardmann-Wolfe agent? Why, that lying, scum-sucking, low-life *bastard*!"

"I take it," Armstrong said grimly, "my reputation has been compromised?"

Skeeter snorted. "You might say that. Senator Caddrick's telling the whole world you're *Ansar Majlis*."

The look that passed across Noah Armstrong's face set Skeeter's hair on end.

"I see," Armstrong said very softly. "I suppose it's fitting, after all, since he put them on our trail in the first place."

"Senator Caddrick?" Malcolm asked sharply. "In league with the *Ansar Majlis*?"

"It's true," Jenna whispered, her watery eyes haunted with terrible shadows. "Daddy ordered his hit men to dress like *Ansar Majlis*."

"I was sitting right beside Cassie Tyrol when they burst in through the door, shooting," Noah Armstrong said heavily. "She was dead before I even had time to draw my pistol. If I hadn't thrown the table in their faces, they'd have shot me down, as well, then they'd have found Jenna and killed her. They did kill dozens of people standing near us as we escaped the restaurant.

Caddrick and the men paying him off have stirred up the real *Ansar Majlis*, as well. Fed them money, munitions, transportation, names and locations of targets, helped them to attack Ianira on the station."

Margo was frowning. "Wait a minute. Am I the only one confused, here? I know I've been in London for quite a while, but what possible connection is there between Jocasta Tyrol and Ianira Cassondra? Would you mind starting at the beginning? Because this isn't making much sense to me."

Noah Armstrong spoke quietly. "Miss Tyrol came to me three years ago; at least, it was three years ago for Marcus and the girls and myself, just a few weeks ago for Jenna and Ianira." Grey eyes flicked toward the senator's daughter. "Miss Tyrol was curious about some very ugly things she had uncovered about her brother-in-law, Jenna's father. She hired me and also helped a young friend of hers get a job in Senator Caddrick's office. An actor doing role research. The boy stumbled across some very nasty evidence. He sent it to her, but was murdered for it. I'd been doing my own investigations, along the same lines, and as soon as Mr. Corliss was killed, I persuaded Miss Tyrol to go into hiding until we could take the evidence to the authorities."

Jenna said bitterly, "Aunt Cassie tried to warn me. She slipped away from Noah and called, arranged to meet me. *I'm* the reason she's dead! Aunt Cassie and Carl, both . . ." Tears tracked messily down her face, dripping into her surgically-implanted sideburns. "Carl McDevlin was going to marry me, in spite of my father's nasty habits and the chaos of the press following everything we Caddricks do. And my doting *father* gave the order to murder him, just on the chance I might have told him something."

Armstrong brushed wet hair back from Jenna's face, the gesture eloquent of the trust that had grown between them. "Miss Caddrick and I managed to get into TT-86," Armstrong sighed, "with the tickets for London she and her fiancé were planning to use, but the assassination squads followed. Two of them almost killed Miss Caddrick the night she arrived."

Jenna shivered. "I managed to shoot my way out of the Picadilly Hotel or I'd be in a morgue someplace. And so would Ianira."

Malcolm said very quietly, "I hope you have proof?"

"Yes." Jenna whispered. "Noah does."

The Wardmann-Wolfe detective nodded wearily. "There've been quiet rumors for years about Senator Caddrick's association with organized crime. The evidence Alston Corliss gathered is enough to hang Senator Caddrick and several of his cronies, particularly a paid enforcer named Gideon Guthrie. And Guthrie works for Cyril Barris, who has mob connections on three continents, just for starters. Ties to the Yakuza and the Russian mafia, you name it, he's diddling in it. Barris has been paying off John Caddrick for a couple of decades. Unfortunately, Alston Corliss was a total amateur up against seasoned killers. The pieces were found in several different locations."

Margo shuddered.

"What Alston Corliss found," Noah added, "were payoff records made through companies the senator owns, monies deposited into accounts only he had access to, as majority shareholder and CEO. Construction companies, mostly, both in the States and abroad, Asia and Japan, in particular."

This finally started to make sense to Skeeter. In the aftermath of the orbital accident that had formed the time strings, the whole Pacific Rim had been hard hit by earthquakes and tidal waves. The rebuilding had been going on for most of Skeeter's life.

Malcolm was nodding, as well, face set in weary lines.

"And the construction industry in Japan is controlled by the Yakuza gangs, has been for centuries. The senator allied himself with these gangs?"

"Yes. There and in the States, in South America, anywhere the Yakuza gangs were active. In the States, particularly on the west coast, local gangs of American thugs started affiliating themselves with the Asian gangs coming in, running drugs, prostitution, and gambling. Years back, even before he launched his political career, the senator had ties to a local mafia boss in Los Angeles, a man who later affiliated his gang with a prominent Yakuza family. It turned out to be a very profitable affiliation. For all parties concerned. It certainly financed the senator's campaigns."

"Yes," Margo frowned, "but how does Ianira tie into all of this?"

Jenna's mouth thinned to a bitter line. "Think about it. You know what she was responsible for starting. The Lady of Heaven Temples are the fastest growing international religion in the world. What better way to smuggle drugs halfway around the planet, launder money, ship American girls out to Asian brothels—"

"Ianira's not involved in that kind of garbage!" Skeeter snapped.

Jenna was crying again. "No. I never said she was. But my father is. He's using the Temples as a cover. Several congressmen have been calling for an investigation of Templar possessions and financial activities, something Daddy couldn't risk. So he decided to turn the Templars into martyrs, so public sentiment would crucify anyone who dared investigate Temple finances."

Skeeter swore aloud. It made abrupt, sickening sense.

"I see you've tumbled to it," Armstrong nodded, holding Skeeter's gaze. "Miss Caddrick's father also knew he was being investigated by one of the best detective agencies in the business and he knew Miss Tyrol had put us on his trail. But he couldn't order an ordinary gangland hit on a woman as widely popular as Cassie Tyrol. There'd be far too much press, not to mention police asking questions, if he simply had his regular paid thugs kill her. His one piece of luck was that both Jenna and Miss Tyrol were prominent Templars, and so was Miss Caddrick's fiancé. Miss Tyrol donated her share of the profits from *Temple Harlot* directly to the Temple."

Skeeter's blood ran cold. "So he used the *Ansar Majlis*. Of course. They were a perfect front."

"Yes. They made it look like a terrorist hit. Only the bastards in that restaurant were never part of the actual *Ansar Majlis*. Neither were the hired killers who came after us on the station. They activated real *Ansar Majlis* moles already in place on TT-86, of course, so the riots on station would look like the genuine thing. The senator targeted Ianira as one of his primary public martyrs, since the *Ansar Majlis* exists specifically to destroy everything she's responsible for starting. He knew very well what public sentiment would be if the deified prophetess of the Temple were murdered, along with her entire family." The bitterness in Armstrong's eyes was terrifying. The shame in Jenna Caddrick's was infinitely worse. Silence spun out like filaments of glass, waiting to be shattered.

"So that's the whole, sordid story," Noah finally shattered it. "We're in hiding, with Miss Caddrick posing as a gentleman and me posing as Marcus' sister, trying to stay alive long enough to put Senator Caddrick in prison where he belongs."

Malcolm rubbed the bridge of his nose for a moment, eyes bleak when he met Armstrong's gaze again. "According to Skeeter, there have been multiple riots and murders on TT-86, with a number of cults, including the

Angels of Grace Militia, at odds with supporters of the *Ansar Majlis*. Now we know why. Everything we've built on TT-86 is at enormous risk. The senator is making threats, very serious threats, to close down the station."

Jenna said in a low, hard voice, "He's been looking for a way to shut down time tourism for years."

"He doesn't even need to do it, himself," Skeeter muttered. "The riots and murders alone are likely to shut us down. He brought federal marshals with him and arrested Bull Morgan, the station manager, on trumped-up tax charges. I.T.C.H. has been brought in to investigate and God knows where that will end. The Inter-Temporal Court has shut down stations before, replaced their whole management operations. And with Bull Morgan and Ronisha Azzan out, only God knows what would become of the down-timer community on station. I.T.C.H. sure as hell doesn't care—down-timers have no legal rights to protect and not enough financial clout to influence a gnat, never mind the Inter-Temporal Court."

Malcolm added heavily, "Down-timers on other time terminals I could name live like animals, compared with TT-86. Most 'eighty-sixers have no idea how fortunate our down-time population really is."

"We must stop this!" Marcus cried, moving protectively to Ianira's side.

"Yes, but *how*?" Margo wondered, frustration burning in her eyes. "You're a detective," she swung abruptly toward Armstrong, "and you say you've got proof. What do *you* suggest we do? You can't hide forever and you certainly can't expect *us* to sit and bury our heads in the sand like a bunch of ostriches. Marcus and Ianira are our friends. We won't sit around and do nothing!"

Noah's lips thinned. "No, clearly we *can't* just sit here, not now. The senator and his assassins know we're in the city, since they sent you through to look for us. Hiding in London was only a stopgap measure, we knew that from the start. All we've done by coming here is buy ourselves time. We would've been gone before now, if Ianira hadn't been kidnapped her first night in London. It took us days, tracing and rescuing her. What has to be done is simple. I have to go back with the proof. Make sure the senator and his gangland bosses are arrested and stand trial for murder." Armstrong frowned. "Getting the evidence to the authorities is going to be a major battle, even if someone else takes it to them. And you know what mafia trials are like. Clearly, the senator has taken pains to ensure I'm shot on sight as a dangerous terrorist, so I won't live to testify." With a bitter twist of lips, Armstrong added, "I really do appreciate your not shooting me out of hand and asking questions later."

"I started wondering about Caddrick's story even before we went chasing halfway across Colorado on your trail," Skeeter muttered. "I was standing next to Ianira when that first riot broke out. What I saw didn't tally with the line Caddrick fed us."

"For that, I am deeply grateful, Mr. Jackson. I also suspect," the detective added darkly, "there will be at least one hired killer in London trying to trace us."

"Oh, yeah," Skeeter said softly. "There is, all right. And I know his name. At least, the name he's been using. Mr. Sid Kaederman. The senator's so-called detective. A Wardmann-Wolfe agent, so he says."

Noah Armstrong's brows twitched downward. "Sid Kaederman? There's no Wardmann-Wolfe agent by that name."

"You know them all?" Malcolm asked quietly.

"I'd better. The agency's founder, Beore Arunwode, is my grandfather. I know that agency and its employees better than most people know their own kids. Part of my job was running security clearances on every agent we hired."

"Great," Skeeter groused. "I *knew* there was something wrong with that guy, I just couldn't figure out what."

Malcolm favored him with a faint smile. "I've never known your instincts to fail, Mr. Jackson. It seems they were right on target, once again. The question is, how to deal with Mr. Kaederman? If he's a hired gun, the proof you have, Mr. Armstrong, isn't likely to incriminate *him*. At least, not directly. Which means we need to trap him into committing a crime we can hang him for. Or I should say, trap him into *trying* to commit that crime."

"Like what?" Jenna asked bitterly. "The only thing he's here for is to murder me. And Noah. And Ianira and her family."

The answer skittered across Skeeter's mind in a jagged lightning strike, a notion so wild, he actually started to laugh.

"Skeeter Jackson," Margo asked sharply, "what are you thinking?"

"He wants Jenna Caddrick and Noah Armstrong. So, let's give him what he wants."

"*What?*" Jenna came out of her chair so fast, it crashed over. "Are you *insane?*"

"No," Skeeter said mildly, "although I know a few people who might argue the point. When your father showed up, he mistook me for Noah. And Paula Booker's here in London with us. Kit insisted she come along."

Margo gasped. "*Skeeter!* You're not thinking what I *think* you're thinking?"

Malcolm moved sharply. "You *do* realize the risk?"

"Oh, yeah," Skeeter said very softly. "But do you

have a better way to trick him into trying to commit murder, without risking the real Noah Armstrong's life? Not to mention Marcus and Ianira and the children, and Miss Caddrick, here. Noah's got to testify. He's the only one who can put a noose around Caddrick's neck. We can't risk *Noah*, but we can sure as hell hand Sid Kaederman a life-sized decoy. If you have any better ideas, I'm all ears."

Malcolm didn't. Neither did anybody else.

"All right," Malcolm said tersely. "I'll have to get him out of the road long enough for Paula to work her magic on your features. When Kaederman tries to murder you, we'll nab Kaederman, dead to rights, with enough evidence to hang him."

"Where do we spring the trap?" Margo asked, brow furrowing slightly as she considered the problem.

"Someplace open enough to give him a shot at Mr. Jackson," Malcolm mused, "but not so open he could give us the slip too easily. A public place, with plenty of witnesses, but not a crowd so large he can lose himself in it."

"Train stations are out, then," Margo frowned. "Victoria Embankment or maybe Chelsea Embankment?"

Malcolm shook his head. "Access to the water taxis is too great. He could jump into a waterman's boat and be gone before we could lay hands on him. It'll have to be someplace he wouldn't expect a trap. A place we could tell him we've found a clue to Armstrong's whereabouts and have him believe it without question."

"What about the Serpentine? Or Boating Lake in Battersea? We could say he's been seen there with Ianira and the children."

"I've got a better idea," Skeeter said suddenly. "We tell Kaederman you've discovered the counterfeit banknotes, which is something Kit and I kept secret. So we tell him you're running short of cash. Kaederman already knows you're in disguise as a man, Miss Caddrick, and we also know that Noah Armstrong can assume any disguise he feels like, male or female. So the two of you have been hitting the gentlemen's clubs, gambling, as a way to dump the counterfeits and make up your losses, fast."

Jenna frowned. "Gambling? But why would we do that? Gambling is a good way to *lose* money."

"Not—" Skeeter grinned, abruptly merry as any imp, "—if you cheat."

Chapter Fifteen

The tunnels beneath Frontier Town were a maze of immense glass aquaria, ranks upon tiers of them, which had been empty the last time Kit had searched Shangri-La Station's basement. Now they held all the live fish the station could import through its gates. Between the flock of crow-sized pterodactyls and toothed, primitive birds and the enormous *pteranodon sternbergi,* whose wingspan rivalled that of a small airplane, pest control had been hard pressed to import enough fish. Sue Fritchey had turned the corridors and tunnels beneath Little Agora and Frontier Town into a miniature biological preserve where pterodactyl lunches swam by the thousands.

In this dim-lit world of glass walls and gleaming fish scales and the patterned reflections of water on tunnel walls and ceilings, the caged *sternbergi's* weird, primordial cries vibrated eerily against the stacked aquaria, each cry drifting through the basement corridors like the soundtrack from a bad horror flick. The noise set teeth on edge as once-extinct screams echoed and reverberated for hundreds of yards in every direction, distorted by distance, inexpressibly strange.

Kit hunted the alien terrain with a team of four, Sven Bailey and Kit out front with riot shotguns, Kynan and Eigil behind them with bladed weapons and a couple of old-style wooden baseball bats, to reduce the chances that an attack would put friends in the line of fire. They had searched about a hundred yards of cluttered corridor, finding no trace of Jack the Ripper or his manaical worshippers, when they came to an intersecting tunnel. Kit held up a hand. "Stay back until I've had a look."

He had just eased to the corner when they came boiling out of hiding, at least a dozen of them, brandishing knives and hurling murderous threats into Kit's teeth. Kit fired into the thick of them. Men screamed and went down as Sven, too, loosed off a load of buckshot. A baseball bat smashed into an aquarium at Kit's elbow. Water and wriggling fish flooded the corridor floor, stained red where several attackers had fallen, gutshot and screaming. Kit fired again, trying to drive the madmen back. Eigil was shouting in Old Norse; the Viking *barsark* was lopping off limbs and smashing more aquaria to the floor. Screams and moans echoed amidst the shattering noise of smashing glass. Then the Ripper cult broke and ran, with Sven and Kit hard on their heels. Eigil and Kynan, their borrowed weapons dripping blood, were right behind.

Pounding footsteps echoed, distorted by the piled aquaria. Kit put on a burst of speed, rounded a corner on Sven's heels, and piled into the middle of a seething mass of bodies. The Ripper cult had turned at bay, blocked by the massive bulk of the *pteranodon sternbergi's* cage. Kit slammed into a would-be killer and they reeled against the cage. The gigantic pterosaur screamed, shattering eardrums, and lunged in a state of maddened agitation. The immense beak, longer than a man's body, shot between the bars as Kit flung himself aside. The Ripper cultist screamed, impaled on a razor-sharp beak. The *sternbergi* reared backwards, scraping the body off against the bars. Kit staggered off balance, buffeted by the backdraft of immense leathery wings. One of the cultists snarled and slashed at his throat. Kit dropped to the floor, under the blow, and fired his riotgun upwards into the man's gut. Kit's attacker reeled backwards against the bars, then screamed and dropped his knife as the pterosaur struck again, its wicked eye gleaming like a poisoned ruby. Its beak snapped shut with a clacking sound like two-by-fours cracking, taking off the man's arm at the elbow. He screamed and went down in a puddle of arterial spurts.

Kit rolled, trying to come to his feet, and heard Sven's shotgun roar. More screams rose, then a group of men burst around the corner and slammed full-tilt into the battle. Kit caught a glimpse of flying burnooses and grim, dark Arabic faces, then Mr. Riyad, foreman of the Arabian Nights construction crew, was fighting his way to Kit's side. A group of his workmen, proven innocent of terrorist affiliations, mopped up the remnants of resistance. Kit staggered to his feet, wiping sweat and someone else's blood, and met Mr. Riyad's gaze.

"Am I glad to see you," he gasped out.

"We came as quickly as we could, when we heard the screams and the shooting."

"Thank God."

They'd taken five men alive, having left a trail of nine dead and wounded behind them. Kit fumbled with his radio. "Code Seven Red, Zone Eleven. We've got prisoners and a helluva mess, down by the *sternbergi's* cage."

"Roger, Zone Eleven. Sending reinforcements."

"Better get a medical team down here and tell Sue

Fritchey to bring a tranquilizer gun. The *sternbergi's* out of control." The immense pterosaur was still screaming and trying to attack anything that moved near its cage.

"Copy that, we'll do what we can. We've got casualties all over the station."

"Roger, understood. Anybody find Lachley yet?"

"Negative.

"He's not with this group, either. We'll keep searching once we've turned these guys over to security. Kit out."

"Roger, security out."

As Kit clipped the radio to his belt, Pest Control arrived with a dart gun. They shot three separate tranks into the immense pterosaur, which gradually ceased hurling itself against the bars. Its wings and head drooped to the cage floor, its baleful ruby eye heavy lidded and closing. Security arrived a moment later, taking charge of prisoners with rough efficiency. The battered cultists stumbled off in handcuffs and shackles, too dazed to protest. Pest Control agents opened up the cage and began treating lacerations on the *sternbergi's* hide and wings. A weird grunting moan issued from the pterosaur's immense throat, then its wicked little eyes closed completely and it lost consciousness.

"We'd better regroup and keep searching," Kit sighed.

The construction foreman nodded. "Yes. We should perhaps search together, this time? These men are completely mad," Riyad gestured at the dead Ripper cultists. "They fight like demons."

Sven Bailey, who was wiping blood off Kynan's gladius while Kynan wrapped a shallow cut in his ribs with makeshift bandages, muttered, "You just said a cotton-pickin' mouthful. Never saw anything like it."

They sorted themselves out, then spread into a loose fan, moving down the corridor past the open cage. As they searched, grim and silent, Kit couldn't help worrying about Margo's safety in London and cursed himself for not asking Dr. Feroz. He'd have to wait, now, because he couldn't clutter up security channels with a personal request. Besides, he needed to focus his entire attention on this lethal search for the Ripper and his maniacal followers. So Kit thrust the worry aside as best he could, telling himself that she was in good company with Malcolm and Skeeter, and kept hunting.

"You want me to *what?*" Paula Booker stared.

Skeeter grinned. "I want you to make me look like Noah Armstrong."

She blinked at him, eyes still blank with astonishment. "*Here?* In Spaldergate House?"

"Yeah. Here. Tonight, after everyone has gone to bed. Mrs. Aldis, the housekeeper, will let us into the vault, that's no problem. It's a little crowded right now, because the Ripper Watch Team is down there, but we won't be in their way. They aren't using the surgery, in any case, just the computer facilities. The surgery's modern, has all the amenities. And Mrs. Aldis is a surgical nurse, assists Dr. Nerian all the time."

"I know that," Paula said impatiently. "I've been down there already. But . . . *Tonight?*" The request had clearly thrown her off stride. Clearly, she thought Skeeter had taken leave of his senses.

He let his grin fade away. "Paula, we learned something tonight that . . . Well, let's just say I'm not going to sleep very well 'til this is over. Sid Kaederman isn't what he's pretending to be. If we don't trick him into giving himself away, he will literally get away with murder. And if we don't stop him, it'll be Ianira and Marcus on his hit list, them and their kids. And that's just for starters. This is one helluva mess we're stuck in, Paula. Believe me, I wouldn't ask you to rearrange my face with a scalpel if it weren't necessary. I happen to like my face, whatever anyone else thinks of it."

Paula Booker's eyes widened. *"You found them, didn't you?"*

"Shh!" he motioned frantically to keep her voice down.

She darted a worried glance at her closed bedroom door. Like Skeeter, she was on the third floor, bunking in the servants' quarters. Sid Kaederman, as a VIP, had been given the last available room on the "family" floor, one level down and at the opposite end of the house, overlooking Octavia Street rather than the rain-choked gardens at the back.

Paula whispered more carefully, "You *did* find them today, didn't you?"

Skeeter nodded. "Yeah. They're mostly all right. Once you're finished rearranging my face, though, Malcolm wants to talk to you. He wants you to run a checkup on everyone, make sure no lasting damage has been done. Particularly Ianira. She's had a rough time in London. Malcolm will explain all that later. Right now, I need that new face, so we can lay a trap for Kaederman. The sooner he's in cuffs, the sooner we can all go home."

Paula sighed, pushing back her hair in a weary gesture. "All right, Skeeter. I don't have everything I'd like, not to do a face job of that magnitude, but I think we can do a creditable job of making you look like Armstrong. Enough to suit, anyway. Fortunately, your bone structure and coloring are very similar, as you've pointed out. And we do have good photos of Armstrong to work from. That'll help. Let me get my medical bag. I brought through a lot of instruments and medicines to supplement Spaldergate's supply. You realize, this is going to put you out of commission for about a week? It'll take that long for the swelling and bruising to fade and the stitches to heal where I nip and tuck."

"Yeah, we figured it would take a while. That'll give Malcolm and the others a chance to lay the trap for Sid. And it'll give you time to work with Ianira, too."

"All right, Skeeter. We'll have to tell Sid something so he won't grow suspicious about your absence."

Skeeter nodded. "We'll spread the word I was hit by a carriage or a wagon and had to be rushed into surgery."

"That should work. Let's go down to the Vault, then, and get started."

Eight hours later, Skeeter woke up in recovery to a dull throb of pain all through his face and the muffling, claustrophobic feel of bandages. As he swam toward full consciousness, with the sounds of a heart monitor beeping somewhere beside his ear, his gaze focused slowly on Margo, who sat beside his bed.

"Hi," she said quietly. "Don't try to say anything, Skeeter."

He wouldn't have moved his face on a dare.

"Sid bought the story about you being hit by a freight wagon. The creep actually chuckled and said it was about time you got your comeuppance. Malcolm was extremely rude to him."

That surprised Skeeter, even as it warmed his heart. He still couldn't get used to the idea that Malcolm Moore and Margo Smith were giving him their friendship. Margo smiled. "Paula's gone to Spitalfields to check up on Ianira and the others. They're all moving to Malcolm's flat in Belgravia, just in case there's trouble about the counterfeit banknotes."

Skeeter regretted the necessity of ruining his friends' down-time cover.

Margo patted his hand gently, taking care not to disturb the I.V. leads. "Rest for now, Skeeter. We've got everything under control. I'll visit again tonight, after Paula gets back." She gave him a cheery smile, then vanished from his line of sight. Dr. Nerian appeared and spent several moments fussing with his I.V. lines, then injected something into the heplock. Whatever it was, it eased the deep ache in his face and left him drifting.

Skeeter fell asleep wondering what he really would look like, a week from now.

Goldie Morran was having the worst week of her life. I.T.C.H. agents had been prowling through her books, finding discrepancies she would have to explain, and Interpol agents had been breathing down her neck, curious in the wake of the Inter-Temporal Court's investigation. She would have been deeply thankful for the reprieve brought about by the Ripper, but for one detail. The entire station was locked down, leaving her trapped for three solid days in her shop, which she'd had the foresight to equip with a well-stocked back room, including a convertible sofa bed, a wet bar, and plenty of food.

But all business was suspended for the duration of the search, which meant she was losing thousands of dollars, same as every other merchant on station. So Goldie sat in her back room in splendid solitude, listening to her Carolina parakeets chirp, tried to straighten out her books, and brooded over what news might arrive about Jenna Caddrick when the Britannia Gate opened again.

Skeeter, thank God, had kept his mouth shut about the counterfeits, but Goldie was terrified she would end up facing charges over them. She hadn't done anything so *very* wrong—she hadn't printed them, after all. She'd simply tried to recoup some of her own losses, passing them to that idiot, Benny Catlin. Goldie cursed her luck and poured another brandy from her rapidly dwindling supply. Who'd have dreamed that moronic little graduate student would turn out to be Jenna Nicole Caddrick, in disguise? Making an enemy of Senator John Caddrick was a dreadful business move. Worse, even, than attracting the attention of Interpol agents and the Inter-Temporal Court.

Her nerves were so frayed, when the telephone rang she actually dropped her brandy snifter from nerveless fingers. She left it lying on the carpet and lunged out into the shop where the telephone sat. "Goldie Morran!" Her voice came out breathless and unsteady.

"Goldie? Mike Benson, here. No wonder we didn't get an answer at your apartment. How long have you been trapped in your shop?"

"Since that maniac arrived, of course!"

"We're conducting a room-by-room search of the station. You're alone, I take it."

"Of course I'm alone! Did you think I'd be giving wild parties, back here? I want out of this shop, Mike. Send somebody over here to escort me home, for God's sake."

"I'll send someone," Benson retorted, "to search your shop, then your apartment."

"Thanks for the royal treatment!"

"Don't mention it, Goldie. Be ready to unlock your door."

"I'll be waiting," she promised grimly.

Five minutes later, a young BATF officer arrived, security radio in hand. Goldie unlocked her doors and stood tapping one foot impatiently while he searched her shop. She followed him into the vault to be sure he didn't appropriate anything.

"Nice birds," he commented with an avaricious twinkle in his eyes. "Carolina parakeets, aren't they?" He scribbled something into a notebook. "Mr. Wilkes will be very interested. He loves birds, you know." The arrogant booby was laughing at her.

Goldie seethed. It was perfectly legal for her to have them on station. But Monty, curse him, would be watching her like a hawk from now on, curtailing her profitable sideline in viable egg smuggling.

"All right, you can lock up, now," he said, snapping his notebook shut and pocketing it. She closed the vault door while he radioed in that her shop was clear. "I'll escort Miss Morran to her apartment and clear that, as well."

"Roger."

They left through the front door, which she bolted, then she rattled down the big steel mesh doors and locked them, as well. "I can't tell you how much I'm looking foward to a hot shower and a real bed," she muttered.

"You think you've had it rough," the BATF officer complained. "We've been running on two hours of sleep a day since that maniac got here. And things were no picnic before he crashed the Britannia."

They hurried across Valhalla, the fastest way to reach the section of Residential where Goldie lived. The emptiness of Commons was downright eerie. Their footsteps echoed. She could hear other security patrols in the distance, mostly when their radios sputtered where patrols reported in. "How much of the station has been searched?" she asked uneasily as they started around the end of the big wooden ship housing the vacant Langskip Cafe—

They ran slap into someone coming the other way. Goldie staggered under the impact. She had only a split second to register wild, inhuman eyes in a narrow, darkly Eastern-European face, then a wicked knife flashed and the BATF officer went down, throat cut to bone. Goldie drew breath to scream and he slammed her against the wooden hull of the ship. She hung there, stunned, while he pressed a gore-covered hand across her mouth and nose. She choked on the stink of blood.

"*Do you live here?*" he hissed.

Goldie nodded, so terrified she could barely keep her feet. He dragged her away from the ship, shoved the knife against her ribs, and stooped to secure the dead BATF officer's radio and pistol. He then marched her rapidly across Commons toward a Residential corridor. "My followers have told me much about your Primary Gate. Unfortunately, your guards have deprived me of my acolytes, so *you* will have to assist me through that gate. Take me there. And hurry up, bitch! The gate goes in ten minutes."

She glanced despairingly at her shop, safe behind its locks and steel-mesh doors. If she could get to the shop, she could trip the silent alarm, summon help. And she kept a pistol in the shop. When she tried to change direction, he pressed the knife against her ribs again. "Not that way! I saw him take you from your shop. I shan't allow you to summon help, woman, a fact you had better learn *now*. Take me to Primary, by a safe route. If you do not oblige me quickly, I will find someone else." The blade cut through her blouse. "Do you understand me?"

She nodded, still half-choked by the bloodstained hand pressed across her mouth. The entire left side of her face ached, where he'd slammed her against the side of the Langskip, and her eye was starting to swell closed. Senses whirling, Goldie took the nearest route into Residential, moving woodenly along with the Ripper's knife under her ribcage. Goldie staggered frequently, but her captor made no offer to assist her. He simply held the knife against her ribs and hissed, "Cry out and I will kill you where you stand." She guided the killer through twisting corridors until they reached a passageway that emerged at the junction between Edo Castletown and Primary Precinct.

She pointed toward the gate, since he hadn't freed her mouth.

He eased to the corner and peered around, surveying the stretch of open Commons beyond. Goldie, too exhausted even to try running, hung in his grip and waited to die. Tremors threatened to send her to the floor even sooner. As she sagged against the wall, waiting, the public address system blared to life.

"Your attention, please. Primary is due to open in three minutes. Be advised, all station passes through Primary have been revoked for the duration of this emergency. Remain in your hotel room or your current place of shelter with the door locked. Do not make any attempt to reach Primary . . ."

The Ripper jerked Goldie around to face him. "*Explain this!*" He laid the sharp steel against her throat and drew his hand away from her mouth.

She shook her head in a stupor. "They've shut down the station," she mumbled, voice shaking. "Locked down all the gates, so no one can leave. They'll have security officers swarming all over Primary, to keep anyone from coming in or going out."

Goldie could, in fact, see a whole cordon of security officers blocking the gate access, armed to the teeth with riot guns. The Ripper swore savagely, then gazed down at her through cold, implacable grey eyes. "You said you live in this insane place?"

"Yes—"

"Where?"

"Back—back that way."

"Take me there!"

Goldie's heart sank. Tears blinded her. "Please don't kill me . . ."

"Stop snivelling, you stupid harridan! If I had

intended to kill you, I would have cut your throat already. Since my worshippers have been killed or taken prisoner by your station guards, I require shelter and someone to explain the operation of this infernal place! Now take me to your flat or I'll find another hostage!"

Goldie limped toward her distant apartment, hardly able to keep to her feet. By the time they reached it she was weaving so badly, all that kept her on her feet was his monstrous grip on her arm. She stumbled to a trembling halt in front of her door.

"Open it."

She fumbled with the lock, turning the key from her pocket, then he kicked the door farther open, dragging Goldie inside and shutting the door with a slam that echoed. He hunted through the apartment swiftly, then shoved Goldie into the bedroom. He threw her onto the bed and tied her to it, leaving her shaking in a film of sweat.

"Have you a name?"

"G-Goldie Morran . . ."

"What trade are you in?"

Humor him . . . that's what they always say, humor a madman . . .

"I change currency," she quavered out. "Up-time money for whatever a tourist needs down a gate . . ."

"Tell me how to operate this device." He held up the stolen security radio.

"You press the talk button," she gulped. "Then someone from security answers."

He pressed the button. The radio sputtered. "Security."

"I've searched Goldie Morran's rooms. There's no one here."

"Roger."

Even if she'd dared scream for help while the radio was live, he gave her no chance, switching it off immediately and setting it down on her dresser. He considered her coldly where she lay sprawled, bound hand and foot to her own bed. "Where might I find a map of this accursed place?"

Goldie swallowed down a dry throat. "The computer would be best."

She had to show him how to use it. He tied her to the bed again, afterward, then returned to the living room and spent hours sitting in front of Goldie's computer. She heard keys clicking, listened numbly through a haze of terror to his soft-voiced verbal commands, not really taking in anything he said. Then the living room fell silent. Goldie strained to hear, trying to catch any hint of movement beyond the open bedroom door. Nothing came to her ears except the hum of the air-conditioning fan.

How long she lay rigid on the rumpled bedspread, Goldie wasn't sure. She couldn't see a clock from her angle. Pain and fright began taking their toll of her strength. She was nearly unconscious when the sound of footsteps jolted her back to full awareness. *Oh, God, he's back, he's going to hack me to pieces . . .*

The Ripper smiled down at her. "You've done very well, my dear. Now, then, show me how to operate the devices in your kitchen. I could use a cup of tea."

"I'm in pain," Goldie whimpered. "I can't feel my feet and hands and my eye is swelling shut."

He frowned slightly, then pulled loose her bonds. He examined her ankles and wrists, then traced the extent of the bruising along her face with surprising gentleness. "Mmm . . . A bit swollen and there will be a bad bruise, I fear, but you're in no danger of losing the eye. Beg pardon for handling you so roughly. Have you an icebox?"

Goldie stared, trying to comprehend the shift of attitude. "What?"

"An icebox. You need a cold compress to bring down the swelling. And a tincture of laudanum would ease the discomfort. I fear I left my medical bag in London."

Goldie managed to whisper, "I don't keep any laudanum. You need a prescription for something like that. There's ice in the freezer. In the kitchen."

He tied her to the bed again, although less tightly than before and he wrapped her wrists and ankles first with scarves from her closet to keep the skin from chafing, then headed for the kitchen. She heard rummaging sounds as he searched through cabinets and finally tried the freezer door. "Ah . . . What an ingenious device! How is it powered, I wonder?" She heard the clink and rattle of ice cubes, then the hush of running water. A moment later, he was back in the bedroom, carrying a wet towel packed with ice cubes. He laid it carefully against her face, stroked her hair back from her cheeks and tested her pulse. "You've suffered a shock, dear lady. We really must bring the pain level down."

"In the bathroom," Goldie whispered. "Aspirin . . ." Nausea and pain were setting the room to lurching like a capsized boat.

More sounds of rummaging drifted to her, then he forced something between her lips and held a water glass to her mouth. She choked and swallowed a handful of aspirin tablets. He covered her warmly with her own blankets and checked the icepack, as though genuinely concerned for her welfare. Goldie closed her eyes as he searched her closets and bureau drawers, whistling contentedly to himself. "Have you been through many gates?" he asked at length, rousing her from near stupor.

"No. I don't go down time." Not since that disastrous trip to New Orleans a few years back. The gate had gone unexpectedly unstable, forcing her to leave behind a young historian she'd taken with her. She'd felt worse pangs of guilt, trapping him there, than she'd ever felt in her life, but there really hadn't been anything she could have done, or anyone else, for that matter. "I stay on the station and run my shop," she added with a shiver.

"Ah. How soon before Primary opens again?" he asked at length.

"Three days."

"In that case, my dear Mrs. Morran, make yourself comfortable while I learn the vagaries of your ingenious cookstove."

Goldie lost consciousness to the sound of rattling pots and pans.

Six days after Skeeter's surgery, on the tenth of October, Malcolm baited the trap. Sid Kaederman had made no secret of his disgust with the lack of modern amenities and repeatedly criticized the search efforts in scathing terms when Malcolm and Margo returned to Spaldergate each night to report their "lack" of progess. When Skeeter's new face was finally healed and ready, Malcolm returned to Spaldergate with news of a major and unexpected "break" in the case: Armstrong had been spotted.

"Who saw the bastard?" Kaederman asked eagerly. "*Where?*"

"An inquiry agent," Malcolm said smoothly. "We ran across the chap this afternoon. Runs a small agency out of Middlesex Street. He's done work for hire before, on behalf of Spaldergate."

"What did he say? How did he find Armstrong?"

Malcolm poured brandy as he explained. "Essentially, he was hired by an irate merchant to discover who'd been passing counterfeit banknotes."

"Counterfeit banknotes?" Kaederman's brows twitched upward in startlement.

"Indeed. It seems the money changer he used on station was somewhat less than scrupulously honest. She slipped a number of counterfeit banknotes in amongst the genuine article. Just before Skeeter Jackson left the station, the money changer asked Mr. Jackson to look into it for her. She was afraid Jenna Caddrick might have been arrested for passing counterfeit money. We'd hired this particular inquiry agent before, looking for Benny Catlin, so this afternoon I hunted him up. Mr. Shannon had been hired recently by a local merchant, trying to trace a foreigner passing fake banknotes. The merchant was irate, wanted to find the counterfeiter to recover substantial losses."

Sid Kaederman laughed quietly, utterly delighted, judging from the glint in his eyes. "Imagine Armstrong's shock when he discovers he was swindled by a money changer!"

Malcolm frowned. "You appear to misapprehend this situation. Counterfeiting is a serious charge, Kaederman. If we don't get to Armstrong before the police, he will be in more trouble than we'll be able to get him out of—and God knows what that will mean in terms of recovering his hostages. We must move quickly. Mr. Shannon has identified him and only a substantial bribe kept him from reporting what he's learned to his client and the police."

"Where's he hiding?"

"He *was* staying somewhere in the East End, but moved out of his lodgings very suddenly, with his entire family—or rather, obviously, his hostages. According to Shannon, Armstrong has discovered the difficulty with his cash supply and may well have passed counterfeits to his landlord without realizing it. Clearly, he wanted to disappear before his landlord could create trouble. Shannon managed to locate him again and saw him purchase a fancy suit and silk top hat. Armstrong subsequently wrangled an introduction at one of the Pall Mall gentlemen's clubs and has been gambling at the gaming tables. Loses here, wins big there."

"Sounds like he's trying to get rid of the counterfeits without having to go to a bank."

"Precisely. Which means we should be able to lay hands on him tonight, when he returns to the gaming tables. Shannon overheard him make an appointment with some of his new acquaintances for the Carlton Club tonight. Unfortunately, when Armstrong took the underground railway out of Blackfriars Station, Shannon lost him in the crush of the crowds, so we still don't know where he's moved the hostages."

Kaderman ignored that last piece of information, eyes glinting with feral excitement as he latched onto the useful item in Malcolm's story. "Tonight! The Carlton Club, where's that?"

"Pall Mall, just west of Waterloo Place. All the fashionable gentlemen's clubs are found in Waterloo Place and Pall Mall. It's an ideal setup to pass counterfeit banknotes. So much money changes hands at the gaming tables, a man would be hard pressed to determine just who had passed the counterfeits. Are you a gambler, Mr. Kaederman?"

A small, secretive smile came and went. "Often."

"Might I suggest, then, that we arrange to play cards this evening?"

Kaederman chuckled. "With pleasure."

"I'll arrange for a hansom cab to take us down at eight o'clock, then."

"I'll be ready."

Malcolm wondered if Kaederman would wait until they approached "Armstrong" at the Carlton Club's gaming tables or if he'd try a hit from some distance, before his victim could realize Kaederman was there. They hadn't been able to search Kaederman's luggage—

he kept both his room and his cases locked—so he could easily have any number of modern weapons stashed away. They were putting Skeeter in body armor, which Kit had thoughtfully sent along, but Malcolm still worried over the problem like a Staffordshire terrier with a soup bone. He hoped Skeeter knew what they were all doing. Far too many lives were riding on the outcome of this trap, Margo's and Malcolm's own, among them. With a final worried glance at Sid Kaederman, Malcolm arranged for the hired carriage and settled down to wait for showtime.

Skeeter fiddled nervously with his watch fob as he climbed out of the Spaldergate barouche into the elegant bustle of Pall Mall. He was a man transformed. His formal black jacket was the forerunner of the modern tuxedo and his diamond horseshoe stick pin, high collar, and heavy gold watch and chain marked him as a man of considerable wealth. The expensive macassar oil that slicked his hair back glinted in the dying light of sunset as his reflection wavered in the Carlton Club's windows. He did an involuntary double-take—his new face startled Skeeter every time he glanced into a reflective surface.

At least the swelling had gone down where Paula had tugged and snipped his flesh into a different shape, and the bruises had faded. He could even talk without pain and had finally graduated to solid foods after nearly a week on liquids, unable to chew without the aid of opiates. As the Spaldergate House carriage rattled away, returning to the gatehouse, Skeeter told the butterflies in his belly to settle down and behave. Any other night, he would've been thrilled beyond measure to play the role of wealthy gambler in one of London's finest gaming establishments. But springing a trap on Sid Kaederman left Skeeter scared to the bottom of his wild, adopted-Mongol heart. He'd accepted the risks when he'd set this in motion, but that didn't stop every monarch and swallowtail butterfly in the northern hemisphere from doing a rumba under his ribs.

Douglas Tanglewood, the Time Tours guide assigned to Skeeter for the night, flashed him a wan smile. "Feeling a bit keyed up?"

"A little."

"It's to be expected," Tanglewood said with forced cheeriness. The guide had been pressed into service with a critical role to play. He would provide Skeeter with the necessary introductions at the Carlton Club, since Malcolm had another mission tonight. Malcolm was bringing in Kaederman. As they crossed the pavement toward the Carlton Club's doorman, Tanglewood kept darting glances at Skeeter, clearly disturbed at seeing him wearing another man's features.

The entrance to the Carlton Club was crowded with laughing gentlemen, opportuned on all sides by unfortunates who made their living—such as it was—off the spare change flowing like wine through Pall Mall. Bootblacks and eel-pie vendors jostled shoulders with flower girls, all crying their wares while newsboys hawked the latest shocking reports out of Whitechapel. Skeeter spotted Margo in heavy disguise as a bootblack boy, diligently polishing some gentleman's shoes in the glow from the club's gaslights. Her unsuspecting customer had stepped up with one foot on her overturned wooden box, reading his newspaper while Margo darted quick looks through the crowd.

Margo caught his gaze and nodded imperceptibly. Skeeter nodded back, then followed Tanglewood into the opulent interior of the Carlton Club. The Time Tours guide greeted the liveried doorman by name as the man opened massive mahogany doors. "Good evening, Fitzwilliam. I've brought a guest this evening, Mr. Cartwright, of America."

Fitzwilliam accepted a small tip from Tanglewood's gloved hand. "Good evening, sir." The doorman spoke politely, his accent as carefully cultured as his gleaming livery. "Welcome to the Carlton Club."

"Thank you." The instant Skeeter stepped across the threshold, he knew he had just walked into *money*. The game rooms were in full swing with lively conversation and gambling activities, the air thick with cigar smoke and the smell of wealth. Skeeter and his guide checked their overcoats and wandered through the busy rooms to acquaint themselves with the club's floor plan, then paused at a craps table where Skeeter tossed a few rounds, just to "keep the hand in." He paid his losses with a polite smile, then, as they walked off, muttered, "Don't play that table. I tossed four sets of dice and every one of 'em was loaded."

The Time Tours guide shot him a startled stare. "*What?*"

Skeeter chuckled. "Never try to con a con. He'll spot you every time. The first ones I tossed were weighted, probably with a mercury tumbler inside. Did you notice how that portly guy with the mutton chops kept tapping them? Dead giveaway. It's why I asked for a new set. Second pair was shaved on the edges. I could feel where they'd been rounded off on all corners but two. That means a better chance they'll roll until they hit a true squared edge, skewing the odds."

Tanglewood was gaping at him.

"Then there was a set where they'd shaved a few of the faces just slightly convex, causing 'em to tumble more readily along the bulged sides. The one concave face creates just the tiniest vacuum against the table's surface, causing the die to land on that face. Wouldn't happen every time, of course, but over a long enough period of throws, you'd get a consistent win. Or loss, if you're trying to prevent sevens or elevens from showing."

"And the fourth pair?" Tanglewood asked, visibly astonished.

"Weighted again, very subtle, though. The paint didn't quite match on all the dots. Your basic slick operator made those. Used heavy lead paint on the dots for the sixes on that pair, so they'd consistently end up on the bottom." Skeeter gave the gaming room they'd just left a disgusted glance. "I didn't say anything, because we're not here to create a scene and I didn't particularly feel like getting involved in a duel of honor with some stiff-necked British lord. But I think I'll avoid the craps tables from now on, thank you."

"Good God, Jackson. Where do you learn such things? No, don't answer that. I'm not sure I want to know. Ever consider a career as a detective?"

"As a matter of fact," Skeeter chuckled, "Kit Carson hired me to work security for the Neo Edo."

Tanglewood let out a low whistle. "I am impressed."

Ten minutes later, Tanglewood had introduced him as "Mr. Cartwright, of New York City, America" at the card tables and Skeeter found himself wallowing happily in a rip-snorting game of stud with the scions of several noble houses, all of them happy as clams to be playing "cowboy poker" with a genuine Yank. In the third hand, one of the players lit a thin, black cigar and gave Skeeter a friendly glance. "I was in America, once, had business in San Francisco. Met a fellow there who played this game very well, indeed. Perhaps you know him, if you've played cards widely over there?"

Skeeter glanced up. "What was his name?"

"Kiplinger. Mr. Kiplinger."

Skeeter sat back in his chair. "*Kiplinger?* Why, yes,

I have heard of him, although we've never met." The corners of his lips twitched. "Quite a gambler, Mr. Kiplinger." Skeeter's eyes twinkled as a positively wicked mood stole over him. "Do you suppose you'll ever be going back to San Francisco, sir?"

The card player smiled. "No, Mr. Cartwright, I think it exceedingly unlikely. An uncle of mine had gone out there during the Gold Rush of '49, you see, made a fortune selling whiskey and victuals to the miners. Parlayed it into an astonishing sum, buying shares in mining operations. When he died last year, I went out to see to the estate, since I was named in his will. He'd never married, poor old Uncle Charles, left a fortune with no heirs but a nephew. Black sheep of a very fine family, let me tell you. But he added ten thousand per annum to my baronetcy when he passed on. Quite an astounding country, America."

Skeeter grinned. "Well, since you don't plan on going back, mind if I let you in on Mr. Kiplinger's secret? Quite a scandal it was, too. Happened just before I came over here." The other gentlemen at the table leaned foward, abruptly intent. Even Tanglewood, whose job was to keep watch for Malcolm and Kaederman, listened with keen interest. "Mr. Kiplinger," Skeeter warmed to his subject, "is what's known as a machine man."

"A machine man?" the baronet frowned. "What the deuce is a machine man?"

"In short, a cheat, a swindler, and a fraud. Maybe you've heard the term 'ace up your sleeve'? Well, what Mr. Kiplinger did was invent an ingenious little machine that fit around his forearm and wrist. It had a little clip in the end of it, to hold a playing card or two, and it could be extended down along the inside of his wrist, like so," Skeeter pointed to his own forearm, "or pulled back again, to hide whatever cards he'd slipped into the clip. He tied a string to the end of the sliding arm of his machine, ran it down his coat and inside his trousers, to a little mechanism at his knees."

The gentlemen had forgotten their own cards, staring in open-mouthed delight.

"The devil you say! How did it operate?"

"The string was attached to a tiny little hook sewed to the inside knee of his other trouser leg. If he wanted to slide the arm of his machine down to his wrist, so he could palm a hidden card into his hand, he squeezed his knees together, which took the tension off the string and lowered the sliding arm with the cards clipped to it. When he wanted to sneak a card up his sleeve, all he had to do was pull his knees apart and presto! Away went the card, slick as a whistle. He practiced with that little contraption until he got so good at it, he could slip three or four cards into that clip during the course of a round of poker and nobody was the wiser."

The gentlemen at their table were gasping, both delighted and scandalized.

"Eventually," Skeeter chuckled, "he got greedy. About two months ago, it must've been, he decided to enter a really high-stakes poker game in San Francisco. And he kept winning. Every single hand. There were a number of very fine card players in that game, professional gamblers, all of them, and several of these professional gentlemen started to get just a little suspicious of Mr. Kiplinger and his phenomenal run of luck at the cards. So at a prearranged signal, they jumped him, dragged off his coat, and found his little machine with three aces and a queen clipped into it."

"Good God! Did they shoot him on the spot?"

"Oh, no." Skeeter grinned. "Not to say that didn't cross their minds, of course. Men have been shot for cheating less seriously than that. No, what they did was tell Mr. Kiplinger he had a choice. He could either die, right then and there, or he could earn his life back."

"How?" That from a heavy-jowled gentleman whose peerage earned him the right to wear a jewelled coronet in the presence of the sovereign. He'd told them so, within five minutes of their having joined the group.

Skeeter sat back, grinning triumphantly. "All he had to do was build one of these machines for each and every one of them. Which he did."

Laughter and exclamations of astonishment greeted the pronouncement.

"But I say, Cartwright, however did you find out about this?"

Skeeter laughed easily. "One of those fellows was my uncle. Black sheep of *my* family. Hell of a card player." He winked. "One hell of a card player."

Doug Tanglewood joined in the laughter as Skeeter scooted back his chair, gracefully slid off his coat and removed his cuffs, revealing no trace of Mr. Kiplinger's infernal contraption, then replaced cuff and cufflinks and evening coat and resumed his seat.

"All right, gentlemen, let's play poker, shall we?"

Kit was jolted from sleep by the insistent shrill of his telephone. He groped, bleary-eyed, for the receiver. "Mmph?"

"Kit? Are you awake?"

"No." He started to fumble the receiver back onto its cradle.

"Kit! Dammit, don't hang up, it's Bull Morgan. I need you in the aerie."

Kit hadn't slept more than ten hours during the last five days. In fact, he had just spent four of those days combing the station for Jack the Ripper, placating and browbeating by turns panic-stricken, infuriated tourists in the Neo Edo, and working gate control to keep any in-bound tourists from coming back into the station. Tours had backed up not only in New York, where in-bound tourists were refused admittance, but also in every down-time location TT-86 operated, leaving literally hundreds of tourists stranded down time, unable to return until the station neutralized the Ripper threat. Having just fallen into bed after nearly twenty hours of non-stop work, Kit told Bull Morgan exactly what he thought of the station manager's latest request. In graphic and shocking detail.

Unfortunately, Bull didn't speak medieval High German, which was Kit's favorite language for cursing. The moment he wound down, Bull said maddeningly, "Good. I'll see you in ten minutes. Caddrick's on his way with I.T.C.H. They're shutting us down, effective today, unless we can figure a way to stall 'em off."

"Oh, God . . ." Kit propped his eyelids open. "If I'm not there in ten, send an ambulance."

"Thanks, Kit. I owe you."

"You sure as hell do. I'll collect on this one, too, just see if I don't."

The line went dead and Kit crawled out of bed, feeling a certain kinship with a recently squashed garden slug. He dragged on the first clothes that came to hand, staggered in search of footgear, and finally stumbled out onto Commons, heading at a drunken pace for the aerie. He was halfway there, repeating to himself, *I will not fall asleep on my feet* every few seconds, before he woke up enough to realize he wore nothing but a loosely belted kimono that covered entirely too little of him and house slippers that had been new when Queen Elizabeth the First had taken the English throne. He'd stolen them, himself, from an Elizabethan house he'd entered under very unhappy circumstances.

"Ah, hell . . ." He pulled the belt tighter, which at least kept the more private bits of him from showing, and scowled at his hairy shins. No time to go back and change, now . . . He couldn't even stop somewhere and beg a pair of jeans. Commons remained eerily quiet, shops and restaurants resembling darkened caves behind their steel security-mesh doors. Scattered patrols of security, BATF, and Pest Control officers stood guard over major gates due to open, to be sure no one got into or out of the station. After that dead BATF officer had been found beside the Langskip Cafe, a few days back, not even Commons security forces made the rounds without partners along. A slow, door-to-door search of every hotel room and Residential apartment on station was underway, looking for both Lachley and a handful of Ripper cultists still at large, but the search was taking forever, with no guarantee that the Ripper wasn't simply changing lodgings to a room already cleared.

By the time Kit reached the aerie, he was almost asleep again, leaning against the elevator doors for the ride up from Commons. The elevator doors slid open, dumping Kit unceremoniously into the room. He staggered, recovered, and hitched the kimono around with an irritable twitch, then met the astonished gazes of John Caddrick, three armed bodyguards, and five I.T.C.H. agents impeccably attired—respectively—in six-thousand dollar suits and neatly pressed uniforms. Kit scratched absently at a thick growth of stubble, yawned, and wove his way toward a chair, where he promptly collapsed.

Caddrick glared. "You're drunk!"

"God, I wish," Kit muttered. "I just haven't been to bed in about five days. Thanks for waking me up. Now, what's this bullshit about closing Shangri-La?"

Caddrick glanced at the highest-ranking I.T.C.H. officer. "Agent Kirkegard has agreed to shut down this station. TT-86 is dangerously out of control, thanks to gross incompetence among the managerial staff."

Kit just looked at him. Then switched his attention to the immaculately groomed Kirkegard, her blond hair pulled back into a severe knot at the nape of her neck. "You wouldn't mind, would you, if I toss this jackass through the window?"

"This is not a time to joke!" she snapped.

"I'm not joking," Kit growled. "The only thing wrong with this station is John Caddrick's butt, sitting on it."

Bull Morgan stood up hastily, clearing his throat. "Kit, I know how hard you've been working during this crisis. I asked you to join this meeting to present your case as a station resident and business owner, before I.T.C.H. makes its final determination."

"I see. Tell you what," Kit leaned forward, holding Agent Kirkegard's gaze. "You people have been probing around in our books and our private vaults and auditing our tax returns until you've dug down to Himalayan bedrock. I'd like to issue you a *real* challenge."

"A challenge?" Kirkegard echoed, her Nordic brow creasing briefly.

"Yep. A real barn-burner. I'd like you to figure out why John Caddrick, here, would lie to the press, the FBI, Interpol, and I.T.C.H. about the circumstances of his little girl's disappearance."

For a long moment, utter silence reigned in the aerie. Every mouth in the room had dropped open, including Bull Morgan's. Kit was beyond caring if he'd just signed the station's death warrant—not to mention his own. He was simply too tired to keep pussyfooting around what he knew about Jenna Caddrick's vanishing act, and he was fresh out of other options. And it looked to Kit like he'd struck paydirt, with this one.

Senator Caddrick's face had utterly drained of color, leaving him virtually transparent for long instants. Then a scarlet flush darkened toward purple. He came out of his chair, snarling. "Why, you miserable, drunken, washed-up *has-been*! How dare you insinuate any such thing!"

"Sit down," Kit growled, "before you step close enough to call it assault and I retaliate in ways we'll all regret."

"Don't sit there and threaten me!"

"All right." Kit stood up. "I'll stand here and do it. Maybe you'd care to explain a few facts. You say your daughter's so-called kidnappers came to this station and tried to murder Ianira Cassondra, but we've got eye-witnesses who'll swear in court that your daughter came into this station of her own free will. Moreover, she came armed with a loaded revolver she used to *kill* the terrorist about to murder Ianira. Or what about Noah Armstrong, who's supposed to be a ringleader of these same terrorists? Armstrong shoved Ianira to safety, just as the man Jenna killed tried to shoot her. And why did Julius, not to mention Marcus and his children, voluntarily run to Denver with Noah Armstrong in disguise, smuggling the girls out in their luggage and setting up Julius as decoy for your daughter? For that matter, why was Jenna, who was supposed to be held hostage, allowed to wander around this station at will, changing money all by herself in Goldie Morran's shop just minutes before the gate departure? Furthermore, she strolled into Paula Booker's cosmetic surgical studio and paid for a new face, again totally on her own. She was all by herself when she stepped through the Britannia Gate, too—we've got witnesses who'll swear to that, too, in a court of law. Nobody forced that girl through any gates on this station. How about it, Caddrick?"

Caddrick's cheeks faded to the color of dirty ice. *"This is preposterous!"*

"Is it? Your story doesn't add up, Caddrick. I wonder what we'd find out about Noah Armstrong if we went back up-time and started digging? The man can't be an *Ansar Majlis* terrorist, not when he's kept Ianira's whole family from being murdered by *Ansar Majlis* operatives, and he can't be a kidnapper since he let Jenna and Ianira walk through the Britannia gate without armed guards. She was seen on the departures platform by one of the baggage handlers. There wasn't anybody close to her who could've been holding a gun on her. And she walked out of Spaldergate House in London with no escort except a Time Tours driver. No kidnappers in sight, nothing. She was followed, of course. Two men who trailed her out of this station, working as baggage handlers, tried to kill her at the Picadilly Hotel. Only Jenna shot both of them, with the same revolver she used to kill the *Ansar Majlis* gunman on station, killed both men and got away clean. Personally, Caddrick, I'd like to know why your story doesn't wash with the facts."

"I will not stand here and be slandered!" Caddrick shouted, causing dust to jump on the surface of Bull's immense desk.

"Good!" Kit shot right back. "I'll personally escort you to Primary and kick your butt through, the second it re-opens!"

Ms. Kirkegard stepped between them, holding up an imperious hand in either direction, forestalling whatever shattering curse was about to erupt from Caddrick's mouth. "Silence! All of you! Mr. Carson, these are very serious allegations."

"You bet they are. Believe me, I know exactly how serious they are. I wouldn't risk making such accusations lightly, because too many people who thwart John Caddrick's plans end up conveniently dead."

"I will sue you for every goddamned cent you own!" Caddrick snarled.

Kit grinned into Caddrick's teeth. "Like to see you try it. We're outside American jurisdiction, here. You'll have to convince the Inter-Temporal Court, if you want to sue my butt."

Agent Kirkegard said forcefully, "I want to see these witnesses, immediately."

"Sorry. They're in London. Looking for Jenna Caddrick. And keeping a very suspicious eye on the senator's private detective, Mr. Sid Kaederman. Caddrick rammed him down our throats with threats to shut us down if we didn't send him along. The man had never stepped through a single gate, was monstrously unqualified for a down-time search mission. I spent a couple of weeks in Sid Kaederman's company, on horseback in Colorado. Maybe the senator, here, can explain why Mr. Kaederman recognized the man who murdered one of our station residents in an abandoned Colorado mining town? Recognized him and didn't expect to find him dead? That man had committed cold-blooded murder of a sixteen-year-old boy, I might add, who went to Colorado as decoy for Jenna Caddrick."

"There are perfectly good reasons why Kaederman might not say anything," Caddrick began.

"Really? If Kaederman were legit and had recognized one of the terrorists, he'd simply have said so. But he didn't say anything. In fact, he took pains to make sure no one realized he'd recognized the man. Why? Mr. Sid Kaederman's story doesn't add up, either, does it? We sent him to London to avoid having your federal goons shut us down, but I sent Skeeter Jackson and Paula Booker through to keep an eye on him. Skeeter knows this case better than anyone—he's been at hand when every key piece of this mess has unfolded. And when it comes to Ianira Cassondra, Skeeter's the only man on this station I can guarantee no amount of money will buy off. A boy doesn't get adopted by twelfth century Yakka Mongols without adopting their moral codes. For Skeeter, clan is sacred, and someone's already killed one member of his adopted station-side clan and tried to murder several others. Believe me, Caddrick, that boy will kill to protect Ianira and her family, if he has to. And he *will* find Jenna and Noah Armstrong. The question is, what will they tell him when he does?"

"You're mad!" Caddrick shouted. "Completely insane! My God, Carson, is this the only way you can find to keep your precious pocket-book from being shut down around your ears? By making wild accusations and threatening me?"

"Why don't we let Jenna settle it?" Kit smiled coldly into Caddrick's eyes.

The senator swung on the I.T.C.H. agents. "Are you going to listen to this garbage? I insist you do your job! Shut down this station right now, before any more lives are lost! As for Carson," he flung a pitying look over his shoulder, "it's clear he's cracked under the strain. Up-time hospitalization is what he needs."

Agent Kirkegard frowned. "Senator, I cannot believe Kit Carson has gone raving mad in the space of one week. Not when he has worked so heroically to save lives on this station. No, do not interrupt!" she snapped, as Caddrick started to protest. "Grave charges have been made, charges which must be investigated. If what Mr. Carson says is true, your actions on this station must be considered highly suspicious. Until this delegation is satisfied that no evidence exists to prove these accusations, my fellow agents and I must take them seriously. You will return to your hotel, Senator, and you will not leave it unless you are summoned by this delegation. Is that clear? Mr. Morgan," she turned her attention to Bull, leaving Caddrick sputtering in naked shock, "I believe your security system records events on Commons?"

"It does," Bull nodded. "We recycle the tapes on a weekly basis, but we've kept the footage of every riot on station, for legal purposes."

"Very wise. I hereby subpoena all security tapes showing the disturbance surrounding Ianira Cassondra's disappearance."

"But she's a down-timer without rights!" Caddrick protested.

Kirkegard turned an icy gaze on him. "Indeed. But if your daughter and Noah Armstrong are shown in that tape doing what Mr. Carson claims they were doing, your entire story will come under serious suspicion. And they are not down-timers, but up-time citizens with full legal protection. Therefore, that tape is critical evidence. Mr. Morgan, if I may suggest it, the senator should not be privy to any further discussions this commission has with station management, until such time as these charges are proven or dismissed."

"You can't be serious!" Caddrick blustered.

She levelled a cool stare back into his seething grey eyes. "I would suggest you remove yourself to your hotel, Senator. Or I will have you removed."

Caddrick stood sputtering for several incoherent moments, then stalked to the elevator. His stunned bodyguards hurried in his wake, exchanging worried glances. The elevator swallowed them down and took them mercifully away. Kit ran a hand through badly disheveled hair. "Thanks. And now, if you don't mind, I'm going back to bed. You can subpoena me to testify later."

And without waiting for a by-your-leave, he stalked

to the elevator and followed Caddrick's abrupt exit. Ten minutes later, he was sprawled in bed once more, his last conscious thought a worried one, wondering what he'd just unleashed on them all.

Chapter Sixteen

The cold night wind chilled Margo through her thin
bootblack's disguise. She shivered and wished she could
walk through the ornate doors to the Carlton Club, just
long enough to get warm. Instead, she danced in place,
hugging herself for warmth, and called out to passing
gentlemen, "Shine, guv'nor? Farthing for a shine?"

She had just secured a customer and was diligently
blacking his boots when Skeeter and Douglas Tanglewood arrived in a rented hansom. They nodded imperceptibly in her direction and vanished into the warmth
of the club. Margo worked briskly, as much to keep
warm as to maintain her disguise. The pistol inside her
trousers was held snug against her abdomen by a belly-
band holster and the dagger in her boot rubbed her
calf as she moved about. She kept close watch on the
arriving carriages, impatient for Malcolm to arrive with
Sid Kaederman. More than a quarter of an hour passed
without a trace of them, leaving Margo more and more
uneasy. She was busily blacking another gentleman's
boots when a hansom cab rattled to a halt some distance

from the kerbside and a well-dressed gentleman swung himself down.

"Driver," he called out, "my friend wishes to continue on to London Docks, to catch his steamer."

Even as he spoke, he thrust his arm back into the dark cab, which jolted slightly on its high wheels. Margo slowed her strokes with the buffing brush, puzzled. The cab started down the street and the gentleman turned, heading toward the club entrance. Margo gasped. *Kaederman!* He strode past, nodding to the doorman. "I shall be joining friends this evening, a Mr. Cartwright and his companions."

"Very good, sir."

Margo dropped the buffing brush, abandoning her astonished client. She darted after the hansom cab, terrified of what she might find. It took her half a block to catch up and she only did so then because the cab was caught in a jam of carriages trying to turn into Waterloo Place. Margo flung herself onto the step and lunged up, ignoring the driver's startled demand to get out of his cab.

"Malcolm!"

He lay slumped against the side of the carriage, cheeks ashen in the gaslights from nearby club windows. "Margo," he whispered in a terrible, weak voice. "Sorry, love, took me by surprise . . ." He had fumbled one hand beneath his coat, was holding himself awkwardly. Blood had spread across his shirt, was dripping down his arm and spreading across the back of his hand. "Get back to . . . Carlton Club . . . warn the others." He sipped air. "I'm not hit bad. Managed to fling myself aside . . . when he told the driver to go to the docks . . . would've had me through the heart, otherwise."

Even as Malcolm was explaining, Margo was ripping his coat and shirt off, using her dagger to cut the shirt into bandage strips. She wound them around Malcolm's chest, folding a couple of thick pieces to act as compresses over the wound. Her hands shook violently, but she managed to tie them off snugly.

"Go, Margo," Malcolm wheezed. "I'll take the cab to Spaldergate. Go!"

She swore aloud, recognizing the necessity. "Driver! Your passenger's been shot! Take him to a surgeon! Battersea Park, Octavia Street! And hurry those horses!"

The driver let go a voluable flood of invective and cracked his carriage whip, urging his horses up onto the pavement to bypass the crush of carriages in the street. Pedestrians scattered, cursing, as Margo shoved her knife back into her boot sheath and flung herself down to the street, pelting toward the Carlton Club once more. She dodged carriage wheels and horses, gained the pavement, and slung herself around startled gentlemen strolling from club to club. She finally gained the Carlton and hurled herself at the doors— only to be snatched back by Fitzwilliam.

"Here, now, where d'you think you're going? This is a gentleman's club! Take yourself away, you filthy bootblack!" He dragged Margo by the back of her shirt collar and shoved her roughly to the pavement, where she landed in an undignified sprawl.

"Listen to me!" she shot back to her feet. "I have to get a critical message to Mr. Tanglewood and Mr. Cartwright! Send a message, yourself, if you won't let me in! Tell them Kaederman shot Mr. Moore and he's going to kill Mr. Cartwright! They're in terrible danger—!"

"Take yourself off before I summon a constable, you little lunatic!"

Margo darted past, but Fitzwilliam was quick. He trapped her between his body and the wall, pinning her like a bug on display. He boxed her ears so soundly, Margo's head rang and her eyes streamed. She swore in gutter langage, then bit his hand, flinging herself around him and running toward the now-unguarded door.

"Stop that boy! Stop him, I say!"

A group of startled gentlemen just leaving the club made a grab for her. She slithered past, cursing them, and dragged out her pistol—then someone seized her shoulder and spun her around and pain exploded through her head, sending her sprawling across the pavement like a ragdoll.

Goldie rapidly discovered that John Lachley, while certifiably mad, was nevertheless no fool. Killing her was thankfully the furthest thing from his mind. She spent most of her captivity tied to the chair in front of her computer, teaching him everything he demanded to know about the up-time world. He needed her— for a while, anyway. And that gave her the courage to hope she might somehow survive.

"This," Lachley demanded, touching a finger to the glowing computer screen, "is the schedule for the various gates, then?"

Goldie nodded. "Yes." Her left wrist was bound to the chair, her right tied to the desk with a short length of rope, just enough to operate the mouse.

"Three different dates are given for each gate," he frowned.

"There have to be three. One is the time-frame of the up-time world, where the tourists come from, one is the time-frame of the station, and one is the time-frame of the tour destination beyond the gate."

He studied the readings for a moment. "This one has only two dates."

"That's Primary, of course. Gate One."

"Ah, of course . . . The way into the up-time world which your guards have so churlishly denied me. Of course there would be only two dates given. Yes.

Show me how one obtains a proper gate pass for your Primary."

Goldie bit her lip nervously. "I can't. You get one in New York. When you come into the station. And a down-timer *can't* get one. Down-timers are never permitted to step through Primary. It's against up-time law."

Lachley scowled. "Deuced awkward. I shall simply have to obtain one from a tourist or station resident, then. No matter. A trifling detail. Make this machine show me what your up-time worlds looks like."

Goldie explained how to put in a CD encyclopedia which contained photographs and movie clips, since she couldn't reach the shelf where they were stored, then clicked into various files to show him what he demanded. As he frowned at the screen, she suggested nervously, "You'd get a better idea, watching videotaped movies on television."

Ten minutes later, Goldie sat bound hand and foot on her couch, while John Lachley sprawled at his leisure beside her, watching Goldie's movies. He exclaimed often, sitting forward with interest whenever cars or jets or cityscapes appeared, took particular note of new machinery and gadgets, and demanded explanations of everything he saw until Goldie's mind whirled in exhaustion. He watched videotapes until she fell asleep in her bonds and when she woke again, stiff and aching, he was still watching. He also spent hours at her computer, reading station library files, and studied every book on Goldie's shelves. Lachley's growing knowledge of the up-time world terrified Goldie. He correctly identified every item in the videos, explained each item's proper use, and had picked up modern slang and idiom with an ease that left her shaking. If he got loose in New York . . .

She couldn't see any way to stop him, short of

reaching a telephone to cry for help, and since he was already familiar with their use from London, he hadn't allowed her near one—once he'd recognized hers for what it was; it bore no resemblance whatsoever to an 1880's telephone. When operating the computer, she wasn't even able to send an e-mail to station security. He'd grasped the e-mail concept with terrifying rapidity and had forced her to delete the programming from her hard drive.

Goldie knew the entire station was being turned upside down, searching for him, but no one had come to her apartment, thanks to his trick with the dead BATF officer's radio, and no one had called her, either, not even to commiserate over lost profits. It hurt to realize that in such a crisis, not one of the station residents had thought to check on her, to see if she was alive or dead. People she'd thought of as friends had completely ignored her. Bitterness choked Goldie, but there was nothing she could do except wait and hope that her captor grew careless just long enough to scream for help.

Every day's passing, however, left Goldie sinking further into despair. He never relaxed his vigil for even a moment and Goldie entertained no doubts about what he'd do if he caught her trying to telephone. Lachley would cut her to ribbons so small, there wouldn't be enough to fill a casket. On the other hand, if she didn't anger him, he would probably let her live, at least until he made the attempt to crash Primary outbound. And he couldn't try that as long as Bull Morgan kept the tourists in their hotel rooms and refused to let anyone through. Goldie's greatest terror was that Lachley would simply kill her, waylay a security agent and steal his uniform, then slip through Primary that way.

As days passed, the intolerable situation left John Lachley deeply impatient, forced as he was to sit through two cycles of Primary without anyone allowed near it. He paced agitatedly, muttering under his breath, then finally snatched up another videotape from her rapidly dwindling supply. Lachley poured himself a generous brandy from the last bottle in the cabinet and slid in Goldie's copy of *Temple Harlot,* which she had just recently acquired through a video pirate. When the pre-movie interview of Ianira Cassondra flickered across the screen, Lachley jerked so violently, he knocked the glass to the floor. He stared at the screen and ripped off a shocked oath. "*God's blood!* It's her!" He turned a wild-eyed stare on Goldie. "Who is that woman?" He stabbed an unsteady finger toward the television.

"Ianira Cassondra. One of the station's down-timers. A member of the Found Ones, the down-time community of refugees. She sits on the council as their speaker."

He ran the tape back to listen to the interview in its entirety, then stopped the video and demanded a full explanation. Goldie told him everything she knew about Ianira, her flight from a murderous husband in Athens, her arrival on station, her marriage to Marcus, the adoring acolytes who had named her their prophetess, hailing her as the Goddess incarnate. "They flock to the station," she quavered. "When she was kidnapped, they went berserk. Staged protests and started brawls with the *Ansar Majlis* and half the station. The Angels of Grace Militia has sworn to defend Templars from harm until Ianira is restored." Goldie wanted to ask why he was so abruptly interested, but couldn't find the courage to open her lips again.

Lachley sat staring into empty space for long moments, mind clearly racing. At length, he murmured, "It is possible, then, to wield that much power, even in this strange world . . . If a mere chit can be taken for a goddess, then I shall certainly rule as a god." He smiled, laughed softly to himself, eyes twinkling. Then untied Goldie from the couch and hauled her unceremoniously into her bedroom, where he dumped her onto the mattress and tied her down again. He stroked Goldie's wild, unwashed hair back from her face and smiled down at her. "You have done very well, my pet. According to the time tables on your computer, Primary opens again tomorrow evening. You and I shall be ready, dear lady. Whether they permit it or no, I *will* step through that gate."

Goldie was too exhausted, too numb to ask how. She hadn't forgotten how he'd created his last diversion— or the severed human head he'd flung down into the crowd, its plunge caught vividly on SLUR-TV's cameras. It had been a woman's head, with once-beautiful blonde hair. Goldie knew in her creaking bones he would cut *her* to pieces, too, if he could find no other way through Primary.

Despite Goldie's soul-deep weariness, sleep was a long time coming.

Skeeter was winning the latest round of poker, hands down, when a liveried servant carrying a folded slip of paper on a silver tray entered the card parlour. "Message for Mr. Cartwright!" He spoke just loudly enough to be heard, without disrupting conversations under way over the cards. The servant was peering around the room, trying to locate the recipient. At the sound of his assumed name, Skeeter jerked his glance up.

"What is it? What message?"

"Ah, Mr. Cartwright? A message, sir." The man handed Skeeter the folded slip of paper and waited for the tip Skeeter produced, then departed with a slight bow. Skeeter glanced at Doug Tanglewood, who was frowning already, then opened the note. Every droplet of blood drained out of his face. *There's serious trouble at home, come at once, someone's taken the children . . .*

The table flipped over with a crash. Cards and money went flying. Skeeter hit the floor running and took the stairs five at a time, leaving Tanglewood to follow in his wake. Skeeter was ruthless with elbows and shoulders. "Let me through, damn your eyes!"

Shocked gentlemen scattered out of his path, staring after him. Then he was on the ground floor, retrieving his coat, rushing toward the door. He was nearly there when a voice at his ear said, "Where's the fire, Armstrong?" He jerked his gaze up, startled, to find Sid Kaederman at his elbow. An instant later, something hard, cylindrical, and terrifying jabbed his ribs, as luck would have it, between the front and back panels of his hidden body armor.

"Make any noise at all and I'll blow a hole through your liver," Kaederman hissed. "Outside, Armstrong. We're going have a friendly little chat someplace quiet. About your friends."

Shaking with fury at his own stupidity, Skeeter walked into the cold October night. The jaws of the trap had slammed shut, all right—only Skeeter was the one caught and where the hell was Malcolm? Nothing was going down the way it was supposed to! How had Kaederman gotten the drop on them all, leaving Skeeter off balance and everyone out of position? Kaederman pushed open the door and shoved Skeeter through, gun still jammed into his ribs. Skeeter raked the pavement with his glance, searching for familiar faces and not spotting any. Kaederman was lifting a hand and whistling for a hansom cab when Margo appeared, running toward them.

"Kaederman!"

The killer stiffened—and the damned, interfering doorman grabbed Margo by the shoulder, slugging her so hard, she sprawled across the walk. Her little .32 top break clattered across the pavement and into the street. Men were shouting, calling for a constable, and someone cried, "Good God! The boy had a gun!"

Kaederman shoved Skeeter away from the fracas, toward a hansom cab waiting for a fare, the horse's head bent low, the cabman bundled against the cold wind. Skeeter's fury faltered into the beginnings of real fear.

"I say," a familiar voice said from behind them, "did you drop this, sir?"

Kaederman started to glance around, an instinctive response to the polite inquiry—and Doug Tanglewood kicked Skeeter's feet out from under him.

He went down with a startled yell, no more expecting that sudden move than Kaederman. A brief, sharp scuffle exploded above him. The muted *clack!* of a silenced pistol reached him. The scent of burnt powder and hot metal filled the air as the gun discharged almost soundlessly. Tanglewood gripped Kaederman's gun wrist with both hands while swearing savagely, oblivious to the hole through the loose side of a once-fine Prince Albert coat. The crowd of gentlemen on the steps stood like spectators at a sporting event, thinking this was an ordinary brawl; not one of them recognized the anachronistic, suppressed semiautomatic pistol as a dangerous weapon.

Skeeter kicked out and managed to clip Kaederman's ankles with one thrashing foot. Kaederman tripped, flailing for a moment off balance. Tanglewood suddenly had his opponent's full weight slipping through his hands and only slowed Kaederman's fall enough for the assassin to control it, leaving Tanglewood the one off balance and Kaederman rolling back up. Skeeter scrambled to his feet just as Margo rushed in low, under Kaederman's gun arm. She prevented his second shot from catching Tanglewood between the shoulder-blades. The gun fired wild as Kaederman tried to avoid her. A giant's fist punched Skeeter in the chest and sent him sprawling, saved from the bullet by the Kevlar panel under his fancy dress shirt. Margo was still struggling with Kaederman. Shrill whistles sounded, police whistles, and someone shouted, "Constable! Over here!"

Tanglewood lunged at them just as Kaederman punched Margo in the solar plexus. She doubled up with a gagging sound and he dragged her back with the gun to her head. "Get back, damn you, or I'll kill her!"

Skeeter tried to crawl to his feet, stunned and gasping against pain to his ribs, bruising pain from that shot to his body armor. Kaederman kicked him in the gut, dumping him to the ground again, and dragged his hostage into the street where he flung her into a cab. Then Kaederman lunged up and shouted at the driver, who sped away with a clatter, swerving into traffic at a reckless pace. Skeeter and Tanglewood bolted in pursuit— and found their way blocked by two burly constables.

"What's going on, here?" the taller policeman demanded.

"That man's a killer!" Skeeter gasped, pointing at the vanishing hansom cab. "He's taken a girl hostage! We have to stop him!"

Tanglewood dashed into the street, scooping up Margo's revolver in one fluid movement while flagging down another cab. "Skeeter! Come on!"

The constables grabbed for him and missed. A moment later, the cab driver was racing down Pall Mall in pursuit. Skeeter clung to the side of the rocketing hansom to avoid being flung out as they whipped between carriages at a reckless pace. Douglas Tanglewood was swearing nonstop. "Goddammit, what a bloody *mess*!"

"What'm I gonna tell Kit?" Skeeter groaned, closing his eyes against the very thought. "What in the world

am I gonna tell Kit? And the others . . ." He could hear
the voices already, could picture the freezing contempt.
*And where were you, Skeeter, when Margo was abducted
by that killer? Ah, gambling . . . Well, of course you were,
Skeeter, who could expect anything better of you . . .*

He had to find her. Before Kaederman tortured her
to learn where Jenna was. Skeeter wouldn't give a
plugged nickle for her life, once Kaederman knew.
Skeeter clenched his jaw. He vowed to hunt Kaederman to the ends of the world, if necessary.

And kill him.

Chapter Seventeen

Primary was due to open at eight-fifteen P.M., station time. Goldie spent the day in a mute daze, watching John Lachley prepare his escape. He had raided Goldie's wardrobe, finding a pair of her jeans and a sweatshirt that fit him reasonably well. He carefully studied the identification papers and cards in her wallet, requiring Goldie to explain the purposes of each. He knew, now, about the BATF kiosks and medical stations he would be required to pass, with identification in hand. Goldie didn't see how he could possibly fool anyone with her ID, but he clearly had a plan and that scared her even more thoroughly. If he used her ID, he wouldn't need her.

Lachley also tucked into her wallet all the loose cash Goldie had left in the apartment. He'd already appropriated her private stock of jewelry, gemstones, and rare coins, some of which she kept separate from her shop inventory in case of robbery or other disaster to her storefront. She reflected bitterly that the one contingency she hadn't planned for was kidnapping and armed robbery by Jack the Ripper. He was packing Goldie's suitcase, chatting almost gaily about the up-time world and his plans, when the buzzer sounded at her apartment door.

Goldie jerked her head up from the mattress. Lachley whipped around, transformed in the blink of an eyelash to a cold-eyed, ruthless killer. He snatched up his knife and advanced on her with a terrifying, soundless movement, a snake that had abruptly sprouted legs. The door buzzer sounded again, followed by an impatient pounding. Lachley dragged her from the bed and hauled her, trembling, into the living room. He laid the razor sharp blade at her throat and whispered, "Call through the door. Say you're ill and can't open it."

"Hello?" Goldie called, voice cracking with terror.

"Security!" a man's voice came back through the door. "Mind if we check the place again, Goldie? We sent you an e-mail, but you never answered, so we thought we'd check on you."

"Could you come later?" she choked out, shaking so violently the knife knicked her throat in a thin red line. "I'm not well. I slipped and fell and can't move around much."

"Do you need a doctor?" the security officer called back, sounding worried, now. "I'll send for someone . . ."

Lachley pressed the steel tighter against her jugular. "No!" Goldie cried. "I'm fine! Just bruised and shaken, is all."

"Open the door, Goldie," the man demanded maddeningly. "We'll let the doctor decide. And I have to search the apartment, no exceptions allowed."

Lachley cursed under his breath, then shifted the tip of the knife to Goldie's spine and slid around behind her. "Open it," he hissed.

Goldie's hands trembled violently as she reached for the locks and the doorknob. Lachley stood hidden from sight as the door swung open. She shuffled aside for the security team. Wally Klontz and a BATF agent stepped inside, the BATF officer entering first. Wally had barely crossed the threshold when Lachley shoved Goldie brutally to the floor. Lachley sank his knife into the BATF officer's throat in a lightning attack, leaving Goldie screaming and covered with spatters of blood. Wally flung himself at the killer, but Lachley twisted aside and slashed out. The blade tore Wally's shoulder to the bone, sending the security officer reeling back in shock and pain. Then Lachley was out the door and running. Wally fumbled with his radio while blood poured down his arm and spread across the front of his shirt.

"Code Seven Red!" he screamed. "Goldie Morran's apartment! Lachley killed Feindienst and laid my shoulder open, then bolted!"

Goldie dragged herself to Wally's side and tried to stanch the bleeding with her hands. The radio crackled. "Roger, security teams are responding. Medical's on its way. Did he kill Goldie?"

"Negative, but she's pretty shaken up."

Goldie's hands trembled violently against Wally's torn shoulder.

The radio sputtered. "Roger. Sit tight, help's on the way."

Ten minutes later, Goldie lay strapped to a gurney in the back of a medi-van, headed for the infirmary. Wally Klontz occupied the gurney next to hers, where EMT's worked over his gashed shoulder and threaded an I.V. into his elbow. Goldie still didn't quite believe she had survived. As terror finally dropped away, Goldie's mind gradually came back to life again, presenting her with several startling, lucrative possibilities. After all, very few people could claim to have survived a week as Jack the Ripper's prisoner. Why, there might be television appearances in this, exclusive magazine and newspaper stories, books, perhaps even a movie . . .

Feeling more like herself than she had in a full week, Goldie settled down to enjoy her notoriety.

For long moments, shock held Margo motionless on the floor of the cab. The driver had whipped his horse to a gallop, urged on by Kaederman's shouted promise of reward. By lifting her head, she could just see over the footboard. It was dark beyond the open side of the hansom, which swayed and jolted badly as they rattled over uneven paving, but as they whipped around a corner, she caught a glimpse of the Atheneum gentlemen's club. They'd turned onto Waterloo Place, then, which meant they now raced northward along Regent Street.

The long, gentle curve of Nash's Quadrant left her slightly queasy as the windows and street-level doorways flashed past. A dizzy swing through Picadilly Circus sent them plunging past the County Fire Office into a broad, sliding turn down Shaftesbury Avenue. They rattled down Shaftesbury at a terrific clip, the SoHo district flying past on their left hand, then the cabbie swung sharply into a skidding right-hand turn that left them racing down High Holborn.

Margo was beginning to recover her breath, at least, despite the terrific jouncing against her ribs as she was jolted around on the floor. Her wits returned, as well, stirring into anger. She was alive and if she wanted to stay that way, she'd better do something fast. She'd lost her pistol, thanks to that idiot doorman, but she might still have the boot-knife, if all that thrashing around hadn't knocked it out of her boot sheath. He hadn't searched her yet, which was a small miracle. If she hoped to use that dagger, she'd have to do it quick. His silenced pistol frightened her, his prowess with it even more so, but they were in a flying cab with her sprawled across the floor, supposedly stunned and terrified out of her wits, so he probably wouldn't expect her to try anything yet. She groped cautiously toward her boot with one hand, trying to brace herself with her other arm to reduce the bone-shaking jar of the ride.

Cor, I'll 'ave bruises from me thri'penny bits to me toes... she thought sourly, lapsing into the Cockney she'd been speaking almost more than standard English, this trip. Margo stole her hand into her boot and closed her fingers around the grip of the little dagger Sven had given her. It wasn't a large one, only four inches or so of blade, thrust into a leather sheath sewn to the boot lining, but it was a weapon and she certainly knew how to use it, after all those lessons with Sven Bailey. Just closing her hand around the stout wooden handle lifted her flagging spirits. Kaederman shouted up to the driver, "Turn south! And you can slow down, now. We've shaken the bastard following us!"

"Can't turn, guv," the driver called down, "we're on the Viaduct, no way to turn 'til we come to Snow Hill an' Owd Bailey!"

The Viaduct! Margo's hopes leapt like bright flames. Built to eliminate the treacherously steep drop along Holborn Hill, the Viaduct was essentially a bridge fourteen-hundred feet long, with shops and even a church built down the length of it. Where the Viaduct's single open space of visible ironwork crossed Farringdon Street—itself the covered-over course of River Fleet—there was a sheer drop of some fifteen feet. No carriage could get off the Viaduct anywhere between Charterhouse Street and Snow Hill, with the Old Bailey Criminal Court just beyond.

But a lone person on foot could.

Stone steps descended to Farringdon on either side.

The trick would be to create such confusion, he couldn't shoot her. She considered—and swiftly rejected—three separate plans of attack before settling on the one likeliest to work. It was also the riskiest, but she wasn't afraid of risk. If she didn't escape, Kaederman would kill her. Probably after torturing her for Jenna's location. So, as the cabbie slowed his horse to a swaying trot past St. Andrews' Church, she quavered out, "P-please, can I g-get up? I'm hurt, down here . . ." She slid the dagger out of her boot and held it tight in the hand farthest from him.

Kaederman muttered under his breath, "Try anything and I'll put a bullet through you." He grasped her wrist and levered her up. She swayed, losing her balance deliberately—which wasn't hard to do. Hansoms were notoriously tippy contrivances and they were still going at a fair clip. She slipped sideways with a gasping, frightened cry. She flung out one arm to catch her balance, which put the knife exactly where she wanted it.

Right over the trotting horse's rear quarters.

She slammed the blade home, hilt deep.

The horse screamed, a tearing, jagged sound of pain. It kicked and reared violently, sheering wildly to the right. The cab flung sideways. The maddened animal was kicking, lunging, trying to get the steel out of its flank. The whole carriage crashed sideways. Margo grabbed for the edge of the roof above her head as they went down. She lost her grip when they slammed to the street. The force crushed Margo back across the seat, with Kaederman under her. She kicked anything that moved and dragged herself up over the lip of the toppled hansom. The driver was yelling from his seat at the rear of the cab. From the sound of it, he was pinned by the weight of the carriage.

Then she was out and running, with no time to be sorry for the driver or the horse and no time to recover the dagger. Kaederman was shouting, cursing hideously. The iron railings over Farringdon Street flashed past, then she was skidding in a desperate lunge for the nearest of the step-buildings flanking Farringdon, plunging down the steep steps, clutching at the railing for balance. She heard thudding footfalls above, pounding in pursuit across the bridge and down the stone staircase on her heels. *Oh, God, help me, please* ... She expected a bullet to slam through her back any moment. Margo reached the street and cut back toward Shoe Lane and St. Andrew Street. If she could just reach Holborn again, she wasn't far from the Old Bell. The ancient coaching inn would be busy, with lots of people coming and going. Famous along all the old coaching roads, the Old Bell beckoned as her only safe haven. The proprietor and his customers would help her and there might even be a constable, in for a bite of supper. She flew up St. Andrew, gasping for breath at the steep climb back up Holborn Hill.

Just short of Holborn Circus, a heavy hand closed around her shoulder. Kaederman spun her against the side of a closed shop, snarling and backhanding her brutally. Margo punched and kicked, screaming bloody murder—and a shrill whistle sounded, practically on top of them. A constable pounded down Holborn Hill, straight toward them, shouting at Kaederman to halt immediately. Kaederman swore and ran, instead, vanishing down a side street. Margo staggered and slid down the side of the shop toward the pavement, reeling with the shock of her near escape.

"Are you hurt, boy?" the constable cried.

She sat on the cold stone pavement, shaking violently. "N-no ... He was going to kill me ..."

The constable crouched beside her, than said in a surprised voice, "Cor, it's a girl!"

She glanced down and realized Kaederman had torn her shirt open during the struggles. She blanched and clutched the edges closed, hands shaking violently.

The constable's eyes widened abruptly. "Dear me, miss, was he—was that the *Ripper*?"

Margo's head whirled for just a moment. She found herself giggling shrilly and fought to get herself under control. "I don't . . . I dunno," she gulped, deciding she'd better stick with Cockney, given her current appearance. "Said 'e would give me somefink to eat, but 'e never. Just tried to kill me. Dragged me into 'is cab, only I got away an' run down the steps from 'igh 'olborn t'Farringdon. The cab tipped over, y'see, an' I think the driver's 'urt, up there on the Viaduct."

"You're all right, then, miss? Truly?"

She nodded. "Just shook, is all. You'd better go an' see about that cabbie, mister."

"Stay here, please. I'll see you're taken someplace warm and I'll certainly want a description of your attacker."

She nodded again, leaning against the shop wall while the bobby hurried up the steps toward the Viaduct. The moment he was out of sight, she dragged herself to her feet and headed the opposite way, walking as fast as she could push herself. Margo was still badly shaken, but she had to get away before that constable returned and started asking questions she didn't want to answer. She had to report Kaederman's escape, too, and Malcolm was injured, on his way to Spaldergate for treatment. She groaned aloud. It was a long way from Holborn to Battersea, which left her with far too much time to worry about Malcolm on the way. He had to be all right! Just had to be . . .

I blew it, Kit, she wailed silently, *I really messed up! Worse than South Africa!*

Castigating herself every step of the way, Margo walked faster.

At Skeeter's harsh insistence, they moved Jenna Caddrick and the others into the vault beneath Spaldergate House within half an hour of the attack at the Carlton Club. Spaldergate's vault was, at the moment, quite literally the safest place in all of London. "Kaederman's got Margo hostage, which means he'll find out exactly where you're hiding," Skeeter had said ruthlessly, overriding Noah Armstrong's objections. The detective, shaken at seeing his own face mirrored in Skeeter's newly rearranged one, reluctantly agreed, even handing over the damning proof that would condemn Senator Caddrick. They packed up and moved yet again, returning to the gatehouse only to find another crisis underway. Malcolm had arrived twenty minutes earlier by hansom cab, shot through the chest and barely conscious. Both Dr. Nerian and Paula Booker were in surgery, working to save his life. Skeeter tightened jaw muscles over a whole spate of curses and carried his honorary nieces down the stairs leading to the vault.

The Spaldergate housekeeper took charge of Ianira, Jenna, and the others, settling them down on sturdy cots in one corner, but nothing Skeeter said would induce Noah Armstrong to stay in the vault, as well.

"No!" The detective glared at Skeeter, expression haggard. "Dammit, what kind of coward do you think I am, to hide down here when he's holding Miss Smith hostage! God knows what he'll do to her! I've only stayed in hiding this long because of *them*," he jerked his head toward Jenna Caddrick. Ianira and Marcus sat on one of the temporary cots, holding their frightened little girls close.

"What you've done for my friends . . ." Skeeter said quietly. "Nothing I do will ever repay that. Except, maybe, catching this bastard. But if Kaederman kills you while we're chasing him, you won't be able to testify and all of this will have been for nothing."

In the brief silence, while Noah Armstrong ground molars together, the vault's telephone shrilled. One of the housemaids on duty with the Ripper Watch Team answered. Her eyes lit up as she gasped, "*Margo's back?* But we thought she was a hostage!"

Skeeter ran for the stairs, Armstrong pounding right on his heels. They found Margo in the parlour, where Hetty Gilbert was fussing over her, wrapping a quilt around her shoulders and putting an icepack to her bruised face, while Mr. Gilbert brought a generous brandy and forced it between her teeth. She was shuddering, from cold or shock or both. "Malcolm's really all right?" she was asking anxiously as Skeeter and Armstrong burst into the room.

"He's in surgery, dear," Hetty Gilbert soothed, brushing back Margo's hair with one hand. "Doing fine, they said. Hold that ice *on* the bruise, child."

Margo noticed Skeeter and bit her lips, startling him when tears welled up. "I'm sorry, Skeeter. Kaederman got away."

"Thank God *you* got away," Skeeter said fervently, collapsing into the nearest chair and upending the brandy Gilbert poured for him. "*Shalig*, what a night! How in the world did you escape?"

She told them succinctly, glossing quickly over any details that might have betrayed her own terror during the experience. Margo was one tough cookie, all right, for all that she was barely seventeen. Malcolm was luckier than he knew, to have a girl like Margo. She sighed, at length, nursing her own brandy and shifting the icepack on her cheek. "When that constable shouted, Kaederman ran off and disappeared down a side street. I sent the constable up to check on the poor cabbie, pinned under the wreckage, then got out of there as fast as possible and came back here."

"Quick thinking," Marshall Gilbert nodded approvingly. "Very quick thinking. You not only saved your life, you kept the authorities from asking uncomfortable questions that might have led them here. And God knows, we've been under enough official scrutiny as it is, thanks to Benny Catlin's shooting spree at the Picadilly Hotel."

Margo nodded and leaned her head back against the chair, drained and pale, but her hand on the icepack was rock steady. "They'll assume it was the Ripper, I suppose. That's what the bobby thought, anyway, and I didn't disabuse him of the notion. Look, we've got to find Kaederman. And we have to get Ianira and the others to safety—"

"They're in the vault," Noah said, attracting her attention for the first time.

She did a double-take, then laughed weakly. "God, that's startling. You really do look like twins, now."

"Do you have a photo of Kaederman?" Noah asked, voice grim. "Something we can duplicate and use, the way you traced us?"

Skeeter nodded and rescued his scout's log from his room, replaying their arrival through the Britannia Gate. Noah swore. "Good God! That bastard really must be desperate!"

"You know him?"

Armstrong tapped the screen on Skeeter's log. "That's Gideon Guthrie. Provides security for the L.A. gangland boss who's been doling out Senator Caddrick's payola. For Guthrie to be handling this personally, they're running *scared*. He hasn't actually dirtied his own hands in years. Maybe," Armstrong mused darkly, "he simply ran out of hit men to send after us?"

"And now he knows we're onto him," Skeeter growled. "Want to bet he bolts? Jumps on the nearest ship and runs?"

Armstrong shook his head. "He's got a helluva lot to lose, if he just ditches."

"Yes," Skeeter countered, "but he's gotta figure Caddrick will do time, over this, and maybe his own boss, as well. There's no way he can get back onto the station, not without somebody putting him in cuffs. So he's down to just a couple of options. He can run for it and start over, in this time period. And surely a guy like Kaederman has enough experience to set up shop someplace like New York or Chicago, even San Francisco, maybe, put together a sweet little gang of thugs with all the up-time tricks he's accumulated. Or he can do what Marcus and you did, getting *here*. He can hot-foot it to New York by the first trans-Atlantic steamer, board a train headed for Denver, and slip through the Wild West Gate in disguise, try and get back through Primary to New York."

"Will the Denver gate still be operational in 1888?" Armstrong asked quietly.

Mr. Gilbert answered. "I don't see why not. The Wild West Gate is very stable, has been for years, or we wouldn't be using it as a tour gate. I can't imagine it going suddenly unstable and closing."

"Then our boy might try it," Skeeter mused. "All he'd really need to do is mug a Denver tourist for his ID to get through the gate."

Armstrong gave him a grudging glance. "Not a bad point. So, we comb the steamship ticket offices?"

Margo eased the icepack into a new position as color returned to her cheeks. "It's a start," she nodded. "And we'd better put one of the groomsmen in each major railway station, in case he tries to catch a train for another port city. Liverpool did a lot of trans-Atlantic shipping, passenger as well as cargo." She grimaced, wincing slightly under the icepack. "James Maybrick certainly shuttled back and forth between Liverpool and the States for years. In fact, he met his wife on one of the crossings, poor woman. I wonder how many trains leave tonight? Or how many ships are scheduled to sail? It's going to be a long night."

Fortunately, the Gilberts were able to produce a table of scheduled ship departures from the day's newspapers. Hettie Gilbert copied them out while her husband retrieved a map of the docklands. He spread it out across his desk, then turned up the gaslight for better illumination. Skeeter stared in rising dismay at the immense stretch of land to be searched. Wapping, the Isle of Dogs, Poplar and Limehouse and Shoreditch, not to mention Whitechapel, of course, and Shadwell. St. Katharine's Docks, London Docks, Wapping Basin, Shadwell Basin, and the Old Basin below Shadwell. And there was the great West India Docks complex and the smaller Junction Dock, Blackwell Basin, and Poplar Docks. And east of there stood the *East* India Docks, the Royal Victoria and Albert Docks, and south of the Thames, the vast Surrey Commercial Docks . . .

Skeeter groaned aloud. Hundreds of acres, tens of thousands of people to question if the ticket offices didn't pan out, and very few of those teeming thousands likely to part with a word of information without palm grease of some sort, even if it were only a pint of ale or a glass of gin. "My God," he said quietly, "we'll never cover all of that."

"It isn't quite hopeless," Marshall Gilbert insisted. "Look, we can probably discount this whole complex, and this one," he swept a hand across the map. "They're cargo facilities only, no passenger services offered. And these, too, no point in searching naval shipyards. No commercial traffic, just military vessels. I'll get Stoddard

in to help, he knows the docklands better than anyone
else on staff. And we'll put Reeves on it, as well as all
the groomsmen, footmen, drivers, and baggage handlers.
I would imagine," he added, glancing from Skeeter to
Noah Armstrong and blinking mildly at their startlingly
matched faces, "Miss Smith will be keen to assist, as
well."

"You'd better believe it," she muttered.

Twenty minutes later, Hettie Gilbert handed over
her finished list. "There's only one ship scheduled to
sail tonight, leaving in an hour, but a dozen are due
to sail tomorrow."

Skeeter nodded. "We'll just have time to reach the
docklands, if we leave right now."

Groomsmen and gardeners and footmen were already
clattering out of the stable yard on horseback, dispersing
for every train station in the city. A woman in a
housemaid's dress was leading more horses from the
stable, saddled and ready as riders were assigned. Iron-
shod hooves rang against the paving stones. Skeeter
mounted in silence as Margo, who had changed into
warmer clothing, hurried out of the house and took
her own horse, still in masculine disguise but looking
now like a young man of the middle classes, rather than
a ragamuffin bootblack.

"All right," Skeeter said tersely, "we'll follow your
lead, Margo."

They set out in silence.

Kit was in his office at the Neo Edo Hotel, trying
to placate outraged tourists and worrying about the
rapidly dwindling supply of foodstuffs in the hotel's
larder, when word came: Lachley had been spotted at
Goldie's apartment. The security radio he carried
everywhere crackled to life with a generalized call to
every member of the volunteer security force.

"*Code Seven Red, Residential Zone Two.* Lachley's on the run, last spotted heading into the subbasements. All teams are hereby reactivated. Report in for a zone assignment."

Kit clattered the phone down in the middle of a wealthy dowager's tirade and snatched up the radio. "Kit Carson reporting."

"Kit, take Zone Seventeen again, same search team and pattern."

"Roger."

He picked up the telephone and started calling members of his team. They met on Commons, which stretched away in an echoing, empty vista of deserted shops and restaurants, the floors scattered with refuse no one had yet cleaned up. Alarm sirens hooted at intervals and lights flashed overhead, red and malevolent. Sven Bailey arrived first, followed by Kynan and Eigil. To Kit's intense dismay, Molly and Bergitta were with them, both women moving with a determined grimness that boded ill for reasoning with them. "We aim t'help," Molly said without preamble, "an' nuffink you say will stop us."

Bergitta, who had finally recovered from a terrible beating and gang-rape at the hands of the *Ansar Majlis*, gave an emphatic nod. "I will not stay hidden when this man attacks our home. We will help drive him out."

Molly added, "We got Viking ring-mail shirts on, underneath." She plucked at her loose-fitting dress. "Connie give us the loan. Didn't 'ave no other armor would fit under a frock, so she didn't. B'sides, I know somefink about this 'ere bloke, might be important."

Kit rocked back on his heels. "You *know* him? John Lachley?"

Molly shrugged. " 'Corse I knows 'im. Come up out of Whitechapel, 'e did. Called 'imself Johnny Anubis. Read fortunes and suchlike. Nasty little blagger. Wot's more, 'e ain't a normal man, so 'e ain't. I walked them streets, 'eard wot the girls said about 'im. They said 'is male parts weren't made right. Were 'alf woman, 'e were, wiv an Hampton Wick small as your little finger and wot a lady's got, besides, only that ain't made right, neither. A couple of girls wot laughed at 'im ended floating in the Thames wiv cut throats. Never could prove nuffink, but I say 'e done 'em, 'is own self."

Kit frowned. Had John Lachley been born an intersexual? He had to force aside quick pity. It didn't matter—couldn't be allowed to matter—what Lachley had suffered in London's East End, growing up with a blurred gender. Too many people had died already. Kit said quietly. "Whatever he once was, John Lachley is now Jack the Ripper and it's our job to end his career. All right, ladies. You just might help us flush him out, acting as bait. I know Bergitta started training with you, Sven, after that *Ansar Majlis* attack, and I'd trust Molly in any scrap. Bergitta, you and Molly take the middle. Sven, you and I will take point, Kynan and Eigil, bring up rear guard. We're searching Zone Seventeen again."

Sven grunted. "Just remember to stay away from that damned pterosaur's beak. I don't want any of *us* skewered."

"Amen to that," Kit muttered, leading the way.

They moved warily past barricaded shops and restaurants, past ornamental fountains and ponds and secluded alcoves formed by shrubbery and statuary and mosaic tile floors. They'd just reached Little Agora when the overhead sirens screamed.

"*Code Seven Red!* Zone Thirteen . . ."

"That's just downstairs!" Sven yelled above the ear-splitting howl of the siren.

Kit jammed his radio against his ear, trying to hear.

"Down-timers have spotted him! He's in the tunnels under Frontier Town!"

They rushed down the stairs, sprinting past stacked aquaria where idling fish watched curiously as they raced past. Someone was screaming, a high and hideous sound that brought Kit's hair on end. Garbled shouts echoed and floated down the long, twisting corridors, then Kit burst around a curve and skidded to a halt. Two down-timers lay twisted on the floor, one man's neck obviously broken, another gutted and lying with sightless eyes. A third, the young Greek hoplite, Corydon, clutched at a gash across his arm, which had been laid open to the bone.

"He ran . . . that way . . ." Corydon gasped, nodding with his head. His radio lay on the floor, sputtering with static. "I called . . . security . . ."

Bergitta dropped to her knees beside him, ripping her own skirt and using a comb from her pocket to form a tourniquet band just above the massive wound. "Go!" she snapped. "I will watch Corydon until medical comes!"

Kit keyed his radio even as he pelted in the direction Lachley had taken. "Medical emergency, Zone Thirteen. Two dead, one serious casualty. Tell medical to shag butt, Corydon's nearly lost an arm!"

"Roger that. Medical's on the way."

Kit slowed when the corridor branched off in three directions. "We don't dare split up, Lachley'd just gut us one by one," he muttered, listening for any sound of footfalls. All he heard was echoing silence and an occasional, distant mutter and weird cry from the immense pteranodon's cage. "We'll take the left-hand fork," he decided, "and come back if we run into a blind alley without finding him."

They did not run into a blind alley. In fact, they ran into a deep maze of tunnels twisting through the bowels of the mountain, past doors where machinery chugged and hummed and rumbled and a distant rush and tumble of water could be heard through pipes and fittings. Kit marked the corridors they'd searched by scrawling on the walls with an ink pen, trying to sort out the tangle of passageways. Storage rooms were locked tight, but the heating and cooling plants, the sewage works, the generator pile all had to be searched painstakingly. Which they did, as time piled up in their wake.

The gigantic pteranodon was asleep when they eased past its cage, wicked red eyes shut inside their whorls of brightly colored, leathery skin. Bloodstains still marked the concrete floor from the pitched battle fought with the Ripper cultists, but they found no trace of John Lachley.

"He can't have vanished into thin air," Kit muttered as they pressed on past the pterosaur's cage. He'd begun to feel a superstititous prickle of sympathy with those befuddled London constables.

Kit glanced at his wristwatch and scowled. Upstairs in Commons, security would be preparing to turn back the incoming tour from Denver as the Wild West gate dilated open. If they could just find Lachley *before* the gate opened, they could end this monstrous blockade and get the station back to normal.

"Molly," he frowned thoughtfully. "You told me Lachley grew up in the East End. Is there something we could use to drive him into the open, maybe goad him into attacking?"

Molly's eyes began to glitter. "I can't flush 'im out, nuffink ever will." Molly drew a deep breath and let go a flood of Cockney gibberish. "C'mon, then, let's 'ave yer 'ideous Cambridge an' Oxford out where we can 'ave a butcher's, eh? I grassed on you, so I did, Johnny Anubis! You an' your disgustin' Kyber, 'ope you like it in a flowery, corse yer lemons 'as done caught up wiv you, so they 'ave!"

Sven cast a dubious glance at Molly. "Do you really think any of that's going to flush him out? Somehow I don't think he cares about the crimes he's committed."

Molly's eyes flashed with irritation, but she changed her approach. "Eh, Johnnie, you got no cobbler's t'show yer ugly boat to a frog-chalkin' fanny like meself? Shouldn't wonder, you weren't born wiv none, was you, Johnny Anubis? An' you ain't pinched none from them fancy friends of yours, neither, 'ave you? I shouldn't wonder you *don't* show yer Kingdom Come! Corse you bloody well can't chalk, wiv as bad a case of Chalfont St. Giles as ever you saw, wot you got off lettin' a toff like yer lovin' Collars an' Cuffs run 'is great Hampton up yer bottle."

"This isn't working," Sven muttered.

"You got any better ideas?" Kit shot back.

Molly was still trying to goad Lachley into the open. "I don't give an 'orse an' trap, so I don't, Johnny Boleslaus, not for you nor your tea-leafin' ways, takin' a starvin' woman's last 'apenny an' tellin' 'er t'bend over again so's you can tell 'er she's fore an' aft, wivout a brain in 'er loaf. Gypsy's kiss on you, an' you'd better Adam an' Eve *that*, so you better. An' yer bubble an' squeak friends, 'ere, says the same to you!"

"Kit, Molly's just wasting her breath—"

He came in low and fast, lunging from a dark alcove where the corridor snaked around in a tight twist. Molly screamed and went down. Lachley's blade flashed in the dim light even as Kit whirled, trying to bring his pistol to bear on the struggling figures. Sven's gun shattered the silence. The bullet whined off the concrete wall. Molly was in Kit's line of fire, kicking and screaming at Lachley. Eigil waded in as Lachley rolled to the top, knife slashing again at Molly's

unprotected throat. The Viking *barsark* snatched him
up by the neck. Lachley rammed his knife into Eigil's
gut and the Viking went down with a sharp grunt of
pain. Kit fired, but Lachley was already moving again,
slamming the point of the knife toward Sven. The
blade just grazed the weapons instructor as Sven flung
himself down and back, away from the knife's arcing
path. Sven's pistol went clattering and slid into the
pteranodon's cage. Kynan was dragging Molly away,
sliding her across the floor on her back. Kit might have
gotten another shot off, but Eigil was in his line of
fire, clutching at his belly while blood poured out
between his fingers. Kit lunged past, trained his pistol
on the maniac—

And Lachley was away and running, knife in hand,
twisting around a corner and vanishing even as Kit
fired. The bullet shattered a door at an oblique angle,
driving splinters outward. Kit swore and shouted into
his radio, "*Code Seven Red! Zone Seventeen!* Converge
on my signal! And get a Medical team down here,
we've got casualties, bad ones!" Kynan was already
stripping off his own shirt and shoving it as a compress
against Eigil's gut wound. Molly was bending over Sven,
saved from worse injuries, herself, by the chain mail
under her dress. That steel-ringed undershirt had done
exactly what ring-mail armor was designed to do:
deflect the slashes of a bladed weapon. *Connie Logan,
I'm gonna buy you a whole* case *of champagne, maybe
even a keg of Falernian through the Porta Romae* . . . The
boom and rumble of the station's public address system
came echoing eerily down the open stairwells to the
tunnels.

"*Code Seven Red, Zone Seventeen, repeat, Code
Seven Red, Zone Seventeen!* Station medical personnel,
report to Zone Seventeen, stat, for transport and
emergency triage. Please be advised, Gate Three cycles

in seven minutes. All tour passes are hereby revoked until the station emergency has ended. Repeat, all visitors are required to stay in their hotel rooms until further notice. Shangri-La Station is operating under martial law. Code Seven Red, Zone Seventeen . . ."

Sven was muttering under his breath and brushing Molly's hands away. "It's just a scratch, dammit! I can't believe I let him get that close to me in the first place!"

"You were a little distracted," Kit grunted, wiping his brow with a sweating arm. "We've got to trail him. Sven, can you move?"

"Hell, yes," the weapons instructor growled, coming to his feet to prove it. Kynan, shirtless and holding compresses against Eigil's gut, handed up his borrowed gladius. "Kill that son of a bitch, please."

Sven saluted him with the blade.

Kit muttered, "We'll give it our best shot, Kynan." He didn't add what he was thinking: *We shot at that maniac from close quarters and missed. Maybe he can't be killed, after all. God help us . . .*

Then they whipped around the corner, following the Ripper's bloody footprints.

Chapter Eighteen

Grey dawnlight spilled like dirty bilge water across thousands of chimneys jutting up from factory roofs, refineries and foundries, from ironworks and shipyards as Skeeter entered the docklands, accompanied by Margo, Noah Armstrong, and Doug Tanglewood. Their search the previous night had turned up no trace of Sid Kaederman, either at the train stations or the docks near Wapping Old Stairs. Skeeter carried a list of ship departures scheduled for today, convinced Kaederman would be on one of them.

A forest of masts stabbed skyward, dark silhouettes against clouds which promised more rain before the morning grew much older. Furled sails and limp rigging hung like dead birds on all sides, marking the berths of hundreds of sailing vessels used mostly as cargo transports, now, too antiquated and slow for passenger service. The heavier, stubby iron snouts of steamship funnels jutted up alongside passenger quays, cold and silent until coal-fired boilers were heated up for departure.

Douglas Tanglewood led the way toward the main

offices of St. Katharine's docks along St. Katharine's Way, Wapping. Carts and draymen's wagons bumped and jockeyed for space on the crowded roads. Surrounding the dockyards lay a jumbled maze of factories, foundries, food processing plants, icehouses, shipbuilding yards, and shops that fed, clothed, and supplied thousands of industrial workers.

"St. Katharine Docks," Tanglewood said quietly, "is the oldest and now one of the smallest dock complexes. More than twelve hundred homes were razed to build it. Left eleven thousand Londoners homeless and destroyed some of the oldest medieval buildings in the city." He shook his head, clearly regretting the historical loss. The dockyard gate, an arched entrance of stone, was surmounted by elephants on pedestals. Immense brick warehouses abutted the waterfront across from berthed ships. "On these small docks, like this, there's no room for transit sheds between water's edge and the warehouse doors. That gives our quarry fewer places to hide. It'll be much worse, if we have to search the other dockyards."

Skeeter watched a confusion of sweating stevedores off-loading valuable cargoes into vast, echoing warehouses, then asked, "Where do you buy tickets?"

"The Superintendent's office and transit offices are this way," Tanglewood nodded, pointing out the buildings beyond a stone wall that separated the dockyards from the street. "Mr. Jackson, please come with me. Perhaps Miss—ah, Mr. Smith and Mr. Armstrong could ask around for word of an American trying to buy passage."

Margo and the enigmatic Noah Armstrong, both decked out in middle-class businessmen's wool suits, moved off to talk to the dock foremen. Skeeter followed Tanglewood into the transit office.

The clerk glanced up from a ledger book and smiled a cheerful greeting, his starched collar not yet wilted under the day's intense pressures. "Good morning, gentlemen, how might I help you?"

Tanglewood said, "We're hoping you might be able to assist us. We understand there is a ship scheduled to leave St. Katharine's this morning at six-thirty, a cargo ship. Do you know where we might discover if a certain man has tried to book a passenger berth on her? Or maybe hired on as shiphand?"

The clerk's smile reversed itself. "You're trying to find this man?" he asked cautiously.

"We are. He is a desperate criminal, a fugitive we're trying to trace. He kidnapped a young lady last night and shot a gentleman, leaving him nearly dead, and we have proof that he is responsible for several other deaths in the recent past. The young lady has escaped, thank God, made her way to safety last night. We have reason to believe he'll try to book passage on any ship that will have him, to escape the hangman. This gentleman," Tanglewood nodded to Skeeter, "is a Pinkerton Agent, from America, one of the Yanks' best private inquiry agencies."

Skeeter dutifully produced his identification.

The transit clerk's eyes had widened in alarm. "Dear God! Have you contacted the Metropolitan Special Constabulary, sir? The river police should be notified at once!"

"If this ship proves not to be the one we're looking for, we certainly shall. But it's nearly six already and the ship sails in half an hour, so there's hardly time to go and fetch them."

"Yes, of course. Let me check the books." He was opening another stiff ledger, running a fingertip down the pages. "The *Milverton* is the ship you want, just two years old, so she's new and fast for an iron sailing vessel. Western Dock, Berth C, opposite East Smithfield Street, north of the offices. Go along the inner perimeter at water's edge, is best. You'll have to go right round the basin, there's no way across the inlet on foot. Watch your step when you're out by the warehouses, we're very busy this season, and the stevedores will cause trouble if you get in their way. As to a passenger . . ." He was consulting another ledger. "There's no record of anyone booking passage on the *Milverton* this crossing, but a desperate man might well approach the captain privately, rather than risk transit office records or the presence of river police." The clerk shook his head, frowning. "Plenty of men are still shanghied off the streets round here, by commercial captains desperate for shiphands. A man asking for a berth or offering to work for his passage wouldn't even be questioned."

"Wonderful," Skeeter muttered. If Käederman offered to work his way or paid a tidy sum the captain wouldn't have to report to the ship's owner, not a captain in the docklands wouldn't jump at the offer, no questions asked.

"You've been very helpful, sir," Tanglewood thanked the clerk, slipping him a half crown for his trouble. The young man pocketed the coin with a nod of appreciation and returned to his ledgers. Tanglewood opened the door and stepped quickly outside.

"We'd best hurry. They won't welcome interruptions at this late hour."

They hailed Armstrong and Margo, who stepped smartly out of the way when sweating stevedores cursed at them. The *Milverton* was a sleek ship, her iron prow and bowsprit jutting so far out over the wharf, the tip end of the bowsprit nearly scraped the warehouse opposite. Men bustled across her, shouting commands and unfurling her great sails in preparation for departure. Loading was still underway, stevedores by the dozens manhandling huge casks and crates out of the warehouse along her port side, hauling them up into her vast iron holds. Skeeter kept a sharp watch for Kaederman. The captain, when Skeeter and the others climbed the main gangplank, was not amused by the interruption. "Get the bloody hell off my deck! I sail in a quarter hour and we're behind schedule!"

"This won't take long," Tanglewood assured him, producing a conciliatory five-pound note and holding it up. "Have you taken any passengers aboard in the past twenty-four hours? Or a new crew hand, a Yank?"

"I bloody well have not and if you don't get off my deck, I'll toss you into the basin!" He snatched the five-pound note and stalked off, shouting at a hapless crewman who'd snarled a coil of rope leading from the capstan to the mainsail, which rattled lopsided in the rising breeze.

They searched the ship anyway, dodging irate ship's officers, but were finally forced to admit that if Kaederman were aboard, he'd stowed away as cargo. They jumped back to the quay with minutes to spare before becoming stowaways, themselves. Standing on the quay, they watched until the *Milverton* pulled slowly and majestically across the basin toward the river, under tow by steam-powered tugs. They held vigil to make sure Kaederman didn't show up at the last minute, but he remained a no-show. When the ship passed through the locks into the river, Skeeter pulled a rumpled list from his coat pocket and scratched off the *Milverton's* name.

"London Docks," he said quietly, "a ship called *Endurance*. She leaves Wapping Basin at seven."

London Docks, down in the heart of Wapping, dwarfed little St. Katharine's. The immense, double-armed Western Dock alone was larger than all the basins of St. Katharine's, combined. The smell of tobacco was strong in the air, coming from the central basin and its warehouses. When Skeeter mentioned it, Tanglewood nodded. "That's Tobacco Dock, of course. Rented out by Her Majesty's government to the big trading companies. You said the *Endurance* leaves from Wapping Basin? This way, then."

The appalling noise overwhelmed the senses. Beneath the level of the quays Skeeter could see vaulted cellars where stevedores trundled great casks of wine and brandy. Transit sheds stood between waterside and warehouses, temporarily sheltering a vast tonnage of goods and providing a maze in which one man could hide almost indefinitely.

Lock-keepers worked incessantly, regulating the flow of ships in and out of the great basins, while draymen arrived with wagonloads of luxury goods for export to Britain's far-flung mercantile markets. The stench of raw meat and blood and cooking vegetables mingled with the smells of coke-fired furnaces from vast food-packing plants. Whole wagonloads of salted sea-turtle carcasses rolled past, off-loaded from a ship out of the Caribbean basin, destined for the soup canneries and luxury manufacturers who made combs, hair ornaments, boxes, ink-pen barrels, and eyeglass rims from the shells.

Past the canneries were great icehouses, bustling with men and boys loading ice into insulated wagons. Every time the doors opened, cold rolled out in a wave across the road. Skeeter began to realize just how overwhelming London's docklands really were as they passed the Ivory House, with its immense stockpiles of elephant tusks, and warehouses where eastern spices and enormous pallet-loads of exotic silks were trundled off the quays. The number of places Kaederman might hide was distressing; to search all of it would take a small army.

The *Endurance* proved to be a squat little tramp steamer, its days as a passenger boat eclipsed by vastly larger luxury ships. The hectic pace of loading was no less frantic than it had been aboard the *Milverton*. The captain was no less harried, either, but was slightly less brusque. "A Yank? No, I haven't laid eyes on a Yank today nor yesterday, neither, and not a paying passenger the last three crossings. New crew hired? Not a single hand, no, sir, I've a good crew, treat 'em right. They've turned down offers of more money working for harsher masters and that's a fact . . . No, no! The deliveries for the galley go into the center hold, not the bloody prow! You'll break every egg in that crate, storing victuals in the bow, that's where she takes the brunt of the waves!"

And off he went, correcting the error, leaving them to question crew hands. No one had laid eyes on anyone answering Kaederman's description.

"Strike two," Skeeter Jackson muttered, crossing the *Endurance* off his list. "Next stop, Regent's Canal Dock, Stepney."

Rain began falling in earnest, plastering Skeeter's hair to his forehead and horses' manes to their necks. Draft horses strained against their harness collars and slipped on the wet streets. Drivers shouted and cursed and wagon wheels churned piles of dung into a foul slurry carried into the nearby river and the sewers underfoot. They struck out at Regent's Canal Dock, as well: the *High Flyer*, sailing for Hong Kong, produced no trace of Kaederman.

Perhaps it was only the grey and dirty rain soaking through his coat and snaking in runnels down his collar, but Skeeter began to think the task of finding one murderous lout in this overcrowded, reeking maze of humanity and bustling commerce was impossible. He tried to protect the ink on his slip of paper from spatters of rain gusting in beneath the broken eaves of a pub where they'd taken momentary shelter. "Next ship departs out of Quebec Dock."

"Where's that?" Noah Armstrong asked, rubbing hands together absently in an attempt to warm them. The October rain was cold. Keening wind cut through their trousers and coats.

"Surrey Docks, that's south of the river," Margo said, shivering. "We'll have to cross at London Bridge, there isn't any bridge closer. Which is why Tower Bridge is being built, to shave miles off the round trip from London Docks to Surrey Docks, for the draymen. But it's still just an iron shell, doesn't even span the river, yet. We'll have to backtrack. When does the ship go?"

Skeeter consulted his pocket watch. "Three-quarters of an hour from now."

"We'd best not walk it, then," Tanglewood muttered, "that's a bloody long way from Stepney to Rotherhithe and Bermondsey. There's a tram line nearby, we'll catch the next tram heading west. When do the other ships go, Jackson?"

He used his cap to protect the ink on his list. "Eleven o'clock, Blackwell Basin, West India Docks. Two p.m., Import Basin, East India Docks. Seven o'clock this evening, Royal Albert Dock."

"He might try for a later ship," Margo mused as they located the tram stop. "Just to give himself time to pull together the kit of goods he'll need. Money, clothing, sundries, a packing case or duffel bag to hold them in."

"We might get lucky at the secondhand shops, if the transit offices don't pan out," Noah Armstrong said quietly. Armstrong didn't say much, but listened with an almost frightening attentiveness and the detective's ideas were always sound. The tram arrived a moment later, glistening a wet, cheerful red, its sides covered in advertisements. They managed to secure seats on the lower level, where they could sit out of the rain. Passengers on the upper deck sat huddled under the open sky, with rain pouring down their collars despite umbrellas that turned the top of the tram into a lumpy, domed canopy. The horses snorted, shaking their great, dappled heads against the downpour, and chewed at their bits, jingling their harness bells and tugging at the reins, then the tram rumbled into motion along the tracks.

They crossed the Thames, its grey water choppy in the storm. Hundreds of river taxis and sailing ships bobbed like forlorn, waterlogged birds. Steamers chugged and churned their way through the leaden water, spewing coal smoke into the dark sky. Rain spattered against the tram's windows, bringing Skeeter's spirits even lower as he caught sight of the vast Surrey Commercial Docks on the southern shore of the river. Surrey was exclusively commercial, offering no passenger service, which meant security would be tighter.

Skeeter spotted only a few gates along the access roads, used by draymen and their wagon teams. It occurred to Skeeter that Surrey Docks could become a trap to anyone caught inside, if a security force could be thrown across those few gates. The four of them, however, did not comprise such a force, and they clearly couldn't involve the river police. How would they ever find one man, in all that immense sprawl? Surrey was bigger, even, than London Docks.

Entering the Surrey complex was like walking straight into a foreign land. Spoken English was in the minority, with half-a-dozen Scandinavian languages battling for dominance over harsh Russian and garrulous French as fur traders and timber importers argued tariffs with stolid dock foremen. And permeating it all came the scents of raw lumber and cured animal skins and dark, dirty water lapping and slapping against the sides of iron hulks tied up at the quays.

They entered through Gate Three, out of Rotherhithe, and found the Superintendent's office. "Berth 90, Quebec Dock," the clerk read from the ledger. "The clipper ship *Cutty Sark*. Yes, they've registered a new hand, galley cook from America, name of Josephus Anderson. He signed on as crew this morning after the regular cook took suddenly ill. Says he can't read, but he signed his name on the books." The clerk showed the signature, a laborious scrawl that was nearly illegible.

"Could be trying to disguise his handwriting," Skeeter said thoughtfully as he and Tanglewood rejoined the others. "Make himself look less educated than he is, so he won't attract as much attention. He wouldn't need to know a thing about sailing to work as a galley cook. And it would be just like him to drug or even poison the real cook, so they'd have to hire a new one in a hurry. Josephus Anderson sounds like Kaederman, all right."

When Skeeter told Armstrong and Margo which ship they were looking for, Noah Armstrong gave a start of surprise. "My God, the *Cutty Sark?* Bastard has a real sense of style, doesn't he? Haven't they retired her by now?"

Tanglewood said, "Oh, no, she's a few more years of work left in her career. The *Cutty Sark's* days as a trading clippership are numbered, of course. She might've been the fastest to make the tea run in her day, but they'll put her in drydock in a few years, never fear."

A passing trader who overheard the remark laughed heartily. "Drydock, eh? What on earth would you put a useless ship in dry dock *for?* Charge sixpence a tour?" He continued on his way, laughing and shaking his head.

Tanglewood chuckled. "Well, that *is* what becomes of her, thank God. Imagine, ripping up a ship like her for scrap!"

Skeeter led the way past the end of Canada Dock basin, toward berth 90. Rain pelted down harder as they headed down Redriff Road, dodging heavy wagons and piles of dung and sodden masses of sawdust heaped into ruts and holes. Mud spattered their trousers and squelched underfoot. Wet lumber towered in stacks higher than their heads; stevedores were throwing tarpaulins across piled crates in the shadows of those lumber stacks. French Canadian sailors grumbled and groused about the foul weather and asked for directions to the nearest pubs and whores. Near the immense warehouse beside berth 91, casks marked *Black Powder, Explosive!* formed a squat pyramid under the transit shed. A ship's officer was giving instructions to the stevedores.

"We've got an iron hull, boys. I don't want any man jack of you striking sparks or you'll blow my ship and half this dock sky high. Black powder is shock sensitive and friction sensitive and we're packing three tons of it into those holds. Thank God for this rain, it'll dampen down static electric charges. Be damned sure your men are wearing leather-soled boots, no steel heel plates, no hob-nails, no copper-toed work boots, have I made myself clear . . ." Skeeter edged past the massive pyramid of powder kegs, where unhappy stevedores were already grumbling about having to change footgear in the middle of a driving rainstorm thick enough to put out hell's own fires.

Berth 90 stood in Canada Yard South, opposite Bronswick Yard, Greenland Dock. The two yards were separated by Redriff Road, which snaked and twisted its way between Surrey's various basins. They found the captain on the quay, deep in discusssion with dock officials regarding fees the captain insisted were sheer piracy. One look at the captain's wrathful countenance and Tanglewood suggested, "Let's try one of the crew hands first, shall we? I'd say that chap's in no mood for polite inquiries."

A crewman passed them, headed up the gangplank toward the *Cutty Sark's* beautiful decks, and Margo darted forward. "Hey, wait a second, could I ask you a quick question?" Money changed hands, then Margo waved them over. "This gentleman," she nodded at the puzzled crewman, "will escort us down to the galley to meet Mr. Anderson."

Skeeter pressed elbows against ribs, where his pistols lay concealed in twin shoulder holsters: the Royal Irish Constabulary Webley he'd carried to Denver and a larger Webley Green borrowed from Spaldergate, a commercially popular revolver predating military models carried by British army officers. And snug against the small of his back, in a sheath worn sideways beneath his coattails, rode one of Sven Bailey's Bowie knives. Going after Kaederman, he would've felt happier carrying a Maxim machine gun, as well.

As they climbed the gangplank and crossed the holystoned decks, Skeeter's pulse kicked in at triple time, jumping savagely in anticipation of Kaederman's violent reaction. Then they were climbing down into the ship's dark interior, following the narrow passageway to the cramped galley. Skeeter stole his hand into his coat and gripped the butt of his Webley Green, fully expecting trouble to break out the instant "Anderson" caught sight of them.

"Hey, Anderson!" the sailor poked his head into the galley. "You got company, mate!" He then sauntered away on his own business, jingling Margo's coins in his pocket.

"I comin', suh, I comin' . . . can I help you all, some-how? I got work to do . . ."

Anderson's voice was soft, respectful, almost obse-quious. And the moment Skeeter caught a glimpse, his spirits plunged toward despair. Their new galley cook was a Yank, all right. A very black one, at least sixty years old, with grizzled white hair, missing half a tooth in front. He spoke in a broad, drawling dialect that sounded like the deep South. Anderson proved to be a former plantation slave who'd signed as cook aboard the first ship out of Savannah after his manumission. Said he wanted to see something of the world, have a few stories to tell his grandchildren.

While Tanglewood thanked the cook and apologized for interrupting his work, bitter disappointment sent Skeeter striding back topside, fists clenched as he reached the rain-slick deck. A ship's officer sporting a vulcanized rubber rain slicker was telling someone, "Your bunk's below, stow your gear and report to the quartermaster for a uniform. Then shag your arse back topside and find the first mate, he'll tell you what your job's to be."

A man with a heavy sea duffel across one shoulder turned to locate his new bunk below decks . . . and Skeeter gasped. Then yanked loose his big Webley Green revolver, aiming for Sid Kaederman's heart. "Don't move! Don't even breathe, God damn you!"

Sid froze in astonishment. The officer in the rain slicker was staring at the Webley, slack-jawed. "Here, what's the meaning—"

"Tanglewood!" Skeeter shouted. "Get up here! He's on deck!" Running footsteps sounded below. The deck officer started forward, plainly furious. "What is the meaning of this outrage? Put away that pistol, sir, or I'll have you put in irons!"

"Stay back!" Skeeter shouted. But it was too late. The officer had stepped straight into Skeeter's line of fire. Kaederman dropped the heavy duffel with a thud and raced across the rain-slick deck, heading for the gangplank. Skeeter lunged around the officer and fired.

Splinters flew as lead struck the ship's rail. Kaederman plunged down the gangplank and hit the quay running. Skeeter cursed and followed as Armstrong and Tanglewood ran across the wet decks of the *Cutty Sark* at full tilt, guns drawn. Tanglewood fired, as well, missing the fleeing Kaederman clean. Tanglewood skidded wildly across the slick decking and Skeeter's feet did a creative skid of their own, slowing him down so badly, Armstrong beat them both to the gangplank. The detective plunged down toward the quay on Kaederman's heels. Douglas Tanglewood was swearing as he scrambled up from the deck. Margo appeared just as Skeeter rushed down the gangplank in pursuit, shoving aside shocked stevedores and ship's crew to reach the quay.

Skeeter glimpsed Kaederman ducking through the transit sheds alongside berth 91. Armstrong plunged in after him, shoving his way past angry stevedores trying to shift heavy casks from a dwindling pyramid. A scant instant later, the detective came racing back Skeeter's way, white-faced and shouting. *"Get down! Get down!"*

A massive explosion rocked berth 91. Fire belched outward in a solid wall of destruction. The concussion hurled Armstrong to the ground. The shockwave knocked Skeeter flat, crushing the breath from his lungs. Heat seared his sodden coat as he flung both arms over his face. Then rain was pouring over him again, slashing down at the mass of flames that had, seconds before, been an immense transit shed. Blazing timbers and tin shingles crashed to earth in a deadly rain. The rigging and sails of the ship at berth 91 were on fire. Stunned sailors were already struggling aloft with buckets and heavy knives, chopping at the ropes, trying to put out the inferno before it reached the holds.

"Armstrong!" Skeeter yelled, scrambling to his feet. The detective stirred sluggishly, but staggered up. Skeeter braced the Wardmann-Wolfe agent when Armstrong nearly fell, again, reeling and dizzy on his feet.

"Was Kaederman in that shed?" Skeeter shouted, barely able to hear his own voice.

"What?" Armstrong shouted back, voice tinny and distant through the ringing in his ears.

"*Kaederman!* Was he in there?"

"No! Saw him bolt for Redriff Road, right after he broke open one of those casks. Struck a match and threw a damned blazing rag right onto the loose powder, then ran out the other side!"

"*Black powder?* Good God!" No wonder the whole transit shed had gone up like a bomb. Unlike modern, smokeless powders, black powder was genuinely explosive, deadly as hell in that kind of mass. *How many stevedores were killed in there?* Skeeter wondered as he dodged and jumped across burning timbers and twisted, smoking tin shingles.

He reached the terminus of Redriff Road and searched wildly for any trace of Kaederman. He swore... Then heard shouts and curses drifting down from the direction of Greenland Dock. Any disturbance was a good bet. Skeeter raced that way and pelted slap into an angry group of Scandinavian sailors, cursing to make a Viking raider proud. A whole stack of crates had been knocked down, breaking open to strew their contents of valuable furs into the mud, white ermine and sleek mink and glorious black sable. Then Skeeter caught a glimpse of Kaederman far ahead, running down Plough Way through Commercial Yard on a direct course for Gate Eighteen.

And Kaederman's diversionary tactics abruptly backfired right into his face. He hadn't quite reached the gate when a whole squadron of irate constables burst through, inbound. London's river police, responding to the emergency. Kaederman, clutching an up-time pistol in one hand, skidded to a halt. For an instant, Skeeter thought he meant to shoot the entire police squadron. Then he doubled back, instead, and raised his gun directly at Skeeter.

Shit—!

Skeeter ate mud. He skidded face-first on his belly and tried to bring up his own pistol. There were too many innocents in his line of fire. He spat filthy muck and rolled frantically as Kaederman dodged past, firing at him on the way and shoving aside the furious sailors busy rescuing their sodden furs. Kaederman fired at Armstrong, Tanglewood, and Margo, too, as he ran toward them. The hail of bullets sent all three headlong into the mud. Then he raced along the very rim of the quay at water's edge and reached Redriff Road again before they could turn their weapons on him.

Swearing and spitting, Skeeter propelled himself to his feet, covered head to foot in slimy, foul mud that carried a rank stench into his sinuses. He didn't want to consider what might be *in* that mud. Armstrong was in the lead as they burst out of Commercial Yard in pursuit. Kaederman was a sizeable distance ahead, but even Tanglewood and Margo were gaining ground and Skeeter, abruptly in the rear thanks to the about-face, was steadily catching up.

Kaederman headed this time for Gate Three, the principle entrance to Surrey Commercial Docks. And once again, his delaying tactics with the black powder backfired. A horse-drawn fire engine, bells clanging madly, charged through, followed closely by four more. The fire engines completely blocked the way as they swung into the dockyards. Trapped inside the walls, Kaederman turned north toward the warehouses alongside Albion Dock. River police had taken up the hue and cry, as well, shouting at the fire officials to send word for another squadron.

"We've got us a bloody arsonist!" a policeman behind Skeeter yelled, fury lashing his voice. "Damned Fenian bomber, blew a shed of gunpowder to hell! Try and head him off at Gate Two . . ."

Rain slashed down across Skeeter's face in blinding gusts and unpredictable squalls. The mud under his boots sent him slipping and sliding for purchase in the choppy mess. At least it washed the reeking stuff off his face. Kaederman didn't try any delaying tactics at Albion Dock. He passed the warehouses and a gang of startled stevedores at full tilt, racing for Gate Two and escape. They charged past another huge basin in a straggling, strung-out line, then Skeeter caught up to Doug Tanglewood and Margo. They ran—as he did—with guns clutched in wet, muddy hands.

"If he gets out of this dockyard, we're sunk!" Skeeter gasped.

"Looks like we're sunk, then!" Margo spat back.

Kaederman had just slipped through Gate Two, with Armstrong hard on his heels. Skeeter put on a burst of speed and drew ahead. By the time Skeeter shot through Gate Two, a second squad of river police had put in appearance, running north from the direction of Gate Three. They were still in the distance, however, nowhere close to Kaederman. He was just visible on Rotherhithe Street, dodging past startled pedestrians on the pavements, cutting around large groups by ducking into the street. Horses flung their heads up and reared, shrilling a sharp protest at his erratic flight. Skeeter had just caught up to Armstrong when Kaederman cut sharp south again, leaving Rotherhithe Street.

"Where the hell is he going?" Skeeter gasped. "The river police are down that way!"

For a long moment, Armstrong didn't answer, too busy dodging past a protesting carthorse and its cursing driver. Then a startled expression crossed the detective's face. "Surely not?"

"What, dammit? Where's he heading?"

"The *tunnel?*"

It took a few seconds for Skeeter to call up his mental map of the area, memorized before leaving the station, then he had it: Isambard Kingdom Brunel's Thames Tunnel, connecting Rotherhithe and Wapping. Twelve hundred feet long, it had taken eighteen years and countless lives to build. It was also the only way to get from Rotherhithe's Surrey Docks to Wapping without detouring to London Bridge—or swimming.

"Isn't that a railway tunnel now?" Skeeter asked as they ran, heading helter-skelter straight for the tunnel's entrance.

"Yes! Trains from London to Brighton, owned by East London Railway Company. But the railway uses only one of the tunnel shafts! The other's still a pedestrian tunnel!"

"Aw, shit, you *are* kidding, right? If he makes it to Wapping . . ."

Unfortunately, Armstrong was not kidding.

He was also correct. Sid Kaederman plunged into the circular structure that housed the Rotherhithe entrance to the Thames Tunnel and vanished from view. They followed at a run, clattering past startled men and women in working-class garb. Skeeter and Armstrong pounded their way through the vast entrance, with Margo and Doug Tanglewood on their heels.

The entrance was a circular shaft at least fifty feet across. Skeeter peered past wrought-iron railings as they plunged down the broad, double-spiral stairs. The shaft was a good eighty feet deep and Kaederman was already halfway down, plunging three and five steps at a time. Skeeter's muddy boots skidded on the stone treads. Down and around, in a broad, lazy spiral, a dizzying gyre that would prove fatal if he put so much as one foot wrong. *Down, down to goblin town . . .*

He was beginning to pant for breath when they finally reached the landing where the double spiral came together. Half-a-turn more and they were on the ground, paving stones clattering underfoot. The Thames Tunnel loomed before them, a double-barreled shotgun nearly a quarter of a mile long. The air was dank, foetid, cave-like. The tunnel walls exuded a chilly sweat, moisture running in tiny rivulets like the condensate on a beverage glass. Twin tunnels receded into infinity, dimly lit at regular intervals with gas lamps. Railway tracks ran down the center of one side.

"Which tunnel?" Skeeter gasped as Tanglewood and Margo bounded down the last few steps to join them. "Which one did he go down?" They listened intently at each entrance for the echo of footfalls. The chugging of water pumps growled and echoed. They couldn't distinguish anything like a sound of running footsteps against the background noise.

"That one!" Armstrong finally decided, pointing to the pedestrian tunnel. "I doubt he wants to risk meeting a train. He's no coward, but he's no fool, either."

Dank, chilly air closed in as they pelted down the echoing brickwork and stone tube in pursuit. A few handcarts loaded high with coal and wooden crates jockeyed for space in the narrow tunnel. Gas lamps gave plentiful if rather dim light the length of the shaft, which had been constructed as a series of connective arches beneath the river. Nearly forty-five years old, the long pedestrian tube remained the province of footpads, thieves, and innumerable prostitutes who led a troglodyte's existence beneath the river. They passed sleeping drunks huddled in the brick archways, women who'd set up stalls at which tawdry goods and cheap jewelry could be purchased. Ragged children begged for money. A pair of roughly dressed men eyed them as they shot past, then thought better.

A train deafened them as it roared past on the other side of the brick supporting wall. If Kaederman had chosen the other route—or if they had—they'd have been crushed under the wheels. Then they were through, emerging on the Wapping side of the river, somewhere to the east of the great London Docks. The eighty-foot climb up the dizzying double-spiral of the Wapping shaft, a twin of the Rotherhithe entryway, winded Skeeter badly halfway up. He staggered on with a stitch in his side and cursed Kaederman with every upward step of burning thigh muscles. They caught a glimpse of him from time to time on the way up, moving doggedly toward the street high above.

The raucous noise of workaday Wapping drifted down in distorted echoes and clangs, human voices and riverboat whistles and the slam of cargo being offloaded at the docks. The rumble and clatter of freight wagons mingled with the roar of the train chugging through the tunnel far below. Then they reached the street. Sunlight, dim and watery, replaced the gaslights of tunnel and shaft. Rain was still pouring in wind-blown gusts. A vast throng of people and horses and overloaded carts clattered wetly through the narrow streets, past ships parked at dead-end roads.

"Where *is* the son of a bitch?" Armstrong gasped, face contorted with frustrated anger. "We'll never find him in that stinking mess!"

Skeeter was too busy dragging down enough air for his starving lungs to answer. They started asking passers-by and finally obtained a lead from a ragged and muddy girl of twelve, totting bunches of bedraggled flowers in a basket over her arm. She pointed down Wapping High Street. "Cor, 'e went that way, mister, knocked me down an' never said nuffink, spilt me flowers all over the frog, 'e did, ruint' the lot, and never 'pologized, neither . . ."

Skeeter tossed a couple of shillings into her basket, eliciting a soprano squeal of astonishment, then pelted down Wapping High Street through the driving downpour. They finally caught a glimpse of Kaederman—just as he made a flying leap at a cart rattling smartly northward. He caught the tailboard and dragged himself in. The cart shot forward at twice, three times the speed a man could run. Cursing, Skeeter and the others lagged farther and farther behind, searching for some transport of their own. For an entire block, Skeeter staggered along with a butcher's knife of a stitch in his side, beginning to despair. Then a shopkeeper who'd clearly arrived a short time earlier came out to back his horse and cart up onto the pavement, unloading a pile of crates directly into his shop.

Skeeter dove toward the horse with a gasping cry of relief. A quick snatch at the Bowie knife concealed under his coattails, a few slashing blows at harness straps, and the startled horse was free, front hooves coming up off the pavement as it tried to stand on rear legs. "Whoa, easy there . . ." Skeeter stepped up onto the cart pole, its front end digging into the street, and threw a leg over, clutching the grip of the fighting knife in his teeth until he could slide it back into the sheath. The shopkeeper shouted just as Skeeter urged the horse forward with knees and heels.

"Hey! Wot you doin', that's me 'orse!"

Skeeter kicked the nag into startled motion even as he dug banknotes out of a pocket and tossed them onto the street as payment. "Come on, let's go . . ." Obedient, if puzzled, the horse slanted an ear back to catch the sound of Skeeter's voice and broke into a shambling trot, probably its top speed while harnessed. A solid thump of heels sent the horse into a surprised canter, stiff-legged and jolting from the unaccustomed gait. Skeeter gained ground rapidly on Kaederman's cart, while the shopkeeper screamed curses after him.

A swift glance revealed Noah Armstrong halting a hansom cab at gunpoint. Margo and Doug Tanglewood piled in. Then Skeeter gave all his attention to guiding his aging carthorse through the crowded street, cutting and weaving between high-piled wagons, shabby cabs for hire, even a few gentlemen's carriages. Businessmen or merchant traders, probably, come to check on arriving cargo or oversee outgoing shipments. Gaping pedestrians and liveried drivers stared at the sight of a carthorse lumbering past at its top, stiff-kneed speed, trailing harness straps and the end of long reins which Skeeter was looping and pulling in to prevent their being caught in a passing wagon wheel or carriage axle. He had no desire to end his ride that abruptly.

Skeeter pushed his shaggy mount to a rumbling gallop. The carthorse burst past the boundary between Wapping and Whitechapel, steadily gaining ground on Kaederman. The cart made a right-hand turn, swinging smartly into Whitechapel High Street, which was jam-packed with hay wagons, oxen pulling loads too heavy for horses, and fast-moving hansoms. There was a near-collision that sent Sid Kaederman sprawling against the side. Skeeter saw his mouth move and the cart's driver turned his head sharply. The driver started shouting, then turned to crack his cartwhip at the stowaway. Kaederman's answer was to pull loose his pistol and fire at the irate driver, point-blank.

Either the jostling spoiled his aim or the driver was one of those down-timers who couldn't be killed, because Sid missed him clean from a distance of twelve inches. The driver, white-faced and still yelling, performed a diving roll that landed him on the cobbled street, spitting curses and running for his life. The carthorse picked up speed without a guiding hand on the reins. Kaederman's transport careened out of control down the congested road. Kaederman, thrown violently from side to side as the carthorse dodged and shied away from other wagons and horses, crawled awkwardly over the seat, trying to reach the reins. Skeeter leaned low over his horse's flying mane and urged the draft animal to greater speed. *If I can just catch up while he's distracted . . .*

They raced down Whitechapel High Street in a grim, jolting chase. Kaederman's cart plunged into Whitechapel Road, careering past screaming women on the pavement and cursing draymen who swung violently wide to avoid collision. Children scattered like ants, shouting curses after Kaederman's runaway horse. Truant boys and chimney sweeps scooped up mud clots and pieces of broken brick, hurling them in Kaederman's wake.

The inevitable disaster struck just as Skeeter pulled alongside. A heavily laden team of drays, moving ponderously down the middle of Whitechapel Road, couldn't swerve fast enough. The driver tried. Tried hard, in fact. He succeeded in pulling his team broadside to the onrushing cart.

The shock of collision drove Sid's horse slam against the other team's harness poles. Wood splintered. Horses screamed. The heavy wagon toppled. Its driver and a stack of crates six feet high were hurtled under the wheels and hooves of other wagon teams. A human scream tore the wet morning air. The horses were still screaming, crashing down as wood splintered like shotgun blasts.

Sid's empty cart jacknifed around, airborne. It smashed down across the upturned drayman's wagon. Crates broke open under the force of the cart's landing. Hundreds of shoes and ladies' skirts, cheap dresses and steel bustles, men's trousers, and warm woolen coats spilled out into the mud. Sid, thrown violently airborne by the cart's twisting gymnastics, landed asprawl in a heap of dark, wet skirts on the other side of the broken wagon. The spilled garments cushioned his fall, probably saving his life.

Then Skeeter's galloping horse, presented with an impassable barrier, jumped the upturned wagon. The horse's rear hocks clipped the top boards, then they landed roughly on the cobbles beyond and slipped on the wet stones. The horse skidded and went to his knees with a ringing scream of pain. Skeeter was thrown forward across the horse's neck. His superb riding skills—mastered on wild, half-broken Mongol war ponies—and a desperate grab at the harness collar kept Skeeter from smashing face-first onto the cobbles. His horse neighed sharply again, a sound of pain and fright, then heaved and scrambled up, bleeding down both torn knees. Skeeter, badly shaken, slid down the horse's forequarters and landed on the wet street.

Poverty-stricken children, shrieking women, and idle louts from nearby gin palaces descended on the wreckage, a swarm of devouring locusts intent on carrying off as much as they could cram into their arms, toss over their shoulders, stuff into gunny sacks, or simply pull on over their own clothes. Hundreds shouted and cursed and scurried for the choicest pickings, using prybars to open unbroken crates or simply hauling them off, contents unseen.

Kaederman's horse, badly wounded, was lunging, trying to climb over the backs of the toppled drayman's horses. All three animals were down, kicking and neighing shrilly, trying to regain their feet. Harness lay tangled, fouling their legs, which kept them from scrambling up. A man in a blood-stained leather apron hacked at the harness leather with a broad meat cleaver, trying to free the trapped animals. Wagons and carts, blocked by the wreckage, piled up on either side, their drivers shouting curses or jumping down to help shift the broken cart and wagon out of the way. Someone mercifully shot Sid's mortally wounded carthorse, ending the agonizing, bone-grating screams. Skeeter—limping where metal harness fittings had torn a gash through his trousers and thigh—hunted through the wreckage for Sid.

Kaederman had regained his feet, bleeding from cuts down his face and arm. His coat was torn, smeared with mud and dung slurry from the street. The hired killer stumbled, visibly dazed, through the crowd of riot-happy scavengers, then drifted erratically toward the edge of the road. He staggered at every step, clearly having wrenched a knee on landing. He was still running, though, moving raggedly and glancing over one shoulder to locate Skeeter. At least with a bad leg, he couldn't run fast or far.

Skeeter abandoned his own injured horse and fought his way on foot through the near-riot. A hansom cab shoved and clawed its way forward along the crowded pavement, scattering irate pedestrians into the jam of wagons and carts on the street. It halted six feet behind Skeeter's limping carthorse, which an opportunistic girl of fifteen was leading swiftly away. The cab disgorged Margo, Douglas Tanglewood, and Noah Armstrong; the latter tossed a wad of bank notes to the driver before jumping down to join the pursuit.

"He's heading that way," Skeeter pointed as they slithered through the crowd of spectators and fighting

scavengers. "Hurt and limping, but still on the move."
The up-time killer had reached a three-story, eighteenth-
century structure that might have once been a grand
house, built of grey-painted stone and mellow brick. Coal
smoke and soot had stained wide windows and trim a
dingy grey. Kaederman peered through the windows,
clearly trying to decide whether he should bolt inside or
continue down the street. A semicircular, cross section
of metal from what might have been the rim of a wagon
wheel or maybe a large bell, had been mounted above
the door.

Kaederman spotted them and thought better,
limping past the entrance and rounding the corner to
parallel a whole series of longer and lower, grey-painted
buildings attached to the rear of the main structure.
Skeeter and the others had already reached the corner
when Kaederman found a set of double doors into the
third building back, a three-story factory of some kind,
judging from the noise and the smoke bellying up from
a forest of chimneys. A wagon and team of horses stood
in the open doorway where men drenched with sweat
were loading heavy crates. Kaederman sidled past and
plunged into the dim interior beyond.

Despite his own limp, Skeeter was at those wide
double doors in a flash. On his way through, he caught
a fleeting glimpse of a sign painted in neat white letters:
*Whitechapel Bell Foundry, est. 1420, these premises
since 1570, home of Big Ben, Bells of Westminster, the
American Liberty Bell* . . .

The appalling noise and stench of a nineteeth-century
smelting plant struck Skeeter square in the face. Intense
heat rolled outward in a visible ripple, distorting the
foundry's interior for just a split second. Then he was
inside, breathing the fumes of molten metal and
burning charcoal. Rows of windows high up did little
to dispel the gloom. The vast, clangorous room, fully

three stories tall, remained in near darkness, aided and abetted by the wet, cloudy day outside.

Men shouted above the crash and slam of immense machines, heavy conveyors, and the boom of newly cast bells being tested for trueness of sound. Molten bronze—and possibly iron and silver and brass, judging from the color of the ingots on those conveyors— glowed in immense vats, surging like volcanic rock, seething and malevolent in the near darkness. Enormous, pulley-driven crucibles of liquified metal swayed across the room some eight feet above the foundry floor, moving ponderously down from the smelting furnaces to row after row of casting molds, some of them six and seven feet high. Filled molds were jammed and crammed to either side, forming narrow aisles—canyons in miniature—stacked high to cool.

Men with long, hooked poles tipped the crucibles to pour their glowing, gold-red contents into the open snouts of bell molds, every pour sending cascades and showers of sparks and molten droplets in a deadly rain that sent foundry workers scattering back for safety. Others used heavy iron pincers to lift smaller, filled molds aside for cooling, making room for new, empty molds beneath the I-beam pulley system on which the crucibles rode. Catwalks hung like iron spiderwebbing above the smelting furnaces. Conveyors brought heavy ingots up to be tossed by sweating men and half-grown boys into the fiery furnaces. They dumped ingots, secured returning crucibles from the pulley line for refilling, regulated the temperature in the huge furnaces, and fed charcoal from enormous mounds to keep the fires burning hot enough to melt solid bronze for pouring.

And straight down the middle of that hellish inferno, Sid Kaederman was limping his way toward escape. Skeeter plunged in after him, tasting the stink of molten metal on his tongue and in the back of his throat. *We could die in here*, he realized with a gulp of sudden fear. *Every one of us*. If Kaederman succeeded in ducking out of sight long enough to go to ground, he could use the darkness and that ear-numbing noise for cover, lay an ambush and pick them off one by one with that silenced pistol of his and nobody'd even hear the bodies hit the floor.

"Split up!" Skeeter shouted above the roar as Kaederman dodged and ducked past startled foundry-men, darting into the maze of miniature canyons. "Try and cut him off before he can get out through a back door—or go to ground and lay in wait someplace nasty! And for God's sake, be careful around those furnaces and crucibles! Go!"

Tanglewood and Armstrong turned right and jogged warily into the near-blackness. Their shadows flickered and fled into the surrounding darkness as they passed a backdrop of fountaining sparks from another massive pour. Margo followed Skeeter. "Are you all right?" she shouted in his ear. "You're limping!"

"It's nothing, just a shallow scratch! Stings a little is all!" He'd suffered worse as a boy, learning to ride in the first place. Skeeter had the big Webley Green out, held at the ready, up near his chest, elbows folded so Kaederman couldn't knock it out of his hands should he come around a corner where the killer was hiding. Leading with a gun, sticking it out in front of you with locked elbows, was a fast way to disarm yourself and end up seriously dead. Only idiots in the movies—and the idiots who believed them—were stupid enough to lead with a firearm.

Skeeter and Margo edged their way into the wood-and-iron ravines between cooling bell molds. They worked virtually back to back as they advanced, moving one haphazardly strewn row at a time. Molds of differing sizes and shapes jutted out unpredictably, threatening knees, elbows, shoulders. Heat poured off the stacks like syrupy summer sunlight, deadening reflexes and hazing the mind. It was hard to breathe, impossible to hear above the din of the foundry floor. Down the room's long central spine, bright gouts of light shot out at random, throwing insane shadows across the stacked molds to either side.

Skeeter moved by instinct, hunting through the alien landscape. Sidle up to a junction, ease around for a snap-quick glance, edge forward, check the floor for droplets of blood, peer along the rows down either aisle for a hint of motion . . . Then on to the next junction, row after row, sweat pooling and puddling, the wool of uncreased trousers raw on bare skin and stinging in the wound down his inner thigh, hands slippery on the wooden grips of the pistol . . . Another fast, ducking glance—

The bell mold beside Skeeter's head splintered under the bullet's impact. Iron spalled, driving splinters across his cheek and nose. Pain kicked him in the teeth, then he was dodging low, firing back at the blur of motion three rows down. The big Webley kicked against wet palms, the noise of the foundry so immense he barely heard the sharp report. Skeeter blinked furiously to clear his vision, waved Margo back and down. Wetness stung his eyes, sweat mingled with blood burning like bee-sting pain from the jagged slivers in his cheek where the bell mold had spalled. He blinked and scrubbed with a muddy, torn sleeve. When he could see again, he dodged low for another look, down at hip-height, this time. Sid Kaederman was leaning around a stack, waiting to shoot him, but he was looking too high. Skeeter fired and a wooden pallet splintered six inches away from Kaederman's chest. Skeeter cursed his blurring, tear-blocked eyes, and the sweat that had let the gun slide in his hands, and his lousy aim . . .

"Go!" Skeeter yelled as Kaederman ducked back. They rushed forward and ran flat-out, gasping hard for breath in the stinking, steaming air. Down three rows, risk the peek . . . Kaederman was running, stumbling every few strides on his injured leg. Skeeter sprinted after, gaining fast. The paid killer glanced back, but failed to fire at him.

He's out of ammo! Skeeter realized with a rush of adrenaline. There was no other rational reason for Kaederman not to whirl and fire dead at him. A surge of confidence spurred Skeeter to draw ahead of Margo, relentlessly whittling down Kaederman's lead. The hit man ducked down a sideways aisle, vanishing from view. Skeeter swore and closed the distance, ducked low through his own skidding turn. Harsh, sulphurous light flared, momentarily blinding him. The smelters were dead ahead. Workers with iron poles nearly four feet long, hooked on one end, and men with heavy prybars snagged a big crucible and tip-tilted it, pouring its blazing contents into the mouth of a bell mold four feet across, using the prybars to control the angle of the tilt.

Sid Kaederman reached the newly-filled mold and started waving his gun at the stunned foundrymen, shouting that he would shoot them if they didn't get out of his way. The men stumbled back, away from the apparent lunatic. Then Kaederman ran along the line of pulleys, toward the far end of the foundry where access doors led to the street. Blistering hot crucibles, just filled with molten metal, swayed down from the smelters toward another big bell mold waiting to be filled. Kaederman glanced back, realized Skeeter was gaining . . .

He whirled around and snatched up a long iron pole from the floor where a terrified bell caster had abandoned it with a clatter. Kaederman dropped his useless pistol and reached with the hooked pole, instead. He snagged the lip of a brimming crucible swaying its way toward him, a big one that must've held a bathtub's worth of blazing liquid metal. Pulling hard, Kaederman slammed the rim down and ran. Molten bronze flooded out across the floor. Liquid metal splashed and crested in a wave of destruction, spreading across the entire narrow space between stacked, newly-cast bells, an inch deep and still flooding outward. There was no way around it and no way to climb those red-hot iron molds to either side. Skeeter's forward momentum was too great to avoid the deadly lake in his path.

So he jumped straight toward it.

Toward it and *up*. He stretched frantically, reaching for the massive iron I-beam of the pulley system overhead. *It's too high, I'm gonna miss it, oh Christ, don't let me miss* . . . He dropped the Webley, needing both hands free. It fell with a splash and vanished into the scalding, hellish glow. Then his palms smacked against the I-beam and he grabbed hold, swinging his feet up in a frantic arc. He clamped arms and ankles tight, then just hung there, sloth-like, panting and sweating so hard he was terrified his grip would slide loose. Uncurling his fingers long enough to wipe first one hand, then the other, against his coat took a supreme act of will.

Then he wriggled himself around, managed to crawl up and over the top of the narrow iron beam, and balanced on hands and knees, all but prone above the hellish puddle. A black crust had formed along the top, a thin scum of solid metal that seemed to breathe as it cooled. The molten metal beneath flashed and flared in a scaly pattern like the scutes on a crocodile's back. Kaederman had turned to run, dropping the long iron pole into the edge of the molten flood splashing back toward him, but he wasn't moving very fast, clearly tottering at the last of his strength. Margo, thank God, had dodged the lethal flow, ducking sideways into another canyon between bell molds.

Breath regained and balance secured, Skeeter moved forward along the beam in a scooting crawl that was taking far too long. Swinging himself cautiously down once more, he passed hand over hand above the heaving mass of cooling metal, moving ape-like along the beam, swinging up again only to avoid pendulous crucibles.

Kaederman, who'd managed to stumble maybe a dozen paces beyond the far edge of the puddle, glanced back . . . and tripped, sprawling flat. His mouth moved soundlessly as he scrambled up again. Then Skeeter was across and jumping down to face him. Kaederman lunged forward, snarling curses and giving him no time to draw his other gun. They grappled for long moments, gouging and punching.

A blow from Kaederman's knee grazed the cut along Skeeter's thigh. Pain shot through the abused flesh. Skeeter staggered back a step and tangled his feet over the iron pole Kaederman had used to tilt the crucible. His stumbling footsteps kicked its far end askew, out of the puddle of molten bronze, trailing lethal beads across the foundry floor. Skeeter danced a wild jig-step and finally righted his balance, just a boot heel shy of the malevolent lake. The cool end of the long pole rolled and bumped into Kaederman's foot, a weapon ready for the snatching. Kaederman's face twisted in triumph. An unholy laugh broke loose. Before Skeeter could fling himself forward to stop him, Kaederman stooped and snatched up the pole in a two-handed grip—

By the wrong end.

Glowing and still half-molten, the pole dripped liquid bronze which flowed over both of Kaederman's hands. A terrible scream burst loose. He tried to let go.

Kaederman staggered back, away from the puddle, face contorted, still screaming. The stench of cooking hair and meat struck Skeeter's nostrils. Then Kaederman's damaged fingers unclenched enough to let the pole drop. The skin of both hands sloughed away with it. Kaederman's knees gave way. He hit the floor and nearly splashed headlong into the glowing, syrupy-thick bronze. Skeeter snatched him back, dragging him bodily out of danger, and shoved him to the floor. Then held him there. Skeeter smiled down into stunned grey eyes.

"Hello, Sid."

He'd stopped screaming. Broken, gasping sounds tore free in their place. Shock was setting in fast, leaving him shaking and clammy under Skeeter's hands. Skeeter shook him slightly to get his attention. When that didn't register, he used the bastard's real name and shook him again. "Gideon! Hey, Guthrie! Look at me!"

Dull eyes focused. His mouth moved, but nothing came past his lips except those strangled, hideous whimpers. "Listen, pal. You got a choice," Skeeter slapped his face gently to keep his attention. "You listening?"

He nodded, managed to force out a single coherent word. "W-what?"

Skeeter fished out his little RIC Webley and let Kaederman see it. "What I *ought* to do is shoot you where you lie, pal. You don't rate the oxygen you're breathing. But I'm gonna offer you a choice. Your pick all the way. If you like, I'll step away and let you crawl out of here, free and clear. No charges for murder. No prison time. No gas chamber. Of course, with the state of medical care around here, you'll lose both those hands for sure. And even if you didn't, you'd probably die from shock and infection and gangrene."

Kaederman's eyes had glazed. "Wh-what's the—?"

"What's your other choice?" Skeeter's grin sent a shudder through the injured man. "Why, you get to come clean. Tell the cops everything they want to know about your boss. Hand them Senator Caddrick and his mafia cronies on a silver platter. Give us enough to send *them* to the gas chamber, instead of you."

Ashen lips moved, mouthing the words. "Goddamned little bastard . . . should've killed you on sight, Armstrong."

Skeeter grinned down into Kaederman's glazed eyes. "Too bad, ain't it? What'll it be, then? I'll trade the medical care you need to save your hands, trade you a surgeon and a burn-care unit, for Senator Caddrick in prison. That's a fair trade, I think. One of those new prisons he helped fund, a no-frills, maximum security cage without television or libraries or anything to distract a guy except Bubba's hard-on in the next cage over. Couldn't happen to a nicer bastard, don't you agree? Maybe you'll even get a reduced sentence for turning state's evidence. How about it? We'll keep you out of pain, stabilize your hands for you, keep you alive long enough to get you to a burn specialist. Otherwise, I'll just leave you here."

He jerked his thumb at the stench of the Victorian-era foundry. As the ashen killer shuddered, rolling his eyes at the grimy room, Skeeter added off-handedly, "Oh, and by the way. *If* you decide to stay here, and *if* you manage to survive shock and infection and amputation of those hands, I'm told Scotland Yard still hangs a murderer. And I know a couple of folks who'd be delighted to rat on you."

Kaederman didn't answer for a long moment, just lay there sprawled on his back, trembling and sweating, his skin grey and his hands curled into meaty, scorched claws. He glared up at Skeeter while making horrible, strangled sounds and bit his lips until they bled. His body twitched spasmodically, his whole nervous system overloaded with the pain of the burns.

"Okay," Skeeter shrugged, rising from his crouch and sliding his RIC Webley back into his shoulder holster. "Have it your way. Maybe you can actually crawl to the door. Dunno what you'll do once you're outside, though, with all that manure in the streets to drag yourself through and Whitechapel's toughs kicking you into the mud, just for chuckles . . ."

Skeeter started to step away.

Kaederman lunged up onto an elbow. *"Wait!"* He shook violently, eyes wild and desperate. "For God's sake, Armstrong . . . wait . . . Go ahead and take your revenge, curse it, kick my ribs in, smash my teeth, do whatever makes you happy—*just don't leave me to die in this hellhole!"*

Skeeter stood glaring down at him, drawing out the man's terror with cold, calculated loathing. How much pity had this bastard shown any of his victims? When Kaederman fell back, eyes closing over a moan of despair, Skeeter finally decided he'd had enough.

"Okay," he said softly, crouching down again. "But you're gonna have to walk out of here on your own pins, Sid, because I'm not carrying you." He tugged the man by his coat lapels, levering him up to his knees and bracing him under one armpit. Noah Armstrong and Doug Tanglewood, their faces flushed from the intense heat of the bell molds, skidded up just as he got Kaederman onto his feet. Margo was close on their heels, having gone around the long way to avoid the puddle of cooling bronze. Skeeter glanced up. "Hi, Noah. Got a present for you. Sid, here, is going to teach us all a new song. Goes like this: 'All I want for Christmas is my boss in jail. . . .'"

Sid Kaederman stared from Noah Armstrong's face to Skeeter's matching one and back again, eyes widening as the import of their ruse set in. Then his eyes turned belly up and his knees went south and Skeeter ended up carrying him out of the bell foundry, after all.

Chapter Nineteen

Kit hurled through Shangri-La's basement corridors, Sven Bailey pounding along in his wake, both of them grim and silent. John Lachley's footsteps echoed up ahead. He didn't have much of a head start. Kit flung himself around a twist in the corridor and caught sight of the quarry down a long straight-of-way, maybe fifty yards ahead. Easy shot. Kit fired—and missed. Three times. Sven's gun was back in the pteranodon's cage, in a spot nobody wanted to retrieve it from. Lachley whipped into a side corridor. Kit and Sven reached it seconds later. They were gaining on him. Kit lined up the pistol sights as best he could while running full tilt, and tried again.

He succeeded in blowing out the sides of four aquaria in rapid succession.

Water and fish flooded across the floor as Kit spat curses. "Goddammit! I shouldn't have missed! Not *seven times*!"

"Maybe he's got to go back to London, after all?" Sven growled. "And you're out of ammo, by the way."

Kit glanced down. The slide had locked back. He'd shot the pistol dry. When he groped in his shirt pocket, he discovered nothing but emptiness. The spare magazine had fallen out during the fight and he hadn't noticed. *Careless is stupid,* he snarled at himself, *and stupid can be fatal.*

He mashed the send button on his radio.

"Kit Carson reporting. We're in pursuit, heading into Zone Eighteen! Sven and I are both out of ammo— looks like the bastard can't be killed, after all!" Either that, or he was phenomenally lucky.

"Copy that, we have search teams triangulating on your location." In the background, he could hear the station announcer again. *Gate Three is opening in three minutes . . .*

"Set up blockades out of Zones Seventeen and Eighteen," Kit gasped as as they skidded around a corner. He slammed one shoulder into a ten-foot wall of stacked aquaria, which shifted with an ominous groan. Water slopped out of the topmost layer. A door slammed back and Lachley's footsteps receded upward. "Oh, hell, he's gone up a *stairway!*"

"Come again?" the radio sputtered.

"He took the stairs, heading for Commons!"

"Copy that and relaying."

Why was Lachley headed for Commons? Just running blind, heading *up,* same as many another fugitive, or was he planning something . . .

Kit's eyes widened. "Holy—Sven, *Gate Three!*"

He mashed the transmit button again. "I think he's headed for Gate Three! And even if he isn't, leave a corridor open, try to herd him into it!"

"What?" the radio sputtered. "Right into the middle of an *incoming tour?* Kit, are you out of your— Oh. Roger that. Kit, you are one devious bastard."

"So give me a medal—if this works. Sven, be ready for anything. I'm going to try something dangerous."

"Chasing Jack the Ripper *isn't*?"

He had a point, there . . .

How much time? Kit wondered frantically as they plunged up the stairs four at a time. *Christ, how much time's left?* They burst out onto Commons at the edge of Frontier Town. Chronometer lights flashed steadily overhead. The vast open floor lay deserted, as empty of life as a midnight cemetery. Their footsteps slapped and echoed off the distant girders high overhead. Kit jumped a decorative horse trough filled with goldfish, which Sven whipped around, too short to go over it.

He knew they were close when he felt the savage backlash of subharmonics from the gate. The sound that wasn't a sound vibrated through the vast, echoing stretch of Commons. A security team stood waiting at the entrance to the Wild West Gate's departure lounge, charged with keeping the in-bound tour from re-entering the station. Behind the security officers, the massive gate dilated slowly open, right on schedule. Lachley, running flat out, ran straight toward the rapidly widening black chasm which hovered three feet above the Commons floor and whipped through the open lanes snaking outward from the departures lounge. He clearly intended to shake pursuit by jumping through the moment it opened wide enough.

Kit shouted into the radio, "Get those security officers away from the gate! For God's sake, move 'em out before he veers off!"

Too late! Lachley had seen them. He skidded sideways, trying to vault over a row of chairs. Kit charged, frantically trying to recall where he'd been in early August of 1885. It didn't really matter. He was the *only* one in position to take out the Ripper. Kit's flying tackle caught Lachley's knees—and sent them both reeling straight through the gaping black hole of the Denver Gate.

They fell headlong down the dizzying drop. The station end of the tunnel lay at the end of a spyglass inverted, far away and shrinking. Lachley brought the knife up even as they fell like doomed meteors. The Denver end of the gate loomed huge. Kit tried to brace himself, wondered what it felt like to die . . . Then jarred his back. He sprawled, badly winded, across the dirt floor of the Time Tours livery stable. John Lachley snarled above him, teeth bared, knife poised to strike—

And almost made it to the floor.

His whole body wavered like candle smoke and vanished, a shadow eaten whole by a moonless night. For just an instant, a lingering look of shocked surprise floated where Lachley's face had been. Then his blood-stained knife clattered to the dirt beside Kit's ear and a heavy pouch thumped down beside it, inside a flutter of stolen, up-time clothes.

Sven thudded into the stable at Kit's feet, grunting on impact.

Kit lay flat, just gulping air, oblivious to the shocked demands erupting on all sides. Furious guides tried to calm hysterical tourists who had just watched a man die, shadowing himself. Several women were sobbing, abruptly too terrified to go anywhere near the open gate. Kit shut his eyes for long, shuddering moments, trying to convince his own muscles that it was safe to move, now.

He was still alive.

Jack the Ripper was finally dead.

Slowly, wincing at pulled muscles and bruises, Kit picked himself up and dusted himself off and gave Sven a hand up, as well. Tour guides were shouting above the general roar. Kit picked up Lachley's knife, plucking it out of the dirt with trembling fingers, and managed to retrieve the heavy pouch. He said to the nearest guide, "It's safe to bring them into the station, now. Quarantine was just lifted." Then he jerked his head once at Sven, turned his back on the whole shouting mob, and stepped back through the open Wild West Gate to go home.

Once there, he intended to get quietly, massively drunk.

I must be crazy . . .

Jenna Caddrick couldn't believe she'd agreed to this. Couldn't believe she'd just stepped through the Britannia Gate to confront her father in front of half the world's television cameras. Camera flashes and television crews lit up the whole departures lounge, illuminating a sea of spectators beyond the velvet-rope barricades. A sniper could be lurking anywhere in that vast, heaving mob. Noah Armstrong, silent at her side, descended the stairs with eyes narrowed, intent on the business of keeping them alive long enough to testify. She rubbed her chin nervously, wishing Paula Booker had left her muttonchop whiskers in place. But Noah had inisted the surgeon remove the implanted disguise and restore Jenna's face to her own appearance, for the benefit of the cameras. Jenna felt naked, defenseless.

Below them, Malcolm Moore's gurney had nearly reached the Commons floor, followed closely by Sid Kaederman's—or rather, Gideon Guthrie's. The man who'd trailed her from Colorado to London, bent on murder, was unconscious, his burnt hands cradled in special harnesses above his chest. Margo Smith walked beside her fiancé's gurney, holding his hand as they carried him down to the station's medical crews. Jenna's throat closed at the thought of what these people had risked for her sake. Malcolm had nearly been killed and Skeeter Jackson had undergone plastic surgery, rearranging his whole face. Skeeter had been shot outside the Carlton Club, as well, saved only by his Kevlar vest, and had almost been killed at the bell foundry . . .

She and Noah had nearly reached the floor when the inevitable shout came.

"It's Jenna Caddrick!"

The roar hurt Jenna's chest. She flinched back from the solid wall of noise, having forgotten during the weeks in London just how terrible it was to face a sea of screaming reporters.

"Steady," Noah muttered at her elbow. "I don't see a sniper anywhere."

Not yet . . .

She glanced back and found Skeeter Jackson right on their heels, his face still a mirror of Noah's. He gave her a brief, tense smile. "You've got that Kevlar vest of mine on, right?" She nodded and Skeeter muttered under his breath, "Good. I *know* it works." Then they were down the last of the steel-grid steps and pushing foward between a cordon of security guards.

Questions battered her from every side. Reporters screamed her name, demanding to know where she had been, how she'd escaped the *Ansar Majlis* death squads, a thousand, million questions that raked up old wounds and inflicted new ones. Then her father was there in front of her, open-mouthed and staring. Shock had dilated Senator John Paul Caddrick's grey eyes. A white pallor washed across his face as he met her gaze. She wondered how she had ever looked him in the eye without a reptilian loathing.

Then he recovered his composure. Her father presented the cameras with a smile worthy of an Oscar and cried, *"Jenna!* Oh, thank God, baby, you're safe . . ." He rushed forward, arms outflung. Jenna had no idea what she intended to do or say. She'd been thinking about this moment for weeks, drenched in sour-smelling terror sweat each time she imagined it. But when he rushed at her like a demon from her worst nightmares, Jenna reacted without a moment's hesitation.

She slugged him, point-blank. Slammed her fist so hard into his nose, the shock jarred her shoulder and left her hand numb. He staggered back, blood welling from both nostrils. For just an instant, a sewing needle dropped to the concrete floor would have sent echos bouncing through the vast station. Even the reporters had turned to stone, stunned motionless.

Jenna drew a sobbing breath. *"Don't touch me, you murdering son-of-a-bitch! You* paid those bastards to kill Aunt Cassie! *You* paid them to pose as *Ansar Majlis,* so the hit couldn't be traced back to you. Damn you to hell, you *murdered* her, and you murdered my fiancé, then you put out a contract on *me,* you sorry sack of shit! I've got enough proof to bring you down, you and your mafia pals with you. Gideon Guthrie's been singing for his supper and believe me, they're gonna throw away the key! If they don't pull the switch on the electric chair. And frankly, after what you did to Carl and Aunt Cassie, I'd pull it in a heartbeat. I hope you fry!"

Her father stood swaying, waxy-pale, mouth working soundlessly. As the crowd roared its shock, his face twisted in a blurred grimace. Then he snatched open his coat and jerked out a small-caliber handgun. Noah Armstrong flung himself forward. The detective slammed Jenna down, away from the discharge of flame erupting from the muzzle. Another shot exploded as her father snarled, "Goddamn you to *hell,* Armstrong!"

Then Skeeter Jackson was on the floor beside her, swearing in some language she didn't recognize, with a hole torn through his coat where her father's shot had barely missed him. Jackson's reflexes were *good*— he twisted aside even as her father fired again, mistaking him for Noah. The real Armstrong lay full length on top of Jenna, face down to protect her. Then a swarm of security officers buried her father, shoving him down under an avalanche of live bodies. The mob went mad, shrieking and hurling abuse that left Jenna numb. Skeeter Jackson grunted once, lying prone practically on top of Noah, and muttered. "I gotta get my own face back . . ."

Jenna just shut her eyes, quaking under Noah's weight, too exhausted to move.

"C'mon, kid," Noah's voice finally broke through, "you've got to testify, make it official."

"Yeah . . ."

Security officials were pulling them to their feet, surrounding them in a ring five bodies deep, hustling them out of the danger zone to a waiting security cart. Skeeter dragged himself up and followed. Through the numbing roar of the mob, another shocked cry went up.

"Ianira Cassondra!"

Then Jenna and Noah were thrust into the cart. Skeeter slid in after them and scooted over as Ianira and her family crowded in. The children sat on the floor, dark eyes wide and scared. The driver cranked the siren up full blast and the cart shot down Commons, taking them away from the whole screaming mess. Ianira leaned down to wrap both arms around her frightened children and Marcus held Ianira. Jenna's vision blurred as she met the *cassondra's* gaze. Ianira, at least, had come home. The *cassondra* and her family would be welcomed by people who loved them. Jenna had no one left in the world who cared about her. No one at all. Except her unborn child.

And Noah Armstrong.

Jenna leaned her elbows against her knees and buried her face in her hands and cried. *Welcome home, Jenna . . . welcome the hell home.*

A quarter of an hour later, Jenna told her story to a roomful of station officials, Interpol officers, and a whole, terrifying retinue of I.T.C.H. agents. Jenna would've frozen up, tongue-tied and shaking, if Noah hadn't been there, backing her up and presenting their evidence. Her father was in jail, sedated and under heavy guard. Skeeter Jackson was with Jenna, testifying under oath. Margo Smith and her grandfather, Kit Carson, had already given their sworn affadavits. When everyone had finished their preliminary testimonies, Skeeter handed over the tape from his scout log, recording Gideon Guthrie's confession to posing as Sid Kaederman in order to murder her and Noah.

A long silence fell, finally broken by Agent Inga Kirkegard, the senior ranking I.T.C.H. officer. "I'll start by acknowledging the courage it took for all of you to do what you've done. You've saved countless lives, shut down a major international terrorist organization, exposed a ruthless conspiracy between mob interests and government officials, and kept this station operational. Not to mention ridding the world of Jack the Ripper. And you did so with surprisingly little loss of life, when the Ripper cults are taken into account." One corner of her mouth quirked slightly as she inclined her head toward Kit, acknowledging his pivotal role in on-station events Jenna had learned about on the way to the station manager's office.

Then Kirkegard's eyes frosted over and she stared coldly at Jenna. "However, your methods are something else entirely. We won't even list the number of laws and temporal-travel regulations broken in this unfortunate situation. I suspect most charges will be dropped, since it is quite clear you and Mr. Armstrong acted in self defense, killing the contract murderers sent after you. There is also a matter of jurisdiction, since the killing was done down time.

"In light of the large number of mitigating circumstances, I will recommend a judicial review and waiver of fines, rather than formal charges. That goes for all station residents who participated in the efforts to extract you and Mr. Armstrong alive. Now, Senator Caddrick brought a number of charges against the management of this station," Kirkegard said, turning her gaze to Bull Morgan and Ronisha Azzan. "After a thorough investigation of those charges, as well as countercharges filed by Mr. Carson, this team has officially dismissed all criminal counts initially brought by the senator. Those charges were clearly part of the overall fraud he perpetrated upon the public, including those made personally against you, Mr. Morgan."

A weight visibly lifted from the station manager's broad, squat shoulders. Bull Morgan settled back in his massive chair and switched his cigar to one corner of his mouth. "Much obliged."

Kirkegard nodded. "Ms. Azzan will be receiving a commendation from the Inter-Temporal Court for her superb handling of the multiple crises which struck this station in rapid succession, while Mr. Morgan was incarcerated. So will Mr. Carson," she glanced gravely at the world-famous former time scout, "for safeguarding hundreds of lives and restoring the station's normal economic operations through his ingenious solution to the Ripper difficulty. We've taken into custody those members of the Ripper cults your searchers apprehended. They will be prosecuted to the full extent of up-time law. As will Senator Caddrick and Mr. Kaederman, or rather, Mr. Guthrie."

She then turned her attention to Skeeter Jackson, who sat up straighter in his chair and swallowed hard. "It has come to our notice that you have led a rather, ah, checkered career, Mr. Jackson. We uncovered several old warrants and complaints filed, regarding your activities during the past several years." Sweat popped out along his brow. Kit Carson sat sharply forward, the brooding look turning his eyes abruptly dangerous. Jenna gulped, abruptly thankful she wouldn't be the one on the receiving end of Kit Carson's temper. Agent Kirkegard flicked a glance up at Kit, then smiled slightly. "Given the pivotal role Mr. Jackson played in this case, plus the character testimonials filed by this entire group, I believe the Inter-Temporal Court will vote to grant a general pardon and amnesty, in lieu of a commendation for services rendered."

Skeeter relaxed so abruptly, Jenna thought he'd fainted.

"I would suggest, Miss Caddrick, that you and Mr. Armstrong consider remaining on TT-86 for some time. Until the members of Mr. Guthrie's organization are rounded up and jailed, this station is without doubt the safest place for both of you. I.T.C.H. and Interpol can provide additional security to screen persons entering the station from New York. You will need to testify at the trial, of course, but I suspect you would prefer staying here to being placed in a witness protection program."

Jenna shuddered. "No contest."

Noah gave the I.T.C.H. officer a wan smile. "After my experience in London, I may just switch careers and offer my services as a temporal guide."

Kit chuckled, startling everyone. "I'd say you've stumbled onto a lucrative career opportunity, there. Granville Baxter is always happy to find guides who know how to disappear in a down-time crowd."

Armstrong grinned. "I hadn't thought about guiding in quite that way."

"Consider it. I'll tell Bax to give you a call. You'll stay at the Neo Edo, of course, until permanent quarters can be found in Residential. Penthouse suite. And don't even try to argue. My pleasure."

"Thank you," Jenna said quietly. "There isn't much I can do or say to show how deeply grateful I am to all of you. You helped save all our lives. My father may be a sorry bastard, but I won't forget that kind of debt. Ever."

"Neither will I," Noah agreed. "And I suspect Mr. Jackson wants his own face back, after nearly taking a bullet meant for me. Twice, in fact."

Skeeter grinned. "Now you mention it . . ."

The meeting broke up with Bull Morgan handing around congratulatory drinks, then they crowded into the elevator. Noah slipped an arm around Jenna's shoulder where they stood jammed together in one corner. She leaned her head against the detective's shoulder, grateful for the warm gesture and so weary she could have fallen asleep on her feet. Kit Carson was saying, "Malcolm is still in surgery, but the orderlies left word. He's doing just fine."

"Thank God," Margo breathed out.

"By the way, if you're interested," Kit chuckled, "I've got another little job lined up for you, in a few weeks. A real field test of your scouting skills."

"The Ripper Watch *wasn't*?" she shot back, causing even Jenna to smile.

"Well," Kit shrugged, "we had a major new gate open up while you were chasing Jack the Ripper."

"We did?" she asked breathlessly. "Are you really going to let me scout it?"

He shook his head. "Sorry, imp, but Ripley Sneed already did." His apology visibly deflated her hopes. "But it's a real dilly. Ought to give you a good workout for your final field test."

Margo caught her breath sharply in the crowded elevator. "*Final* field test?" It came out tiny with breathless hope. "As in, final exam before I really start scouting?"

He chuckled. "If you pass. And no solo work for a good long while, yet, even if you do pass the field test. Malcolm goes with you or you don't go at all. I'll conduct the field test and put you through your paces, myself. And this is one gate you won't have to worry about shepherding tourists through. Bax has already agreed. Scholars and scouts only, for the next couple of months."

"Just where does this thing lead?" Margo asked warily.

"Chicago. 1871."

Intrigued despite herself, Jenna sifted back through her skimpy knowledge of American history, randomly absorbed during her academic career. What was so special about Chicago in 1871?

Margo's eyes had narrowed, however. "What *month* in 1871?"

Kit grinned. "October."

Margo's eyes shot wide. "*Really?* Omigosh! How soon do we leave?"

"Four weeks. You'd better hit the books hard, imp."

"You're on!"

Jenna couldn't stand the suspense. "Where are you going? What's so special about Chicago in October of 1871?"

Kit chuckled. "Well, Miss Caddrick, my granddaughter and I intend to discover whether Mrs. O'Leary's cow did or did not start the Great Chicago Fire."

Jenna's eyes widened. Skeeter grinned. Noah started to laugh.

"I have a feeling," Jenna muttered, even as her lips

twitched, "that living on Time Terminal Eighty-Six is going to prove very interesting . . ."

She fully intended to enjoy every minute.

Epilogue

At four o'clock in the morning on November 9, 1888, the Ripper Watch Team's video cameras captured James Maybrick committing the brutal slaughter of Mary Kelly in the cramped little room at number thirteen, Miller's Court. At eight o'clock that morning, those same cameras captured the arrival of a midwife who was known to perform illegal abortions for girls in trouble. The woman let herself in with a key Kelly had taken from Joseph Barnett after he and Kelly had quarrelled and separated.

The horrified midwife, who slipped in the blood and gore, badly staining her clothing, changed into one of Mary Kelly's dresses and shawls and burned her own in the hearth before fleeing the room, too deeply shocked and terrified to go to the police or even scream for help. Doing so would have required explanations for her arrival in the first place, which would have led to a stiff prison sentence. Mrs. Caroline Maxwell, a neighbor in Miller's Court, glimpsed the midwife leaving Kelly's room and mistook her for Mary Kelly, herself, thus confusing police with sober testimony that Mary Kelly had been seen alive at 8:00 A.M.

London police never solved the Ripper mystery and never made a major arrest, although many suspects were named. The case destroyed Sir Charles Warren's career as police commissioner and sparked a massive social reform movement to alleviate the appalling conditions of poverty in which the Ripper's victims—and more than a million other souls—lived. The following spring, James Maybrick died of acute arsenic poisoning. His complicity in the Ripper case did not come to light for another century. His innocent American widow, her unfortunate affair with Mr. Brierly having come to public notice, was convicted of murder—largely because of her adultery—in a trial that shocked all of England and sparked a decade and a half of protests from the American State Department. Florie Maybrick served fifteen years in prison, then returned to the United States and lived in quiet anonymity under an assumed name, never realizing she had lived in the house that Jack built.

When it comes to the best
in science fiction and fantasy,
Baen Books has something for *everyone!*

IF YOU LIKE ...
YOU SHOULD ALSO TRY...

Marion Zimmer Bradley ....Mercedes Lackey,
Holly Lisle

Anne McCaffrey ....Elizabeth Moon,
Mercedes Lackey

Mercedes Lackey .....Holly Lisle, Josepha Sherman,
Ellen Guon, Mark Shepherd

Andre Norton ....Mary Brown,
James H. Schmitz

David Drake ....David Weber, John Ringo,
Eric Flint

Larry Niven ....James P. Hogan,
Charles Sheffield

Robert A. Heinlein ....Jerry Pournelle,
Lois McMaster Bujold

Heinlein's "Juveniles" ....Larry Segriff,
William R. Forstchen

Horatio Hornblower ....David Weber's
"Honor Harrington" series,
David Drake, *With the Lightnings*
and *Lt. Leary, Commanding*

The Lord of the Rings ....Elizabeth Moon,
The Deed of Paksenarrion

IF YOU LIKE . . .
YOU SHOULD ALSO TRY. . .

Lackey's "SERRAted Edge" series . . . . . . Rick Cook,
Mall Purchase Night

Dungeons & Dragons™ . . . . . . "Bard's Tale"™ Novels

Star Trek . . . . James Doohan & S.M. Stirling,
The Rising and *The Privateer*

Star Wars . . . . Larry Niven, David Weber
The "Wing Commander"™ series

Jurassic Park . . . . Brett Davis, *Bone Wars*
and *Two Tiny Claws*

Casablanca . . . . Larry Niven, *Man-Kzin Wars II*

Elves . . . . Ball, Lackey, Sherman,
Moon, Cook, Guon

Puns . . . . Rick Cook, Spider Robinson
Harry Turtledove, *The Case of the Toxic Spell Dump*

Alternate History . . . . Gingrich and Forstchen, *1945*
James P. Hogan, *The Proteus Operation*
Harry Turtledove (ed.), *Alternate Generals*
S.M. Stirling, "Draka" series
Eric Flint & David Drake, "Belisarius" series
Eric Flint, *1632*

SF Conventions . . . . Niven, Pournelle & Flynn,
Fallen Angels
Margaret Ball, *Mathemagics*
Jerry & Sharon Ahern, *The Golden Shield of IBF*

Quests . . . . Mary Brown, Elizabeth Moon,
Piers Anthony

Greek Mythology . . . . Roberta Gellis, *Bull God*

E E

 BAEN.COM

VISIT THE BAEN BOOKS WEB SITE AT:

http://www.baen.com
or just search for baen.com

Get information on the latest releases,
sample chapters of upcoming novels,
read about your favorite authors,
enter contests, and much more! ;)